Uncivil War

Southern Sudan is rife with civil unrest, isolated pockets of guerrillas fighting government forces to achieve self-rule for their provinces. Desperate to have their rights as Sudanese reinstated, they accept the secret help of a group of powerful men . . . and become pawns in a game of international intrigue.

"Mack Bolan stabs right through the heart of the frustration and hopelessness the average person feels about crime running rampant in the streets."
—*Dallas Times Herald*

Accolades for America's greatest hero Mack Bolan

DON PENDLETON's

MACK BOLAN.

ANVIL OF HELL

A GOLD EAGLE BOOK FROM
WORLDWIDE.

TORONTO • NEW YORK • LONDON • PARIS
AMSTERDAM • STOCKHOLM • HAMBURG
ATHENS • MILAN • TOKYO • SYDNEY

First edition April 1988

ISBN 0-373-61411-X

Special thanks and acknowledgment to
Peter Leslie for his contribution to this work.

For modes of faith, let graceless zealots fight;
He can't be wrong whose life is in the right:
In faith and hope the world will disagree,
But all mankind's concern is charity.
—Alexander Pope 1688-1744

The world is full of avaricious men who would prey on
the innocent and trusting. Humankind cannot allow
this. *I* will not allow this.
—Mack Bolan

To those struggling to throw off
the yoke of oppression

PROLOGUE

Night in Marseilles. Rain swept down the deserted, neon-lit length of the Canebière toward the old port, bouncing high off the sidewalks, chasing the whores back into clip joints and doorways. It was late anyway; few gamblers remained to ogle the bared thighs and painted faces. A Mercedes taxi shot a red light, fanning spray over the roadway. In a narrow, cobbled alley traversing the Arab quarter below the Saint Charles railroad station, the clatter of running footsteps drowned the gurgle of rainwater in the gutters.

Two sets of footsteps—hunter and hunted.

The hunter was tall, dark, muscular, his hair plastered to his skull by the downpour. He wore a shoulder rig and a harnessed hip holster beneath a light Windbreaker. In his right hand, the stainless steel of a .44 AutoMag snared a gleam of light from a distant street lamp.

His quarry was fifty yards ahead, a short wiry man whose outline was blurred by the rain. His pale, sodden shantung suit clung to his limbs as he ran, and he glanced desperately over his shoulder each time the alley twisted and changed direction between high windowless walls.

The hunter's black combat boots pounded the glistening stones. He was gaining. He had been gaining slowly for more than a week. Now—after a chase halfway across Europe—he was within range for the first time.

The hunted man erupted from the mouth of the alley and hared across a brightly lit street. Brakes squealed as a car slewed across the wet pavement, narrowly missing the hunter and causing him to break his athletic stride. He vaulted over the hood of the stalled auto, ignoring the curses of the driver, and plunged down a dark lane in pursuit of his quarry.

The man on the run was traveling in Europe under the name of Rafael Carvalho. His passport was Portuguese, but he was, in fact, a South American from Caracas, Venezuela. He was also a big-time operator in the hard drugs retail business, acting as liaison between the Mafia suppliers stateside and the Unione Corse distributors who hawked the stuff in southern France. Two weeks ago he had cold-bloodedly gunned down a high-school senior and his younger sister, ex-junkies who had agreed to testify in a Paris show trial that would convict a ring of pushers and compromise Carvalho himself.

The father of the murdered children was a friend of the man with the AutoMag, and he had sworn to even the score.

His present mission was simple: catch up with Carvalho and exterminate him.

He would have no compunction. Through his evil trade, Carvalho was a murderer many times over. And the law wasn't going to touch him now. *If there ain't no witnesses, there ain't no case* had been the Mob maxim during the gang wars of the Prohibition era. Times hadn't changed. And this was a case in point.

The high-school kids had been the only prosecution witnesses.

There were no witnesses to their deaths.

Everybody knew that Carvalho was as guilty as hell...yet there was no proof.

But the man in black didn't require any proof. He handed out justice to those who thought they were beyond the law.

He was Mack Bolan, the Executioner.

He ran effortlessly now, easily, his breathing controlled, his tuned muscles relaxed. But his mind was diamond-hard with concentration.

Carvalho had gained a few yards while Bolan had negotiated the stalled car, but he was flagging now, his lungs laboring while his out-of-shape body tried and failed to deal with the unaccustomed exertion. He was less than thirty yards ahead of his pursuer.

As the lane turned a corner, Carvalho leaped for a brick wall bounding a backyard, grasped the top and dragged himself onto the coping. For an instant, teeth bared in a wolfish snarl, his wizened features were visible as the headlights from a car in the next street swept across his face. Then his right arm came up and flame spit twice from the gun in his hand.

The Executioner had hurled himself sideways before the twin reports echoed off the stone facades of the surrounding buildings. He shoulder-rolled a short distance and came up on his knees, the AutoMag held out in a two-handed Weaver's grip as one of Carvalho's slugs ricocheted off the cobbles and screeched away into the night.

Blasting off two shots from the big autoloader, he sprang to his feet and ran for the wall as Carvalho dropped out of sight on the other side. There was a metallic clatter and a smothered curse as galvanized trash cans fell to the ground. Footsteps receded, ceased.

The Executioner was over the wall. Leaping down into the yard he heard the South American fire again, three shots cracking out from behind a stack of crates by an outside washroom. A bullet splatted against the wall a foot from his head, and he felt the wind of another fractions of an inch in front of his chin. He dropped to the ground, squeezing out a single thunderous round in reply.

As the first gunshots roared into the night, lighted windows in the nearby houses had gone dark. Wooden shutters slammed home. Gunfire after dark in Marseilles usually signified what the French called "a settlement of accounts" between rival Arab and Corsican gangs competing for territory, and the wise man looked the other way.

Bolan lay among potato peelings, smelling the odors of rotted fruit and spiced meats cooking. He reckoned the yard was in back of a neighborhood couscous restaurant. He could hear the jangle of Arab music faintly in the distance.

Beyond the washroom, a paler rectangle was printed against the dark: Carvalho had opened a door in the far wall and slipped through. The big guy followed and found himself in a vacant lot behind a low-rent six-story apartment building. The dope dealer was running, dodging between the rusted wrecks of abandoned automobiles. He was heading for a fire escape zigzagging down the rear of the apartments.

In the poor light the fleeing figure was too indistinct to make a good target for a handgun. The Executioner, too, sprinted through the rain toward the building.

He holstered the AutoMag on his right hip as he ran and plucked another gun from his shoulder rig. This was a specially modified Beretta 93-R that was equipped with a perforated suppressor, and springs machined to cycle subsonic cartridges. It packed a punch less devastating than the huge AutoMag, but it was more accurate, over a longer range.

Carvalho raced across a rain-slicked concrete playground and made the wall immediately below the fire escape. The lowest flight of the iron stairway was counterbalanced to remain horizontal, out of the reach of children, until weight was put on the treads. Carvalho leaped upward with outstretched hands and grabbed one of the spars. The flight swung down, and he scrambled aboard.

The Executioner halted at the edge of the playground and flicked a rapid glance over the facade of the building. Lights still showed in several windows on the upper floors. Where was Carvalho headed? Was there a safehouse someplace in this gaunt building? Or was the guy simply panicking, bolting for the nearest refuge he could find?

There was no way of telling. None of the intel the Executioner had gleaned suggested that Carvalho had contacts in this part of town. But it was better not to take chances: if there *were* confederates on one of the upper floors, he could be in big trouble himself. He dropped to one knee and raised the Beretta.

His quarry paused on the iron grid at second-floor level that separated the two lowest flights of the stairway. He spun around, and the gun in his hand spit fire once more.

A slug whined off the concrete, and glass in one of the automobile wrecks shattered. But the Executioner's crouched form was no more than a blur against the dark shapes littering the vacant lot. The killer's aim was way off.

Carvalho had forgotten one important detail in his frenzy to get away: while standing there on the grid, his head and shoulders were silhouetted against the diffused light that shone through the armored glass window in the fire exit door.

The Executioner flicked the Beretta into 3-shot mode, then steadied his right wrist with his left hand. He aimed carefully, holding his breath. In his concentration, the sound of the rain clattering on the ironwork of the escape seemed magnified.

He squeezed the trigger.

The gun bucked in his grasp as the triple burst from its silenced barrel streaking for the target.

Glass shattered onto the fire escape as the first 9 mm parabellum slammed into the window. The second slug tore away the left side of Carvalho's face and the third cored the upper part of his torso, penetrating the heart and killing him instantly.

He folded forward over the rail and dropped, but one of his feet caught in the ironwork. There was an audible crack as his shin snapped, and the body hung head-downward, arms trailing, the rain-soaked jacket flopping down to cover the head. His automatic skittered across the grid and fell to the ground.

Ramming the 93-R back into his shoulder rig, the Executioner rose and walked across to retrieve the gun. It was an old Colt Cobra revolver with live rounds in three of the six chambers. The guy must have reloaded in the yard, when there was only a single round left in the cylinder.

He straightened, a finger hooked through the trigger guard . . . and froze.

There were two of them: a tall, thin man with a bushy black mustache, who wore a dark raincoat that hung loosely on his frame, and a short, rat-faced man in Levi's and a leather jacket. They must have walked around the corner of the building while his attention was centered on the gun. Each man sported a snap-brim fedora black with moisture, and each held a standard-issue Browning automatic.

"Police," the one with the mustache growled, flashing a plastic-wrapped card with red, white and blue stripes slanted across one corner. "Brigade des Moeurs."

"Vice?" the Executioner echoed.

"Shut your mouth," Rat face cut in. "You're Mack Bolan, an American citizen." It was more a statement than a question.

Bolan said nothing. He looked beyond them to the roadway outside the apartment block entrance. A Mercedes taxi with the for-hire sign extinguished stood beneath a streetlight, its engine idling. Plumes of exhaust curled up into the rain from the muffler tail pipe. A husky man cradling a short-barreled submachine gun lounged by the open door, one elbow resting on the roof. Another man in plainclothes sat at the wheel.

Bolan weighed the chances. A kick, a swift blow, a sudden break for the vacant lot?

With his own guns holstered and Carvalho's revolver still dangling from one finger? No way.

"You're to come with us," Mustache ordered gruffly.

"On what charge?"

"Did I mention a charge?" The cop jerked his head at his companion. "Take the hardware, Serge."

Rat face twitched the Colt from Bolan's grasp and relieved him of the AutoMag and the Beretta. "You customarily carry these when you take a stroll at night?" he asked.

"Sure. Especially in Marseilles," Bolan growled. "What's this all about?"

"I told you to shut up," Mustache said. "Into the car now. Move."

"What about him?" Bolan nodded toward the body of Carvalho, which was still suspended from the fire escape.

"Forget it," Rat face replied. "We have no orders relating to bodies. That's for homicide. Our brief is to bring you in."

Bolan shrugged. As Mustache seized his arm, he began walking toward the Mercedes. There was nothing else he could do.

He sat on the rear seat, between the two cops. The man with the SMG, who was beside the driver, twisted around to face the Executioner, the barrel of the weapon supported on the seat back. The Mercedes hissed through the wet, deserted streets, passed a housing development, sped downhill toward the docks and then climbed to a raised six-lane expressway.

Over the red shingled roofs of ancient houses, Bolan saw light gleaming on black water, the yellow glare of sodium lamps where crane men working the night shift unloaded a freighter. When it became clear that they were heading north, out of town, he said mildly, "You guys sure patrol a long way from your precinct house."

"No talking."

Twenty minutes later, past the fringe of limestone mountains circling the city, they emerged from a tunnel and drove toward the Etang de Berre, the huge lagoon at the mouth of the Rhône that curls around Marseilles. Low clouds blanketing the sky ahead reflected a blaze of light from factories, refineries, a power station strung along the waterside. The control tower of Marignane Airport rose in the distance like a grain silo, above fields of brilliance where high-power lights illuminated the parking lots and taxiways surrounding the terminal.

The Mercedes took the next exit off the expressway to reach an approach road leading to the airport. Bolan remained nonplussed. If these were real cops, why had they ignored the dead man hanging from the fire escape? They had barely looked at him.

If they weren't, if this was some underworld variation of the old take-him-for-a-ride routine, what were they waiting for?

On the outskirts of the field, neon letters behind a grove of trees spelled out the word Sofitel.

The cop at the wheel turned the Mercedes into a driveway and parked at the end of a line of cars. Beyond them was the floodlit facade of a two-story luxury motel.

"Out," the cop with the mustache ordered. "And no tricks."

Rat face opened the door. He got out to stand beside the guy with the SMG, and covered the Executioner as they all proceeded past the motel's entrance hall and around the back of the building.

Thin strips of light escaped from behind the shutters that covered some of the first-floor windows. In one room that had the draperies drawn back, a woman holding a champagne glass stood smiling at her companions. Somewhere inside the motel Ella Fitzgerald was singing "I Didn't Know What Time It Was."

Bolan and his captors passed a floodlit pool, then rounded one end of a wing projecting from the main block and stopped outside a curtained French door that opened onto the garden. The rain had stopped, and a cool breeze blew through the wet grass.

Rat face rapped a code knock on the French door: three quick taps, two widely spaced, then two more quick ones.

The door opened.

Silhouetted against the discreet glow of a floor lamp in a tastefully furnished bedroom, Bolan saw a bulky man in a rumpled brown suit, an unlit cigar clamped between his teeth.

"Striker! I thought you'd never come!" Hal Brognola exclaimed.

PART ONE

IDENTIFICATION

CHAPTER ONE

Brognola was a Fed who had the President's ear. When the Executioner had been actively involved in a covert antiterrorist campaign that operated from Stony Man Farm, in Virginia's Blue Ridge Mountains, Brognola had been the sole liaison linking him with the Oval Office.

The two men were longtime friends. They remained in contact after Bolan made the decision to quit that particular hot seat and strike out on his own. When the big guy needed intel on the underworld, Brognola supplied it from the worldwide Stony Man computer complex. But at a point when America really needed him, the Executioner came in from the cold to establish an arm's length relationship with the government. Bolan vowed never to be at the mercy of the Administration and refused to work within the confines of the system. He'd help Brognola with situations that were too hot for the intelligence agencies to handle, but he'd always be his own man—free to refuse certain missions, and free to pursue those of his own choosing.

"Hal, don't you think this strong-arm cop routine is something of an overkill? Why the vice squad?"

Brognola shrugged his heavy shoulders. "I knew you'd chased Carvalho this far. The vice squad boys know the back street runs better than anyone. Plus the fact that half the other services here are in cahoots with the Mob, and security was important."

"Okay," Bolan said. "But they could have passed on the message, given me your location."

"Uh-uh. Nobody can know we're working together, that's vital. The local cops were asked, as a favor, to locate you and hand you over into my care. Those guys' orders were to bring you in. No questions. End of story."

Bolan nodded. "Got it. So could we dispense with the window-dressing now?" He held up his wrists, which the French police had handcuffed before they left.

"My pleasure." Brognola produced a key. "Take a seat, Striker, and please hear me out. This is dangerous stuff."

"One more question," Bolan said, rubbing the circulation back into his wrists. "Why here? An airport motel is secure?"

"It has to be. Question of time. I'm really supposed to be in Istanbul on a drug-busting conference along with police chiefs from Damascus, Vientiane, Ispahan...and Marseilles. It's important that the local guy doesn't know I've been here. Right now—" Brognola glanced at his watch "—it's 3:45. The next session of the conference is scheduled for 11:00 a.m., in seven hours. If I'm going to make the plane that'll get me back there in time, I can't risk getting too far away from the airport."

The Executioner nodded again, dropping into a deep-seat easy chair. The room was comfortable enough: burnt-orange draperies and bedspread, tobacco-colored wall-to-wall carpet and a chromed floor lamp that stood beside a long desk.

The Fed was unpacking a home movie projector from a fiber suitcase. "Just how close are you to getting Carvalho?"

"The case is closed," Bolan said gruffly.

"And the dealer?"

"No longer with us."

"Terminated with prejudice?"

"Extreme prejudice."

Relief flooded across Brognola's worry-lined face. "That's just fine," he said. "You'll have time on your hands. So relax and pay attention. I have news for you."

Bolan sighed. "Pour it on."

"I'll drop you in the deep end," Brognola said. "There's a nuclear angle, and it could be serious. We discovered a gradual series of thefts of uranium 235."

"Gradual?"

"Over the past three years. We hadn't paid all that much attention until the Stony Man computers came up with a rundown. We'd run a random trace, and it showed tiny, but consistent, losses of the fissile isotope. Each one with an identical MO."

"I'd have thought even one theft of uranium 235 was worth one hell of a lot of attention," Bolan remarked dryly.

"Oh, sure. Every one was a big deal on its own. On file, top priority, dead secret—with all hell breaking loose to try to identify the thieves and recover the stuff."

"But?"

"Until we ran that trace, the thefts hadn't been regarded as part of a single operation. We hadn't paid all that much attention until we realized the pattern was international."

"*Inter*national?"

"Yeah. They lifted the stuff from all over—from Hanford and Clinton, Calder Hall in England and Dounreay in Scotland, from Châtillon, near Paris, and Pierrelatte here in the Rhône valley. Even from Magnitogorsk in the Soviet Union."

"I guess that last one should tell you something about who *didn't* steal the stuff. You say 'we,' Hal, and 'they,' but you don't give the cast list. Who?"

"Like I say, it started at Stony Man. Then the NSC got interested. After that it was the Company, and ... well, finally, it came back to me. As far as 'they' are concerned, up to this point we drew a blank. One thing is certain, though. Whoever staged the thefts staged them for one purpose and one purpose only—to use in the manufacture of thermonuclear warheads.''

"What kind of amounts are involved?" Bolan asked.

"Individually, pretty small. But if you add them up it begins to look alarming."

"You're certain Ivan's innocent?"

"Certain. Why would the Russians bother? They refine more uranium and plutonium than we do. Some CIA genius suggested that it might be the Chinese, or even the Soviets raiding their own places as a blind."

"There'd be no logic in that," the Executioner agreed. "None of the stuff has been recovered?"

"Not an ounce. They were precision operations, all right. Every one was an inside job, and no one connected with the thefts was identified."

"So what do you have in mind for me?" Bolan asked.

"Relax, Striker. You'll see." Brognola had set up the projector at one end of the desk. Now he unrolled a screen and pinned it to the far wall. "We have reason to believe there's a North African connection. And after the raid on Tripoli, Lebanon and Irangate, the Administration is too scared to openly take a hand in any intrigues centered on that theater. Too many people are eager to accuse us of being fascist imperialist warmongers. Plus the fact that even the small countries are kind of touchy on matters that relate to their own defense."

"So the regular agencies are definitely out. What's the job?"

"Find out who's behind the thefts, check out their plan...and squash it."

"Tell me what you've got."

"We did have one break," the Fed admitted. "A week ago, MI-5 in Britain reported a recent theft of 235—from Aldermaston this time. But for once they did have a line on the guilty man. You remember Harries?"

"The physicist who went over to the Communists when he was on vacation in Hungary last month."

"Yeah. It seems he lost his nerve after he'd taken the stuff, and he tried to pull the political asylum gag in Budapest. But the comrades didn't want to deal with the situation, so they handed him back—which seems to confirm they had nothing to do with the theft."

"Meanwhile..."

"He comes up for trial in a couple weeks. But while he was away his wife turned up something and contacted Scotland Yard's special branch. So when Harries was handed over they were wise to the theft and knew what questions to ask. He could only finger one contact of course, a cutout. But it was a start. They didn't recover the isotope, but they were able to trace it—right here to Marseilles."

"And the cutout?" Bolan asked.

"He woke up with a hole in his head two days later."

"So the trail goes cold here in Marseilles?"

"Not entirely. I hired a private investigator to dig up what he could find before you hit town. I received his first report just before I left for Istanbul." Brognola slotted a spool of 8 mm film into the projector. "I guess they were too close behind him for the guy to risk filing in the clear, so this intel is in a kind of visual code. He was posing as a newsman after colorful feature material for a syndicate. This one small can of color stock and an audio cassette accompanying it were supposed to be samples of what he could offer."

Brognola switched on the projector, and it whirred to life. Letters and figures swirled across the small screen, then it suddenly erupted into a blaze of light and color. A line of camels stood silhouetted against a raspberry-tinted sky in a landscape of date palms and ridged dunes. The camera pulled back to show that the viewer was looking at a poster advertising package tours in North Africa, then cut to a locale-establishing shot of Marseilles—the hilltop church of Notre Dame de la Garde, with its huge gold Virgin topping the bell tower—and then switched to a close-up of dockside cranes loading a freighter. This was followed by a landscape sequence, with the camera—obviously mounted on a truck—panning rapidly across fields of vines to zoom in on a road sign at an intersection. The lettering on the fingerpost read Cannes 235 km.

Next came a street scene, the conventional casbah shot, although the church in the distance showed that it was still in Marseilles. The camera, hand held, threaded its way along a crowded alleyway, with veiled women and gesticulating men in robes thronging two rows of brightly colored stalls.

Cut to a close-up of a revolving postcard stand outside a tourist souvenir shop. The gaudy photos spun slowly to a halt, and the camera zoomed in to pick up a card showing a panoramic harbor scene against an improbable blue sky.

Cut back to the alley, the camera panning along one side, stopping at a booth displaying Arab hardware—row upon row of copper pans, pots and other containers. More camels: a medium-long shot of bedouin loading bales of merchandise onto three dromedaries, a distant view of a whole caravan heading into the sunset. Finally the face of a black African, which was cross-faded with a fierce Arab visage. After that, the screen went blank.

Brognola switched off the projector. "How do you read that?" he asked.

"Three themes come through loud and clear. Transport, freight and Arabs. I think the signpost shot was a tip-off that the freight was your uranium 235. I wouldn't think the town it pointed at was relevant, but—"

"Unless it was a pun," Brognola cut in. "With the Arab hardware booth thrown in, in case we missed the point. You know Cannes...cans...equals canisters. Which is what radioactive isotopes have to be transported in."

"That could be. And camels equal North Africa. So we have that connection, plus canisters of uranium 235 in Marseilles, being transported by freighter to...where? The port on the postcard?"

"We identified it as Alexandria, Egypt."

"Okay, Alexandria. Then camels again, going west into the sunset, if that's significant. What do you think, Hal?"

Brognola shook his head. "You tell me. And I don't get the Arab face superimposed on the black one, either. Maybe the cassette will give us a clue." He took a small tape player from his suitcase and slipped in an unlabeled cassette.

"Most of this is cover stuff," he said, "but there's a message in there, as well." He thumbed a switch.

Bolan heard a man's voice, speaking in exaggerated travelogue style:

"As I stand here in the Arab quarter of France's second city, this historic cosmopolitan seaport where the Phoenicians traded six hundred years before the birth of Christ, it is difficult to resist a twinge of alarm at the evidence of our century's effect on those hundreds of years of tradition. The halcyon days when Marseilles was the gateway to the Orient are gone. Yet even in this nuclear age the Arab influence grows—"

Brognola had cut the sound. "That's an arranged cue," he said. "After the sentence containing the word '*hal*cyon,' it's a message for me." He rewound the tape a few revolutions and flipped the switch again.

"...to the Orient are gone. Yet even in this nuclear age the Arab influence grows stronger. Mustapha Tufik has run a coffee shop in the Algerian ghetto for more than thirty years. He, if anybody, has a finger on the pulse of North Africa and an ear for the Muslim heartbeat within the city. On the dark continent, he says, things are no longer as black as they were. There is nevertheless disquieting news from this Mediterranean imbroglio. The immigrant population has never—"

"That's all," Brognola said, switching the machine off. "The rest is all quasisociological guff for cover. The message ends with the word 'imbroglio.'"

"Okay," Bolan said. "So we have a ship ferrying the stolen 235 to Alexandria in some kind of canister, a strong scent of camels and now Mr. Mustapha Tufik and his coffee shop as a contact for disquieting news." He paused. "I notice you spoke of your private eye in the past tense. Is he off the case now?"

"Permanently. His body was found floating in the old port yesterday morning. He had been knifed. And robbed . . . or so the local gendarmes say."

The Executioner's eyebrows rose. "So somebody knows we're on the trail already?"

"Somebody knows *somebody*'s on the trail already," the big Fed corrected. "That's another reason for using you as a bird dog. So far as this case is concerned, you'll be the X factor."

He unplugged the projector and began to pack it away. "There's a four-star general named Hartley staying a couple days at the Intercontinental. He's one of the Pentagon's nuclear experts. He can fill you in on the possibilities before you start digging for real."

Mack Bolan nodded. He rose to his feet and stretched. "Good to see you, Hal," he said. "Meanwhile, it must be nearing breakfast time. I think I'll go on into town and get a cup of coffee."

CHAPTER TWO

The first attack on Bolan came within fifteen minutes of his meeting with General Hartley. He was in a cab, on his way back to the city center. Banks of high clouds scudded across a sunny sky, though the drying roadway was still greasy from the previous night's rain.

The cab was only a few blocks from the Canebière when it was passed by a Volvo station wagon, its rear loading door propped open. Bolan paid no attention to the vehicle, though his subconscious registered the fact that two men in back of the driver were maneuvering some package near the door.

He barely noticed the Volvo slacken speed when it was fifty yards ahead, and then accelerate away. It was only when the heavy, square, black object fell to the road and came spinning toward the taxi that his battle-honed sense of survival took over and he exploded into action.

There was no time for speech. He leaned over the back of the driver's seat and grabbed the hand brake, heaving it upward.

There was a tortured screech of tires as the rear wheels suddenly locked, the cab slewing sideways across the slippery street. The startled driver overcorrected, and the cab—with Bolan still clutching the lever—turned completely around. Careering backward across a crosswalk, it slammed into a light standard and flipped onto its side.

The noise of the crash was drowned in the explosion, which blasted a ten-foot crater in the roadway. Miraculously, neither Bolan, the cabbie nor any of the people on the sidewalks was injured.

As the rubberneckers swarmed around the wrecked vehicle, the cabbie helped Bolan through the shattered rear window. "I don't know whether that was for you," he said shakily, "but if it's all the same to you, I'd rather you finished your journey by bus."

The Executioner thrust money into his hand. "Just be thankful it wasn't nuclear," he said.

Pushing his way through the excited crowd, he hurried away before the gendarmes arrived on the scene. The thick column of yellow smoke that rose above the rubble-strewn roadway was already at rooftop height. In the distance he could hear the warble of sirens.

The nuclear reference wasn't altogether a joke, he reflected as he ducked into a narrow alleyway. Not if General Hartley's intel was as disquieting as it seemed, let alone whatever the mysterious Mustapha Tufik could reveal.

The Pentagon man had reminded Bolan of a robin—a short, rotund figure with quick, darting movements and a characteristic pecking motion of the bald head to emphasize important points. He had seemed glad of the opportunity to display his knowledge.

"Stolen U-235?" he asked. "More than enough to make your critical mass? Let us consider how this material can be used."

"It won't be used to fuel the atomic pile at a nuclear power station, that's for sure," Bolan said grimly.

"Quite so, quite so." Hartley pushed shell-rim spectacles onto the pale slope of his forehead. "First of all, we can rule out your crude atom bomb right away. That's kid stuff now. Second of all, I think we can forget the cobalt bomb. Most everybody's too goddamned scared to touch it. That leaves us with the conventional thermonuclear fusion bomb. I guess you are familiar, sir, with the principle of this device?''

''Familiar, but not intimate.''

Hartley's question had been rhetorical. He ignored the reply and continued, ''As you will be aware, there are three separate explosions involved—or more properly four, if you count the original detonator. The detonator sets off a charge of conventional explosive that hurls together two quantities of fissile material totaling more than that substance's critical mass. This initiates a chain reaction that produces a fission explosion. And it is only in the immense heat generated by this that the fusion process involving the bomb's main constituents can take place.''

''You mean an H-bomb can only be triggered off by a small A-bomb explosion inside it?'' Bolan asked.

Hartley coughed. ''Well, yes—if you want to put it that way. But the *significant* thing,'' he continued, ''is that the light elements required for the fusion reaction—that is, the main explosive substances in an H-bomb—can be acquired by any country, any organization, with reasonable resources. What stops every half-pint army and militia in the world going nuclear is the difficulty and expense of obtaining the fissile material necessary for the initial atom bomb blast.''

''And that is uranium 235?''

''Or plutonium 239. Precisely.''

''You're telling me that whoever has this stolen U-235—providing they have reasonable resources—could be setting up a plant and manufacturing H-bombs in some secret place...say, somewhere in Africa?''

The bald head bobbed in affirmation. ''Mind you, 'reasonable' resources can be astronomic by ordinary standards. But if they had the means, and a sufficiently isolated site, and the labor, and some way of getting equipment and material there—if they had all those things, then I guess it could be done. But those are big enough 'ifs' just the same, sir.''

"They couldn't make it without the uranium 235?"

"Definitely not. Not unless the resources, the funds, were virtually *unlimited*, and they'd been working on it for years. To start with, you see, you'd have to amass your uranium ores. Then you must extract and refine pure uranium. Then the 235 isotope has to be separated from the natural element in a nuclear reactor, and the yield is minimal, only .7 of one percent. Add to this the cost of the raw materials, the cost of the plant, the time, the labor, the expense of the immensely thick shielding needed for—"

"Okay, General, you convinced me. I guess you made your point."

"I mean, sure, they could get their deuterium, their heavy hydrogen, their cadmium and their graphite moderators easy enough. They could even build themselves a reactor, provided of course that they—"

"Why uranium 235, though?" the Executioner cut in once more, in an attempt to stem the flood. "I thought plutonium was preferred these days on account of the yield from uranium being so much greater."

Hartley shrugged. "Why bother when you're stealing it anyway? Could be because security is even tougher on plutonium. Or maybe the guy masterminding the deal has a personal preference for the other isotope. Whoever it is, he has to be a big brain in nuclear physics. This is no high-school laboratory routine, whatever the scare stories in the media say."

"That does narrow the field some," Bolan admitted. "How many physicists are there in the world capable of directing such an operation? A hundred? A thousand? Ten thousand?"

"You tell me," Hartley said. "My guess would be hundreds. Maximum. But it's only a guess."

He removed his spectacles, snapped them shut and stowed them in his breast pocket. "Whatever you turn up, keep in touch," he said. "Frankly, I can't say I approve of the way Brognola's handling this. Nothing personal, you understand. But any shift, any prospective shift, in the balance of nuclear power is vital information for our strategic planners. Remember that."

"I'm not likely to forget," Bolan said soberly.

"No. Well... " Hartley sighed. "I'd rather it was done through professionals answerable to the Administration, but I can see why Brognola decided against it. The other thing to remember is that the destination of the stolen isotope isn't the only problem. Apart from Harries, every single man responsible for the thefts is still working undercover, undetected, in the nuclear plants where they occurred. It's equally vital that they should be identified."

Bolan nodded. "I'll do what I can," he promised.

It was only then that he asked the hotel doorman to call him a cab.

Back in his hotel, therefore, he was faced with a problem more immediate than the relocation of the uranium trail.

Who could have been so familiar with his movements that they could have traced him from Marignane back to the hotel, where he changed into more conventional clothes, and then on to the Intercontinental?

And who would have had the means to call up a car, a crew and a ready-primed explosive device at such short notice? The men of the Marseilles underworld, certainly—especially bearing in mind the coded message from the private eye and his subsequent fate; or the cops, who knew he was at Marignane and could conceivably have bugged the

motel room. And who could—as Brognola had hinted—
have been in touch with the *milieu* and tipped them off.

But neither of them would have known that Bolan was
anything more than a criminal being handed over to American justice. And even if for some reason the room *had* been
bugged, would anyone have had time to analyze their conversation, draw the right conclusions and act on them?

On the face of it, the most likely character in the cast was
the general himself. He had the knowledge and the opportunity. But did he have the motive?

Hartley had made it clear that he didn't approve the use
of a free lance at the expense of the official intelligence services. But unless he was himself part of the conspiracy involved in the uranium thefts, which seemed kind of
farfetched, would that disapproval have been strong enough
to countenance the *elimination* of the lone wolf?

The Executioner thought not. He hoped not.

But he was left with the uneasy feeling that the mission
entrusted to him by Brognola was much less undercover
than he had thought.

CHAPTER THREE

Mustapha Tufik's coffee shop wasn't listed in the telephone directory. It rated no mention in the city guide. Nobody in Bolan's hotel had ever heard of it.

He had assumed, somehow, after the buildup on the private eye's tape, that it might be something of a tourist attraction, the kind of place known to every hotel porter and cabdriver in town. But he scored zero all along the line.

Finally, standing beneath the sheer forty-foot stone wall of the fort that guarded the entrance to the old port, he got wise. If Tufik ran a coffee shop, he would have to get supplies someplace. The next step was to make the rounds of the coffee wholesalers.

Bolan found a pay phone and removed the entries he needed from the *C* section of the yellow pages directory. He looked around for another cab.

It wasn't so easy. It was raining again, a sullen, relentless downpour, slanting under pressure from a westerly wind that bounced ankle-high off the shining quays and cascaded from flapping awnings over the waterfront restaurants. Every taxi in town seemed to have been booked by office executives hightailing it for the railroad station or hurrying to bars to imbibe an extra predinner martini.

Hunched against the deluge, Bolan tramped past the forest of masts and rigging, and started his odyssey on foot.

Three out of the first four wholesalers were closed already. At the fifth he struck pay dirt. Tufik had been a customer there since the mid-fifties.

By the time he had located a cab, and the driver had found his way to the ancient Arab quarter above the docks, it was after dark.

"I can take you no farther, *monsieur*," the driver said, looking at the Executioner curiously. "The road becomes too narrow. You will find the establishment, I think, up there on the left in a small courtyard. It is not my business to ask, but..." He paused.

"Yes?"

The driver shrugged. "Nothing. It is of no importance." He slammed the big Citroën into reverse and began backing up toward an intersection. "Just keep your hand on your billfold, that's all!" he yelled as the cab drew slowly away.

Bolan grinned. A word to the wise. He thrust a hand between the lapels of his sodden raincoat, checking the Beretta in its shoulder rig.

Rain was still pelting down, streaming over the surface of the lane, which twisted uphill between tall, blank facades. The gutters, choked every few yards with garbage, formed a series of dams that had spread out and flooded the cobbles, and Bolan's footsteps as he splashed up toward a dim streetlight were almost drowned in the gurgle of running water.

Directly beneath the streetlight, an archway led to a paved courtyard with half a dozen run-down houses on each side. Faintly above the drumming of the rain, hard rock warred with Moorish music.

The coffee shop was at the far end of the cul-de-sac. Bolan walked under a second arch piercing the crumbling wall, traversed an evil-smelling passageway and pushed in through the door.

Heat, light and noise engulfed him.

He saw a low-ceilinged, smoke-filled room jam-packed with men of a dozen different nationalities. Arabs, Hispanics, Africans and Northerners crouched over low tables around the walls, crowded a bar and stood in gesticulating groups. A rock number blared from a gaudy juke in one corner, barely audible over the babel of voices.

The noise level dropped abruptly as Bolan came in, but it had resumed its former pitch by the time he made it to the bar. From behind the handles of an Italian espresso machine, a hard-faced individual with the sleeves of his shirt rolled up above tattooed forearms looked at him inquiringly. Judging from the condition of a party of French sailors shouting by the juke, the place served stronger drinks than coffee for the non-Muslims.

"Espresso," Bolan said brusquely, mopping his drenched hair with a handkerchief and shaking the drops from his raincoat.

"Bien, m'sieu."

"The boss here this evening?" Bolan asked a few minutes later. There appeared to be no waiters. Customers wanting refills separated themselves from the brawling crowd and shouted their orders across the bar. And certainly there was nobody who looked as though he might be the owner.

"M'sieu?"

"Mustapha Tufik," Bolan returned. "Is he here tonight?"

The hard-faced barman stared at him. "But of course. He is always here."

"I'd appreciate a few minutes of conversation with him."

"That is not possible."

"I have come a long way to see him. With a message from a mutual friend."

"No."

A tall man with a broken nose, who had come into the den a few minutes earlier, lurched up to the bar and elbowed the Executioner aside. "Here, Jean-Marc," he growled. "Attend to your business. There's thirsty men waiting. Three *marcs* and a large glass of red, and make it quick."

"Would you mind letting the man decide for himself?" Bolan asked when the barkeep had filled the order.

The man scowled. "I told you, no. Nobody sees the boss without an appointment." He moved back to the espresso machine and began to prepare coffee for three Arab laborers.

"There would be a certain amount of money involved—for all concerned," Bolan called, mastering his irritation.

"Keep your money. Tourists are not welcome here, especially American tourists."

"I am not a tourist, and I am no American," Bolan lied. "What I have to say may be of particular interest to—"

The barman leaned his hands on the counter and thrust his face toward the Executioner. "How many times do I have to tell you," he shouted, "that the answer is no, no and again no. Now drink your coffee and belt up, or else get out of —"

He broke off as a high-pitched buzz from below the bar cut through the hubbub. Reaching down, he unhooked a house phone and held it to his ear. "Yeah," he growled. "That's right... What?... Right away?... You're quite sure?... I don't know that you— Oh, what the hell. Just as you like."

The barkeep slammed the instrument back on its hook. "He'll see you," he said curtly, jerking his head toward a bead curtain behind the bar. "This way."

Bolan drained the rest of his cup and followed the man through the curtain and along a dark passageway. They skirted a patio bordered by a grimy glass canopy rattling under the assault of the rain, made it past another bead curtain and stopped in a softly lit waiting room. As they entered, a slim man in a suit rose quickly to his feet, one hand hovering near the unfastened top button of his jacket. Beneath the tarboosh he wore, his sallow face was watchful.

Bolan took in the scene at a glance. The contrast with the coffee shop was extreme. Subtly colored Persian rugs covered the mosaic floor, and the room was furnished with low divans in the Oriental style. There was only one other door: a sheet of beaten copper gleaming dully in a vaulted stone arch.

"For some reason he's agreed to see this tourist, Hassan," the surly barman said. "You take over from here, eh? I have customers waiting in the bar."

The slim man nodded, gesturing toward the copper door. As the barman turned and went back through the bead curtain, Hassan pressed a button concealed in the stonework and the door swung slowly open. Another corridor, stone-flagged and illuminated by wrought-iron lamps on brackets, stretched ahead.

"After you," Hassan said evenly. He kept some distance behind as they walked past a number of closed doors. Other than their footsteps on the stone floor, not a sound disturbed the silence. When they had passed five doorways, the slim man said softly, "The next one on the left. Knock four times."

Bolan rapped on the teak panels. There was a subdued buzz, a click and again the door swung open.

Mustapha Tufik was enormous, one of the biggest men Bolan had ever seen. He must have weighed well over 280 pounds, fat shoulders merging into a bulging neck, the great swell of his belly thrusting against a crumpled sharkskin suit. A few strands of reddish hair were combed across his freckled scalp, and a pair of unexpectedly humorous blue eyes twinkled among the rolls of pale flesh that formed his face.

He was sitting in an electrically operated wheelchair. Most surprising of all, he greeted Bolan in the broad accents of County Cork.

"Well, now, me boy," he called cheerfully, "and what can I be doing for you? Come in, come in, and sit you down—if you can find a place, that is. For it's queer and cluttered it's getting to be in here at all!"

He waved a fat hand around the windowless room. It was a tough job finding a seat, for the entire area, about thirty feet square, was swamped by a great tide of paper. There were a few piles of reference books, matched by corresponding spaces in the bookshelves lining the walls, but most of the litter comprised an endless variety of newspapers, magazines and journals from all over the world. Overflowing onto chairs and couches, covering the floor in untidy heaps, these, Bolan saw, were spidered with scrawled annotations and underlinings in various colors.

Adrift on the flood were dozens of sheets of writing paper crisscrossed with scribbled notes, sheaves of clippings and long telex rolls bearing messages from APA, Reuter, Havas and Tass.

Steel filing cabinets in front of one wall flanked a modernistic console, which looked like the control panel of a recording studio. Oriental rugs hung below the lofty ceiling above the bookcases against two opposite walls. The fourth wall was pierced by an archway masked by the inevitable bead curtain.

The room was airless and hot. Bolan stripped off his soaking raincoat and draped it over the back of a chair that was piled high with old editions of the *Herald Tribune*. He moved aside copies of several different magazines and perched himself on the corner of an ottoman covered in purple silk.

"'Tis a foul night out there, they tell me," the fat man continued, "and you'll be after needing a spot of refreshment." He clapped his hands three times and then turned to the man in the tarboosh. "That's all right, Hassan, thank you," he said. "I'll let you know when this gentleman leaves us."

Hassan bowed and withdrew, closing the heavy door after him. A moment later, a veiled Arab girl of about thirteen pushed through the bead curtain. She was carrying a brass tray loaded with tiny cups and saucers, a copper pot full of fragrant coffee, a stone flask, glasses and a squat bottle half full of pale yellow liquor.

Tufik said something to her in Arabic as she cleared a space on the table and set down the tray. He slapped her familiarly on her silk-clad bottom as she giggled and ran off through the curtain.

"Delightful creature," he said reflectively, staring at the swaying strings of beads. "I keep half a dozen of them to look after me. When you're a big fella like me, there's nothing more relaxing than... Well, sure, I'm forgetting me manners! Turkish coffee now? With a drop of the rose water to settle the grounds? And you'll take a spot of the hard stuff? Izarra, it is, from the Basque country. I have the sweet tooth, as you see."

After pouring the drinks, he spun the wheelchair with dexterity and sped down an aisle left free between the masses of paper to hand Bolan a cup, saucer and eggshell-shaped glass held in a fine filigree cradle black with the patina of age.

"You have a most...unusual establishment here," Bolan observed, sipping the fiery, aromatic liquor.

"Sure, I guess I have and all. Though if it's the girls you mean, I have to tell you they're not—"

"I didn't only mean the girls. There's one hell of a contrast, you have to admit, between the, uh, coffee shop and this room, for example. Then there's the electrically controlled doors, the professional gunman outside, the fact that you knew I was here and invited me to step in just as your barman was about to throw me out."

"Ah, you have to keep a finger on the pulse, boy, in my business—and you have to take precautions, too. Besides, Jean-Marc didn't know who you were, Mr. Bolan. *I* do."

"And just what *is* your business?"

"Well, now, isn't that a question I should rightly be asking you? *You're* the one asked to see *me*. What is it you want?" The blue eyes were suddenly shrewd and calculating.

Bolan decided on the direct approach. "I was given to understand by a friend—a late friend—that you might be able to provide me with some information on a certain subject."

"What was the name of the friend?"

Bolan quoted the name of Brognola's private eye.

The fat man chuckled, the rolls of fat around his neck wobbling uncontrollably as he sucked coffee through pursed lips. "Sure, there's a splendid coincidence then," he said, putting down the cup. "You've come to the right man, you see, for information *is* my business. I'm a merchant of information, to be sure. Wholesale or retail, in gross or by the item. You name it. If it's possible to get it, I'll get it. I play no favorites, I take no sides, I offer no loyalty, no allegiances. A man comes to me and pays for information, I give it to him, no questions asked. I don't care who he is. The customer is always right, and my customers come from all over—police, private detectives, lawyers, intelligence men, dubious characters from here to hell and gone. They all come to Mustapha Tufik."

"That's a fine old Irish name," the Executioner commented dryly.

"And it's my own, I'll have you know, sir. Me mother came from Ireland like they say in the song, God rest her poor soul. And indeed I was brought up in the old country. But me father was a Casablanca man, born and bred—though you'd not think it to look at me now, would ye?"

"No, I wouldn't," Bolan agreed. "But I understand you've been here a great number of years, just the same. In this Arab neighborhood, I mean."

"I have and all. The kind of setup I have here doesn't grow in a day. It's taken a long time to build up. You wouldn't believe how many hundred dollars a week it costs me in wire services and papers alone. And then, of course, there's the informers, the hotel porters, the airport folks, the travel agency men."

"You must have great insight into what goes on in the world just by reading these." Bolan indicated the mass of periodicals around the room.

"Well, you know how it is. You never know when it'll come in useful, knowing who sleeps with whom, who was cleaned out at the tables, who's opened his mouth too wide and got fired. The gossip columns—when you add two and two together from different ends of the world—can tell a man a great deal. Then of course there's the diplomatic and political pieces. There's much to read between the lines there."

"And the coffee shop?"

"Maybe that's the most useful of all. You know what they used to say: if you wanted to know what went on in the big houses, you'd ask in the servants' hall. Well, my coffee shop's a little like the old servants' hall. We get seamen from the boats, waiters from the consulates, porters, hit men, all kinds. Sure, I'm like a recording angel in here, preserving every little thing that comes in—and the coffee shop's one of my main microphones, as it were.''

''I was surprised that you knew I wanted to talk to you.''

''And isn't that the simplest thing! Wait'll I show you.'' Tufik sent the chair wheeling around to the console and flicked a switch. A pilot light glowed red on an indicator board. ''What'll you have?'' he asked. ''The bar? Second table on the left? The far end where the gorillas are standing?''

He thumbed a series of buttons ranged across the board. As each one was depressed, a colored light glowed above it and a snatch of conversation boomed from a speaker at one side of the console.

''*. . . asked the consul's daughter to slip the package into the diplomatic bag, but the bitch doesn't snort herself, so. . .*''

''*Jean-Marc! Three flats and a glass of white!*''

''*Shit, all you have to do is listen at the bedroom door. . . .*''

''*. . .should wipe that damned smile off your face if I were you, or there's one or two of us'll wipe it off for you!*''

''*A goddamn flic, that's what the bastard is. I knew it as soon as I came in. . . .*''

Bolan recognized in the last surly voice the ill-tempered guy who had shouldered him aside at the bar. He had noticed his suspicious glare before the barman led him away, and he had no doubt he was still the subject of speculation. ''Very ingenious,'' he said. ''You have each table wired for sound, and other mikes concealed at strategic points around the room. How do you know when to listen to what?''

Tufik was delighted. He giggled like a high-school freshman. ''Good, is it not?'' he crowed. ''As to listening, all conversations are recorded automatically. I have two secretaries who go through the tapes each morning and transcribe anything they think might interest me." He pointed to two huge spools revolving on a complex deck beyond the speaker. "Multitrack, recording both sides."

"At least that material costs you nothing," Bolan said.

Tufik burst into a wheezing laugh. "That's right. This stuff is gratis—it offsets all the bread I lay out in other directions!"

"There must be one type of intel you can't pass on."

"Something Tufik cannot provide? You name it." The fat man bristled, his professional pride at stake.

"I mean details of what one client has asked you. You wouldn't reveal that information to another client, would you?"

"Ah, no, you're right there. Wouldn't be just, now would it? In a business relying on discretion, I couldn't do that at all."

Someplace amid the jumble a telephone was ringing. Tufik eventually located it beneath a heap of Sunday supplements. "Hello?... Yes, it is.... Good evening, Colonel, and the same to you." He listened for a few moments and then said, "Yes, I think I can. Just hang in there a minute, will you?... Now wait. Where did I put that cutting?"

He hunted among the sheaves of papers, propelling himself around the room with extraordinary speed. At last, with an exclamation of triumph, he came up with a clipping printed in Japanese characters that included a photo. "Got it!" he announced proudly into the mouthpiece. "Model girl from Tokyo who works in New York. Name of Umino Takimoto. They stayed at the Imperial in... Let's see... Yes, from the twenty-first to the twenty-seventh of April last year. Tried to duck out of a group photo in the *Miami Her-*

ald, but they're identifiable top left, walking out of the shot, issue of April 28..."

"Military attaché," he said as he put the phone down. "Now there's some poor politico who's going to have the bite put on him."

"Your work must make you unpopular sometimes," Bolan said.

"It does that. There's plenty who would try to put an end to it, believe you me. They nearly did once. That's why you see me here in this contraption. 'Twas when I was younger and stronger, and I had a mind to even the score with a gang of rascals who was spreading lying tales about me behind me back. They was trying to put me out of business, and I went up there to sort them out—only they had more friends than I did an' somebody put the boot in. Result: a spinal injury and partial paralysis."

"You seem to have plenty of protection now."

"Sure I do. I never go out. I have my girls and my work. I keep in touch, as you might say. Then there's Hassan and Jean-Marc and a couple more good ones to cover me. Wait'll I show you...." Tufik clapped his hands twice. "Bruno!"

A shutter slid open behind a blank space in the bookshelves and the muzzle of a machine pistol, capped by the long snout of a silencer, poked into the room. Above it, watchful eyes gleamed in the reflected light.

"All right, Bruno. Just a demonstration," the fat man called over his shoulder. The shutter snapped back into place. "But there you are, you see. My visitors are covered all the while."

Tufik drained his glass of Izarra and leaned back in the chair. "Now talking of visitors, I don't want to rush you, but I have callers expected. What did you want to know?"

"You must have helped my private investigator friend."

"These many years. I never knew who he worked for—that wasn't my affair—but, sure, I helped him many times."

"I'm following up a lead of his. He was killed before he could take it any farther. My question is simple. He was trailing a consignment of a certain commodity. I have reason to believe it's left Marseilles—or is about to leave—for Alexandria on a freighter. I want the name and address of a contact in Alex who'll be able to finger the consignment when it gets there—and who can fill me in on its final destination. Can you oblige?"

"I can, as it happens. At least the first part. Now we have two systems in this business: we have the subscription account, which is fine for clients like that military attaché, who constantly require snippets of information. But it'll hardly interest you. Then we have the one-off operation, for the flat fee."

"Which is?"

"For every isolated piece of important information, no matter how simple or complicated, off the top of me head or involving research, one thousand dollars. It may seem a lot, but if it's unobtainable anyplace else . . ." He shrugged. "And, as you see, I have my overheads."

Bolan had come prepared. He removed a wallet from his breast pocket and counted out ten hundred-dollar bills, then laid them on the table.

"Plus fifteen percent service charge," the fat man continued suavely. "The boys here are on a percentage. That's one of the reasons I get such good protection. And that's why Jean-Marc spurned your bribe."

The Executioner opened the wallet again and took out another hundred and five tens, placing them on top of the bills already on the table.

"And one percent state tax."

Bolan raised his eyebrows sardonically.

"This is Marseilles. There's different kinds of protection, you know."

Bolan shook his head in disbelief as he pulled two crumpled five-spots from his pocket.

"Right." Tufik's voice was suddenly brisk. "I can answer the first part of your query without any research. We get a lot of seamen in here, see. I can tell you that your consignment—let's just say that it's highly radioactive—left here at dawn yesterday aboard a Panamanian-registered freighter called the *Esperanza*. It's packed in a lead canister that's much heavier than it looks."

"Good. And the contact on the other side?"

"That's something I'll have to arrange for you."

"There's a limit to my largess."

"All part of the service," Tufik said smoothly, gathering up the bills and stuffing them into an inner pocket. "No extra fee. Now what you have to do—you'll be flying to Cairo and then driving to Alex?" At Bolan's nod, he continued. "Good. The day after tomorrow, in the afternoon, you take the Corniche and you go to Stanley Bay. It's the usual sort of bathing beach with a seafront and an esplanade. At the far end, on the landward side of the road, there's a restaurant called l'Oasis. It's a run-down sort of a place, standing by itself. You couldn't miss it. Order a Turkish coffee and an Izarra and wait. You'll be joined by a wee man called Ahmed Ibrahim, who works in the port weights and measures office. When there's stuff to be smuggled ashore by men on the boats, he's the man who fixes the routine. I think he will be able to help you."

"What time in the afternoon?" Bolan asked.

"Well, now, that lies beyond my competence right now, for I can't be after speaking for Ahmed's work schedule. But the harbor at Alexandria's a queer and interesting place, they do say. If you was to take a walk down there in the morning, say around eleven-thirty, and ask where the *Esperanza* will berth later in the day, I shouldn't be surprised if someone contrived to get a message to you that would fix a time."

"Thanks." Bolan rose to his feet. "I congratulate you on your sources, Monsieur Tufik. I'm impressed."

The fat man favored him with an impish grin. "You know what the British say when a child asks how a person finds out something? They tell them 'A little bird told me.' And that's the way of it with me, sure. Because in Arabic, the word *Tufik* means...a little bird!" He smiled again and held out his hand.

Bolan shook it and turned to leave.

When the slim torpedo named Hassan had shown the American out, Mustapha Tufik stared pensively at the papers scattered across his table. He sighed. Then, propelling his chair to the telephone, he lifted the handset.

"Hello?" he said. "Brigitte? Get me the Commissaire Le Brocquet at police headquarters, will you?"

CHAPTER FOUR

Bolan was expecting the attack—Broken-nose and his cronies had been conspicuous by their absence from the bar—but the timing of it and the method took him by surprise.

He had figured on an ambush someplace in the dark lane leading to the intersection where he had paid off his taxi. In fact the assault came from above: four men leaped down on him from a balcony above the archway that linked the lane with the courtyard.

He was sent sprawling to the cobbles by a violent blow in the back. Rolling with the fall, he drew up his knees to protect his groin, so that the follow-up man jumping for his belly tripped and fell heavily beside him. Bolan chopped him viciously in the throat and twisted eellike to his feet as the three others rushed him with upraised arms.

Backing up against the wall, he dragged the Beretta from its shoulder holster. But before he could thumb off the safety, a paralyzing knock on the right arm dropped it from his nerveless fingers.

Blows rained down on his head and shoulders, and from the corner of his eye Bolan saw the lamplight gleam on the length of lead pipe that had crippled his arm.

He drove his left elbow into one man's solar plexus, brought his knee up to parry a kick to the crotch then threw another punch at the first attacker, who was groping for the gun on the cobbles. He grunted and collapsed on his face as the Executioner kicked the weapon spinning into the middle of the lane.

Broken-nose and the two other thugs were trying to drag him to the ground. With a heave of his shoulders, the warrior broke momentarily free and piled a left, with all his weight behind it, to the jaw of the man with the lead pipe. The attacker dropped like a stone, his weapon clattering to the ground.

Bolan had whirled to butt one of the gorillas in the nose, and the man now sat in the roadway with blood streaming through his fingers. The warrior now faced the last thug, who wielded a knife with a wickedly curved blade.

Backing warily away along the wall, Bolan kept his eyes fixed on the murderous face, twisting aside as Broken-nose leaped forward with a tigerish bound. The assassin spun around and crouched for another spring, his knife arm held wide.

The Executioner kept moving until he found himself in front of a recessed doorway. The moment the Arab attacked again, Bolan backed into the entry and then, using a hand on each doorpost as a lever, he launched himself feet-first.

Cold ripped through his raincoat as his heels slammed against the man's chest and knocked him to the ground. Bolan scrambled upright, stamped on the killer's knife hand and took a running kick at his head.

The metal-capped tip of his combat boot connected just below the ear, and Broken-nose was out for the count.

Bolan was panting, and his right arm hurt like hell. Broken-nose lay where he had fallen, and the man with the smashed face sat sobbing into his bloodstained hands. But the other two thugs he had taken out were stirring.

As he searched the dark alley for the Beretta, the Executioner realized that it was no longer raining. Throughout the fight, which had lasted perhaps two and a half minutes, not a single light had come on, not one curious head had been thrust out a window. Now he was suddenly aware of the persistent splash, drip and trickle of water from eaves and broken gutters all around him. From somewhere over the rooftops, a two-tone car horn blared.

But the Beretta was nowhere to be found.

He advanced farther into the lane, bent double to scan the cobbles in the dim light. The Arab's knife had slashed through raincoat and jacket, and the chamois holster for the missing autoloader—which had probably saved his life—was sliced in two. He was covered in mud, had a jagged cut on his forehead and his right arm was useless.

He stood, in order to take in a greater area of the wet stones, and halted abruptly. By the light from the intersection below, he could see three men in long overcoats and wide-brimmed hats advancing toward him. Before he had time to react, a slug from a silenced automatic caromed off the cobbles at his feet and ricocheted past his shoulder.

The Beretta would have to be abandoned. At first Bolan had figured the attackers for minor underworld characters determined to get someone they believed to be a police spy, or two-bit crooks who thought he might have money. Strangers were always in danger of getting rolled in this part of town. But the appearance of the three pros convinced him the attack was directed at him personally. And that it must be connected with his search for the missing uranium.

He turned and sprinted uphill. He heard someone shout hoarsely close behind him. Two of the thugs who had attacked him were on their feet, lamplight gleaming briefly on the steel one of them held.

Snatching the AutoMag from his right hip, Bolan blazed off a couple of shots in the direction of the archway, two more at the goons down below then raced around a corner in the lane.

He thought he'd seen one of the torpedoes in the long coats lurch and fall, but there was no time to check. There were situations where the odds on success were too long, situations from which it was wiser to withdraw. He reckoned this was one of them—if he wanted to stay alive long enough to follow up on the radioactive isotope.

Immediately ahead of him, he saw a low wrought-iron balcony above a barred doorway. He leaped upward, grabbing the sill with his fingers.

For an instant his numb right arm gave way, and he hung by one hand. Then he managed to swing up a leg and place the wrist of his damaged arm between the bars. It was a painful struggle to lever himself to a position that would allow him to slip over the railing.

Light seeped through the slats of shutters across the window beyond. As the sound of footsteps around the corner below drew nearer, Bolan dropped to one knee and peered through. The window inside was wide open.

Voices called out in the dark alleyway. The warrior drew back his right foot and slammed it into flimsy wood halfway up the shutters. The wood splintered and gave way. He thrust an arm through the jagged space and twisted the catch, jerking the shutters open.

Inside the squalid bedroom, a woman with hennaed hair had been admiring herself in a flyblown pier glass. She jumped to her feet, flabby body quivering, as the warrior tumbled through the opening. The face painted over her features cracked open in a smile. "Not without an appointment, handsome, *if* you please," she croaked with mock severity.

"No sweat, honey. Just passing through," Bolan tossed over his shoulder as he walked to the door.

"Mind you, I could always make an exception..." the woman began. But Bolan was already halfway down the dingy hallway, which contained four doors: one in each long wall and one at either end.

Counting on one leading to a stairway, he tried the door at the far end. It opened on another bedroom, and revealed a black man and a blonde lying in bed listening to a transistor radio. A baby slept in a crib near the foot of the bed.

The man started up in terror, clutching the covers across his chest. "I don't want trouble, man," he stammered. "I don't want to get involved in—"

"The stairs," Bolan rapped, interrupting him. "Where are the stairs?"

"Look, I don't want trouble. I don't want to get—"

"The *stairs*?"

"If you want money, man, I don't have none. If you're from the police, this here's my wife and that's our kid. I don't want trouble."

Bolan suddenly realized that these people were probably scared to death because of his blood-streaked face and muddy clothes. He turned to the blonde. "Look," he said. "I just want you to tell me which door leads to the staircase."

She stared at him through sleepy eyes. "Second on the left," she murmured. "Turn right at the bottom for the back entrance. It lets you out on another street."

"Thanks."

"Any time," the woman said laconically. "Emerson, for God's sake lie down."

Bolan jerked open the door leading to the stairs and charged down the steps, bullets splintering through woodwork as he turned right and dashed along another corridor. The rear entrance was an archway off a crude kitchen where an old Arab woman slept upright in a chair by the cooking stove.

Bolan crossed a small yard, climbed a wall with the help of a garbage can and dropped ten feet to a sunken lane on the far side. The lane traced an irregular course between shuttered houses for several hundred yards, finally terminating in a stone stairway that led down to the brightly lit streets of the La Joliette quarter behind the dockyards.

Half an hour later, he was back in his hotel, reflecting on the night's events. He had lost a gun, and he ached all over, but he knew now without any doubt that there was a contract out for him and hired killers were on his trail.

But there was a positive that counterbalanced those negatives and then some—he knew where he was going. And with luck he would find out when he got there where the stolen consignment of uranium 235 was going, too.

CHAPTER FIVE

The Mediterranean at Stanley Bay was no longer blue. Oyster-colored and smooth, the ocean blended with the sky half a mile offshore and the noonday sun, invisible above the haze, transformed the humid atmosphere into a steam bath that left the vacation crowds from the city lying exhausted on the beach.

Bolan parked the rented Corvette a couple hundred yards from the end of the esplanade and walked the rest of the way to l'Oasis. He was in no hurry, but by the time he made it his clammy shirt was stuck to his back and the damp heat had plastered his hair to his scalp.

As Tufik had said, the place looked run-down: the peeling stucco walls were stained, grass grew through cracks in the concrete parking lot, the iron terrace tables beneath their faded parasols were marked with rust.

Half a dozen teenaged Egyptians chattered over gaudy ice creams inside. Bolan ordered his coffee and Izarra, and sat down on the terrace near a large family of French-speaking Lebanese. He watched the sea gather enough strength to flop into a minuscule wave, which sank into the sand before it had time to recede. It seemed a long time before the next wave limped in.

Bolan was early for the rendezvous. He wanted to take the temperature of the place, to check the atmosphere and options, and, finally, to plan escape routes in case the meet went sour.

He had strolled the waterfront, all morning sauntering along moss-covered wharves, gazing at the long lines of big ships ranked in Alexandria's huge dockyard, sometimes pausing to stare at a thicket of masts and rigging outside the yacht club overlooking the inner basin. Once a sentry had warned him away from a bay where two coast guard gunboats were refueling. Otherwise nobody came near him.

Just before eleven-thirty, as briefed by Tufik, he had asked someone where the *Esperanza* was due to dock, and was told it would be at the far end of a wooden jetty in the outer harbor.

A traveling crane had been railed into position outside the customs shed, and coils of rope lay ready by the iron bollards. As yet, there were no stevedores in sight.

Bolan had walked up and down the wharf, playing the part of a rubbernecking tourist. He had bought an inexpensive camera and spent some time maneuvering himself into position to take "artistic" shots of the shipping. It had been a quarter to twelve when a stone wrapped in paper—thrown from somewhere behind him—landed on the wooden deck at his feet.

Bolan had swung around, but had seen no one.

He had unwrapped the paper, which contained no words—just a meticulously drawn clock face with the hands pointing to 1:15. He had returned to his car and driven to l'Oasis at once.

Now it was 1:45. For the twentieth time the Executioner stared over the peeling wooden rail of the terrace at the livid sea. What if there was no contact and Tufik had been stringing him along?

No, that was crazy: if the Moroccan-Irishman had been conning him, there would have been no message on the wharf.

Okay, so there *was* a contact. What if the killers on Bolan's own trail had gotten to him first? Could he pick up a cold trail here in Alexandria, with no names and no addresses? No way.

He'd have to go back to Marseilles, in the hope of choking intel out of some underworld hood.

Bolan's sober reflections were interrupted by the rustle of tires on concrete. A small man in a rumpled white suit carried a pedal cycle out of the parking lot and propped it against the terrace railing. Climbing the steps, he looked quickly around him—a ferrety little guy with dark shades and a ragged mustache smudged across his face.

The Lebanese family was squabbling over which movie to see that evening. Two students who had installed themselves on the terrace ten minutes earlier were ordering mint tea. A crowd of young people inside the restaurant had begun to sing.

The slight man zeroed in on Bolan's table: the small glass of yellow liquor, the copper pan of coffee. He hurried over and dropped into a vacant chair.

"Ahmed Ibrahim?" Bolan asked.

"No names, please," the man said nervously, glancing over his shoulder. "My apologies for the delay. As you can see, someone's blown the whistle." He dragged a folded newspaper from an inner pocket and spread it on the table.

It was that day's edition of *Al Ahram*, turned back to an inside page with a short item ringed in red marker: Bomb Outrages Rock Marseilles.

Following a mystery explosion that wrecked a cab in a main street of the city yesterday, police were today trying to pinpoint reasons behind a bomb blast that destroyed a coffee shop in the old part of the town during the early hours of the morning. Among the victims were six Arab girls and three men....

Bolan stopped reading and dropped the paper onto the table. "I suppose it was a matter of time before someone got him."

Ibrahim's fingers were trembling, "Not someone," he said. "*They* got him. He...he called me and told me what you wanted to know. I think I can help. I can put you in touch.... But I had to find out another way, and it'll cost you."

"I was told there wasn't any more to pay. Tufik—"

"No names, *please*. I know you were told that, but this bomb thing has altered everything." Ibrahim mopped his brow with a large silk handkerchief. "I've got a wife and family. I want out. When I agreed at first, I never expected... It'll cost you," he repeated, looking nervously over his shoulder once more.

"Okay, so it'll cost me. The point is, can you deliver?"

"I told you, yes. But it's difficult. They must know somebody's on the trail. In fact I know they do, because they switched plans. I have friends in the police and Movement Control, you see. That's why I was late. I was checking—"

"Just tell me what you know," Bolan interrupted.

"The...consignment in which you're interested was taken off the ship the moment it docked. That was less than an hour ago. It was lowered onto a dory on the far side from the quay and rowed to the other side of the harbor."

"No suspicions on the part of the customs officials?"

"Everyone was looking the other way. Like I said, these things cost. The stuff was driven out of town on the road to Cairo. There's a helicopter meeting them someplace in the desert to take the consignment aboard."

"They must be rattled to pull something that obvious. Do you know where the chopper's headed?"

"I heard it was Khartoum, in the Sudan. There isn't a lot more that I can.., What do you want to do?"

"What happens to the stuff in Khartoum?" Bolan asked.

"I don't know. I think someone mentioned something about a camel caravan."

"A *camel* caravan? You're serious? Where would they be going? The interior?"

"I tell you I don't *know*. I can pass on only what I heard."

Bolan took a sip of cold coffee. Unlikely though it seemed, the information figured. He remembered the emphasis on camels in Brognola's movie clue. A desert caravan would be as good a way as any to shift hot merchandise from one point to another without attracting attention. Maybe that had always been part of the plan; maybe it was just the method of getting the uranium to Khartoum that had been changed.

"I've got to contact that caravan," he said. "I want the name of someone in Khartoum who can identify it, someone who can fill me in on where it starts from, the assembly point. If possible I want a lead to people who could fix me up with the right kind of disguise, with papers and all that. I need to join that camel train. Can you get me an in?"

Ahmed Ibrahim thought for a moment, drumming his fingers on the table. "It is not easy," he said at last. "And they have spies everywhere. But there is an Englishman in Khartoum. He is local correspondent for the Madison news agency, I think. He would know about caravans and where they go. I cannot say whether he could identify this particular one, and I'm not sure about the papers. What exactly did you want?"

"I don't know until I get there. But two separate sets, for sure. One to justify my presence with the caravan..."

"Oh, Arab papers. The Brit could handle that all right."

"And another set that could pass muster if I had to leave the caravan and assume the identity of a Westerner."

"Ah. That would be more difficult. The Sudan is a troubled area, particularly in the south. Strangers are unwelcome."

"That's why I have to have foolproof ID, the right kind of cover, permits, etcetera."

"Courtney—that's the Englishman—couldn't help you there. You'd have to go to someone more important, a Sudanese in a high position. From the military, perhaps, or the ministry of the interior. But you would have to be very careful. They have infiltrated—"

"You keep saying 'they,'" Bolan interrupted. "Who? Who are these people? Who fixed the port authorities? Who transported the stuff in a helicopter? Who has spies everywhere? Are they part of the same organization as the isotope thieves, or just the hired help?"

Ibrahim looked apprehensive. For the third time he stared at the beach, the terrace, the inside of the restaurant. The Lebanese children—three boys and two girls between the ages of five and ten—had finished swimming and were playing some Mediterranean version of cowboys and Indians around the terrace steps. Their parents were lying flat out on the sand with newspapers spread over their faces. The young people inside had stopped singing and started to play a board game.

"Very dangerous people," Ibrahim said. "They have contacts in many countries. You could find out more, perhaps, from a man called Hamid el-Karim. He is *very* important. A high post in the interior ministry. He also has a high standard of living. He has a great deal of interest in money."

"Tell me something I couldn't guess," Bolan murmured.

"El-Karim can give you any papers you want—at a price. But you must have a good cover reason for asking. And do not on any account mention to him the caravan angle."

"Why?"

"Because he is the man who—"

The Egyptian stopped in midsentence, brushing a hand irritably over his nape as if a fly was troubling him. One of the kids on the steps shouted something triumphantly.

"Who what?" Bolan prompted.

Ibrahim was gazing at him with wide-open eyes. Suddenly his body corkscrewed in the chair and he pitched forward across the table, scattering the Executioner's cup, saucer and glass. The copper pan fell to the wooden deck of the terrace, spilling coffee grounds over the white alpaca suit.

Bolan was on his feet, leaping to the stricken man's side. The two students ran to join him. "What happened?" one asked. "Is he ill?"

"Terminally," Bolan rasped. He ran his hand over the back of Ibrahim's lolling head, withdrawing the tiny feathered steel dart that projected from the neck just below the hairline. There would be a lot less trouble—and his wife and kids would come out of it better off—if the death was read as a simple heart attack. If the quick-acting poison was Rycin, an alkaloid much favored by the KGB, Ibrahim's body would show all the signs of coronary thrombosis.

He ran across to the steps to the boy with the toy pistol, who was crying. "I didn't mean to hurt the man," he sobbed. "It was supposed to be a joke."

"Who said that? Who gave you the gun?" Bolan asked.

The child flung out an arm, pointing along the water's edge. "There. The man with the sun hat."

"The one in the striped shirt?"

"No! The one wearing jeans and a jacket. He said I c-c-could keep this—" the gun was a long-barreled Webley air pistol "—if I pretended to shoot the man at the t-t-table. He said it was a game. We were supposed to be chasing the bad man from the CIA. He g-g-gave me money." Tears streamed down the boy's face. "But he never said the gun was loaded...."

Bolan was already running. "Don't worry, kid," he yelled over his shoulder. "It's not your fault. *He* was the bad man!"

The guy in the jeans and safari jacket was almost one hundred yards away. He was a chunky man, not very tall, but he looked to be in shape. He was carrying a blue airline bag, and the hat on his head was a wide-brimmed straw.

He had been picking his way between the prone sunbathers at a fair pace, although not quickly enough to attract attention. As soon as he heard Bolan shout, he began to run.

He scattered a group of youths playing handball, ran through a family picnic spread out on the sand and bounded up a flight of stone steps to the esplanade.

Ignoring the shouts of protest, the Executioner followed.

Up on the pavement, the killer by proxy sprinted for a red Alfa Romeo roadster parked by the curb. He leaped over the cutaway door into the cockpit, twisted a key already in the ignition and, as the engine burst into life, leaned out to blast off a couple of shots at his pursuer.

Vacationers screamed and flung themselves flat, seeing the tall, grim-faced American leap sideways and draw a large silver automatic. He dropped to one knee and returned the hit man's fire. But the red convertible pulled out into the roadway with a shriek of tires, laying down rubber as the driver tweaked it into a U-turn and roared away toward the outskirts of the city.

Bolan's Corvette was fifty yards away, and he reached it in Olympic time, flooring the pedal to send the sleek sport coupé howling in pursuit.

Street traders, kids playing, a mule with bulging panniers stopped him from closing up as the two cars raced through a shantytown behind the seafront. But once clear of the white, flat-roofed suburban houses that lay among the stands of palm and tamarisk beyond, the Corvette began to gain.

The killer was a good driver: he knew just how fast he could hurl the little roadster into a corner without braking; he could judge to an inch the gaps in the traffic through which he could safely squeeze.

Bolan was as good, if not better. His big, brown muscled hands lay easily on the wheel as he slid around curves, shifted down, gunned the engine and slowly narrowed the gap between them.

Until they made a stretch of higher ground five miles outside the city on the coastal strip, the Alfa Romeo was gaining on the corners and the 233 hp Corvette forged ahead each time there was a straightaway.

But the American car came into its own once the sinuous grades leading up from the plain flattened out. Here the road arrowed straight as a die through orange groves and plantations of cotton, and the Executioner was able to make full use of his vehicle's powerful 5.7-liter V8.

The warm, damp wind screamed past the steeply raked shield and the bellow of the exhaust beat back from stone walls on either side of the road as the coupé surged forward.

The gap between them was reduced to eighty yards, sixty, fifty. Bolan took a hand from the wheel and loosed off a couple of experimental shots from the AutoMag. But they were doing more than ninety, both cars slewing left and right over the poor road surface, and accurate shooting was impossible. If either of the slugs zeroed in on the Alfa, it made no difference to the car's performance.

Bolan was no more than thirty yards behind when the roadster's brake lights blazed, the sloping tail swung out, and the killer wrenched the Alfa onto a dirt road that twisted away between rows of fig trees.

The maneuver was too abrupt for Bolan to follow. He stamped on the brake pedal, fighting the wheel to keep the Corvette straight. The coupé's tires shrieked in protest, streaking black marks along the pavement. Fifty yards beyond the turnoff, the vehicle had slowed enough for him to lock the wheel hard over, haul up on the hand brake and slide the car around in a one-eighty degree turn.

He raced back to the turnoff and swung into the dirt road in a shower of gravel. The Alfa Romeo was no longer in sight. The road breasted a slight rise in the land and then dipped into a valley brimming with acacia, pine and wild cherry. Beyond the trees, the leaden sea reflected a faint gleam of sunshine.

The Corvette hurtled over the brow of the hill and bumped down into a depression. A ten-ton covered truck with the rear doors open and a ramp slanting to the ground stood beneath the pines. The Alfa Romeo had already climbed the ramp and parked inside the truck. As Bolan wrestled the car to a halt at the edge of the clearing, the driver jumped down and joined the two guys with submachine guns, who were lying between the rear wheels.

They opened fire a fraction of a second after the warrior hit the door handle and dived to the ground on the passenger side of the Vette. He could hear the slugs thwacking into the fiberglass bodywork like steel hail.

From where he lay, sheltered by one of the vehicle's front wheels, Bolan could see the flicker of flame blossoming in front of the SMGs, the occasional sharp stab as the Alfa driver choked out a shot from his handgun. Bullets scuffed the dirt beside the Executioner, throwing up chips of stone that stung his cheek.

Bolan held the AutoMag in one hand, and withdrew the Walther PPK automatic he had bought from Marseilles's black market to replace the lost Beretta. He didn't like it as much as the Italian pistol, but it was useful enough at short range, and the 7.65 mm rounds—as the German army had found in World War II—were as lethal as anything that could be fired despite their small bore.

The glade echoed to the sharp stammer of the SMGs and the deeper, single bark of autoloaders. Birds screeched and flapped away from the treetops. Leaves ripped from the lower branches of bushes floated to the ground. Sighting through a hole in the Corvette's alloy wheel, Bolan inserted the Walther's slender 3.5 inch barrel and blasted off three of the magazine's seven skullbusters at the rear of the truck. While the gunmen ducked back into the shelter of the ramp, he shuffled quickly from behind the Corvette on elbows and knees and flung himself into a shallow depression behind a clump of cistus. From there he had a wider angle on his targets without being any more vulnerable himself.

There was now a gap of seven or eight feet between the ramp and the nearest pair of wheels, and the killers had to ease themselves farther back beneath the truck to avoid the punishing 240-grain deathstream being pumped at them from the AutoMag.

One slug pierced the truck's muffler; another ricocheted off a stone and whined away among the trees. Bolan saw a third strike sparks from the axle casing. Then he was obliged to flatten himself against the earth as a hurricane of lead erupted from the SMGs and zipped through the leaves fractions of an inch above his head.

The reverberations of the fusillade were still ringing in his ears when one of the gunners crawled out the side of the truck and, convinced the Executioner would still have his head down, made a dash for a fallen tree, hoping he could enfilade the big guy.

The miscalculation cost him his life.

From the corner of his eye Bolan saw the fleeing figure, rolled onto his back with one arm stretched above his head and emptied the Walther's magazine. Three shots smashed into the killer, tearing away part of his right arm, fisting through his back and coring his skull. He dropped through a spray of scarlet, as inert as a puppet whose strings have been cut.

Bolan twisted around to face the truck again as the engine roared suddenly to life. The second machine gunner had crawled out the front and climbed into the cab.

There was a whine of hydraulic gear, the ramp retracted and the rear doors of the van swung shut. It was already moving when the driver of the Alfa Romeo dragged himself from between the wheels and ran for the cab, a 3-shot burst chugging from his automatic at Bolan as he leaped for the step and the open door above it.

For the first time, the Executioner got a good look at the guy's face. Swarthy, pockmarked, striped with a hairline mustache, the features were those of the gorilla with the lead pipe who had numbed his arm outside Mustapha Tufik's coffee shop in Marseilles.

The AutoMag thundered, heaving in Bolan's two-handed grip. A driving mirror shattered. A .44 flesh-shredder splashed blood from the killer's left arm. He spun sideways, holding on desperately with his right. But the driver reached across and hauled him into the cab before Bolan could finish him.

The truck swung around in a cloud of dust and lumbered along the dirt road toward the ocean.

Okay, the Executioner thought grimly. Right now they were even, with one damaged arm each. But it wouldn't be long before he chalked up an extra score. He ran for the Corvette.

The engine spun, turned, turned again. But wouldn't fire.

Hurling himself from the cockpit, Bolan stretched out an arm to open the hood . . . and then allowed it to drop to his side.

His nose supplied the answer before his eyes.

The bottom of the tank had been cored three times by the first volley from the SMGs. Twelve gallons of gasoline, gushing out to sink into the dry earth, were now vaporizing in the heat of the afternoon.

He shrugged. So it would have to wait until he made Khartoum.

He walked across to the dead man. The submachine gun was a Heckler & Koch MP5—the SD-3 version with a telescopic butt and fitting for a 40 mm silencer.

The muffler itself was in a pouch clipped to the guy's belt, along with a fistful of 9 mm parabellum rounds.

Bolan nodded. A useful weapon. He hoped he'd have the opportunity to use it himself.

He refilled the curved 30-round magazine, stuffed the remaining spares into his pocket, wrapped the SMG in his jacket and started the long hike back to the city.

CHAPTER SIX

The rented car was a Buick Electra sedan. One thousand miles south of Cairo and Alexandria, the scorching dry heat of Khartoum hit Bolan like a hammer and he was happy to trade off a fraction of performance against the Buick's air-conditioning.

He left the car in the underground parking lot beneath David Courtney's modern apartment block and rode up to the eleventh floor in an elevator large enough to hold twenty people.

The British man was tall, thin and immaculate, with iron-gray hair curling just enough at the nape to remain chic. Bolan saw a shrink-wrapped face, a thermonuclear smile and pale suede shoes. He wasn't too happy about what he saw—the guy looked like he was the kind of whiz kid PR type that the Executioner detested—but hell, he was the only lead he had; this was no time to let personal opinions intrude.

What intrigued him about Courtney was the fact that Ahmed Ibrahim was the *second* person to put forward his name as a contact. The first had been Hal Brognola. It seemed that the Brit was used by the CIA for occasional legwork: in a part of the world where even to *be* American was to invite hysterical accusations of espionage and dark threats of counterplots, the Company was happy to channel routine information through the nationals of any friendly country.

In the circumstances, Bolan figured it was okay to pretend he was a roving CIA field agent with special responsibility for the North African theater.

"What I want to know, Courtney," he said brusquely, after the formalities had been completed, "is why your name was given to me by an Alexandria stool pigeon. Why were you the first person he thought of when I asked for a contact to help with certain activities that are not exactly legal?"

The Englishman opened his mouth to reply, but Bolan brushed the interruption aside. His exasperation was partly genuine. "How come you're the guy who can fix fake papers for Arabs, who has all the intel on contraband camel trains?" he demanded. "And if you do, why in hell didn't you report it to Langley? What kind of game are you playing, anyway?"

"Why didn't I report?" Courtney flushed slightly. "Well, actually, because I wasn't asked to, if you want to know." He passed a nervous hand over his hair.

"Weren't *asked* to?" Bolan exploded. "Well, for God's sake! What are you supposed to be doing for us here, if it's not to report things like that?"

"My briefing is to report anything I think would be of interest to Langley. I didn't think this would, that's all."

"Good God, man, if this isn't—"

"By and large," Courtney continued smoothly, "that means a situation report every month. Plus fuller reports on anything specific I'm *asked* to cover. Plus liaison with people like you, if required. Hell, I'm not on the payroll full time. I'm not a field agent like you."

"I know it. But surely a shipment of uranium 235 . . ."

"I didn't know it was 235. I didn't even know for sure it was uranium. Only that it was some radioactive substance.

I mean, it could have been intended for medical research, or for use in a cancer hospital."

"Traveling secretly in a camel train?"

"Perhaps to avoid some kind of import duty . . . or damn fool questions posed by frontier police."

Bolan contrived a sigh. "I suppose so."

"You said yourself, actually, that you didn't know until yesterday, until Ibrahim told you, that the stuff was coming to Khartoum."

"Yeah. But that doesn't alter the fact that you should have reported it."

"I can't report everything shady that happens in the city," Courtney argued. "That would choke the airwaves every day. I mean, so I made an error in judgment. I'm sorry. End of story."

Bolan looked around the room. Stainless steel and black glass; Persian rugs on a marble floor; white hide armchairs. The place looked as rich as the inside of a Rolls-Royce. He walked to the French windows. Beyond the intense shade cast by an awning over the balcony, concrete buildings across the street shimmered in the glaring heat. A rumble of afternoon traffic drifted up from below.

"As far as Ahmed knowing my name is concerned," the voice drawled behind the Executioner, "I really can't see what's worrying you."

"You can't?"

"Absolutely not. I mean, well, you know my cover is a stringer for a news agency. Well, that's a job I do have to do. I have to file every day. Ahmed is . . . was . . . simply one of my informants."

"Did he know you worked sometimes for the Company?"

"Of course not." Courtney's voice was raised. "I'm not that dumb. As I said, he was just a common informer. You lay out the cash, he'll give with the info. Like your man in Marseilles, only on a smaller scale. To him, I was just a client needing inside stuff for my news stories—and of course for other reasons."

"Such as?"

"Well, the sort of questions I sometimes had to ask, he must have reasoned I had other interests. For all I know, he thought I worked for MI-6, or the West Germans, or even the Russians. But his kind don't ask questions. They just take the money and go. I would think he figured I could help you simply *because* he knew the kind of stuff that interested *me*."

"Yeah. But he was wrong this time, wasn't he? Because the stuff *didn't* interest you. Not enough to report it." Bolan looked around the expensive room again. "This informing business with Ahmed Ibrahim," he said, eyeing Courtney's immaculately cut sharkskin suit, "it wouldn't have been two-way traffic by any chance?"

Courtney flushed a deeper red. "I hardly think that question deserves an answer," he said stiffly.

Bolan grinned, then peeled off his own jacket and dropped it on the floor. He loosened his necktie. "Okay," he said affably. "Question out of order. Sorry, Courtney. I guess the heat's getting me down. Next question: how right was Ibrahim? How much do you think you *can* help me?"

"For the caravan? I fancy we should be able to cope, as a matter of fact," the Brit said, looking Bolan up and down. "You're a little tall, and the blue eyes are a minus point. But you've got fairly deep-set lids, you have a...decided...cast of feature and best of all your hair is dark. With the right sort of overall stain, and a fringe of beard to offset that chin, you should pass after my boy's had a go at you. How's your Arabic?"

"Barely passable."

"You'd better be a pilgrim, then. Perhaps a Berber. They come pretty tall. And they keep to themselves and hardly utter a word on these jaunts."

"A pilgrim," Bolan echoed. "Where to?"

"There's a sect that beetle off to some shrine just north of the Zaire border every two months. Kind of a poor man's Mecca. They go with the trade caravans for safety's sake."

"And there's a party of them with the uranium caravan?"

"So they tell me. In any case, that's the only way you could get away with it. Without arousing suspicion, that is."

"Why?"

"Well, I'm afraid the only possible in is for you to substitute yourself for some joker already on the list, as it were. No chance of buying your way in. They're much too religious. But there's a police captain who can be bought. The drill is, you get a set of papers to match some chap who's already signed on, and then the police captain runs the chap in on some pretext and keeps him under wraps until the caravan's gone. Meanwhile, there you are in his place."

"It seems a bit tough on the 'chap,'" Bolan said dryly.

"Yes, well, that's a pity. But they let him go after a couple of days, anyway. Too expensive to feed them inside. The locals are used to incomprehensible police behavior in this part of the world," Courtney said apologetically. "I'm afraid it's the only way."

"I don't want to put an innocent man in jail, even for a couple of days."

"Well, leave it to me. I'll see what I can fix."

"Okay. And you know someone who can get me to the right place at the right time? With the right caravan?"

"Absolutely. It's some way south of the city, the assembly point. We'll get you there. Can you, uh, can you ride a camel?"

"If I have to."

"Splendid. I should warn you, though, that if you're caught impersonating a pilgrim, the consequences can be deuced unpleasant. These Arab johnnies are very strong on Allah and the Prophet. You'd have to leg it like hell for the bush if they did unmask you."

"I'll worry about that if it happens."

"Quite. I just thought I'd mention it," Courtney said.

The Executioner was about to ask him for a rundown on the activities of the highly placed Sudanese official, Hamid el-Karim, but he changed his mind at the last minute.

Courtney had yet to prove himself; he had yet to show Bolan that his instinctive mistrust of the man was misplaced. On a need-to-know basis, el-Karim didn't come within the Englishman's orbit. So why make a present of privileged intel to a man whose loyalty was still an unknown quantity?

For a warrior whose three golden rules of combat were identify, infiltrate and destroy, Bolan was in a difficult position.

He was on the trail of a gang of nuclear thieves; the thieves knew he was on their trail; they had killed his contacts, had tried to waste him, too. But he was no nearer knowing who they were than he had been when he was first briefed by Hal Brognola.

And without identification he didn't have a hope in hell of infiltrating the organization—whatever it was.

Destruction, at the moment, was no more than a penciled-in notice of intention, on a date still to be fixed.

But the date would become specific. Because whatever the difficulties, he was damned well going to crack this one. He would find out who these thieves were if it was the last thing he did.

And, once fingered, they in turn would find out, all right, that it took only one man to make a wave of destruction.

End of story.

CHAPTER SEVEN

Three miles from David Courtney's apartment building, in a shuttered villa behind tall hedges of tamarisk, Mack Bolan was ushered into a study furnished in ornate luxury.

The black Nubian in flowing white robes who had escorted him from Hamid el-Karim's marble reception hall bowed and withdrew.

The man behind the huge glass-topped desk was lean and dark, a narrow mustache emphasizing the chiseled planes of his mouth. Above his sleek head, a horizontal fan with six-foot blades revolved slowly in the hot, dry air.

"Bolan?" he said, glancing at the card the Executioner had presented. "That is an unusual name, *monsieur*."

"It's Russian." Bolan lied smoothly. As an in, he had claimed acquaintance with the Soviet general in charge of the KGB's Eighth Directive. "From the Don basin, originally."

"You know Major General Asimov well?"

"At one time we were very close," Bolan said truthfully. In fact they had been firing at each other over the rubble of a bombed building in West Beirut, where Bolan had foiled a KGB plan to patch in to satellite communications linking the French embassy there with Washington. "The general has been a great help to me."

"I must say that I do not customarily receive visitors unknown to me personally. However, since you mentioned the name of—shall we say?—a mutual friend of great eminence, and since, to be honest, your own name intrigued me, I made an exception.''

"It is an honor to receive such flattering consideration from a highly placed person," Bolan said fulsomely. "And in particular that he should permit himself to be intruded upon at home."

"There are certain . . . transactions . . . better approached in the informality of the home, *monsieur*."

"Precisely."

"In what way may I assist you, Monsieur Bolan?"

"I have a desire to visit the southern part of your agreeable country."

"Indeed? May one ask why?"

"Of course. It's said there may be certain mineral deposits," Bolan said carefully, "to the southwest of the El Marra massif. It seems that these might be well worth exploiting— by those, of course, with practically unlimited resources. The lignite veins, for example, are said to be by no means as poor as the reference books would have us believe. The bauxite, too, is rich enough to interest those with a need for aluminum. To say nothing of more, uh, esoteric ores."

"And you represent such an interest?"

"I do. And might I add that those who cooperate with my gov—with my principals, would find themselves well rewarded. There is a great deal of money involved. A very great deal."

Hamid el-Karim leaned back in his steel-and-leather chair. His tongue flicked once rapidly around his well-shaped lips. "Your, ah, principals have charged you with the task of verifying these reports?" he asked.

"Yes. I guess I don't have to elaborate?"

"No, no. Indeed not. But in this exploratory stage, how can I help you?"

"They tell me there's a certain amount of dissidence down there. I wouldn't want, during my researches, to mix it with rebels. Or for that matter with your efficient troops policing the region. Apart from which, in the normal way, I imagine you would hardly welcome strangers there."

"There are one or two cutthroat bands of renegade blacks," el-Karim said carelessly, flicking a speck of dust from his lapel. "We Muslims here in the north are continually being misrepresented by the backward Negroes of the south. Agitators are sent in to stir up trouble, and the poor fools fancy themselves exploited. But there is nothing that could be called a rebellion proper.... Nevertheless, it is true that a foreigner wandering there without the benefit of official accreditation could run into trouble."

"Just so." Now that he had been dealt the card, Bolan played it. "And since it was not considered desirable at this early stage to make an official approach at governmental level, I'm here to ask your help in my getting some sort of laissez-passer, which would at once identify me, justify my presence in that area and assure those it might concern that I am, as it were, under your distinguished protection."

The Sudanese rose from behind the desk, moving elegantly across the big room to a wall map flanked by a coat of arms and the national flag. "I gather the areas in question would be, roughly, here...and here...and perhaps here?" he said, tapping the map with a manicured finger.

"Right. And also, maybe, in the province of Western Equatoria, nearer the Zaire border," said Bolan, who had pored over maps as well as mineralogical reports in the library. "Would you care for a Russian cigarette?"

"Thank you, I do not smoke. Please do so yourself, if you feel so inclined."

Bolan murmured a polite acknowledgment as he placed the brown tube between his lips. He seemed to have some trouble manipulating his heavy bronze lighter, for it took several attempts before the spark produced a flame.

El-Karim waited by the map, tapping his teeth with a gold pencil. "I see no problem in arranging that," he said when the cigarette was drawing properly.

"You understand why it is preferred to make this initial approach at a . . . personal . . . level? An official *démarche* would inevitably draw attention to the project."

"And signal your interest to possible rivals? Do not worry, Monsieur Bolan. Discretion is assured. If you could go this evening to the regional military directorate at this address—" he moved back to his desk and scribbled a few lines on a sheet from an ivory-framed memo pad "—the necessary documents will be waiting for you. Please take your passport to identify yourself. The staff will themselves take care of photographs and attach a copy to the papers—just to make sure there is no mistake, you understand. And you should also present this. . . ."

He wrote something on a second memo sheet, tore both sheets from the pad and handed them to the Executioner.

"You are very kind."

"It is a pleasure. Oh . . ." Hamid el-Karim paused as if struck by a sudden thought. "There is one thing. Such extramural activities regrettably involve the participant in certain expenses. There are, I am afraid, various charges, payable to the official departments concerned, inseparable from the issue of such papers." He shrugged. "You know how it is."

Bolan knew exactly. Most governments had their fair share of corrupt money grabbers.

Bolan replied, "I quite understand. It's to be expected. I have already trespassed too much on your generosity. But since it's already after office hours and I have no other way of paying these charges, would it be too much of an imposition if I was to entrust these monies to you for disbursement in the right quarters?''

''In the circumstances,'' the Sudanese said suavely, ''I would be prepared to waive protocol and perform this service for you.''

Bolan reached for his wallet.

An hour later, back in his hotel, he unloaded the spool of film from the tiny camera built into the bronze cigarette lighter and developed it in the bathroom. Two of the shots he had taken were too blurred to be usable; the other three were as clear as a bell—two profiles of el-Karim pointing at the map of the Sudan; one full face of him standing by the flag and tapping his teeth with the gold pencil.

Bolan dismantled the miniature lapel mike and the fine wire linking it to the cigarette-pack tape recorder in his breast pocket. Playing back the recording of his interview, he found to his annoyance that the tape had run out in the middle of el-Karim's sentence explaining that ''such extramural activities'' cost money.

Without the part where he agreed to take the cash himself—and the actual amount, which was specified later—the tape wouldn't be much use as a lever, if ever Bolan needed one. On the face of it, the recording showed no more than an official going out of his way to accommodate a foreign prospector.

He sealed it carefully just the same, and he made postcard-size prints of the three photos. In a country where bribery was a way of life and blackmail a way up the ladder of success, there was no way of knowing when they might be of help.

The next morning Courtney came by the hotel to report that one of his spies had discovered the caravan was headed for Wadi Djarzireh, beyond the Nouba Mountains, where the pilgrims were to leave the main body and head west.

"There's only one other trail out of Djarzireh," the Englishman said. "Due south to Ouad Faturah and Oloron. So the other lot must be heading there. You'll have to find out which party the stuff's with before you get there, so you'll know whether to stick with the religiosos or shadow the others south at a distance."

"How long will I have?"

"Before they make Wadi Djarzireh? Several days. They don't exactly aim to break speed records. If you ask me, it *will* be with the other lot, the traders and suchlike. Pilgrims travel light. It'd be easier to conceal a heavy lead canister among bundles of merchandise on pack camels than it would be between a rider and his bedroll."

"Isn't Oloron one of the so-called Forbidden Cities?" Bolan asked suddenly.

"Was, old chap. Was. It's in the middle of the rebel country now. If the canister leads you that way, you're heading for a hotbed of trouble."

"I'm not really into the situation in the south," Bolan admitted. "Just how strong are the rebels?"

"Strong enough, actually. Of course they play it down, here. This is the Mohammedan part of the country, where the money is, and the power. They don't want to know about the blacks in the south, and all this self-determination crap."

Bolan was determined to reveal nothing of his meeting with Hamid el-Karim, and that official's dismissal of the southerners' claims. Nor had he told Courtney about the imposing document he had collected from the military the previous evening. "What do you mean by self-determination? I thought the southern provinces had been granted some form of autonomy fifteen years ago."

"Well, technically of course, that's true," Courtney said. "Gafaar al Nimayri, the general who seized power in 1969, put an end to the full-scale rebellion down there by promising the blacks some kind of autonomy, as you say. But they're never satisfied, are they? They always want more."

"I'm listening," Bolan prompted.

"Well, autonomy in a country that's vaguely socialist-oriented, but where the Arabs up here, down in the Nile Valley, even in the desert, control all the raw materials, all the means of production... It doesn't mean very much, does it? And remember the blacks are all missionary Christians—juju men, witch doctors, that kind of thing. Add the resentment they still feel over the old race war and you can see why the Arabs are still not too popular down there, why there's still unrest in some of the provinces."

"Race war?" Bolan repeated.

"Your actual genocide. As soon as the Raj pulled out after World War II, the Arab military then in power started a systematic campaign of extermination. Sent down squadrons of cavalry to wipe out whole villages at a time—massacre the people, destroy the buildings, fire the crops. Like the death squads in South America."

"I didn't know it was that bad. So the blacks fought back?"

"As much as they could. But they had no weapons to speak of, and no centralized command. A population of five million was halved in fifteen years."

Bolan whistled. "Not the ideal background for a stable society."

"You can say that again. Once you know the form, you can see why your Arab pilgrims ride with a trade caravan that has a military escort. An Arab on his own down there is a dead man. If you have to leave that camel train, Mr. Bolan, I should junk the old borrowed robes pretty damned quick! Can't trust those customers an inch you know."

"It's no sweat guessing where your own sympathies lie."

With the Arabs, you mean? Well, of course. That is to say... Well, dash it, you *can* talk to them, can't you?''

In this town? Only if you had money in your hand, Bolan thought.

AFTER DARK, when the fierce heat of the day had cooled, Bolan traveled to a poor quarter on the riverbank where a man named Nessim stained his skin and bearded him, hair by hair, along the jawline. His teeth were discolored.

"According to the papers I shall give you, effendi," Nessim said, standing back to admire his handiwork, "you have journeyed all the way from Al Khureiba in Saudi Arabia to join the pilgrimage to this shrine. Let us hope this will be considered sufficient excuse for any inconsistencies of accent should you be required to speak Arabic.''

Beneath the heavy, hooded burnoose, the Executioner slung the waist and shoulder rig holstering his AutoMag and the PPK. Next to the skin, he wore a Chubb-locked money belt and a waterproof pouch containing basic survival kit, a miniature transmitter-receiver and spare clips of ammunition.

Later that evening he drove the Buick to the underground parking lot and stole up eleven floors of emergency stairs to David Courtney's apartment.

"I'm going to keep in touch by radio," he told the Englishman. "If there are any developments, I might ask you to forward messages stateside.''

"You think there will be?''

"Developments? Probably. This stolen nuclear material has to be going someplace! If they're building a reactor, or an atomic plant, or some kind of hydrogen bomb, something must be there to see. *Somebody* must have noticed. Those installations spread over a lot of ground.''

"Who will the messages be for?''

"You can send them to Langley in the normal way, using your normal code techniques. But there'll be a prefix drawing attention to the fact that they're destined for a man named Brognola. And an access code that will allow Langley to program them straight into the data banks at his operational headquarters in Virginia."

"Brognola?" Courtney repeated. "Don't think I've run across the chap. Is he on the strength at Langley?"

"Just pass on the messages," Bolan said, then left the apartment.

Back in the basement lot, he crept between the rows of vehicles, hoping to make the Buick unseen. It wasn't unusual to see cars driven by men wearing Arab robes, but the burnoose disguising the Executioner wasn't classy enough to justify the Electra, and he didn't want to risk a brush with the law on suspicion of being a car thief.

He ducked behind the trunk of a Mercedes 190 as a sedan rolled down the ramp and slid into a vacant space on the far side of the lot. Two men and a woman climbed out of the sedan, doors slammed and the three of them strolled, laughing, toward the elevator bank.

Bolan straightened, walked around to the driver's door and slid the key into the lock.

The low-ceilinged parking lot reverberated to the throb of another engine. Bolan cursed and squatted by the door. The vehicle drove down the curving ramp with a squeal of rubber and accelerated along the far side. It was an AMC Cherokee off-roader, and the driver seemed to be in a hurry. He backed into a spot with a squeal of brakes and cut the lights.

Cautiously Bolan raised himself. His head was level with the windshield when the Cherokee's headlights blazed again. The driver gunned the engine, and the tires protested once more. He had seen a space that suited him better. The big Jeep swung around and rocked across the lot.

Bolan hadn't time to duck, but in the instant that the headlight beams swept over the Buick, his eye was attracted by a faint, fugitive gleam below the steering wheel.

Light reflected from something that shouldn't have been there.

The driver switched off the ignition and hurried to the elevators. Bolan pressed his face to the glass of the Electra's window and squinted into its interior.

In the dim light illuminating the parking lot, he saw a thin strand of wire that stretched from beneath the dashboard to the handle of the door.

Very slowly, he withdrew the key and lowered himself to the ground. Lying on his back, he edged beneath the car.

Even in that poor light he could make out the crudely rigged bomb hanging there—four sticks of explosives taped together at the end of another, thicker wire that led upward.

Taking no chances, he unlocked the trunk, dislodged the back of the rear seat and crawled into the tonneau. He reached across the front seats and switched on the interior light.

If the bomb itself was crude, the means of detonating it were ingenious enough. If the door had been opened, jerking the wire, a loop at the far end would have snapped a thin glass stem, allowing a weight to plunge down a tube onto a capsule of fulminate of mercury, which was itself attached by cord to the explosive.

Bolan supported the plunger with one hand while he cut the wire, then removed it from the tube and disconnected the cord. Whoever had rigged the bomb must have worked fast; he must have been tailing the Executioner for some time, and he must have had all the components at hand. But he didn't trust the car's own electrical system as a means of detonating the bomb. That might be indicative of ... what? Some kind of anomaly in the thinking of those sophisticated enough to mess with nuclear physics? He filed the fact away for later examination.

Driving up the ramp and out into the wide, deserted nighttime street, he thought he heard the rasp of motorcycle exhausts. Two hundred yards from the apartment building, he glanced into his rearview mirror. Yeah, there were two of them, just emerging from the parking lot exit at the top of the ramp.

They were riding without lights.

Coincidence? Forgetfulness? Or backup men left to check that the bomb had done its work—and, if for any reason it hadn't, to follow up and finish the job themselves?

Bolan favored the last explanation. The conviction grew after he had turned right at the first intersection. Swerving across the roadway and then back again, he saw that the bikes had closed up to station themselves in the Buick's blind spot between the side and rear windows. Suspicion became certainty after three more right turns, when he was passing in front of the building once more.

The riders were still there.

Bolan goosed the engine and drove toward the embankment where the White Nile and the Blue Nile rivers ran together, maneuvering the AutoMag from beneath his burnoose as he steered with one hand. Crossing a floodlit square flanked by imposing public buildings, he veered left and then right to check out the mirror a second time ... and saw from a telltale gleam of metal that the nearer biker carried a short-barreled submachine gun across the machine's gas tank.

In a split second he mentally listed the options.

They were waiting until he was clear of the city center, where there would be less chance of a police presence, and they could ride up alongside and blast him as he drove.

They had been ordered, if he survived the bomb, simply to tail him and report where he was staying, so that some alternative method of elimination could be used later.

They had been told to wait for the right moment and then jump him, taking him prisoner so that he could be interrogated.

This time number one got his vote. If they had wanted merely to question him or locate his hideout, they wouldn't have tried to waste him with explosives first.

In any case he had to get clear of the car. The bomb and its detonator were still on the passenger seat, and he wasn't too happy at the thought of bullets ripping through the sedan's bodywork. If he threw the explosive out the window, on the other hand, there was a chance the bikers could capture it and still use it against him.

The street curved around a mosque with a dome and four minarets. Beyond it, at the foot of a slight grade, there was a glimmer of light on water. He gunned the engine and sent the Buick hurtling down the slope.

When the vehicle hit the embankment, Bolan wrenched the wheel to the left and raced northward along the riverbank. There was a traffic circle four hundred yards ahead where another street fed in from the left. A grassy mound in the center of the circle was covered with bushes.

Bolan floored the Buick, and the big sedan leaped forward; the seat back slammed his spine.

For a moment the bikers trailed behind. The Buick gained the circle, lurched around with screaming tires and then, as the Executioner stamped the brake pedal flat, slewed across the road, hit the far sidewalk, reared up into the air and hit the parapet at the edge of the embankment.

In a shower of fragmented masonry, the sedan burst through and toppled to the bank below. The crash of the impact was drowned by the thump of an explosion as gasoline spilled over the hot engine and ignited. A livid sheet of flame erupted beyond the shattered parapet, and this in turn was eclipsed by a gigantic detonation when the bomb in the car blasted the wreck apart.

Flame licked redly at the underside of billowing black smoke, and burning debris clattered into the roadway. The bikers skidded to a halt and leaped from their saddles.

Bolan was crouched behind a screen of bushes on the grassy knoll. He had flipped open the door, launched himself out and shoulder-rolled when the Buick first braked. Now he had the AutoMag lined up on the guy with the SMG—a dark leathered figure whose features were hidden behind a black-visored crash helmet.

The big autoloader roared twice in the Executioner's two-fisted grip. The biker spun around and collapsed on the sidewalk, smashed backward by the lethal punch of the 240-grain boattails. Blood pulsed scarlet from the ruin of his chest in the flickering light from below the parapet. The SMG skittered away across the blacktop.

The second man boasted a fast reaction time. He had darted into the roadway, snatched up the fallen weapon and dropped behind one of the parked bikes before the echoes of Bolan's second shot had died away.

The rasping calico stutter of the gun split the night apart as Bolan flattened himself against the ground beneath a shower of twigs and leaves.

While the hellstream ripped through the bushes he sighted his own stainless-steel skullbuster beneath the lowest branch and calmly shot away the motorcycle's kickstand so that the heavy machine crashed onto its side and left the gunman exposed.

He scrambled to his feet and ran for the broken parapet, twisting to fire from his hip as he sprinted across the sidewalk.

But this time the hail of lead sprayed wide. Bolan stood and dropped the man with a single shot that drilled between his shoulder blades, blasting apart three vertebrae and pulverizing the pancreas and one lung before it tore a fist-size exit wound between his ribs. He dropped, lifeless, without a cry.

The Executioner emerged from the bushes and walked across to check out the dead men. Without the helmets, they could have come from any Mediterranean country; each was sallow-faced, mustached, with dark hair and a hooked nose. Neither carried any ID. There were no labels on their clothes.

Bolan remained as much in the dark as he had ever been.

If the would-be assassins were part of the organization shifting the stolen uranium, the group, whoever they were, had to be on the ball. How else would they have gotten on to him as early as his visit to General Hartley?

How had they fingered him at Mustapha Tufik's? How did they know that Tufik had supplied him with intel—and intel important enough to have signed the man's death warrant?

How did they make the connection with Ibrahim in Alexandria . . . and organize themselves so well that they had time to murder him before he'd said everything he had to say?

What tipped them off that Bolan was following the trail as far as Khartoum?

How had they known he was driving to see David Courtney that evening?

Whatever the answers, they would point to two inescapable facts: first, the organization was efficient, fast-moving and widespread; second, even allowing for that, they couldn't have done what they did without the help of someone on Bolan's side of the fence.

Put it another way—and this was what really shook the warrior—there had to be a traitor or a mole in Hal Brognola's camp....

He straightened up; he could hear shouting. The warble of police sirens was growing louder.

Bolan hurried to the undamaged bike. Hitching up his Arab robes, he sat astride the saddle and kick-started the four-cylinder engine. The motorcycle was a Honda Golden Wing, capable of doing more than 130 mph—fast enough and maneuverable enough to leave any patrol cars behind.

He discarded the bike when he was a block from his hotel and walked the last two hundred yards. He took the stairs to his room, collected the Heckler & Koch then left to start the long walk to the dawn assembly point, south of the city on the banks of the Blue Nile, where the caravan was to start its long journey into the interior.

Let the cops scratch their heads over two dead foreigners, a motorcycle and a bombed Buick Electra by the riverside.

By the time they discovered it was a rental, the guy who hired it would be long gone, on the first stage of his voyage into the unknown.

CHAPTER EIGHT

Mack Bolan shielded his eyes against the blazing sun. Under the folds of his djellaba, the Heckler & Koch MP-5 in its improvised sling had worn a sore place on his hip; the Walther and the AutoMag grew heavier in their harness every minute. For the hundredth time he shifted the shoulder rig as the dromedary lurched and swayed, picking its way over the shale slanting up to a massive sandstone cliff one thousand feet above them.

The caravan was a large one—a long line of camels, horses, men and women, some mounted and some on foot, strung out for almost a mile across the desolate plateau.

It was five hours since they struggled up the steep valley from the last mud-walled village, five hours of sweltering torment. The sun had risen in the sky as the caravan climbed south through barren foothills pockmarked with patches of scrub, along a crest of rock and sand where nothing but thorn bushes broke the monotony of the scorched terrain, and now across this bleak upland plain beyond which, he dazedly hoped, their route would at last tilt downward once more.

The furnace heat was almost insufferable, shriveling the skin, hammering in the veins. He eased the harness again, scanning the plateau with red-rimmed eyes. Below and behind them, the dead land fell away in parallel ridges of ocher and tobacco-brown; above, some geological upheaval had left a thin band of richer rock between the weathered shale and the sandstone, and here a streak of dun-colored vegetation daubed the foot of the cliff.

Squinting against the glare beating back off the hot rock, he gazed ahead. A few hundred yards farther on, the line of stunted bushes followed the strata as they dipped toward a fault gashing the cliff. The leaders of the caravan were moving in the direction of this pass.

Between the towering walls of the cleft, the relief from the sun's assault was immediate. It was still stiflingly hot in the shadowed gorge, but the contrast with the blast of direct heat was as refreshing as a shower.

Bolan moistened his lips with tepid water from a padded bottle slung over his shoulder. He could hardly believe it was less than three days since he had been sipping iced bourbon beneath the striped awning shading David Courtney's balcony.

The meeting with Hamid el-Karim, the bomb in the underground parking lot, the bloody encounters in Alexandria and Khartoum were as unreal as the surrealist sequences of a dream; only the dawn meeting with Nessim, when he had paid for the camel, the bedroll and the other outward signs of his adopted Arab existence, were real—and even they faded in his memory under the relentless assault of the noonday sun.

So far they had skirted the blistering western fringe of the Nubian desert, recrossed the White Nile, traversed the lower reaches of the Sahara and were now laboriously making their way across the gaunt massif that separated the province of Kordofan from southwest Sudan. They were due at Wadi Djarzireh the following day.

After the open wastes of the plateau, the rock walls of the long, twisting defile amplified the incidental noises of the caravan: the camels' stony footfalls, the creak and jingle of pack stays and harness, an occasional whinny from an out-rider's horse and the guttural murmurs of Arabic in front and behind. Above them all rose the singsong voice of Mahmoud, the camel master, as he discussed the route with a tall, dark man in Tuareg robes at the head of the column.

It was a mixed caravan, Nessim had told him. There were ivory merchants and dealers in ostrich feathers on their way to the Congo basin, traders leading pack camels loaded with bales of merchandise destined for Bahr el Ghazal and the Central African Republic, tribesmen from as far away as the Atlas Mountains and the usual supernumeraries—individual travelers and nomads tagging on for the ride. For this was, as Courtney had said, dangerous country. Small, isolated groups unprotected by military outriders could easily fall victim to a marauding guerrilla band or even overzealous army details.

The largest single group was formed by the pilgrims. They were on their way to an obscure shrine at Amergu, on the shores of Lake Kundi in southern Darfur. Bolan, in the place of a lone traveler from Saudi Arabia, had changed the anonymous burnoose he had worn in Khartoum for the yellow, white and black djellaba that distinguished the pilgrims from other travelers.

The pilgrims were under a vow of silence until they reached their destination. But there was always a chance that the sullen Tuareg outriders escorting the column might ask for papers or pose questions. The warrior wondered again if his disguise, his reasons for being with the caravan, his knowledge of nomad customs and of Arabic, would be good enough to protect him when they made camp.

Riding at last out of the long, sinuous cleft and into the dazzle of the afternoon, he saw with relief that the trail did in fact lead downward now, across a wilderness of thorny scrub. Here the oven heat was tempered from time to time by a puff of hot, dry wind. Soon the sun would sink.

Two hours later, on a plateau strewn with huge limestone boulders, they stopped for the night.

The caravan boasted entertainers. As the western sky faded through vermilion to pale green above the rim of the wadi where they were camped, the plaintive tones of Arab pipes and strings rose into the rapidly cooling air.

Squatting like the rest of the pilgrims in the outer ring of figures around the fires, Bolan dipped his fingers into the aromatic food filling the bowl in front of him and watched acrobats and tumblers as he ate.

Soon, however, it was time for the woman to perform. And as he had feared—for the same thing had happened the previous night—she sought him out again. It seemed to him that she was directing her act exclusively at him.

She was a belly dancer. Not a very good one, possibly. But the taut body with its lean shivering breasts and eloquent hips spoke as clearly as if she had tossed a card into his lap with her telephone number on it.

Her name was Yemanja. She was probably, Bolan figured, of mixed Negro and Arab parentage. Certainly the name was that of a Yoruba fertility goddess, and while she had the nubile body and high bridged nose of most Arab women, the full-lipped mouth and smoldering eyes were pure African.

What heightened the danger was the fact that she was the "property" of Mahmoud. And the camel master's sullen and glowering regard had already been drawn toward the Executioner too often for his liking.

He kept his face bent low over his food as Yemanja stopped for the third time opposite him. Her well-muscled abdomen heaved, rotated and jerked as the tempo of the music increased, and her hips writhed seductively.

And then, with a final provocative flash of her eyes, the woman was gone and the dance was over.

Bolan sighed with relief. Desperate as he was to avoid attention of any kind, he found the dancer's nightly attempt to entice him a complication he could do without. As he watched a group dance begin on the far side of the firelit circle, he determined to keep well clear of Yemanja for the rest of the journey.

Striving to concentrate on the performers, he clapped with the rest as the music grew wilder and the fires burned low. Then he slipped unobtrusively away to erect his one-man tent beside his tethered camel.

The night was cold. They had come a long way down from the pass, but the wadi was still more than four thousand feet above sea level. Rolling himself into his striped blanket, Bolan eased into the low tent and fingered the miniature transceiver out from the pouch clipped to his belt.

Two minutes later, his head covered by the blanket, he thumbed a button on top of the casing and a faint, barely discernible whine quivered on the cool air. He turned a milled wheel set flush with the back of the instrument, and the noise increased slightly. Rotating the wheel the other way he heard the whine fade, momentarily vanish and then swell once more.

He experimented patiently until he had located the null point, the setting where the noise was tuned right out. Then, lips against the grill piercing the front of the transceiver, he spoke very softly.

"MB to DC," he breathed. "MB calling DC. If you receive me do not, repeat not, answer. Give me the signal specified in schedule T7...."

He paused. After a moment the tiny transmitter-receiver emitted three very faint bleeps in rapid succession. Bolan spoke again.

"Okay," he said. "Now listen carefully. I'm not going to repeat, and I can't talk for long. Transmit this message to

Langley. Usual code. Slugged Priority ProBrognola and followed by the access code I gave you. Message begins. Post office located. Stop. Hope identify package and consignee's address tomorrow before distribution of mail. Stop. Riding with delivery man. Stop. Signed Striker, repeat Striker. Message ends. Acknowledge on T7."

The receiver emitted a single prolonged bleep.

"Okay," Bolan whispered. "Listen again tomorrow between 2100 hours and 2230. Over and out."

He replaced the instrument in his pouch and rolled himself more tightly in the blanket. The AutoMag lay conveniently within reach, under the folded djellaba that served as his pillow.

In a large tent on the far side of the circle of dying fires, the tall dark-robed man who had been riding at the head of the column leaned back from an open document case packed with electronic equipment. His aquiline features creased into a scowl at once petulant and menacing. "As I thought," he said quietly. "Somebody in this caravan is using a radio transmitter. It's on a different wavelength than ours, quite different, but there's no doubt about it." He glanced down at the tuners and dials in the fake document case as if for confirmation.

"Can you get a—fix, isn't it?—on the transmitter with this equipment?" his companion asked.

The tall man looked at him for a moment. Although he was also dressed in Arab robes, the second man was unmistakably an African. "No, Colonel," the tall Arab said evenly. "Unfortunately we cannot. We have the means to establish its existence, but that is all. For an accurate triangulation...that is to say, there is nothing here that could locate the radio source."

The African nodded. "Too bad."

"Nevertheless, as we believed, this proves there are spies in the caravan. They must be identified and taken care of. Perhaps you would be good enough to send Mahmoud to me, so that I can instruct him to be specially wary. Meanwhile, we shall see if we can pick up anything more definite."

He turned back to his dials as the African left the tent, and began experimentally turning the controls.

But this time there were no signals to pick out of the air. Mack Bolan was asleep. Tomorrow the two parts of the caravan would separate, and he would have his work cut out to finger the animal carrying the canister of fissile material before that happened.

CHAPTER NINE

The caravan broke camp at dawn and reached Wadi Djarzireh just before dusk.

Bolan saw an ancient fortress village nestling in a ravine whose course through the highlands was marked by a line of stunted trees. There was even a trickle of water sliding yellow over the flat stones of the riverbed.

The village was a compact mass of bleached battlements, walls, domes and watchtowers surrounded by terraced *regs* of gravel on which nothing grew. Perched above the fringe of vegetation it looked more like a medieval castle than an open community, but as they rode slowly down toward a huge fortified arch protecting the only gateway, the warrior saw it stretch out visually until the course of the narrow streets could be charted by the bands of shadow striping the age-old stone in the setting sun.

The caravan passed beneath the arched gate. There were soldiers armed with modern machine pistols inside and outside—at least a dozen that he could see—and once inside the walls a scene of surprising bustle and activity was visible on all sides. Isolated in its barren environment, the village had from a distance appeared abandoned. But the maze of courtyards and alleyways was thronged with armed tribesmen. Berbers from the High Atlas mingled with nomads, mountain farmers, Tuareg in exotic robes—a dense crowd of figures in white and gray accentuated here and there by individualists dressed in vivid orange, azure, citron or acid green.

In a small central square unexpectedly planted with olive trees, men and women chatted, joked, exchanged news and gossip or bartered the goods they had brought into the village.

As the caravan wound its way through, Bolan saw a Berber warrior dictating a letter to a scribe squatting in a doorway exactly as his ancestors must have done one thousand years before.

They halted in an open space before the mosque. The camels were watered, fed and tethered in rows beneath a line of date palms, and then most of the travelers vanished into the narrow streets. Only the women, a few old men and the pilgrims—sitting quietly among their bedrolls—were left in the dusty square.

Bolan took stock. When the train split into two sections the following morning, he knew that each part was to be escorted through rebel country by a squadron of Sudanese cavalry. So it was vital that he locate the canister that night and identify the animal carrying it. Tomorrow could be too late.

In the center of the square, Mahmoud was talking to Yemanja, the belly dancer, and the dark man who had been riding at the head of the column. Beyond them, one of the armed outriders was having his head shaved beneath the wicker canopy of a traveling barber. Bolan saw the dancer looking his way and turned his back.

If he wanted to check out the lines of tethered camels unnoticed, he would have to get past them and enter the square from the other side, near the mosque.

Should he stay as he was or remove the pilgrim rig while he searched?

He was stuck with the facial, that was for sure. He would never be able to duplicate it once it was removed. And the clothes? The robe would help him remain anonymous. On the other hand his movements would be restricted if he was spotted ... and, identifying him as a pilgrim, the garment would lead any pursuers back to the caravan. In the privacy of his small tent, he shrugged out of the djellaba and drew on his skintight combat blacksuit.

The bivouac was close to a crumbling wall on the side of the open space farthest from the camels. Cautiously lifting the rear flap of the tent, he crawled out and stood between it and the wall, listening. Leaping light from naphtha flares was reflected from somewhere over the rooftops, and he could hear a gabble of voices from the bazaars. Nearer at hand in the darkness, only an occasional murmured conversation punctuated the movement of the tethered camels. It was now or never.

Flexing his knees, Bolan sprang lightly upward and grasped the top of the wall. A moment later he had dragged himself over and dropped to an evil-smelling lane choked with refuse on the far side.

He ran swiftly between the wall and the rear of a line of mud-walled houses. One hundred yards farther on, the lane twisted away from the square, around the bulk of the mosque, to emerge in a narrow street. Bolan paused, looking right and left.

To the left, the street curved away into the shadows. The right-hand branch led toward the hubbub and bright lights of a market. If he turned left, and then left again someplace, he should be able to double back and reach the square on the side farthest from his bivouac. He turned and hurried on.

There were people in the street, Koran fundamentalists in bush shirts bristling with cartridge belts, merchants carrying baskets of food, soldiers and refugees from the southwest. Most of them were on their way to the bazaar; few gave more than a glance at the bearded Arab in black.

Bolan plunged down another alley on his left, squeezed past a veiled woman leading a donkey with bulging panniers and ran on. Soon he was back in the square, crouched behind the nearest line of recumbent camels.

Mahmoud, the woman and the tall stranger had gone. Fortunately many of the traders in the caravan had already unpacked their rolls to take samples to the market, and that made Bolan's task easier: the lead canister would be hidden somewhere in an untouched bale.

Furtively, crawling on hands and knees across the beaten earth between the animals, he searched, prodded and investigated with exploring fingers. After an hour, he was halfway along the third line of camels. The great beasts chewed noisily, turning their eyes to gaze incuriously at the doubled-up human. He was enveloped in the rank odor of their fetid breath.

Toward the end of the line, he pitched forward as his wrist turned under him on a loose stone, and lurched against a bale of merchandise still harnessed to a dromedary. The bulging pack swung away from him in an odd manner. It looked too light; it didn't move the way a tightly folded wad of material should. . . .

Suppressing an exclamation of triumph he gave it his full attention. Fifteen seconds later its secret was revealed. The thin layer of cloths on the outside was stretched over a wicker cage. Inside, the bale was bulked out with some superlight substance such as cottonwool—and buried in the center, his fingers slid down the cool, greasy surface of a lead container.

The canister was as heavy as hell, but because the weight was concentrated in one place the bulk as a whole didn't move as sluggishly as the genuine bale balancing it on the camel's other flank.

Bolan let out his pent-up breath in a long sigh. Unfastening the flap of the pouch at his waist, he drew out a small leather case containing two metal devices each the size of a matchbox. One of them emitted a continuous radio signal; with the dial of the other correctly tuned, the movements of the first could be traced from a distance by following the direction in which the bleeps were loudest.

Where should he conceal the homer? Its magnetic limpet attachment would be useless on lead. Finally he shrugged and thrust it as far as he could into the cotton beneath the container. At least now he could keep track of the animal carrying the deadly load, even if he had to leave the caravan when the column split into two: the radio signal had a range of twenty miles.

But a visual check would help. Taking a penlight from his pouch, he allowed himself the briefest flash. Okay: between the bogus bale and the real one a rolled blanket with red, yellow and black stripes lay across the camel's back. Noted.

Working fast but warily, he replaced the coverings over the wicker cage, tightened the retaining straps and crawled back the way he had come. He was getting to his feet at the end of the line when a flashlight beam blazed at him from behind a tree.

"What are you doing?" a harsh voice growled. "Stay still or I shall shoot." There was a movement toward him in the shadows.

Bolan froze. "Pardon," he said in French. "I was trying to find my way to the central market. Perhaps *monsieur* could direct me?"

"On your hands and knees? A likely story! Come here and let's have a closer look at you. Thefts from caravans are not regarded too kindly here by the military."

The Executioner advanced slowly, thankful he was not wearing the telltale djellaba that would tag him as a pilgrim traveling with the camel train. "I assure you *monsieur*, there was no question of theft," he said. "I had lost my way and I tripped in the dark. When you saw me I was just rising—"

"We shall see about that," the other snarled. "Put up your hands and we shall see what you have stolen."

Bolan raised his arms and remained still. The man came closer, circling him watchfully, the barrel of a revolver gleaming in the light from the torch. Bolan saw that it was Mahmoud, the camel master.

He patted the warrior on both hips and under the arms, running his fingers expertly up the insides of his thighs and across his abdomen. "At least you carry no weapons," he said. "That should reduce the sentence by perhaps five years. Aha! What have we here?" His hand had touched the hard shape of the leather case inside the pouch.

"A transistor radio," Bolan said truthfully.

"I shall believe that when I see it. Take it out."

"You want me to unfasten—"

"Quick!" The gun barrel jabbed Bolan hard in the small of the back.

He lowered his left arm slowly and unfastened the flap of the pouch, drawing out the case containing the tuner between finger and thumb.

Then, before the grunt of satisfaction had left Mahmoud's lips, he dropped the case and his hand streaked down and behind him, knocking the Arab's gun arm aside.

The heavy-caliber revolver roared as Bolan whirled to seize the hand that held it in both of his own. He jerked the man's arm furiously up and down, exerting a paralyzing judo grip on the wrist. When the pistol was pointing at the ground, it exploded again, the slug ricocheting off the stony terrain to whine away among the trees.

As the revolver finally dropped from his nerveless fingers, Mahmoud fisted his other hand to slam the head of the flashlight under Bolan's chin, pushing his head back with agonizing force. The warrior went with the thrust, releasing the Nubian's wrist and rolling onto his back. At the same time he brought up his knees, planted his heels in Mahmoud's crotch and then suddenly straightened his legs.

The camel master flew over his head and crashed to the ground with a clatter that echoed throughout the square.

Pausing only to boot the revolver into the shadows and scoop up the leather case, Bolan leaped to his feet and ran for the alley. This was no time for a prolonged combat: all that mattered was that he get away and return to his tent before he was recognized. Roused by the shots, people were already running toward them from the encampment.

Mahmoud was yelling abuse as he scrambled after the gun. A third shot rang out. The wind of the bullet fanned Bolan's left shoulder, then he was clear of the square and pelting down the alley toward the street that led to the bazaar.

He stopped abruptly and melted into the shadows of a doorway. Half a dozen soldiers with drawn pistols careered into the alley from the street and ran past him in the direction of the square.

Once they had gone, the Executioner slid out of his hiding place and walked rapidly away from the noise. "But you *must* have passed him," Mahmoud's angry voice called. "He ran down that lane only seconds before you arrived...."

Bolan joined the throng eddying toward the bazaar and strove to conceal the fact that he was hurrying. Veiled women, fellahin in striped shifts and tarbooshes and bedouin in flowing white robes jostled him as he walked. There was a commotion behind him as Mahmoud and the soldiers ran back into the street.

He heard arguments, protests, shouts...and then he was swallowed up in the activity of the marketplace, where the shuffling of feet was drowned in the cries of barkers and the traditional haggling between merchants and customers. Hands gesticulated, fingers wagged, palms were upraised in the suffocating press among the stalls of fruit, vegetables, cloth and hardware beneath the blazing naphtha lights.

Bolan had almost shouldered his way through to the far side when three shots reverberated above the heads of the crowd.

There were screams and a stampede as everyone fought to get away from the center of the bazaar. A great stand of copper pots and pans near Bolan toppled over as half a dozen people forced their way between two stalls.

"Stay where you are! Don't leave the marketplace," a voice yelled over the clangor of tumbling hardware and the furious complaints of the merchant. "There is a foreign thief at large here, and we want to find him. This is the military. Stay where you are. You have nothing to fear."

Feeling as vulnerable as a man suddenly exposed in the glare of a searchlight, Bolan edged behind the stall and made for a street that twisted away into the shadows. If he was to run one hundred yards down there and then find a right turn, he might be able to circle back and find the lane that led to the wall sheltering his tent.

"Over there!" another voice shouted. "Look! On the far side of the bazaar. Quick! After him!"

He glanced over his shoulder. The owner of the hardware stall, dancing up and down among his tureens, was pointing his way. Mahmoud and the soldiers were advancing rapidly between the rows of striped awnings.

Bolan himself broke into a run and plunged down the dark street. A fusillade of shots erupted behind him as he made the shadows. Bullets kicked up the dust at his feet, one chipping plaster from the wall by his shoulder.

He gained the first bend and saw there was no turnoff to the right—the street led toward the lights of another square. He dashed into a doorway on the left, hared up a flight of stone steps, crossed a wider street and sprinted through an archway into a maze of unlit alleyways.

The voices and footsteps of the hunters behind him drew near. He had passed plenty of people in the street who could point the way he had gone.

He pressed on, down a second flight of steps, and found himself in a narrow lane lit at long intervals by dim street lamps. All around him a murmur of voices behind closed shutters stirred the warm air. Music rose and fell in the distance.

He halted, panting, the blood pounding behind his eyes.

"Why do you not come inside, stranger?" a soft voice at his elbow intoned in Arabic.

Bolan swung around and heard a faint click. The beam of a pencil flashlight revealed a woman's breast, the swelling contours held toward him by silver-tipped fingers, the nipple and areola purplish in the diffuse light.

Below this a tight swathe of diaphanous material sheathed belly and hips; above, a hint of white teeth, the highlight on a full lip shone through the gloom.

The Executioner caught his breath. He had seldom seen anything more suggestive, more overtly erotic than that breast shamelessly exposed against the dark. He hesitated. The hunters were only a block away, and heavy feet had begun to scramble down the last winding flight of stairs.

He made up his mind. His decision was based on the conviction that a prostitute was unlikely to be well disposed toward the police and the military. It was a gamble—she might prefer to buy a little protection by turning a fugitive in—but what the hell: the entire mission, his whole life in the hellgrounds of the world, was a gamble. "Why not?" he said huskily.

He stepped toward the doorway in which the woman was standing. The light vanished. A door creaked open into blackness. Bolan brushed past her and stood waiting as she closed it.

In the airless dark, the odor of some cloying, exotic cosmetic washed over him. Footsteps scraped to a halt outside. He heard Mahmoud's voice. "Foreign, by his accent . . . a tall man wearing black . . . bearded but with no headdress . . ."

"He came this way. Some pig of a thief."

A woman mumbled a negative.

"But he must be here somewhere! He can't have gotten away. The far end of the alley is blocked."

"He could be anywhere," another voice cut in. "You know where we are? This is the street of the—"

"It does not matter what street it is," Mahmoud interrupted. "You must post sentries at the entrance, too, and search it house by house. There is valuable merchandise with the caravan. The foreign swine must be captured at all costs." The footsteps died away.

The woman, whose breath had hissed in sharply the first time Mahmoud spoke, now moved past Bolan toward the rear of the building. Soft flesh brushed the back of his hand. In a low voice, she said, "This way."

Light stabbed the dark as she switched on the flashlight. Bolan saw a narrow passageway leading to a flight of stone stairs, and he followed the woman up the stairway. Apart from the clip-clop of her slippers and the swish of garments against her naked flesh, there was silence. At the top of the stairs he saw a poorly lit hallway with a number of curtained alcoves. The illumination was provided by a single primitive lamp: a simple wick floating in a small bowl of oil. There was another in the tiny room she ushered him into—a cell no more than eight feet square, furnished only with rugs and cushions strewn across the floor.

As she went to draw heavy draperies over an arched window, he leaned against the wall while he regained his breath. It seemed as if the gamble had paid off. But there was still danger in the air. Judging from the whispers and an occasional muffled cry, most of the other cubicles were already occupied. And there was no way of knowing how the inmates or their clients might react if they knew a wanted man was in the house.

A hazard of a different kind presented itself when the woman turned to face him.

She was voluptuously built, the full breasts heavy on her chest, her taut belly shadowed under the semitransparent skirt. With a start of surprise, he recognized Yemanja, the dancer from the caravan.

"So! It is you!" she breathed. "I knew we were fated to meet again. It is well that you came this way."

Bolan cleared his throat. "I'm glad to see you, too. But I have to tell you, I only want—"

"You are running away, are you not?" Yemanja cut in. "It is you that Mahmoud and the soldiers were chasing? This is no concern of mine. I have no love for the guards or the military, especially Mahmoud and the Nubians, who are brutal men. On the other hand, if it is they who are responsible for bringing you here..."

"Yemanja, I didn't recognize you. I was—"

"Why would you, my friend? How could you recognize what you will not see? But *I* recognize *you*—although Mahmoud evidently does not...yet."

"I don't want you to misunderstand me, Yemanja. When I agreed to come in here—"

"I know. If you had recognized me, you would have run away from me, too. The way you always run away with your eyes when I look at you. Why do you rebuff me? Am I not beautiful? Am I not desirable?" She sank down onto a pile of cushions, staring at him with her enormous eyes.

"You are very beautiful," Bolan said, "and very desirable."

"Then . . . ?"

He hesitated. Dare he trust the woman? If she was genuinely sold on him, might it be worth the risk? On the other hand, they did say that a woman scorned . . . Mentally he shrugged. He had really no choice.

"I'm involved in a certain . . . mission," he said carefully. "In order to complete this, it is vital that I do not in any way attract attention while I'm with the caravan. That's why I was unable to respond to your—"

Yemanja laid a finger on his lips, stopping him in midsentence. "I have told you that this does not concern me. So why do you not stay here? Come. Sit beside me and I will send for some refreshment."

Bolan swallowed. He shook his head. "Yemanja, I can't."

"Cannot? But I wish it. You are not one of the emasculated ones with high voices. You also are beautiful. You have a strong but kind face, effendi. You are different from the Nubians, the bedouin and the other men I meet here. In this place I am forced by Mahmoud of the camels to take whoever chooses to stop. Let me for once make a choice of my own. I ask you once more—do I not please you?"

"I've said that I think you're beautiful."

"Then why do you reject me?"

"It's not a question of rejection. If I . . . become friendly with you, it'll make Mahmoud jealous. And if he becomes more jealous than he already is, he'll notice me all the more in the caravan. And that must not happen. He hasn't yet connected the man he chases tonight with the man his woman so obviously likes in the caravan."

"Mahmoud!" Yemanja's voice was full of scorn. "He is a bad man, that one. He beats me. Look—I will show you. . . ."

"No, no," the Executioner said hastily. "I believe you."

"In any case he is not jealous. Because he sees that I like you, he is afraid that I will take no money from you, that is all. You need not be afraid of Mahmoud. He is a bully, all brag and no courage."

"I'm not afraid of him. It's just that I don't want him to notice me."

"Well, he *cannot* notice you here!" Yemanja cried triumphantly. "While the caravan was traveling, each night you refused to look at me. Well, here we are alone. Perhaps you can find time to look now?"

"Like I said. It's not a matter of desire but of time. . . ."

And then she was pressed against him, kneeling up on the cushions, one arm clasped around his hips, the other hand feeling for his genitals, the fingers moving knowledgeably over the skintight blacksuit, caressing, massaging.

"See!" she cried, her voice suddenly exultant. "You do desire me! Your manhood . . ."

She tensed, leaving the sentence unfinished.

A persistent hammering echoed up the stairway. "The soldiers," she whispered. "They said they would search every house."

Bolan put her away from him gently. "I'm sorry," he murmured. "That's what I was trying to say."

"No, you are right. They must not find you here, my friend. You must go."

"Sure . . . but how?"

Yemanja ran to the window, her eyes wide with alarm. "Nobody saw you come in," she said, pulling aside the draperies. "As far as they know, I have been here alone all the time. If you were to leave through this . . ."

"Does Mahmoud know you're here?"

"Of course. I am here at his command. Now where do you wish to go?"

"Back to the encampment. There's a lane that runs behind the wall."

"Very well." She pushed open the window. "Out here is a flat roof. Below it there is an alley. You cannot go back directly without crossing the lane in front of where the soldiers are. But if you take the alley in the opposite direction, you will find you are in the street circling the town inside the walls. Turn right along this and you will see that the—one, two, three, four, yes, fifth—the fifth turning will lead you directly to the mosque. And from there, the lane you speak of—"

"Yes. I know the way from there," Bolan said.

He thrust money into her hand. "Take this. Please. Perhaps one day you will be able to buy a little freedom with it." The hammering had stopped, and there was the sound of many voices from below. He swung a leg over the windowsill, turning back to the woman. "You're very desirable and very kind. I'm grateful. If there's ever anything I can do . . ."

"You know what you can do!"

He grinned, leaning inward to kiss her briefly on the lips. But once more she was all over him, devouring him with kisses, her body pressed against his chest, her hands cradling the back of his head. For the second time, Bolan disengaged himself. "The soldiers," he reminded her in a whisper.

"I had forgotten." She was panting. "But I will not forget you. The next time you have occasion to visit Wadi Djarzireh . . ."

"It will be a pleasure," he said. Then the warrior jumped lightly to the flat roof and ran to the edge. The curtain dropped over the window.

The alley was about fifteen feet below. The jump jarred him from head to heels, and it seemed to Bolan that he made a hell of a lot of noise. Nobody appeared to have heard, however; no voice questioned and no footstep advanced. He waited ten seconds, listening, and then stole away in the direction of the mosque.

The beaten-earth road behind it was deserted. Just before he reached the square he saw the back of a patrolling sentry silhouetted against the night sky on top of the village's outer wall, but he was swallowed up in the shadows below the mosque before the man reached the end of his beat.

There was one danger point before he was home free, when he had to cross an open space between the domed building and the street that led to the marketplace. But the few passersby were all facing the lights of the bazaar, which showed through an arch halfway along the street. Shouts of command from the soldiers could still be heard above the hubbub.

Bolan passed noiselessly behind the watchers and turned the corner of the mosque. Two minutes later he was back behind the tumbledown houses in the lane, jumping for the top of the wall behind his bivouac. He lowered himself quietly behind the small tent, lifted the back flap and crawled inside with a sigh of relief.

He briefly wondered if he should relay another message to Brognola, but decided against it. He knew which camel was carrying the stolen nuclear material, but otherwise nothing had changed since his last transmission. Until he could identify the "consignee," it was best to keep radio silence.

Everything had finally gone his way tonight; he didn't want to push his luck too far.

Once he had stripped off the blacksuit and donned the djellaba, Bolan looked out the front of the tent. Naphtha flares now flamed where the camels were tethered. One of the horses was restive, snorting and rearing on the end of its rope. A group of soldiers lounged beneath the date palms.

Nearer at hand, Mahmoud paced up and down with the tall, dark stranger. "I don't see how he could have gotten away," the camel master was saying angrily. "We had the whole street bottled up." He flung out an arm to encompass the square. "I think it unlikely, but just in case he did come from here, I am ordering the soldiers to waken all these people—" he gestured toward the area where Bolan and the other pilgrims were quartered "—so that we can get them out and have a look at them."

His companion took his arm. "It is not necessary," he said.

"What do you mean, not necessary? We must catch this—"

"There are plans, my friend," the tall man said, "of which you know nothing. Just leave it, all right?"

Mahmoud stared at him, shrugged, shook his head but said no more.

Bolan shrugged too. What the hell? But he would leave that particular mystery for examination tomorrow. Right now he was bushed.

Withdrawing like a tortoise into his shelter, he rolled himself into his blanket and went to sleep.

CHAPTER TEN

The rendezvous with the cavalry was outside the archway whose watchtowers monitored the only gate leading into Wadi Djarzireh.

From here the pilgrims would continue westward along the right bank of the river, on the first part of their long ride to Lake Kundi and the shrine at Amergu. The pack train was to cross a ford and then climb up into the hills on the left.

Mack Bolan kept his head well down under the hood of his djellaba as Mahmoud rode up and down the long line of camels and horses with a Sudanese officer, separating the travelers and their beasts into two convoys. The dromedary with the red-yellow-and-black-striped blanket roll was one of a string of three led by a bedouin immediately behind the head of the column.

The camel master's features were set in their usual scowl as he maneuvered his horse in among the throng scanning papers and shepherding the riders roughly into the correct line. There was no sign of Yemanja. Perhaps the entertainers were left behind when the caravans traversed a dangerous area.

Bolan kneed his camel as unobtrusively as he could toward the file of pilgrims in an attempt to join them without having his papers—or his face—scrutinized. It would be easier to move off with that section of the train and quit later than it would be to try and stick with the others now.

The moment was well chosen because Mahmoud's back was turned, but the army officer saw him move and called out, "Hey! You there! Where do you think you're going?"

He spurred his horse toward the Executioner, cursing. Mercifully the camel master was arguing with another pilgrim and did not accompany him.

"I wanted to join my fellow pilgrims, that is all," Bolan said meekly, his head bowed, as the Sudanese reined up beside him.

"You wait until you are told. And that is a strange manner in which you speak, friend," the officer added suspiciously.

"I am not of your country. My speech is not as yours because I come from afar, from Al Khureiba, in Saudi Arabia."

"Hmm. Well, see that you do not get out of line again," the soldier grunted. He wheeled his mount and rejoined Mahmoud.

When his turn eventually did come, Bolan showed his papers, still with bent head, and suffered himself to be pushed into the group of pilgrims. The camel with the striped bedroll, as he had expected, was with the other train.

A few minutes later, the pilgrims and their escort moved off along the riverbank while the baggage train with its attendant squadron splashed across the ford and began climbing the rocky trail on the far side.

Bolan deliberately lagged, hoping that he might have an opportunity to break away from the pilgrims and somehow rejoin the other train undetected. Half a mile farther on his chance came. The stream, and the trail beside it, wound through a twisting canyon that cut through the baked rock . . . and all the escorting soldiers were up at the head of the column.

He brought his camel to a stop behind a group of enormous boulders and allowed the others to move slowly around a corner and out of sight. Then, wheeling, he rode back along the trail as fast as the camel would go.

Fording the river, he urged the animal on up the steep path the baggage train had followed. The track mounted steadily past tiny squares of cultivation planted with millet, maize and sorghum, through a patch of scrub and across an exposed slope of bare rock, where it turned sharply to follow a dried-up river valley toward the crest of the ridge.

A natural tunnel through the limestone led beneath the saddle, and on the far side he could see, dwarfed by distance, the long line of camels and horses snaking over the desolate plain below.

If he could manage to link up with the caravan without being noticed there was a slim chance that he could stay with it at least until nightfall.

The trail, although dry, threw up very little dust as the camel passed. Bolan rode on down, steering his swaying mount into the shelter of every rock outcrop and pile of boulders the terrain offered.

Sixty minutes later he was within a quarter of a mile of the caravan. He could hear clearly the sounds of its progress and took the chance to get closer when the route began to twist between pebbled *regs* and areas of thorn.

If only there was no cavalry riding shotgun when he rounded the last bend and tagged on . . .

But when he urged on the camel as the trail straightened once more he saw that his luck had changed: two horsemen in uniform were riding behind the last pack camel.

Before he had time to retreat, one of them turned and saw him. There was no way he could escape—both men carried rifles across their pommels. Besides, a horse could outrun a dromedary anytime. Cursing inwardly, he rode straight ahead until he caught up with them.

How was he going to handle this? He had changed the yellow, white and black *djellaba* for his original dun-colored burnoose when he split from the pilgrim train . . . but the papers he carried were specific: he was on the way to the shrine at Amèrgu.

Was there any way he could fake it?

No.

"Who are you? What do you think you're doing?" the man who had seen him said roughly. "Show me your papers at once."

Bolan sighed. Okay—he was stuck with the pilgrim routine.

While the second man kept him covered, he reached inside the folds of his robe and produced the documents. "But according to these, you should be with the other train!" the soldier exclaimed. "What are you doing here—and who are you, anyway?"

"You can see who I am. I lost my way. I was wandering around, trying to locate a trail, when I heard the sounds of your caravan, and I thought it might be the one I missed. It was—"

"Impossible. The others are miles away, on the other side of the river. You couldn't possibly have arrived here by mistake." The soldier turned to his companion. "Ali, ride up to the front of the column and fetch Mahmoud and the captain while I keep an eye on this man."

The second cavalryman spurred his horse and rode after the disappearing caravan while Bolan remained motionless under the soldier's watchful guard.

The Heckler & Koch MP-5 was slung beneath his robe, but it was dismantled. The AutoMag and the PPK were holstered, but the soldier could drill him before he even got a hand beneath the cumbersome burnoose.

Soon, four horsemen galloped into sight around a bend in the trail: the soldier, Mahmoud, the officer who had remonstrated with the Executioner before the two caravans separated and a tall, dark man on a splendid gray mount— the stranger who had told the camel master not to bother locating Bolan the previous night.

"What is the trouble?" the dark man asked curtly.

"This man was attempting secretly to join the caravan, Excellence."

"Who is he?"

"According to his papers, one of the Amergu pilgrims— who should be riding with the *other* train."

"But I know this man! I had trouble with him before," the officer said. "He was trying then to attach himself to that caravan before it was time. Now he wants this one, you say? And he has changed his clothes. To me that appears suspicious."

"So have I seen him before," Mahmoud snarled suddenly. "I knew the face was familiar, but I had not made the connection." He leaned across and twitched aside the enveloping hood the Executioner wore. "See! The foreign thief is at last unmasked! Foreign thief... and perhaps foreign spy also, eh?"

The cavalry captain looked inquiringly at the dark man, who seemed, out of the four, to carry the most clout.

"I suppose so." The latter sighed. "It was planned otherwise, as you know. But in the circumstances... At least we now have a culprit in connection with the mystery radio transmissions from the caravan. We can search his baggage afterward."

"Dismount," the Sudanese officer ordered Bolan.

Bolan slid from the dromedary, his mind racing. The tuner for the homing device and his miniature transceiver were safe in the locked belt around his waist. The weapons were beneath his burnoose. The rest of his gear would have to be sacrificed along with the bedroll on the camel. Assuming he could get away at all. Unobtrusively he touched the hard, comforting edge of the AutoMag through a fold in the robe.

As his feet touched the ground, Bolan heard the chilling sound of an old-fashioned rifle bolt being drawn back and slammed home. He knew that he was going to die. There was a bullet in the breech; the soldier behind him was preparing to shoot.

Honed on the hard stone of many years of combat experience, the Executioner's razor-sharp battle instinct took over. Mind and muscle and eye, working in perfect combination, directed his movements without conscious thought as he exploded into action.

He ducked beneath the camel's belly, plunged his right hand through a slit in the burnoose and fired at the soldier through the thick material. The man toppled over his horse's neck, his rifle clattering to the ground.

Before any of the others had time to move, Bolan bobbed up on the far side of the animal, and the big autoloader boomed again. The second man, who had been winged while raising his gun, jerked back violently under the impact of the 240-grain slug and then sagged in the saddle, clutching his pulverized shoulder.

An instant later, in a smooth, continuous flow of movement, the warrior had bounded across the space between the camel and the first soldier's horse, hauled the dead man clear of the harness and vaulted into the saddle.

Then, driving his heels into the animal's flanks, he charged straight at Mahmoud and his two companions.

Their horses had reared at the sound of gunfire, and they were trying to draw their weapons when Bolan scattered them, urged his own mount over a four-foot thorn hedge at the side of the track and galloped away into the scrub.

Mahmoud's revolver boomed behind him, the report followed by the sharp crack of an automatic and the duller, flatter explosion of a rifle.

Bolan rode like the wind, zigzagging among the stunted bushes. He was thankful that the soldier's horse—unlike most Arab steeds—was harnessed and saddled. Crouching low over the animal's flying mane, he glanced back over his shoulder.

Two horses had cleared the hedge—Mahmoud's and the officer's—and were galloping in pursuit. The dark man had stayed behind. His head and shoulders were visible over the thorny branches, one eye squinting along the barrel of a rifle. Four more shots rang out. Then for a long time there was no sound but the drumming of hooves on the iron-hard ground.

Bolan was making a big circle through the tinder-dry scrub, planning to come back on a course parallel with the trail but about one mile distant. He hoped to gain a range of low hills some way ahead and keep watch on the caravan for as long as he could before dropping out of sight and relying on the homer. Meanwhile, he had to outdistance his pursuers.

Next time he looked back Mahmoud had dropped a quarter of a mile behind, but the cavalry officer was no more than one hundred yards away and gaining fast. There was a puff of smoke and a bullet sang over Bolan's head.

More alarmingly, a dust cloud moved above the scrub. It was farther away but vectored on a course that would intersect his own. Clearly it was the remainder of the squadron racing to cut him off.

With the reins between the fingers and knuckles of his left hand, Bolan had been maneuvering the MP-5 away from its sling and out from under his robe. Now, controlling the horse—and his own balance—with the steely pressure of knees and thighs only, he slammed in the magazine, pushed home the retractable butt and flicked the compact killer onto 5-round burst mode.

It was tough for the Sudanese. For the continuing success of the mission, it was vital that he get away.

Regretfully he reined back some, waiting for the officer to close up on a straight stretch between the thorn trees. The guy was firing as he rode, but after three shots Bolan twisted in the saddle and hosed a series of 5-shot bursts his way.

The rip-roaring bellow as the 9 mm deathstream zeroed in on the Sudanese scared Bolan's horse. Rearing with a neigh of alarm, it threw him heavily to the ground.

Bolan rolled with the shock, scrabbling for the SMG. But the immediate danger was over. Horse and rider were lying in a grotesque tangle among the thorn bushes fifty yards away. The bare earth, and parts of the prickly trunks, glistened redly in the glare of the sun.

There remained the menace presented by the rest of the squadron. The dust cloud was still half a mile away, but if the cavalry continued on its course they would cut off the Executioner before he could make the hills.

Standing with his horse's bridle in one hand he stared across the desert scrub. The yellow cloud was streaming away behind the squadron. The puffs of hot, dry wind he had noticed the day before were increasing in strength. He spit on one finger and held it up. The wind was blowing from the northeast, scouring the arid wasteland between him and the Sudanese.

He nodded. They were downwind enough for it to work.

He drew the heavy bronze cigarette lighter-camera from his pouch and approached the thickest stand of thorn bushes he could see.

Shielded from the breeze by one of his hands, the flame shot up beneath a desiccated branch, and an instant later the whole bush blossomed with flowers of fire.

The flames spread, teased out by the wind, until the whole stand was blazing.

Burning twigs floated away and ignited the next clump of thorn bushes; brown smoke billowed and roiled toward the cloud of dust. And two minutes later there was a blazing firefront crackling fast toward the distant cavalry.

In a moment Bolan would be safely hidden from them, but he still had to get to the far side of the smoke screen before he made the range of hills. Remounting, he cantered along the sunbaked earth in back of the leaping points of flame.

He was halfway there, and the shouts of the frustrated horsemen were dying away behind the increasing roar of the blaze when a single rider burst through the smoke ahead of him and wheeled his mount to face the Executioner.

There was a Kalashnikov AKM automatic rifle resting across the man's saddle, and before Bolan had time to react to the unexpected apparition, the guy had raised the weapon to shoulder level and blasted a stream of lead his way.

Bolan's response was instinctive. The Arab was more than a hundred yards away—too far for accurate shooting when the marksman was astride a horse, and certainly way out of range of the Executioner's own armory when he, too, was riding. He attempted a maneuver he had learned from the fearless equestrian gymnasts of Turkestan, when he had been on mission for three months in the Soviet Kazakh region.

Flattening himself along the horse's back, he urged the animal into a gallop, heading straight for his antagonist. At the same time, locking his left hand in the harness and gripping fiercely with his left thigh, he slid down the heaving flank until he was inverted beneath his mount's chest.

From there, gritting his teeth, he extended his right arm between the horse's pistoning front legs.

His right hand was wrapped around the butt of the Walther PPK, the forefinger caressing the trigger.

The premise—again he was regretful, but he had no choice if he wanted to stay alive—was that no Arab cavalryman would shoot deliberately at a horse, but only at its rider if he was a visible target.

The Sudanese was hesitating, the barrel of his assault rifle wavering. Bolan squeezed the trigger. He emptied all seven rounds from the pistol's magazine when there was less than forty yards between him and the Arab.

The 7.65 mm cartridges made much less noise than the deafening blast of the AutoMag, but the series of reports cracking rapidly out beneath its tossing head frightened the horse as much as Bolan's earlier volley from the H&K MP-5.

It lowered its haunches, hooves scrabbling to a halt in a shower of gravel on the pebbly ground, reared up, neighing, then bucked with its heels thrown into the air.

Bolan lost his grip and fell, rolling swiftly out of reach of the tattooing legs, allowing the empty Walther to go with the tide, sliding over the rough terrain as he felt for the AutoMag.

He came up with the big gun in his hand, but he didn't need to use it.

Four of the shots from the Walther had flown wide, but the fifth had nicked the sling of the Kalashnikov. The two remaining rounds had scored—one splintering through the horseman's breastbone, the other punching a hole in his throat below the Adam's apple.

Hurled backward off his mount by the impact of the slugs, he lay spread-eagled on the spines of a thorn bush.

The Executioner scrambled to his feet and limped across to the bush. By the time he reached it, the scarlet stream throbbing from the soldier's chest and neck had ebbed and died; the man's sightless eyes had glazed, and even the blood staining his uniform and pooled on the hard ground below had filmed over with dust.

Bolan ached all over and his knees, wrists and elbows were grazed, but otherwise he was unharmed.

The fire was sweeping toward the southwest, rolling a cloud of brown smoke tinged with violet before it. Behind it, the searing heat of the day was tainted with the bitter stench of charred brushwood.

Bolan attempted to remount his horse, but the animal was skittish and shied away. Two shocks in one morning was enough. He had to settle for the cavalryman's mount, which was tractable enough.

He rode toward the hills, the Walther reloaded, the AutoMag now holstered outside his burnoose, the MP-5 on the saddle in front of him. For perhaps two miles, the riderless horse accompanied them, then it careered off across the plain on its own.

At noon, Bolan halted between two monolithic rocks at the top of a cliff in the first range of hills. Allowing the horse to forage for something edible among the desiccated desert scrub, he looked out from the shadows across the great tract of country.

The fire was a smudge of smoke staining the horizon far to the south. Several hundred feet below, the caravan wound its way around the base of a spur projecting beneath the cliff. The camel with the striped blanket still walked just behind the posse of cavalry at the head of the column. It would be twenty minutes or more before the last riders passed out of sight.

He decided to rest the horse and call up David Courtney: Brognola might welcome another progress report, even though the Executioner was still ignorant of the caravan's destination and the identity of the thieves was still a secret.

Sheltered by the rocks from the fierce heat, he sat down, took the transceiver from his pouch and turned the pointer to Receive. He pressed the button that actuated the automatic call sign on their wavelength.

Half an hour later he was still trying.

There was no reply from Courtney.

CHAPTER ELEVEN

"Bolan was supposed to funnel messages to me through your man Courtney in Khartoum," Hal Brognola said gruffly.

John Samson, the CIA sector chief detailed to liaise with the Fed, frowned and compressed his lips. "Nothing came in at Langley as of noon today."

"I know it. I'm not happy about it. That's three days without any news."

Samson sighed. "We can't pass on something we don't get, Hal," he said defensively. Heads could roll fast at Langley when the Man was displeased.

"So why aren't you getting it? Mack wouldn't delay a progress report. Not on anything this important."

"The Brit's not a regular operative," Samson replied. "He's on a retainer, and he files when—"

"I know all that."

"So what do you want me to do? Put in a field agent?"

"Hell, no. Not in that part of Africa! I don't need to tell you what they'd say if—"

"Sure. I know the tune. Imperialist warmonger spies. Fascist interference in the affairs of a sovereign country. All that jazz."

"Right. Especially now that the Sudanese are heavily back into their civil strife routine." Brognola riffled through a stack of newspapers and picked up that day's edition of the Chicago *Globe*. It had been folded back to an inside page with a boxed news item outlined in red marker. He passed it to the Company man.

Samson saw the headline Sudan Bloodbath Feared and beneath it: By Jason Mettner II, Special Correspondent in Central Africa. He read:

The Sudan government in Khartoum is under strong pressure to investigate a recent massacre in Southern Darfur province and punish those responsible. Administration officials admit that between two and three hundred Dinka tribesmen died, but black leaders reckon the murder toll was more like 1,500.

The incident is the latest in a series of bloody clashes opposing guerrillas of the Sudan Peoples' Liberation Army and pro-government Arab troops. The SPLA, fighting for total autonomy, is drawn mainly from the Dinkas, many of whom are more than seven feet tall.

"What the story doesn't say," Brognola said, "is that the folks wasted in this latest killing weren't guerrillas but Dinka refugees from farther south, who were trying to escape from tribal clashes. It seems that seventy Arab militiamen were killed in such a clash, and the refugees had been rounded up and taken to a police barracks to protect them from Arab reprisals."

"Don't tell me," Samson said. "When the local militia attacked, the police joined in?"

Brognola nodded. "Read the rest of it."

The Company man ran a professional eye quickly down the column of print.

Repeated protests by black leaders in the south have been reinforced by the Arab opposition in Khartoum, which has called for a reversal of government policy arming Arab villagers to fight SPLA guerrillas. The situation worsened rapidly after security forces were sent into the southern provinces to root out the guerrillas, driving black peasants to seek refuge in Arab areas, where they are at the mercy of these militiamen.

Foreign diplomats in Khartoum now fear that the SPLA will launch renewed attacks on Arab-dominated provinces to avenge the latest massacre and that this could lead to a further cycle of blood feuds and religious atrocities in a country where more than two-thirds of the twenty million people are Muslims of Arab descent, but most southerners are African Christians or animists.

"Just the kind of situation for rogue shipments of nuclear material to get lost in," Brognola said grimly. "Maybe you can see now why it's so important to renew contact with Bolan."

"Sure I can," Samson agreed. "But I can't see how we can help. If you don't want us to alert Courtney in case he's blown, and you don't want us to send in a personal contact..."

"I think I've got a better idea," Brognola said. "It's a long shot, but right here no news is bad news."

"So?"

"So I'm gonna call a newspaperman I know."

The two men were sitting in Brognola's office at the Justice Department. The Fed lumbered to his feet and crossed to a table littered with photocopied press digests and printouts. He picked up a phone.

"Janice," he said, "I want you to call Chicago, person to person for Allard Fielding at the *Globe*. Scramble the call, okay?" He replaced the handset.

"Fielding is the editor of that guy Mettner who wrote the Sudan piece," he said to Samson. "Imagine a guy who looks like a cross between W. C. Fields and Wallace Beery, add a temper as mean as a rattler on a bad day, and you got the picture. But he's a good man just the same. And Mettner knows Bolan."

The phone rang. He picked up the receiver. "Al?" he said. "Brognola here. I want you to do something for me. Your man in Central Africa. Yeah, Mettner. I want you to cable him a service message on my behalf...."

NINE HUNDRED THIRTY MILES to the south, three men sat by a pool in the roof garden of a condo penthouse in Miami, Florida. One of the men was black; both the others were swarthy, black haired, mustached. Each of them had flinty, expressionless eyes, as animated as an electric lamp with the current switched off.

The older of the two, who was around fifty-five, sipped a highball beneath a striped sun umbrella. Bright light reflected off the ocean winked from diamond and ruby rings, a gold identity bracelet and a heavy gold chain circling his neck. He was wearing white loafers, white sharkskin pants and a salmon-colored herringbone jacket over an open-necked sport shirt.

"I don't like loose ends," Giovanni said. "They louse up the smooth running of the act."

If the younger man disapproved of the mixed metaphor, it didn't show. His orange-peel complexion remained impassive as he bit off the end of a Corona Corona, spit it over the roof-garden balustrade and thumbed a gold lighter into flame. "We've got good people down there," he said. "It's just that the reports don't stack up yet."

"I'm not interested in reports, Lou." Giovanni's voice was gravelly and hoarse. "Either I get results or these good people you talk about get replaced."

Louis Mancini glanced across at the black man. He was wearing a pale lightweight suit and a jazzy foulard, but he looked as if he'd be happier in a uniform. "The colonel here is one hundred percent certain his organization is secure," Mancini said.

"So what am I supposed to do?" Giovanni growled. "Stand up and cheer?"

"You have to understand, sir, that this is a very large tract of land," the black man said. "With communications not always like here. We know there is, or was, a spy with the caravan. We shall find him. He will be interrogated."

"Interrogated? Squeeze the fucker until his heart bursts and he spills all he knows. I want to know who's paying him and why, how they got on to us, who else is in the outfit, the *ganz*," Giovanni said.

"We shall try our best."

"You better. And your best better be good. There's one hell of a lot of money invested in this operation. You want the big payoff, you've got to come across with results. You read me?"

"My plane leaves in one hour," the African said. "In forty-eight at the latest you shall have positive news."

"We better have our own tame soldier check out the other end," Mancini said when the black officer had gone. "See if there's any relation between this and the fuck-up in Marseilles."

"Why would there be? We wasted the bastards, didn't we? But check it out if it makes you feel good."

"I guess so," Mancini said. "You figure he really believes that big payoff routine?"

"Who? The African? People will believe anything, if you string them along and promise a big enough prize."

CHAPTER TWELVE

Bolan guided his horse between the stones of a rubbled slope that led gradually down to a plain. Somewhere ahead of him, the caravan with the camel carrying the container of uranium 235 was winding its way among the tall grasses and scrub oak that had supplanted the interminable thorn trees. At last, it seemed, they had crossed the southern fringe of the desert and were heading for a less desolate tract of land.

The Executioner rode slowly, the homing device open on the saddle in front of him. At first, turning the pointer to check that he was vectoring in on the sector where the bleeps were loudest, was almost a formality: the trail was well marked and there was no other route the caravan could have taken. Later in the afternoon, when he was climbing yet another of the limestone ridges with which the country was barred, he was forced to concentrate, for the track petered out in a wilderness of rock outcrops and it took a lot of effort to check and recheck the route.

Hunger clawed at his belly: the small amount of dried food he carried had been abandoned with the camel. His water bottle was empty. And he was anxious about the horse: apart form a few dried-up leaves on top of the cliff, the animal had neither eaten nor drunk since he escaped from Mahmoud and the soldiers.

Ripping a length of cloth from his burnoose to improvise a turban that would protect him from the scorching rays of the sun, he had buried the rest of his Arab disguise along with the "pilgrim" ID.

Thankful that he had been wearing a bush shirt and khakis beneath the robe, he was again beardless, in the person of Mack Bolan, a mineralogist who was equipped with a *laissez-passer* countersigned by His Excellency Hamid el-Karim, big wheel in the Sudanese administration in Khartoum.

The blacksuit was in the pouch clipped to his belt, both handguns were accessible in their quickdraw leather and the submachine gun was slung across his back. Only the stained skin remained to connect him with the mysterious traveler from Al Khureiba in Saudi Arabia.

Several times during the afternoon he stopped and tried to contact Courtney, but the radio remained obstinately silent.

On the crest of the ridge he reined in the horse and scanned the country beyond, which was becoming definitely less barren. He could see occasional squares of cultivation in the distance; vegetation covered the rolling contours more thickly. Far off toward a line of wooded hills that reared, blue-hazed, against the horizon, a long smear of dust marked the position of the caravan.

He passed the sweat-stained sleeve of his shirt across his brow and headed down. It wasn't often that he found himself in such rough terrain.

This was the exception that proved the rule.

Twice he had to skirt villages—no longer the mud-walled Arab variety but circles of African huts standing in the sweltering heat—but he saw nobody. Once, though, he thought he heard the rattle of distant rifle fire.

He was within a mile of the tree-covered hills when he saw a column of smoke rising above a mealie plantation off to the right. Soon afterward hooves thundered on hard ground and he trotted the horse out of sight behind a corn patch just before a squadron of Arab soldiers galloped past in a cloud of dust.

There were about thirty men, shouting, laughing and waving their rifles above their heads as they rode. Two of them carried the bound bodies of African women across their saddles; a third dragged behind his horse on a length of rope the twisting, lacerated corpse of a man.

Bolan waited in his hiding place until the dust had settled. He switched on the homer again. He was still receiving the bleeps loud and clear. He could afford the time to investigate.

Walking the horse warily between scattered trees, he advanced toward the column of smoke, the AutoMag in his right hand.

When he was about two hundred yards away he found a grassy hollow where the horse could graze. He tethered the animal to a sapling and continued on foot.

The village was completely hidden in a shallow depression. As he made his way down the slope Bolan smelled the bitter, familiar odors of burning and death.

Most of the inhabitants had fled, but there were a dozen bodies sprawled in the dusty space enclosed by a ring of gutted huts. The lucky ones had been shot. Others had been hacked almost to pieces with saber strokes. Two of the men had been castrated. Muslim fundamentalists, the Executioner knew, believed that this grisly rite barred the victim from entry into Paradise. He wondered what kind of nirvana they expected for themselves.

Compressing his lips, he strode farther into the sacked village. The flames had died down, but half a dozen of the smoldering huts still spiraled smoke into the air. The only structure standing was the stone-built end wall of a shack considerably larger than the others.

He walked around the corner of the wall . . . and stopped dead in his tracks.

The African—the village headman? a teacher?—had been wearing a white linen jacket with a shirt and necktie. His pants had been removed and lay crumpled in the dust. He had been impaled on a sharpened stake planted in the ground with his wrists wired together behind his back, and small sacks filled with stones had been roped to his naked feet. The stake was about eight feet high. Once the pointed end had been forced into his body, the killers had left him there, certain that his frenzied struggles, plus the weights on his feet, would gradually force the wooden staff up through his intestines and belly until the point pierced a vital organ.

Blood stained the insides of his thighs, glistened on the peeled wood of the stake and lay congealed on the earth below. The pitiless sun flashed from a pair of spectacles still perched on the nose above the man's soundlessly screaming mouth. The reddened point of the stake had pierced the linen jacket near the center button.

Bolan reckoned it had taken him a long time to die, and that the final release must have been within the past fifteen minutes. Gritting his teeth, he surveyed the remains of the building beyond the wall.

It had been made of wood, but all that remained was a tangle of charred embers from which wisps of smoke still rose. It had clearly been some kind of school. Hardwood desks with iron frames had escaped the conflagration and still stood upright among the debris.

The Executioner turned to look at the end wall.

A scorched teacher's desk had fallen forward among the smoldering timbers of a rostrum. Behind it a slate board was still attached to the plaster. Glancing at the chalked letters and figures, Bolan drew in his breath with a hiss of surprise. The top line read: *Explosive power derived from energy liberated by (noncontrolled) chain reaction.*

Beneath this was a diagram accompanied by the deadly Einsteinian equation that lay at the root of all atomic power: $E = mc^2$.

And then the line: *If beryllium is used to slow down the neutron bombardment when the fission of uranium is...*

The writing tailed off halfway down the board, presumably when the teacher had been interrupted by the Arab attack and dragged out to the stake.

Bolan whistled as he took in text and formulae. "Nuclear physics out *here*!" he murmured. "I guess the trail's warming up at last!"

Hurrying back to the horse, he rounded the smoking remains of a burned-out hut and came upon the body of a woman sprawled on her back. She had a slip of paper clutched in one hand.

Gently Bolan disengaged it from the dead fingers. It was a sheet from a looseleaf notebook. He smoothed it out and read:

Radium Family: Clearly the teacher so cruelly impaled had been giving a course in advanced physics when the village had come under attack.

Bolan had a lot to think about as he remounted and rode off along the trail.

Wherever the nuclear thieves were conveying the stolen uranium 235, it looked as if they were organizing courses of instruction in its use among the dissident Africans. It followed then that the thieves, overtly or covertly, were hostile to the official Sudanese government in Khartoum. Whether the sack of this particular village by the Arab cavalry had anything to do with this, or whether it was merely a coincidence, he had no way of knowing.

Remembering that it was the teacher who had been most brutally killed, the Executioner figured the odds were on the former choice: the raid could have been part of a systematic campaign to "discourage" tribes considered backward from advancing their scientific education.

Whatever, it was an even bet that the final destination of the lead canister and its sinister cargo was not too far away.

A few miles farther among the wooded hills, Bolan stopped once more on a crest and took a small but powerful pair of binoculars from the pouch at his waist. Three ridges away, he could clearly spot the caravan traversing a clearing. The Zeiss lenses showed him the striped blanket still in position on the camel he was trailing.

He rode on down the track, now clearly marked and in more constant use than most of the route he had traveled.

The warrior was within sight of the open space where he had last located the caravan when he noticed that the bleeps on the homer were growing fainter.

Puzzled, he reined in the horse. He knew the train had come this way because he had seen it with his own eyes; and he knew, furthermore, for the same reason, that the camel had still been with it when it crossed the clearing.

They could not possibly have put on speed and gotten so far away that they were out of range. So why should the signal have lost strength if he was on the right track?

He rode on. The bleeps grew fainter still.

Had the camel carrying the canister broken away from the column? He halted again and swung the homer questioningly around. There was no sign of the signal strengthening in any direction tangential to the trail. In any case, he had *already* seen the camel farther ahead than this....

It was only when he wheeled completely around that he stumbled on the answer.

The bleeps increased in volume when he was facing back the way he had come.

Although the camel itself was still with the caravan, the canister—or at least the homing device he had secreted beside it—had been left someplace along the route!

Bolan cantered back along the trail, his pulses quickening at the thought of action at last.

Action he got . . . but not the kind he expected.

It was simple enough to follow the signals—they became stronger as he went along. It looked, in fact, as if the canister was now stationary.

The homer finally led him off the track and in among the trees. As the woods grew more dense, the bleeps got louder. When the signals were registering their maximum, he dismounted, unslung the MP-5 and stole cautiously through the undergrowth as the device directed him.

Bolan was puzzled. He knew he must be almost there, yet there were no signs of the buildings or installations he expected; nothing but the vibrating hum of insects in the steamy shade beneath the forest trees.

At last he walked out into a small glade with a sandy pit in the center—and in the middle of the pit was the lead canister. No camel, no bedroll, no wicker cage. Just the heavy cylindrical container on its own.

It was open, Bolan saw with a momentary thrill of alarm, but the narrow core in the heart of the lead shield was empty.

Except for the homer placed neatly inside it.

The Executioner's scalp prickled. Something smelled. The deserted glade, the canister so conveniently displayed in the sand pit, the absence of buildings . . . it was a setup.

"You had better drop your weapon. There are automatic rifles covering you on every side," a voice said quietly.

Bolan whirled. A ring of soldiers with AKMs at the hip stood in the shadows of the tree trunks enclosing the glade. He pitched the submachine gun away from him and stood waiting.

A squat, powerfully built African wearing a French paratroop beret and the insignia of a colonel on the shoulder straps of his bush shirt stepped forward and picked up the gun.

"We were expecting you to show, so that you could collect your electronic toy," he said affably. "What kept you? We have been waiting more than an hour."

CHAPTER THIRTEEN

Jason Mettner II was a tall, lanky man with a prematurely lined face and jackets that looked as if they had been tailored for a heavier man.

He sat on the porch of a ramshackle hotel in El Da'ein, sipping a warm Coke and scanning for the third time a cable that had been relayed by train from Nyala, in southern Darfur province. The porch railing was blistered and peeling. Below it, scrawny fowls scuffed the dust between two beat-up off-roaders parked in the sunbaked yard.

Mettner eased the collar of his shirt away from his perspiring neck with a forefinger. Fans stirred the stale air beneath the porch roof, but it was still intolerably hot. The sweat dripped from his arm to smear the ink on the handwritten blue cable form as he read:

URGENTEST PROMETTNER HOTEL NASSER EL DAEIN DARFUR SUDAN STOP ESSENTIAL YOU LOCATE CONTACT STRIKER ANOTHER NONPUB EXCLUSIVE STOP LAST HEARD ALEX PROBABLY SOUTHWARDING SUDANWARD TRAIL HIJACKED CHEMICAL SEE MY LAST STOP CHECK IN SOONEST   GLOBE

Mettner lit a cigarette and stared at the cable. It was the first time in his life he'd had a service message brought to him by train. Why had it been ferried by the train returning from the railhead at Nyala, which was farther from civilization than even he was? Probably because there was a two-bit airfield at Nyala and the cable had been flown there from whatever town in the armpit of Africa had the nearest telex that worked.

Characteristically the time and date of filing—and even the town of origin—had been lost in transit.

But it wasn't this that fazed the *Globe*'s ace foreign correspondent. In a stormy relationship with Allard Fielding that reached back ten years or more, Mettner had received some zany messages. But this was the first time he'd been genuinely stumped by the text. He didn't know how to interpret the damned cable.

He read it again, squinting one eye to keep out the smoke that spiraled up from the cigarette that drooped from his mouth.

No problem deciphering Fielding's opening order. And it was clear from the tone of the message as a whole that the editor was being guarded. Guarded? Shit, he was being cagey as hell! Which meant the contents were to be treated as secret, either to fool rival newspapermen or to keep them from the law. But in any case the word Striker could have only one meaning for Mettner. One meaning, one man.

Mack Bolan, a.k.a. The Executioner.

Okay, so he was to locate and then contact Bolan.

But what the hell was Fielding talking about, saying that it was for the purpose of a *nonpublishable* exclusive? Christ, that was exclusive all right, something that couldn't be shared even with your own readers! Big deal.

Wait a minute, though. There was another word, maybe even more out of line than that "nonpub."

The word "another," in fact.

Another nonpublishable exclusive?

That meant that there must have been others before.

Mettner saw some light. He fished a leather-covered flask of tepid bourbon from his hip pocket and poured a shot into the remains of the Coke.

Repressing a shudder, he remembered. Twice before— once in West Africa, once in Hong Kong—he had run up against this guy Bolan. Each time there had been one hell of an undercover story. Each of them had terrorist overtones. In both cases, Bolan had destroyed the opposition.

And in both cases there had been one hundred percent, unanswerable, surefire reasons—reasons of state, of national security, of world peace, of a promise given and respected—why Mettner had been unable to publish the full story.

But that wasn't why he remembered the Executioner so well. Mettner's father had been a crime reporter during the Windy City gang wars in the Roaring Twenties, and many of Bolan's victories had been won against the scum descendants of Mafia torpedoes he had written up.

So where did that leave the goddamn cable? As a tip-off, surely, that the big guy was on the warpath again. That it was top-secret stuff. And maybe that Mettner could help as he had done before. If he could lay hands on the elusive warrior.

And there the clues in the cable were less than helpful.
Last heard Alex probably southwarding Sudanward.

Did that mean that Alex, whoever he or she might be, was expected in this godforsaken country? And if so, what had it to do with Bolan?

Or did it mean Bolan had been in Alexandria, Egypt, and was expected to head south? Leave that in the Pending tray.

Whichever, it related to Allard Fielding's last service message, which Mettner had received in Khartoum a week previously.

He killed his cigarette in a cup of cold coffee and tapped another from the pack. Beneath it was a crumpled cable form. He smoothed it out and read for the fifth time:

COMING YOUR WAY QUERYMARK STOP MAYBE STOP BUT KEEP EYE AND EAR WIDE OPEN PRONUKEM STOLEN CALDERHALL LIKELY DESTINATIONS MEAST OR CENTRAF STOP SHIPMENT DASH ONE MANY DASH ALREADY CARGOED EXMARSEILLES STOP REGARDS FIELDING

Nukem was press cablese for nuclear chemicals, a current euphemism for fissile material. Meast and Centraf were contractions, respectively, for Middle East and Central Africa. As far as the Mettner eye and ear were concerned, this hot rumor had scored zero until today. But if Bolan was concerned with the theft . . . ?

Mettner lit the cigarette and walked out into the heat. Beyond the yard the blackened spars of a gutted railroad observation car—in which thirty-five black refugees had been burned alive by militiamen—lay gaunt against the leaden sky.

Mettner hurried to the nearest of the off-roaders. It was a Toyota Land Cruiser, and the metal of the hood and roof supports too hot to touch. He eased himself into the driving seat and drew on a pair of thin leather gloves. The unwary could end up with seared hands from grasping the wheel of a parked car in El Da'ein.

The tall, knob-tired 4x4 coughed its way past the stained and cracked stucco of apartment buildings, over a bridge spanning the freight yard, along a wide strip of pavement bordering a sinuous *oued*, a dried-up watercourse that turned into rapids when it rained.

Rain? the newspaperman thought. In this furnace where even the camels wear asbestos humps? Don't make me laugh.

He braked the Toyota in a large square flanked by a plantation of dusty palms. Arab women swathed in black walked toward a street market behind the trees. An armored personnel carrier loaded with steel-helmeted soldiers in camous rocketed past on flailing tracks. Otherwise there was no movement to disturb the glare shimmering off the hardtop.

Mettner waved away a cloud of bluebottle flies that had been buzzing over the corpse of a dead dog and went into a flat-roofed brick building that housed the post office and telephone exchange.

Fans whirred above, but it was no cooler in front of the wire mesh grille topping the counter that sealed off one end of the shuttered room. The place smelled of sweat.

He pushed money beneath the grille and waited for the clerk to secrete it before making his request. In this part of Africa, you laid it on the line for openers if you wanted any service—and paid for what you actually had afterward.

It was a far cry from the glittering white high rises and the air-conditioned lounges of Khartoum. Mettner wished like hell that he was back in the capital right now. Since he wasn't—and since he had about as much chance of locating Bolan from El Da'ein as he had of winning the French national lottery—he would follow his own golden rule and hand over the tough part to a legman on the spot.

That was one of the rewards of being an ace: you got the local stringer to handle the research and dope out the background to a story before you even arrived to order your first shot of Jack Daniel's. The *Globe* had a stringer in Khartoum, too, a news agency man who filled in on the side for several British and American dailies.

The post office clerk was an Indian. He was looking at Mettner with raised eyebrows.

"I want to put through a call to Khartoum," Mettner said. "Press. Priority. In care of the Madison Agency: a person-to-person call to a Mr. David Courtney."

CHAPTER FOURTEEN

Mack Bolan choked back to consciousness. He was strapped naked to a ten-foot wooden plank. His ankles were bound and attached to an iron ring at one end of the plank; his arms, stretched above his head, were tied at the wrist and fastened to the other. The two ends rested on a tabletop and the seat of a chair, so that his head was lower than his feet.

Helpless and undignified on his back, he had three times been put through the "liquid persuasion" interrogation—a torture as old as the walls of the Arab village where he was kept prisoner.

The technique is simple . . . and effective.

Plug the victim's nostrils, wedge an iron ring into his mouth so that it stays jammed open. Then drape a long strip of muslin over the face and pour water—gallons of water—through that and into the mouth.

The head cannot be turned because of the arms strapped on either side of it, so the only way to get rid of the water cascading into the mouth through the thin cloth is to swallow it. But as soon as each mouthful is swallowed it is replaced by another.

Meanwhile the victim has to breathe.

The lungs heave and try to drag in air, but the attempt only draws in water.

And with the water comes the muslin, which is remorselessly sucked into the windpipe. . . .

In a very short time the victim, gagging and retching, is half drowned by the water in his lungs and half choked by the cloth.

The Executioner scored low marks as a victim because his iron will was strong enough to allow himself to be choked into unconsciousness before the spasms became violent enough to tip off the torturers that it was time to stop, remove the cloth, and then start again—if they wanted to keep their client alive.

The effectiveness of the treatment as a means of coercion relied not so much on pain as on the fact that it quickly reduced the victim to a gibbering, blubbering, vomiting wreck whose semiconscious mind had room for only one thought: the agonizing need to supply lungs and thundering heart with oxygen.

At any price.

Such as the disclosure of secret information.

Here again Bolan rated a low score.

The Executioner didn't blubber, he didn't plead, he refused to listen to the frantic cries for help relayed by his subconscious.

Sure, he could be made to yell, to howl in the extremity of scientifically applied pain. But indignity alone left his inner spirit, his will to win, unconquered. His reflexes could be controlled and his body made to void itself outside of his conscious will. But the physical domination of his functions left his mental defenses intact.

Put it another way. If his captors wanted results, they had chosen the wrong torture.

The two men administering the treatment had come to the same conclusion. After Bolan had blacked out for the third time, when the gargling groans had died away to a labored wheeze and the plank had stopped thumping from the threshing of his bound body, the Sudanese holding his head straightened up with a scowl.

"This is no good," he said. "We shall never get anywhere this way. The accursed infidel will simply continue to choke himself unconscious until finally his heart gives out."

Mahmoud put down the jerrican and attached hose he had been using to supply the water. "Very well," he said. "We will try something else."

Bolan heard the words as he swam reluctantly back to awareness through the waves of the nausea engulfing him. Mahmoud had helped along the treatment with vicious slaps and squeezes of the Executioner's genitals, and now his belly was on fire as well as the agony sandpapering his lungs and throat.

The first thing he saw was a blurred image of the black officer who had captured him. The man was leaning against a wall at the foot of the plank. Now he levered himself upright and spoke to the Sudanese. "You are right," he said. "The water was quite satisfactory at the time of the Inquisition. Time was not money in those days. You could continue all day and night. Even a will as strong as this man's would ultimately break. It had to. But today we have less time. Those helping us have a right to demand results. And civilization has, after all, progressed. Perhaps we should avail ourselves of one of its most priceless assets."

Mahmoud and his assistant stared at him.

"Electricity," the officer said gently. "The truck that brought us here is of an antique design, but it does have a magneto, a generator. If you were to take a wrench and loosen half a dozen screws..."

Mahmoud nodded. He and the other Sudanese left the room.

It was a small room with a single window set high in the baked mud wall. Apart from the table, the chair and the plank along which the Executioner was stretched, it was bare.

The village was smaller than Wadi Djarzireh, a compact eagle's nest of flat-roofed houses clustered high up in a canyon cutting through a barren range of hills that broke unexpectedly through the wooded landscape where Bolan had been captured.

The officer and six of the soldiers had bundled him onto the floor in back of the worn-out half-track Berliet, which still bore traces on its rusted fenders of divisional insignia that had once identified a unit of the French army in Chad. Facedown, with their boots grinding into his back, he had been able to see nothing of the country they traversed during the thirty-minute drive.

He closed his eyes now. A man who's naked and manacled, and whose bodily functions are totally controlled by others has difficulty preserving his human dignity, not to mention a spirit of bravado.

When a uniform is involved, the situation becomes more acute.

The anonymity of extreme pain soon produces a humiliation so complete that the psychological distance between torturer and tortured becomes immense—the ringmaster and the lion, the scientist and the lab rat. It's no longer possible for the victim to reply to his tormentor's questions on the same "social level."

Bolan knew this. And he knew that if the torture continued long enough, this phase would be followed by a relationship almost sexual in its intimacy: the invasion of privacy is after all more comprehensive than anything achieved in a normal encounter between a man and a woman.

Anticipating the thunderbolts of agony that the electricity would bring, he had closed his eyes in an attempt at least to stave off this obscenity. They were the only organs still under his own control.

The African officer was talking. Bolan knew the script by heart. He was familiar with the scenario from books, from movies and even from real life. It was the one that ran "you're going to sing anyway. They always do.... So why not save us all a load of embarrassment. Why not save yourself unnecessary discomfort and tell us what we want to know *now*?"

What they wanted to know, of course, was who he worked for. How did he know about the U-235 in the caravan? Who were his immediate contacts and how did the rest of the outfit work?

Bolan's problem was special to this one particular mission.

It turned the usual script upside down. Instead of holding out at all costs, hanging in there to keep details of a network secret until its members had time to split, he must at all costs avoid revealing that there was in fact *no* network.

Because once they knew for sure that he was a loner, all they had to do was kill him. End of story.

But as long as they believed he was part of an organization, however small, there was hope that they would keep him alive in the certainty that he would eventually break. And talk.

He was therefore in the unenviable position of a man determined to prolong his own suffering as many hours as he could.

For the longer he agonized, the longer he lived.

Like the old saying had it, while there was life there was hope.

The Executioner never gave up on hope.

There was one thing in favor of a successful deception. There had to *be* a connection because of the homer... but they hadn't tumbled to the fact that Mack Bolan, heavily armed mineralogist, and the Arab spy who had tried to join up with the "wrong" caravan were one and the same person.

Bolan thanked his lucky stars that he had buried the robes and the incriminating ID papers before he took up the chase again.

He hoped those lucky stars would continue to shine.

"A heavy-caliber automatic designed to take a wildcat cartridge, a Walther PPK and a modern delayed-blowback submachine gun complete with silencer—that's a heavy arsenal for a simple prospector," the black officer said. "Add a professional spy bug, its directional counterpart, a short-wave radio transceiver, a one-piece burglar's suit and several . . . unusual instruments in a waterproof pouch, and we arrive, I think, at a number of questions that require answers."

Bolan said nothing.

"Who, for example, do you contact on that radio?"

"I told you—the government department that employs me."

"What government?"

"Make a guess."

"You refuse, nevertheless, to call them up and prove your point."

"I told you again," Bolan said. "They're way out of range. The transceiver's designed for use in Europe."

"Then why bring it here?"

"I came in a hurry. It's part of my normal kit. I have to report back sometimes and—"

"Bullshit!" the African interrupted. "You have a confederate who planted that bug beside a lead canister carried by a pack camel in the caravan. You knew what that canister contained. You must have done because you were following it when we jumped you."

Again the Executioner remained silent. There was nothing to say.

"I want to know where that confederate is now. I want to know how *you* knew about the canister. I want to know who your principals are and why they are interested in us." The officer paused. "Clearly you were put in to check out the canister's final destination. But supposing you had found it, through a more skillful use of the bug your associate planted—what then? What are you going to do about the shipment of an admittedly stolen consignment of fissile material when so many highly placed persons are involved in its safe delivery?"

Bolan lay with his eyes still closed, breathing as deeply as he could, in an effort to prepare himself for the coming ordeal. He remained silent.

"Very well." The black man exhaled exasperatedly through his nose. "You are the one to suffer needlessly the rigors of what we call sharpened interrogation. If you are resolved to make us force the information from you, let us get on with it."

This time the Executioner opened his eyes. Mahmoud and his companion were back in the room. Bolan caught his breath as the officer took two lengths of electric supply cord from one of them and attached the wires to his scrotum and nipples with miniature bulldog clips. The steel teeth bit painfully into his exhausted flesh.

Mahmoud was holding a cast-iron generator with a crank attached to the armature spindle. The officer jerked his head at the table. "Put it down there."

When the generator was clamped to the tabletop, he screwed the free ends of the wires to its terminals. He took hold of the handle. "For the last time," he grated, "who sent you here and where is your confederate?"

Bolan nerved himself for the agony, trying to imagine the pain so that he would be readier to meet it when it came. It was not the first time he had been tortured with electricity. "I have nothing to add to what I told you already—the truth," he whispered through set teeth.

At a survival course with Britain's crack SAS antiterrorist squad once, he had been taught sophisticated techniques of self-hypnosis to overcome situations like this. He could remember none of them. The pressure of the powerful steel clips alone was exceedingly uncomfortable.

As though he were an objective observer watching a movie, Bolan saw the officer start to turn the generator handle.

For a moment there was only a fierce tingling in the area of the clips, and then, as the handle turned faster, he suddenly gasped.

His chest felt as if it had been ripped open; fire flamed through his loins and seared his belly. A cold sweat broke out all over his body and his breath began to sob. Some time later, his spasming muscles convulsed, and his bladder and bowels evacuated themselves.

One of the Sudanese giggled. The black officer laughed aloud. "He thinks that is it," he said. "Think again, friend."

The grinding of the handle rose to a screech.

"HOW THE HELL did you know I was here?" Jason Mettner asked Hal Brognola. "Who are you? And what exactly do you want, that's so urgent I have to get out of bed in the middle of the night?"

"It's almost 7:00 a.m.," the Fed said mildly. "A more interesting question would be *why* the hell are *you* here?"

They were sitting on the terrace of a hotel overlooking the Upemba National Park in the Shaba region of southern Zaire. It was already very hot.

"If you have to know, I'm following up a lead," Mettner said shortly. He hated to get out of his bed early when it wasn't strictly necessary. "My editor wants me to contact a guy, and according to my information he should be someplace around here."

"I know about the lead," Brognola said. "Allard Fielding's a buddy of mine. He sent that service message at my request."

"At *your* request? But I never heard your name before. I mean, you're not part of the publisher's—"

"I *am* part of the Administration," Brognola interrupted gently.

The newspaperman paused with his coffee cup halfway to his lips, staring out beyond the tropical trees to a stretch of savannah where a herd of animals browsed in the heat. "I get it," he said at last. "And Bolan is . . . ?"

"Checking out something for me, yeah. But we lost touch and I figured that you, being already in the area, might be the quickest way to regain contact."

"Why me? Some newspaper guys put in overtime contributing intel for the NSA or the Company. I don't."

"I know it. I also know," the Fed explained, "that you've ran up against Striker before. And I know from what you *didn't* publish that you're regular, a man who can be trusted."

Frowning, Mettner lit a cigarette. "Thanks for the compliment. If you were coming here in person, why ask me?"

"Because there's something screwy going on. How did you get yourself here, ten miles from the railroad station at Bukama?"

"My legman told me there was a chance Bolan would be here. How did *you* know *I* was here?" Mettner countered.

"Like you say, guys here and there put in overtime keeping the Company informed," Brognola said evasively. "Who's this legman of yours then?"

"Guy in Khartoum. A Brit by the name of Courtney."

"Exactly." Brognola breathed heavily. He was wearing a lightweight seersucker suit, but it was creased and he was sweating. He mopped his brow with a silk handkerchief. "Damned heat in this country," he said. "Why I came. I heard you'd moved this way and I guessed it must be on account of a tip-off—yet this same Courtney is also a CIA legman in Khartoum. He's supposed to channel Bolan's reports back to me through Langley, but he hasn't filed, and his control hasn't been able to raise him in more than a week."

"Screwy is right," Mettner said slowly. "Why would he pass on intel to one agency that's paying him and hold out on another?" He shook a second cigarette from his pack and lit it from the butt of the first.

"You smoke too much," Brognola observed.

"How do you know?"

"It's in your file," the Fed retorted.

Mettner laughed. "So that's why you came. But how did you come? First train from Lumbumbashi doesn't hit town until ten. And the Kananga flyer is an hour later."

"I have a contact in Kenya who let me have the use of a chopper," Brognola told him.

The newspaperman's eyebrows rose. "Whatever it is, your man's mission must be important."

"It's damned important. I have to warn you that you might not be able to publish. But since I trust you—and since I need your help—I can tell you it has to do with thefts of uranium 235."

Mettner whistled. "And Mack Bolan's on the trail?"

"When last heard of, he was tracking a consignment that passed through Khartoum, supposedly heading this way. Tell me. Did you talk with this legman in person?"

The newspaperman shook his head. "Uh-uh. Called him from some hick town in Darfur. He called me back pretty soon, like the intel hadn't been too hard to get."

"Would you know his voice?"

"Nope. Never spoke to the man before."

"You're a foreign specialist, Mettner. How would you read shipments of nuclear material directed to this area? Would you rate it a possible destination for stolen stuff? Are there elements here who might want to go nuclear in secret?"

"Anything is possible in this neck of the woods," Mettner said. "Since 1960 you've got Lumumba, Kasavubu, Mobutu, Adoula, Tchombe in power at different times. There are tribal jealousies. The French had to send in paras in 1978 when rebels massacred Europeans in Kolwezi, and that's less than one hundred miles from here." He shook his head. "But for my money it'd be crazy to hump it all the way down through Egypt and the Sudan. Shit, you could fly it in from the Atlantic coast in a couple hours. You could use the Congo and the Kasai and float it upriver from Brazzaville in less than a week."

"That's what I thought. When's Striker due to show?"

"I was told he'd check in to a Bukama hotel around noon, traveling south from Bukavu in a Land Rover. He was to contact a man, an Indian named Devananda Anand, this afternoon."

"What would you say if he *didn't* show?"

"I'd say your Brit was playing a double game. Either that, or he's out of circulation and the man I spoke to on the phone wasn't Courtney at all. Whichever, I'd guess I was sent off on a false trail—believable but false—to get me out of the way."

"I wouldn't argue with that."

A telephone reservation in the name of Bolan had been made at the hotel in Bukama, but nobody checked in.

Police patrols reported that no European traveling south from Bukava in a Land Rover had been sighted.

And no Indian, named Anand or anything else, showed at the Nation Park hotel that afternoon.

"As our Brit himself might say," Brognola announced when nothing had happened by nightfall, "there's something rum going on here, Mettner. Something very rum indeed."

"BOLAN? THAT SON OF A BITCH?" Don Giovanni spit out the words as if they hurt his mouth. Maybe they did. "The bastard wasted Battaglia, Jesse Lobato and Manny Mandone as well as crippling half the families from Vegas to Miami Beach," he snarled.

"If it's the same guy," Mancini said.

"Be your age, Lou. Of course it's the same guy. You figure there's room in the world for *two* meddlesome bastards who operate like that?"

"They said this one was Russian," Mancini objected. Cotton wool tufts of altocumulus whipped past the window as the Cessna executive jet sliced through the rarefied atmosphere thirty thousand feet above the southern Atlantic.

"Russian my ass," Giovanni said. "The ID was Russian. He's using a cover he figures will appeal to the wogs in Khartoum. For some reason he decided to keep on his own name. That's not to say it's a different operator." He bit the end off a cigar, spit it into a cuspidor and clamped the cigar between his teeth. "Wish I'd never heard of the bastard," he growled.

Mancini flamed a gold Cartier lighter. "You said you wanted results," he reminded the capo.

"Yes, results. But all I got is a name." He leaned the cigar into the flame and puffed smoke. "What I don't understand is why we didn't get this name before. We have enough guys working on this deal. We've been with him all the way. Why in hell didn't our man in Khartoum tip us off who it was?"

Mancini was chewing gum. He shifted the wad. "Maybe it wasn't such a good idea, using two different organizations to move the stuff and to cover it in transit," he offered.

"All my ideas are good."

"Sure they are, Don Giovanni. What I mean is, maybe the two don't liaise the way they should."

The don ignored the remark. "Okay," he said, "the monkey man fingers the guy. He lays hands on him. But he doesn't make him sing. We don't find out who the others are, and where. So, I have to go all the way to the Sudan to take charge myself. I ask you, Lou, do I have time to waste?"

"Maybe it won't be so wasted when you get there," Mancini said. He looked up, scenting an odor of sweat mingled with after-shave. A blue-chinned torpedo wearing a white linen steward's jacket was standing in the aisle, proffering a silver tray loaded with two highballs. "Refueling stop in Casablanca in twenty minutes," he announced in a hoarse voice. "Then six-twenty to Khartoum."

"You want to wash under your arms, Joe," Mancini said.

The Cessna's twin contrails curved through the wisps of cloud over the Azores as the pilot followed the air traffic controller's instructions and veered ten degrees farther south when he was above the Sao Pedro beacon on Santa Maria Island.

"Damn right my time won't be wasted," Don Giovanni said. "It's going be my pleasure to finally get rid of Mack 'The Bastard' Bolan. I'll attend to him personally."

CHAPTER FIFTEEN

Bolan lay on the bare floor of his prison and watched the light fade outside the window. He was shivering.

His clothes had been taken away, along with the weapons, the shoulder rig and the rest of his gear, after his captors dragged him from the truck. But the plain white shift they had thrown into the room when the torturers left was not warm enough to neutralize the cold air of the night.

Unless, he thought tiredly, the shivers were simply a reaction to his ordeal. His throat felt as if he had swallowed molten lead, and every nerve, muscle and sinew in his lean, hard frame was aching. Yet he was astonished to find that, apart from a redness around the site of the bulldog clips, the interminable torture session had left no marks on him. So much pain and so little to show for it.

And the immediate future was no brighter. Right now, all he could look forward to was a repetition of the same treatment. Nobody knew where he was; nobody knew he had been taken prisoner; nobody who counted even knew he risked capture.

A character less battle-hardened than the Executioner might have settled at that point for the easy way—the way that was *relatively* easy—aiming for no more than the will to hold out until he had provoked them to an excess that would finish him.

But that was not the warrior's way. Negative thinking found no space on the shelves of his intellectual armory.

He would hold out until the situation changed in such a way that he could seize the opportunity and turn the tables.

What that change would be, he had no idea. There was no point inventing a scenario: it was a waste of mental energy. The important thing was to be ready for anything.

Because, whatever the odds, he was damned well going to get the hell out. Somehow. He owed it to himself, to his unquenchable determination not only to find out who was ferrying the stolen uranium 235 and where it was going, but also to locate and unmask the mole close to Hal Brognola who must be responsible for all the obstacles stacked against him ever since he took on the mission.

So hold on was the watchword.

Hold on and remember—the only thing he had to hide was that there was nothing to hide.

For a fleeting second, recalling the indescribable agonies of the electric current, the thought that he might not make it flashed across his consciousness. He paid it no mind.

It wouldn't be long, in any case, before he put his resolution to the test. "Leave the foreign swine for an hour," the African officer had growled when at last they unstrapped him from the plank and dumped him on the floor. "Then we shall start over."

Fifty minutes of that hour had to have elapsed already.

Bolan pushed himself upright into a sitting position and surveyed the room. They had taken away everything but the table and chair. Could he possibly break a leg from the chair, wrench a length of wood from the tabletop and use them as a weapon? Against the officer's autoloader and a sentry with an assault rifle? No way.

Force open the door? It was fashioned from heavy beams of wood, ironbound, with metal hinges stretching three-fourths of the way across. There would be a sentry outside still, and he remembered hearing the rumble of stout bolts being shot home.

He cocked his head and listened.

Here in this house in the center of the hill village, the everyday noises of the community were muted. But he could make out the cries of barkers in a market, a jingling of harness as someone rode along a narrow street. Nearer, he heard the splashing of a fountain, a murmur of Arab voices.

And something else.

Bolan frowned. He had been subconsciously aware of those other sounds for some time, but now there was an extra component. What was it? How long had it been there? Where was it coming from?

For a moment he couldn't even separate it from the others. He just knew that an additional noise had manifested itself. Then suddenly he had it—a stealthy slithering sound punctuated by soft, barely discernible thumps. He concentrated on the noise, ignored all others.

It was coming from the direction of the small window high up in the wall.

The warrior had already manhandled the table across, stood the chair on it and checked out the window. He knew the room was on the second or third floor of the house, and that there was a sentry squatting in the patio below with a rifle across his knees. There were no pipes, projections or decorations on the outer wall. Now he rose silently to his feet and climbed up onto the chair again.

It was dark outside, but in the diffused light reflected upward from the courtyard below he could see a length of rope dangling in front of the opening.

It was a thick rope, hanging down almost to the windowsill, and it terminated in a double knot the size of his fist. Every now and then the rope twirled and lowered itself a few inches so that the knot bumped against the rough sandstone of the embrasure. As he watched in amazement, the rope swung slowly back and forth, scraping that knot along the sill, producing the sounds he had heard.

Someone, somewhere above, was trying to attract his attention!

He seized the rope, tugging it once. Immediately the swinging motion stopped and the rope hung still.

Bolan clambered up and hauled himself cautiously onto the sill. He leaned out into the night. The window was just wide enough to take his powerful shoulders.

The guard was still below. Bolan twisted his head and looked up. He knew already that between the window and the roof parapet there was a ten-foot stretch of rough sandstone unbroken by any projection. But now the line of the parapet was broken by a head and shoulders silhouetted against the stars.

The rope twitched impatiently several times. The knot rose upward for twelve inches in a series of small jerks.

The message couldn't have been clearer if it had been sung by a Western union boy in a Hollywood movie. Climb up. Escape.

Bolan pulled hard on the rope. It was rock solid. The unknown rescuer must have wrapped it around a chimney or some other stable feature on the roof.

The soldier below was still nodding over his rifle. Bolan was barefoot. If he could make those few yards of sandstone without a single sound, without dislodging the smallest fragment, before the torturers returned to the room . . .

If he couldn't, he would be a sitting duck. But what the hell. Anything was better than what lay in store for him below. This was the break he had been waiting for. Wrapping both hands around the rope, he swung out over the void, braced his feet against the wall and began dragging himself hand over hand toward the parapet.

The ascent took him seven minutes and nine seconds. Every silent inch was an achievement, a triumph of determination and muscular effort over fatigue and the laws of gravity.

It was the vital need for a silence that was absolute, a delicacy of touch that would not permit the tiniest morsel of frangible sandstone to fall and alert the sentry, that made it rugged. Without that qualification, Bolan could have made the climb in thirty seconds flat and eased himself over the parapet.

As it was, by the time he swung a leg over and subsided, panting, on the roof, his shoulder muscles were shrieking for relief and his feet were raw.

Once the thundering behind his eyes had quietened, he raised his head and stared at his rescuer. There was no Western Union cap, but it was certainly a boy.

The slight figure coiling up the rope was that of an Arab child no more than twelve years old. "What the?" Bolan whispered.

The boy laid a finger across his lips. Jerking his small head imperiously, he stole away to the far side of the roof. Bolan got up and limped after him. The kid was paying out the rope over another parapet. Below, the Executioner could just make out a huddle of smaller buildings, more flat roofs, and then a raised walkway edged with battlements.

"I'm obliged," Bolan murmured. "You'll never know just how much I'm obliged, kid. But who *are*—?"

"Shh!" the boy hissed. "Very dangerous." He waved a hand at the walkway. "Soldiers come here on patrol, yes? We wait until they pass. Then we go down."

"Okay, okay. But what are you doing here? Who are you?"

"I come from Wadi Djarzireh," the boy said in a low voice.

"Yeah, but how did you know that I was here? And why should you help me?"

"My sister tell me I shall look after you."

"Your sister?"

"Yemanja."

"Yemanja!" Bolan was thunderstruck.

"I am in same caravan with the effendi," the boy explained. "I see what happens when they capture him again after the fire. So. Small boy can go many places, hear many things. They bring always prisoners to this village, so I help because the effendi is friend of my sister."

"As simple as that," Bolan mused. "Well—" He broke off as the boy grasped his shoulder and forced him to duck down behind the parapet. From over the wall they heard the tramp of feet and the clink of equipment as an army detail marched along the battlement. When the noises had died away in the distance, the boy rose to his feet. "We go," he said.

Bolan swarmed down the rope and found himself on the roof of a mud-walled shack overlooking a narrow alley. The sweet stench of vegetable refuse wafted to his nostrils. As the boy joined him at the edge of the roof, a confused hubbub broke out above and behind them. Voices shouted: feet clattered on a stone stairway. The officer and his torturers must have returned to find that the bird had flown.

It gave the Executioner some pleasure to imagine their bewilderment, finding the prisoner had vanished from a locked room with guards posted at the window and door. But he didn't have long to relish the thought.

"Quick!" his young rescuer urged. "They call back that patrol from the other side of the village. Very soon they guess how you escape. We go again, yes?"

"We go," Bolan agreed hastily. Together they dropped down into the alley. Already they could hear footsteps of the returning patrol racing along the battlements at the far end of the lane. "There is just one thing," he added doubtfully. "In that house there are things that belong to me. Important things. If there was any way, while they are out searching...?"

"The clothes, the papers, the talking machine and the small sack you will find in a doorway at the end of the alley," the boy said. "I could only bring one gun, the large silver one."

"You are a good boy."

Bolan tore off the shift and shrugged hastily into the bush shirt and pants while the boy waited outside the doorway, gazing impatiently up and down the alley. He buckled the belt and shoved the AutoMag into its holster. "What's your name?" he asked.

"It is a long name, not of this region. Men here call me Ali."

"I guess I can make that myself." The Executioner grinned. He unbuttoned one of the shoulder straps on the shirt. The thin sheaf of bills wadded inside the double thickness of material had been overlooked by his captors. He peeled one off and held it out. "Ali," he said, "this American money is worth a great many piasters. If I give it to you, do you think you could rent, buy or steal a horse for me? I've got to get away from this place very quickly."

"Yes, effendi." The boy nodded eagerly. "Come this way and I will show you."

Bolan thrust his feet into his combat boots, clipped the pouch to his belt and followed him out the alley.

Ali led the way across a broader street, through a deserted courtyard and into another lane from where the flaring lights of the market were visible. Over the clamor of the crowd they heard an outburst of shouting behind them: the patrol must have discovered the rope.

"Quick," Ali said again. "You must go around the market. On the far side is the mosque and beside this there is a jacaranda tree. From the lower branches you can cross the wall without passing through the gate. Below is a wadi. I will bring the horse there in one hour."

"Ali," said the Executioner warmly, "I owe you!"

"It is nothing. I obey my sister." There was a gleam of teeth in the dark and the boy was gone.

The market was on a much smaller scale than the big fair at Wadi Djarzireh. The naphtha flares illuminating stalls of fruit, vegetables and sweetmeats in the center left pools of dark shadow all around the square. Bolan edged cautiously from shadow to shadow behind the crowd of fellahin and their black-veiled women. Instead of continuing to the far side, he took the first lane he came to, figuring he could make the mosque on a cross street—because dressed as he was, in a hill village as remote as this, he couldn't afford to be seen by anyone. Not if he wanted to get out of the place alive.

Placing the rubber soles of his combat boots carefully among the dimly seen piles of garbage, he hurried away from the lights.

There was no cross street.

The lane led straight to an alleyway that circled the village immediately below the wall. And from the left, above him, he could hear the tramp of a second patrol approaching along the battlements.

Bolan turned right toward the mosque and ran, sprinting beneath a curved strip of sky spangled with stars. He passed two narrow openings, the curve of an onion-shaped dome shining faintly in the starlight. He dashed past a third alley—and cannoned into two Arab women walking out through an archway to head for the market.

One of the women was carrying a stone jar on her head; the other had looped an arm beneath the handle of a wicker basket full of fruit. The impact sent them both spinning.

The jar fell to the ground and smashed on the cobbles; the woman with the basket stumbled, sprawled and sent a cascade of dates and lemons rolling along the alley. Bolan tripped, skidded on a flood of oil from the broken jar, put his foot on a lemon and went down with a clatter that seemed to him to shake the ramparts.

Over the shrill protests and squawks of dismay from the two women, he heard a shout from the battlements and a rush of booted feet. The patrol, alerted by the noise, was running to investigate.

Bolan scrambled to his feet and dashed on. The mosque was two hundred yards away.

A man's voice called out a question. From the ululating screams and the rush of Arabic pouring from the women he was unable to say whether they were merely complaining about the behavior of a lout too brutish to stop and apologize for his clumsiness, or whether they had recognized a foreigner in the gloom and were reporting that.

He couldn't take any chances; he had to make that tree beside the mosque and disappear before the patrol gave chase.

For the right reason or the wrong, the army detail was after him. He heard guttural commands, acceleration in the running footsteps, a flashlight beam lanced the dark.

The AutoMag was in his right hand. Should he dive for cover, turn and shoot it out?

No way. He'd last as long as his ammunition, no more. He had to keep running and hope his luck held.

The square in front of the mosque was deserted. Bolan turned out of the alley, hared across and pulled himself frantically up among the branches of the giant jacaranda.

He lay there, holding his breath, as the patrol rounded a curve in the battlements, clattered beneath with the light beam probing the darkness of the alley and ran out of sight around the far end of the mosque. Ten minutes later he was slithering down the dried-up bed of the wadi.

It was an hour and thirty minutes before the boy showed. And even then—doubts were beginning to gnaw at the Executioner's mind—it took a faint whinny from the far side of a huge boulder to guide him to the rendezvous. The horse was saddled, and there was a djellaba and burnoose flung across its back.

"Ali," Bolan said fervently, "thank you. Now tell me. Do you know of the oasis called El Glouai? It lies in a stretch of desert beyond Raga, not far from the frontier of the country they call the Central African Republic."

"I have heard men speak of it," said the boy, "but I have not been there. It is very far, beyond the tall mountain and the place where they make flame come from the earth."

"Flame from the earth?" Bolan's pulses quickened.

"It is a place where they suck out the liquid that they feed to trucks."

"Ah." False alarm, the Executioner thought. "That would be a well. For gasoline and oil. Now can you tell me how to get to the trail that leads to El Glouai? I haven't done what I came here to do, but it is necessary now that I leave and return by another route."

"I think so," Ali said. "You must follow this wadi until it joins the river that flows on the other side of the town. You will have to lead the horse, for it is too rough to ride and would in any case make much noise. The river makes a ravine and after that it crosses a *hamada* with thorn trees. On the far side of this plateau you will find a caravan trail leading away and over the mountains. Beyond the pass you descend, and there you will see the track that goes toward El Glouai and the southwest."

"How far is it to that track?"

"Perhaps one day's ride, perhaps a little less," Ali said. He hesitated. "Effendi... I did not have to pay for the horse. It will not be missed until tomorrow morning." Bolan felt a crumpled bill thrust into his hand.

"Keep it, Ali," he said. "Perhaps you can buy something for yourself that you really need." He smiled, taking the horse's bridle. "And maybe some gift for your sister!"

"Allah go with you," said the boy.

CHAPTER SIXTEEN

Wind, scorching hot and blowing hard out of the wastelands to the north, rolled a long cloud of dust across the *hamada* as Mack Bolan kneed his galloping horse between the thorn trees scattering the plateau.

The pilot of the helicopter saw the telltale cloud when he was still a long way off—it was the only moving thing in all that desolate tract of country that spread from horizon to horizon five hundred feet below his whirling rotors. He nudged the man sitting next to him and pointed ahead through the Plexiglas bubble. The second man nodded. He unhooked a microphone from the powerful shortwave transmitter at one side of the controls. "We got a contact, heading southwest by west," he reported. "Closing to check it out. Stand by for confirmation."

Replacing the mike, he picked a stubby Ingram MAC-10 from the floor and rammed a magazine loaded with thirty .45 ACP rounds into the butt. The chopper banked, floating sideways under the pressure of the wind, then settled down to overtake its ten-mile-distant objective.

More than half the distance had been covered before Bolan became aware of the rotor clatter above the thunder of his horse's hooves on the stony ground. He glanced over his shoulder and saw the helicopter, a speck in the molten sky that was rapidly growing larger, approaching crabwise as the pilot corrected the wind thrust.

Ahead, the range of hills between him and his oasis target had to be a good fifteen minutes' ride away. The lower slopes were densely wooded, but he didn't have a hope of making them before the bird overtook him.

Bolan was betting the chopper was on a recon mission with instructions to locate him. But was it? Wasn't there a chance that this could be no more than some routine flight? Police checking out the movement of nomads, a military patrol on the lookout for SPLA guerrillas, a TV team on their way to report the fighting in Chad?

Maybe, but it was a chance he couldn't afford to take. Because right now he had to get out of the Sudan. In every sense the country was too hot to hold him.

He had been strung along, fooled, led into a trap—all without gaining the slightest intel on his objective. He was no nearer solving the mystery of the stolen uranium than he had been when he left Alexandria.

But he would be back. You could lay your money on that. The Executioner didn't cry quits halfway through the first round. He would make it into a neighboring country and then reenter the Sudan from a different direction, playing another role. He would trace that isotope to its destination, and find out who it was for and why they wanted it—if it was the last thing he did. He would track the stuff down if he had to quarter the whole southwestern tip of the country, from top to bottom and from side to side.

The way the chopper had been quartering the area around the Arab village in search of the infidel who had escaped?

Probably. Because he was certain now the ship was following him. How many lone riders in Arab robes would there be galloping through this wilderness when the sun was at its burning zenith?

Another swift glance behind enabled him to identify the craft. It was a two-man Dassault reconnaissance type, small, maneuverable, originally designed as a spotter for the French colonial army.

Only this ship carried no squadron insignia or military registration letters. Behind the bubble, the skeletal fuselage was painted matt black and it bore no identification.

Bolan dug his heels into the horse's flanks and coaxed the last ounce of energy from the willing animal. The sure-footed Arab steed sped straight as an arrow between the thorn trees.

Bolan lay flat along the stretched neck, the burnoose billowing behind him above the animal's long tail, streaming in the wind. Beneath him he could feel the powerful muscles quiver, the blood pulsing with every herculean stride.

The helicopter was four hundred yards away. If he wanted out of the country in one piece, the men flying it had to be bested.

It wouldn't be enough—even if this was possible and the woods could be reached in time—just to make use of the shelter and hide; whether they had orders to capture or to kill, now that he was located the fliers could box him in and keep him cornered until reinforcements could be called up to finish the job.

So how could a horseman with a single automatic pistol dispose of a modern flying machine crewed by at least two men who could be heavily armed? In a landscape as bare of cover as the most barren wastes of Utah?

By playing it cool.

If the lucky cards came out of the shoe his way.

There was one chance, and it was a slim one. Bolan took it.

Fifty yards ahead, forty, thirty, flat slabs of rock thrust through the shaley crust of the plateau to form a series of long, shallow steps that dropped through a clearing between the thorn trees about the size of a baseball park.

The sound of the helicopter, almost directly overhead, was deafening. Bolan swung a leg over the saddle, sent the horse careering on its way with a thwack of his hand and launched himself into space. He hit the ground with a shock that blasted the breath from his body, shoulder-rolled and came up beside the nearest rock.

The outcrops carried no overhang and offered no cover from a watcher directly overhead. But they cast iron-hard bands of shadow across the foot of each step, and these could conceivably be used to screen a hunted man from pursuers at ground level.

More importantly, the overhead watcher might think the hunted man *believed* himself to be screened also from above....

Bolan dived for the bar of shadow nearest to him, the AutoMag in his right hand.

He wedged himself into the crevice between two steps.

The chopper was immediately above him, at a height of fifty feet, hovering with its Plexiglas bubble turned into the wind. The hatch slid back. A man stood in the open space, with one foot braced against a former, and an SMG with its telescopic stock extended cradled in his arms.

Bolan fired four shots from the AutoMag, the muzzle-flashes livid in the shadow. He didn't have a hope of crippling the chopper with single shots from a handgun, but he did hope the crew might believe he harbored such a fantasy.

The machine sank lower. The thorn trees on either side of the clearing rattled dry branches and dust swirled across the rocks, driven by the rotorwash. Bolan shifted his position and fired again.

Flame stabbed back from the muzzle of the SMG. The gunner hosed a deadly hail downward, stitching a figure-eight killstream over the slabs of rock. Bolan moved just ahead of it, his hands and face peppered with stone splinters.

Before the killer corrected his aim, he took the wildest gamble of his fighting career.

With the lethal .45-caliber submachine gun still menacing him, Bolan staggered out from the shadow into the full glare of the sunlight. He reeled, flung up his arms and collapsed on the ground beside the rocks.

The next few seconds were the most suspenseful of his life. He was motionless, out in the open, a perfect target. Would the gunman, making doubly sure, fire another annihilating burst into his inert body? Or would he be smug in the conviction that he had scored and simply have the pilot put him down and walk over to check the kill?

Mack Bolan's whole future was bet on the second choice.

The chopper remained above him. Waves of dust washed over the dry ground, threatening to make him choke or sneeze. Some kind of horned beetle, blown onto its back by the airstream, righted itself and began crawling up the side of his face.

Bolan tensed, his muscles anticipating the impact, the flail of the iron whip across his back that would pulverize his organs and sever his spine, the pain that would be the last thing he'd feel.

The whine of the rotors changed in pitch, the blades' chatter was slowing. The pilot was putting the helicopter down.

It settled fifty yards away at the edge of the clearing, bounced once on its shock absorbers, then stayed still. The rotors slowed, the turbojet groaned into silence. Bolan heard the thump as someone jumped to the ground. Footsteps crunched toward him.

The Executioner was lying half on his face, his right arm doubled beneath him. He had rolled his eyes so that only the whites showed between slitted lids. He took a deep breath and held it as the footsteps drew near.

He was cut and scratched in a dozen places, the results of his fall from the galloping horse and the storm of fragments gouged from the rock by the volleys from the Ingram. He reckoned there was enough blood staining his shirt to lend credence to his "death."

The beetle, pausing to wave its feelers when it was halfway across his left eyelid, added the finishing touch.

Bending over the recumbent body, the gunman took in the bloodstains, the stillness, the insect over the dulled eye.

Arrogant in his triumph, he failed to notice the small black opening beneath Bolan's left armpit, where the muzzle of the AutoMag was squeezed between biceps and ribs.

With the hand doubled under him, the warrior gripped the big autoloader's butt. His forefinger was curled around the trigger.

Hot breath played over his skin, and he smelled the odor of some cologne as the killer flicked away the beetle and thumbed open the eyelid.

He was staring death in the face.

The pupil of the eye contracted. Flame belched from the muzzle of the AutoMag, and Bolan yelled involuntarily as pain like a red-hot iron seared the flesh of his arm.

Hot blood spurted over him. The gunman's throat disintegrated under the terrible assault of the 240-grain boattail, flying apart in a cloud of cartilage and shredded flesh. He fell heavily on top of the Executioner, the Ingram skittering uselessly away over the shale.

Bolan exploded into action.

He was out from under the body before the echoes of the gun blast died away among the thorn trees. From the corner of his eye he saw the shape of a second man silhouetted in the hatch of the helicopter, frozen in astonishment by the speed of his companion's death.

Bolan had hurled the body onto the nearest rock shelf and flung himself facedown behind it before the pilot got it together enough to react.

There was no SMG this time; the guy was armed with a small-caliber automatic—Bolan figured it for a Browning—and he was using it like an amateur, firing from the hip as he jumped to the ground and sprinted for a screen of dried bushes beneath the trees.

Bolan felt the shock as the slugs thudded into the body of the dead gunner, jerking it on the rock.

Supporting his weight on both elbows, he steadied his right wrist with his left hand, sighting the stainless-steel .44 over the corpse's chest.

A second burst from the Browning smashed into dead flesh, and then Big Thunder roared.

Once, twice, three times the outsize pistol bellowed, bucking in his grasp to send waves of pain flaming through the seared muscles of his left arm where the first shot had burned him.

Number one plowed through the flesh of the chopper pilot's left upper arm, spinning him sideways. Because of this, number two went wide. But the third drilled the center of his chest, smashing a fist-size exit wound between his shoulder blades. Slammed backward by the savage impact, he lay with outflung arms, eyes staring at the sky.

The gun had flown out of his hand and lay ten yards away. Bolan rose to his feet and walked warily across the clearing, the AutoMag poised, alert to counter a knife thrust, a surprise shot from a second gun, a physical attack.

But the man on the ground this time wasn't playing possum.

Pink froth bubbled at the corners of his mouth. The blood welling out from beneath him flowed more quickly than the dead earth could absorb it. Already his eyes had begun to glaze.

The face contorted in a spasm of agony as the Executioner drew near.

"You want me to finish it, guy?" Bolan asked. "Okay, tell me who sent you, what outfit you're with, where your base is."

"Go to hell," the dying man rasped.

"Where's the uranium headed?"

"Drop dead."

"Another time," Bolan said. "Who's using the stuff and why?"

"Go fuck yourself."

Bolan sighed. The voice was now as faint as the whisper of dry leaves stirred by the wind. Once more the features convulsed. Experience among the mad wolves of the underworld told the warrior that he was wasting his time. This man was one of the tough ones who would never speak.

In any case there was nothing anybody could do for him now.

Well, there was one thing. And only the Executioner could do it. He raised the AutoMag and fired the mercy shot.

Bolan was frowning as he dragged the bodies beneath the trees and piled stones over them. Neither of these men fitted the scenario as he read it. It was as if the director at Central Casting had sent heavies to the wrong studio.

The men were neither Arab nor African. Each wore a pale, sharp suit, a flowered necktie and two-tone shoes. There were wraparound shades in the pilot's breast pocket.

With their blue chins, heavy jaws and hairy wrists, they would have looked more at home in the Bronx or Chicago's Little Italy than here beneath the blistering sun in southern Sudan.

There was one additional anomaly. The pilot had died like the hardest of mafiosi, yet he'd handled his gun like a beginner.

Bolan's hawk face was still creased in thought as he recovered the Ingram and walked slowly toward the dragonfly shape of the chopper.

There was a first-aid kit behind the pilot's seat. He dressed the gunshot burn under his left arm, swabbed disinfectant over the cuts and abrasions covering his body, stuck adhesive strips on the deeper cuts. Then he settled down behind the ship's radio.

It took him fifteen minutes to pinpoint the exact frequency to which his original transceiver had been tuned. "MB to DC," he said quietly. "MB calling DC. Zero speech, but if you receive me signal as before."

The three acknowledging bleeps came almost at once.

"Okay," Bolan said. "I don't know where the hell you've been, but try to stand by to receive at the right hours in future. Here is a message for Langley, to be relayed to Brognola with the usual access code...."

The message was a long one. He repeated it twice. Once the single prolonged bleep had acknowledged its reception, he switched off the radio and moved to the pilot's seat.

He checked out the controls, studied dials, flipped levers and thumbed switches. No problem.

The turbojet whined to life. The rotors revolved. The thorn trees flattened.

As the helicopter lifted off, Bolan saw through the curved Plexiglas that vultures were already planing down out of the clear sky to keep watch over the two piles of stones.

Thirty minutes later he passed over El Glouai at five thousand feet and flew into Central African Republic airspace.

PART TWO

INFILTRATION

CHAPTER SEVENTEEN

The frontier was a collection of wooden huts straddling the dirt road; the border was defined by a barbed-wire fence interrupted by a striped pole with a counterweight at one end. Outside the hut nearest the highway, a squad of soldiers lounged by a trestle table, joking around with a handful of frontier guards. Soldiers and guards wore British-style khaki uniforms; all of them were African.

Mack Bolan slid the Land Rover to a halt in a cloud of dust and climbed out of the furnace heat. Something had gone badly wrong with the arrangements. There had been no message from Brognola at Zemio, the largest town in the Mbomou region of the Central African Republic; none of the personal items or equipment he had asked for in the message passed through Courtney had arrived; nobody knew anything about the turbocharged off-roader he was expecting.

He had wasted three days vainly trying to contact Courtney—out of range, now, for the transceiver—Langley or Brognola. But neither the clerks nor the post office facilities available seemed capable of raising a reply stateside or even from Khartoum.

Telephones, radio, cables relayed through half a dozen different countries were all equally ineffective. Fuming with impatience, the Executioner had finally telexed for money to be sent from an account of his own in Switzerland, then he had got what he needed as best he could from the local stores. The Land Rover was fifteen years old; it had cost him ninety dollars.

Sweat clogged his dark hair and trickled between his shoulder blades as he tramped across the scorched earth to the guard hut. It would be dark in three hours, yet it was still hotter than hell.

Bolan wished he still had the use of the helicopter he'd abandoned in the bush ten miles short of Zemio; he wished he'd made it across the Asa River into Zaire earlier, and waited out the three days in relative comfort in Niangara; he wished a cloud would blow up from someplace and blot out the sun for a half hour.

Now, reentering southwestern Sudan fifty miles north of Niangara, he also wished that he'd paid the bribes for his new ID in Zaire rather than the Central African Republic. Were the papers good enough to fool the tall African wearing the three stripes of a sergeant on his arm? The man had been deliberating over them for what seemed like an eternity.

Bolan was about to say something when the NCO glanced past him, stiffened and snapped out a parade ground salute.

The Executioner swung around. Although the face was dark, his first impression of the man he now faced was all brightness and light. His belt and the straps crossing his compact chest gleamed; the riding boots winked in the sun; the insignia of a major general shone from his shoulder tabs and from under his arm the silver-knobbed head of a cane glistened. Brilliantly white teeth flashed as the cane reached out to touch the papers on the trestle table.

"And what have we here, Sergeant?" he asked. "A *foreigner* seeking entry?" The voice was deep and mellifluous, overlaid with a caricature of British English.

"Yes, sir."

The smile vectored through sixty degrees and zeroed in on Bolan. "Ismael Halakaz," the voice continued. "Officer commanding troops rightfully in charge of this region. May one ask your reasons for wishing to enter the Sudan at this particular point?"

"One may, General," the warrior returned. "The answer is simple. I am a photographer of animals. Certain of the beasts I want to shoot can only be found around here."

"For example?"

"Certain types of white rhino, cave baboons, elephant, various members of the deer family." Bolan had done his homework over a bottle of bourbon shared with a big game hunter in Niangara.

"But all these, my dear fellow," the officer protested, "can be found in other parts of Africa. Rhinoceros, elephant, monkeys—we have no monopoly, you know."

"Oh, sure." Bolan shrugged. "In game preserves. Shabby, half-tame creatures with threadbare hides. What I want are pictures of *wild* animals, not those stereotyped images of a blurred rhino charging or a lion hanging its head by a water hole. I'm prepared to wait for what I want. I'm a patient man. What I'm looking for is a pictorial record of animals believably behaving *as* animals in their natural state—as hunters, as beasts in fear, as family creatures—not just one more chapter for a child's geography book."

"It would be an approach overdue," the general admitted. "What camera are you proposing to use for these photographs, Monsieur—?"

"Belasko. Mike Belasko," Bolan replied. It was the name on his new papers, an alias he had used before. He snapped open the leather case at his side.

"Ah! A Hasselblad. With all the extras. Do you know, old chap, that the money that camera would bring could feed one of my villages in there for a month?" Halakaz stabbed the cane toward the rolling savannah across the frontier.

"I know things in this area are...difficult."

"Difficult! The Arabs in the north are still engaged in a war of extermination down here in Equatoria. They're systematically killing my people off. Each week they descend on another village and...*pouf!*" He shouldered the cane like a rifle and shot down an imaginary adversary.

"I didn't know it was still that rugged. Just the same, I guess I was expecting Arab troops to be guarding the frontier."

"They were, old chap. They were. Until yesterday." The stick swung toward a row of freshly turned mounds of soil on the far side of the huts. "We show the flag occasionally, you know, just to emphasize our rights. These good fellows—" the general pointed at the guard hut "—will remain here until another troop descends on them. There will be another little skirmish, and another row of graves on our African soil. Then we will take another post..."

"What's the background to this?" Bolan asked.

"The two R's, old chap: rapacity and religion. My people here in the south are Christian or pagan. The people turning this into a police state are of the Mussulman faith—muscle men, that's good, eh?—and they want all infidels eliminated."

"And so you...?"

"We would have accepted some kind of federation, if only the 'autonomy' they offered involved genuine government of our own three provinces. But too many in Khartoum do nothing but line their own pockets and mouth promises they have no intention of keeping. We shall accept nothing less than secession after what they have done now."

"It's *that* bad, is it?"

"Bad?" Halakaz had a trick of repeating the last word uttered by the person he was speaking to. "So bad as to be unbelievable. It's not an *official* policy, you see. But the Arab officers quartered here are in fear of their lives, so they lounge about in the towns and leave their troops to burn, loot and kill as they want. You think you have terrorists in Europe and the Middle East? Let me tell you, they have destroyed, completely eradicated, more than two hundred villages here and in southeastern Sudan. They have murdered more than one hundred thousand blacks, leaving the survivors to wander in the bush and starve. There were between five and six million of us, old chap, when the British pulled out. Murder, disease, starvation and a drain of refugees fleeing across the borders into Zaire, Chad and the CAR has reduced that population by fifty percent. Fifty percent, Monsieur Belasko. That's half our people gone!"

"Isn't there a strong underground movement?" Bolan asked. "And what about the SPLA?"

"The Sudan People's Liberation Army?" General Halakaz pronounced the words with distaste. "Too far off beam politically for us, old chap. They take their orders from outside, if you get my meaning. Then of course there's the Nya Nyerere, over to the east in the Dongotona Mountains. Lazzari is a skilled guerrilla leader, but he has two RPG-7 grenade launchers and a handful of automatic rifles among a few thousand irregulars. What can such groups do against the fifteen to twenty thousand heavily armed Arabs in the region? Could they prevent the Juba massacre, twenty years ago, when fourteen hundred Africans were slaughtered in a single night? They fight in derby hats and shorts." The general was contemptuous.

"And here in the southwest?"

"Here we order things better. A little better, old chap. The Anya Nya—the force I command—is six thousand strong. But armed, disciplined, efficient." The cane snapped back under the arm.

"I can see that," Bolan said admiringly glancing at the general's Sandhurst-style turnout.

"But today numbers are nothing. Efficiency is next to nothing. It is weapons that count, and the men who know how to use them. Soon, very soon, the Anya Nya will be as sixty thousand men, as six hundred thousand. And then the politicians in Khartoum will bewail their fate. We shall grind the oppressors into the dust and become masters of the whole Sudan!"

For a moment Oxford University, England, went out the window and in its place pure African mission school showed through.

"You are planning a coup, General?" The Executioner strove not to betray his interest, but the little Alert bells in back of his mind, actuated by a combat tactician's sixth sense, had started to ring.

"Ah, it's early days, early days, old chap," General Halakaz said vaguely, conscious, perhaps, that he might have revealed too much. But he could not resist adding, "Now if you were a *news* photographer... But never mind, never mind. Just keep your eyes on the headlines in a few weeks' time, that's all. Meanwhile, we *are* still an underground army. I must be off."

Bolan still retained the laissez-passer in his own name bought from Hamid el-Karim in Khartoum. It would be invaluable if he was questioned by Arab troops policing the region. But he figured it was safer for Mike Belasko to get at least a verbal okay from the guerrilla chief temporarily in the driving seat. "I have your permission to proceed?" he asked.

"So far as I am concerned," the general said, "you may go ahead and shoot your pictures. But I can offer no guarantee for your safety. You would be wise to stay the *minimum* amount of time, and keep your eyes open very wide. *Caveat emptor*, old chap! *Caveat emptor*, don't you know!" The cane was switched from the right arm to the left, the right hand swept up in a crisp salute, and Halakaz strode smartly away.

Bolan smiled, remembering the old Latin tag from the schoolroom. *Caveat emptor.* Let the buyer beware.

Like, it's on your own head, man.

But surely it would be naive to think there was *no* connection between thefts of nuclear material and a professional soldier with a chip who boasted about undreamed-of military power in the near future?

The link was something the Executioner could buy all right.

Right now, nevertheless, the number-one priority was to find where the fissile isotope was. Halakaz, in any case, would certainly clam up if more questions were fired at him.

The guards had raised the pole. Bolan recovered his papers, climbed back into the Land Rover and drove on.

For fifteen or twenty miles the rolling grassland continued. Then the clumps of trees grew farther and farther apart, the herds of antelope vanished, the grasses thinned, and soon the trail was twisting up into the desolate foothills of a range that had showed only as a blue smudge on the horizon at the border.

Three times, Bolan passed the burned-out shells of African villages, only rings of scorched earth and a few crumbling mud walls remaining to show where they had been. Outside the last, on the edge of a mealie patch that had gone to seed, buzzards had picked clean the bones of a man who had been crucified on the lowest branch of a huge banyan tree.

After that the route grew steeper, dipping from time to time into a rubble of stones and rocks flooring a dried-up riverbed, then rising again toward a saddle that pierced the cliffs of volcanic rock topping the ridge.

Once through the pass, the warrior found himself descending yet again to one of those upland plains so characteristic of this part of Africa—a featureless wilderness of thorny scrub broken at intervals by piles of enormous boulders. He would have to make camp for the night soon; the sun had dropped out of sight behind the crest and the heat had already gone from the air. He pulled up and killed the Land Rover's engine.

After the boom of the exhaust and the continuous whining of first gear it was very quiet. Wind rattled the spikes of thorn trees beside the road.

He spread out a map. Two hundred miles farther on, the track ended at Wau, in Bahr el Ghazal province. Ninety miles before that there was a fork, where he would take the right-hand trail for Ouad Faturah. After that he was on his own, for there were no roads to the one-time forbidden city of Oloron, nor was it marked on the map.

It was where he was headed just the same, for it had been in that direction the caravan with the canister had been going. It was as good a place to start as any, and he reckoned that if he kept on going he'd have to cross the caravan trail at some point.

As long as he recognized the point when he got there.

Bolan shivered and restarted the engine. He was unwilling to spend the night in this godforsaken place. But when night fell with tropical suddenness an hour later, he was still driving through the interminable scrub. To continue with headlights would make him visible for fifty miles. Reluctantly he turned off the trail and parked the vehicle out of sight behind a pile of rocks.

He opened a baggage roll in back and ate. Then, wrapping himself in blankets, he settled down as comfortably as he could in the passenger seat and tried to sleep. The Ingram lay within reach on the Land Rover's central seat. Big Thunder was holstered on his hip.

For a long time he huddled there in wakefulness, listening to a family of baboons coughing and chattering uneasily somewhere among the flat rocks above him.

He would have liked to call up Courtney on the transceiver, but it was the wrong time. He was wary—after his experiences with the caravan and the chopper—of alerting the enemy that he was back in the Sudan, and in any case, he thought he was still way out of range. A progress report, and the mystery of the inexplicable absence of news from Brognola, would have to wait.

At last he fell into a fitful sleep...to awake later to the sounds of a stealthy scuttling noise behind the seats. Grabbing the Ingram, he switched on a pocket flashlight.

A prowling jerboa, one of the desert rats that somehow eked out an existence in the wilderness, was trying to get at the food in his baggage roll. He chased the animal away and found that he was shivering with cold.

After he had pulled another blanket from the roll, he looked at the illuminated face of his watch. It was still only a quarter after ten.... By midnight he was asleep again.

Bolan awoke finally before dawn and waited in a fury of impatience for the sun to rise. It was still extremely cold. Moisture had penetrated the perspex side windows, beading the instrument dials and controls, chilling him to the marrow.

He flung off the blankets, clambered stiffly to the ground and stamped up and down the barren earth, trying to restore his circulation and bring some warmth back into his body. The baboons chattered with anger and swung away over the rocks.

The sky was becoming visible at last—a mud-colored expanse tinged with saffron above the scrub to the east. Slowly the mountains he had crossed the previous evening assembled themselves in undulations of purple and ultramarine. By the time the sun eventually blazed into sight above a dark cloud bank, Bolan was already in the driver's seat with the ignition key inserted.

But the ancient Land Rover was reluctant to start. Extremes of heat and cold had made the engine temperamental. Afraid of draining the battery, he got out again and swung it with the handle.

At the fifth attempt, the engine caught. He scrambled back inside and pumped the gas pedal for a few minutes to warm up the space beneath the hood and chase moisture from contacts and leads.

Then, bumping over the stony ground, he steered slowly around the rock pile and back onto the dirt road.

Braking suddenly, he stared left and right.

Strung out across the trail in two lines, barring his escape in either direction, were a score of African soldiers armed with Belgian FN automatic rifles.

AFTER TWO DAYS without news, Jason Mettner decided to call it quits.

Brognola had returned to his drug-busting conference in Istanbul twenty-four hours previously. "Like you say, I figure it for a bum steer," he told the newspaperman. "Hell, why not mix a couple metaphors and say it's a red herring! Something, anyway, to keep you out of circulation, to make sure you're nowhere near the action. The interesting thing is, why tip you off? Why lay a false trail on you and not on the Company?''

"Maybe because I'm here and the Company's in Langley, Virginia?" Mettner offered.

"Could be. I'd like you to hang in a while, just in case," Brognola said. "Stick around maybe one more day, okay? It'd be tough if it really had been a regular tip and something simply happened to louse up both parties' travel arrangements.''

"Check." Mettner nodded. "Though I don't buy Bolan *and* this Indian running into travel trouble at the same time, for the same amount of time.''

"Unless the tip *was* genuine and a third party fixed the delays to stop them from getting here as they'd planned, fixed it in the hope that you'd read it as bogus and take off before they finally showed."

"It's a thought. Except the only person who knew I *would* be here was the guy who tipped me off—our legman, or whoever took his place. I'll stick around, anyway. And if they don't show I'll do my best to nose out where the action *is*. I'll keep in touch, anyway."

"You do that," Brognola said.

While he was waiting, Mettner filled in his time with routine investigation.

How was the reservation in the name of Bolan made at the hotel in Bukama? By telephone? Okay, was it possible to trace the origin of the call? What language did the caller speak? What kind of voice? Male or female? Had there been written confirmation, and if so where was the letter posted?

Were there any Indians at all—or anyone with a name that might be Indian—booked into the Upemba National Park hotel in the next few days?

The last question was easily answered. The answer was no.

The desk clerk at the Bukama hotel was a Nigerian woman with big breasts, straightened hair and features that could have been copied from a Benin fertility carving. She was learning the hotel business, filling different jobs at different hotels in the chain. She thought Jason Mettner was kind of cute.

"Why, sure I remember the call," she told him. "We don't get all that many long-distance reservations. Mostly they come from our own central bureau in Lagos, or locally from Kinshasa or Kananga. You know, folks who want to do the game reserve."

Mettner lit a cigarette. "You wouldn't by any chance be able to trace that call?" he asked. "Find out how long the distance was? Better still identify the town where it was made?"

There was a possibility, the woman said. The call had been put through manually. Theoretically it should have been logged, and she had a girlfriend who worked at the telephone exchange.

"Was it a guy or a gal speaking?" Mettner said.

"A man."

"An American?"

"He had a cute voice. I liked it. I'm pretty sure it wasn't a brother, but I don't think he was American. He spoke in English just the same."

The reservation had been confirmed by letter. "It's a rule of the house," the receptionist said. "Otherwise folks could just call in from anyplace and then never show. You can't imagine how many rooms you have vacant that way." The cover had of course been thrown away, but the letter itself was on file.

The headed paper was that of an international hotel in Khartoum. Mettner wouldn't know if the signature was genuine or not.

"I'll check out the call with my friend when she comes off duty at four," the woman said. "Myself, I'm free after six."

Mettner fielded that one. "Maybe we could get together over a drink someplace?" he suggested.

The drink led to dinner in a smoochy Thai restaurant with red-shaded table lamps and samisen music on tape. While they were toying with their Kenya coffee and South African brandy, the friend left a message. If Mettner would care to call by the telegraph and cable office during the lunch break next day, she thought she could maybe help him.

Mettner did not sleep at his hotel that night.

Neither did Mack Bolan. When he hadn't shown by noon, the newspaperman decided to pack it in. Even if the call was traceable, what would it bring him? He would be no wiser as to whether Bolan himself had made it, had meant to come to Bukama and been prevented, or whether, as Brognola thought, it had been made by somebody else. Probably the latter, as the receptionist thought the caller wasn't American.

In fact the call had been placed in Zemio, in the Central African Republic. The woman who dug out this intel for Mettner was tall and slender, with an Afro haircut, a miniskirt and a dozen necklaces carved from different woods. "If there's something else you want to ask," she said, "I quit at four."

"Baby, I'll be long gone," Mettner said. "I decided to take the train to Kinshasa this afternoon. What you can do, if you want to do me one more favor, is file a cable for me to the United States. The addressee is Hal Brognola. I'll spell that—"

He stopped. The woman was staring at him wide-eyed.

"Well, they talk about the long arm of coincidence," she said, "but this really beats them all!"

"Come again?" Mettner invited.

"Zemio. A place nobody ever heard of in the CAR. You ask me to check out a telephoned hotel reservation that comes by chance from there. That's coincidence number one, because only a few days ago we have another call from Zemio. It seems they want to connect with someone stateside and they can't make it, so they try to route it through us. As it happens, neither can we. But—wait for it, here comes number two!—the person they wish to contact, it's the same name as the one on the cable you just gave me. Brognola. I remember it because it's... Well, it's not an African name. What do you know about that!"

"Are you telling me—" Mettner leaned across the counter in his excitement and blew smoke in the woman's face "— are you telling me that, apart from this hotel reservation, someone in Zemio tried a few days ago to contact this guy Brognola in the U.S.A.?"

"That's what I said."

"You wouldn't...you don't have a record? You wouldn't know if it was the same person speaking?"

The Afro shook from side to side. "That other call was a relay. It was the Zemio operator calling. But I remember the name of the sender. It was kind of unusual, too. It was Bolan, the same as the one on the hotel reservation. You don't think that was a crazy coincidence?"

"Crazy!" Mettner echoed. "Sweetie, you put me in touch with someone can rent me a lightweight private plane and you got yourself a dinner date." He grinned. "As of four o'clock!"

CHAPTER EIGHTEEN

The transceiver in Mack Bolan's pocket began to bleep after he had been arguing for more than an hour with the officer in charge of the detail that was preventing him from resuming his journey.

Colonel Mtambole was short and bulky, with fierce, bright eyes in a very dark face. He was a volatile man, speaking in short, sharp bursts, constantly throwing out his arms to make a point before he smoothed the creases in his rumpled bush shirt. From time to time he snatched the French paratroop beret he wore from his head, only to jam it back on top of his close-cropped hair once the point had been made.

The issue between them was simple. Bolan wanted to go on; the colonel wanted him to go back. Either that or be arrested, for he was not entirely satisfied with "Mike Belasko's" store-bought credentials.

"What do you want to go on for, man? What for?" Mtambole said. "This is dangerous country. We got a civil war on our hands, man. You could say the whole place is under martial law. Okay, technically the province is still ruled by the Arabs." Off came the beret. "Technically, I say. But possession is nine-tenths of the law, even martial law. *Specially* martial law. And we're here, and we're in possession of *you*."

"Sure, sure," Bolan soothed. "I see your point, Colonel. But for the tenth time, I have pictures to take. I have a contract. The way I see it, the only place I'm going to get those pictures is farther on in this—"

"Where farther on? How far are you going? There's nothing to photograph around here—unless you want shots of the villagers murdered by the Arabs."

"I told you. I take this trail as far as the bifurcation, where I keep left on the road for Ouad Faturah. According to my map, that road crosses a range of volcanic mountains and then skirts a big forest before it makes the town ninety miles farther on. There are no roads through the forest. They tell me it's hardly explored, and certainly not by Europeans. And *that*'s where I figure on getting the animal pictures I want."

The colonel flung out his arms. "Pictures, animals, photographs!" he cried. "I tell you there's a race war going on here! You'd do better to shoot some of the atrocities—"

At this moment the call sign on Bolan's radio began bleeping.

"What's that?" Mtambole demanded suspiciously.

"A transistor radio. I must have forgotten to switch—"

"Give it to me."

"But it's my personal property..."

"There's no personal property in a war," the colonel shouted, dragging off the beret and slapping his thigh with it. "When will you Europeans realize this is *Africa*? Give it to me, I say."

One of Mtambole's soldiers moved a step forward, jerking up the barrel of his automatic rifle. Reluctantly Bolan drew the transceiver from his pocket and handed it over. He was mystified by the call. By his calculations, they were still way out of range of Khartoum, and he was angry that he couldn't respond. Courtney might have invaluable intel to pass on.

The African put the red beret on his head and examined the compact device, turning it over in his hands. As the bleeping continued, a hot, dry wind stirred eddies in the dust at their feet and agitated the stilettolike spikes of the thorn trees.

"But this is not a music radio," Mtambole said at last. "This is a talking radio. Somebody is talking to you, calling you up. Who?"

The Executioner contrived a sheepish look. "I guess I'll have to tell you after all," he said. "It's my partner."

"Partner? What is his name? Where is he? What do you mean 'partner'?"

"A journalist—the guy who's writing the story to go with my pictures," Bolan improvised. "Guy by the name of Courtney. He's supposed to be up there in the forest already. I guess he's calling me to say he found the right place for photographs."

"Answer him, then."

Bolan took back the transceiver and turned the pointer to Transmit. "Hello, Courtney," he said, his mouth close to the microphone grill, "this is Belasko. Hello, Courtney... Come in, please...."

He turned the pointer back to Receive, but only the bleeps continued. No voice answered from the tiny speaker, which was not surprising, as he had kept his thumb firmly on a small button set into one side of the casing. Unless the button was released, the radio would not transmit.

"Try again," Mtambole ordered.

Bolan repeated the procedure, and again the high-pitched bleeps provided his only reply. After a time they ceased.

"It must have been damaged, some wire disconnected while jolting over the rough roads," Bolan said, shaking the small plastic device. "I will take charge of it," the colonel said, holding out his hand.

"But it will be of no use to you. It can't be tuned to different frequencies. You can only use it in conjunction with similar sets that have been synchronized with it. By itself it is useless."

"Radios are always useful in guerrilla warfare."

"But it's broken."

"Then you will not be inconvenienced by the lack of it."

Mtambole took the transceiver and put it into his pocket. "I have decided," he said. "I will permit you to proceed and seek your friend, but only because of what you told me earlier—that you had received the personal accord of General Halakaz. This will be checked, and I must warn you that if it should prove untrue you will regret it."

"It is true."

"Good. Then apart from one small formality I need detain you no longer. As underground forces, you understand, we must not remain too long in the same place. However, the day of deliverance is at hand. Soon the Anya Nya will be marching openly, the acknowledged force for law and order throughout the land."

"And the formality"?

"We must search your effects, lest there might be something that could menace us. Or be of use to us."

Bolan shrugged angrily and gestured toward the Land Rover. There was no way he could stop them. He stood in the scorching sunlight, sweat plastering his hair to his forehead, as the soldiers expertly unrolled his baggage and handed over the contents for Mtambole to examine.

The mercurial colonel "requisitioned"—as the Executioner had feared—the Ingram and its magazine. He also took the binoculars, a commando knife, a weighted wire garrote and a bundle of phosphorus lock-destroyers, which had originally been in the pouch Bolan wore at his waist.

"You appear, Monsieur Belasko, to anticipate hostile reactions from your subjects," he said dryly.

"The area is far from any human habitation and practically unexplored, as you know. A man has to be prepared for anything."

"You will be able to move the better without the excess weight," the officer said. "For you can't take the vehicle the whole way, you know. It's rare to see wheels at all around here. Which being so, we shall relieve you also of one of these." He pointed at a pair of fourteen-gallon jerricans of gasoline racked against the Land Rover's flat tail. He jerked his head, and one of the soldiers lifted a jerrican from the rack.

"But I won't be able to replace that," Bolan said angrily. "The tank will need refilling in another ten miles, and I have maybe two hundred to cover. Plus at least another four hundred before I find a gas station on the way back."

"As I said, you won't be able to drive the whole way to the forest. Shortage of fuel now will ensure that you do not stray into areas where you have no business, in any attempts to find an alternative route. Besides—" he favored the Executioner with a bland smile "—you have the pleasure of knowing that you are advancing the cause."

Bolan compressed his lips and said nothing.

There was no point arguing; they had the drop on him. And if he provoked Mtambole too far, the chunky little officer, with his alternations of blandness and menace, was quite capable of taking the vehicle itself and abandoning him in the wilderness.

At least they were leaving him the holstered AutoMag and the Hasselblad, which would support his Belasko cover if he was stopped again.

It was only after he had driven a few miles and decided to brew himself some coffee on the portable camp heater that he discovered the entire contents of the baggage roll, including all his supplies, had been taken.

Mastering his rage, he climbed back behind the wheel and continued. Three hours later he reached the junction where the trails for Wau and Ouad Faturah separated. There had once been a settlement here, but all that remained now was the familiar patch of blackened earth, pockmarked with jagged stumps of walls. The bodies of five hanged men dangled from a branch of a charred tree. They were naked and decomposing, their eyes plucked out by vultures. Bolan shuddered, swinging the Land Rover around the grisly sight to take the left-hand track toward Ouad Faturah.

The scrub had been replaced by squat trees separated by dried-up undergrowth as the road wound upward. Now the trees thickened and the angle of incline grew more steep. Soon the Land Rover was laboring in first gear up what appeared to be a channel carved in solid bedrock.

Several miles later the trail flattened out, though it grew no smoother, and the warrior saw that he was about to cross a plateau of bare volcanic lava surrounded on all sides by steep, sugarloaf hills covered in dense vegetation.

He wrestled with the wheel, striving to identify the route in the stony waste. The tires scattered fragments of basalt, and the vehicle's progress was reduced to a jolting crawl.

Beyond the hills was another thorn tree desert, flat and featureless, stretching as far as the eye could see until it was swallowed up in the trembling heat haze.

Bolan drove on, his bush shirt dark with sweat, his wet fingers sliding on the oven-hot wheel. Dust penetrating the floorboards clogged his throat. The air he breathed seared his lungs.

He was almost twenty-five miles into the desert when the engine's pitch grew harsh. In the sweltering cabin the odors of burned gasoline mingled with exhaust fumes were swamped by the acid stench of overheated metal. He braked, killed the engine and checked the radiator. The rusty water was near the boiling point, but the header tank was still full.

He shrugged, slid back into the driver's seat and twisted the key. The engine was reluctant to restart. When finally it did, the beat was harsher still. He lifted his foot. Should he stop and allow it to cool?

Cool? Beneath the blazing sun? On a flat shadeless plain where the earth was so hot it burned his foot through his combat boot?

In that temperature, there was more chance of the engine cooling if he went on driving, even speeded up. If he stopped there was a risk it would get even hotter, and he himself would go crazy under the hammering assault of that harsh sun.

He trod the pedal and coaxed the scrabbling, bucking Land Rover up to fifteen miles an hour.

Ten minutes later clouds of steam burst from beneath the hood. There was a sudden hollow rumble followed at once by a shriek of tortured metal, and the Land Rover slewed across the track and ground to a halt. The engine was dead.

Cursing, Bolan jumped to the ground. When he managed to pry open the blistered hood, his nostrils were burned by the stench that filled the engine compartment.

It didn't take him long to find out what happened. Someplace along the worst parts of the route, the oil pan had bottomed on solid rock, tearing a hole in the metal sheeting. Backtracking down the rough trail, it was easy enough to find confirmation in blackened grass clumps and occasional stains on the dusty surface.

The engine oil had gradually leaked out. No longer lubricated, one of the main bearings had run in the extreme heat, and the engine had then seized up.

Bolan stared at the stricken vehicle. He was surrounded by total silence, which was broken only by the diminishing hiss of steam and the ticking of cooling metal.

Without an expert mechanic, hydraulic hoists and the correct spares, the old Land Rover was as dead as a headless rattler. And here in the center of southern Equatoria it was going to stay that way.

Without food, water or other supplies, the Executioner was marooned in the wastes of the thorn tree desert.

CHAPTER NINETEEN

The sun flamed out of a sky the color of molten lead. At two o'clock the heat was even less supportable than it had been at noon.

Bolan lay sweating beneath the blistered wreck of the Land Rover, breathing in dust and the odor of melted grease and gasoline fumes from the fuel vaporizing through the breathing hole in the tank filler cap. He knew that he must remain there at least another four hours before it would be safe to move.

He was rated a survival expert, but his training and his particular skills were based more on the steaming jungle conditions of the Far East than those in the arid and desolate wastes of Central Africa. He had, nevertheless, attended that course at the "survivor's school" in Hereford, England, organized by Britain's crack antiterrorist unit. And the lessons on desert conditions spelled out by the SAS lecturers had stayed in his mind as part of his mental armory.

The most important, the most vital, were concerned with water. "Life expectancy in desert conditions depends on water," they told him. "If you want to stay whole, you must replace all the moisture you lose by sweating. So keep out of the sun to minimize perspiration. And eat as little as possible because water is used to break down the food in digestion."

Bolan remembered the grim statistics. Without water, a man will last about two and a half days at a temperature of

120 degrees Fahrenheit—provided he rests the entire time in the shade.

If he has to walk to safety, the distance he makes will relate directly to the water available. With none, in the same temperature conditions and moving only at night, he might cover twenty-five miles before collapse. If he attempted to walk by day, he would be lucky to cover five miles. At the same temperature, given a half gallon of water, he might last three days and cover as much as thirty-five miles.

In terms of those parameters, the Executioner's position was perilous in the extreme.

It was much hotter than 120 degrees; it was more like 140.

Digesting food posed no problem: all his had been stolen. But the only water he had was the coolant in the Land Rover's radiator. There might be half a gallon, but it would be rusty and contaminated. He'd have to distill it to make it drinkable. To do that he'd have to improvise a solar still.

A solar still required digging while the sun was still up, and this in turn would further deplete his bodily supply of moisture. It was a risk, just the same, that he would have to take.

The toughest decision he had to make was concerned with direction. A golden rule for travelers stranded in the desert has always been: don't wander off in the hope of reaching safety; stay with your vehicle until the people looking for you locate it.

Nobody was looking for Bolan.

Okay, so he had to get out. This involved balancing different sets of unknowns one against the other.

Most important, which way should he go? Forward or back?

Visually there were no clues to help him with this decision. The thorn tree desert stretched as far as he could see in every direction. But how far *could* he see? It was difficult to say. The last range of hills he had passed through—he reckoned the Land Rover had made twenty-five to thirty miles since then—had vanished in the heat haze; no change in the flat landscape was visible ahead or on either side. It was the same when he climbed onto the vehicle's hood and stood upright: 360 degrees of stunted thorn trees, motionless under the hammering of the sun.

The map he had was not precise. Making a rough estimate of his own position, he guessed the plain continued for another forty miles before the land rose into a series of ridges intersected by steep ravines that were probably wooded. But there was no indication of the vegetation to be found in the desert. It could become bare, like the lava plain he had crossed, more varied, with larger, greener trees—or stay with the thorns all the way.

He was, of course, following a trail. According to the map, it continued to the far side of the plain and then threaded its way between the hills to Ouad Faturah and the forest. But he had seen no indications that anyone had used the trail recently—or was likely to in the immediate future. No tire marks, cigarette packs, empty Coke cans; no signs of broken brushwood, extinguished camp fires or bivouac sites.

Allowing that he could distill two quarts of water from the radiator, he should be able to make the hills, back the way he had come. But what happened then?

The hills, the lava plain, another, steeper, range of hills...and another plateau covered with thorn trees. The colonel and his detail would be long gone. And apart from the jerboa and the baboons, he hadn't passed a single living creature, had seen no sign of human habitation since he crossed the frontier.

And the other way?

He was damn near halfway across the desert. With luck he might make the far side, and the unknown country beyond. Villages were marked on the map. They might have been destroyed, like those he had passed already, since the map was printed. But he *knew* the first group had gone; those ahead were an unknown quantity.

There was a fifty-fifty chance they would still be there. Or some of them, one of them, would.

What the hell. He would go ahead into the unknown.

He had taken chances before, and they had worked out. Any continuation of the mission lay ahead. Challenges were there to be met. The warrior had a gut reaction against any kind of retreat.

Come nightfall he would forge ahead on foot.

But first he had to make—and use—the solar still. For this the sun must be low enough in the sky not to knock him out while he worked, but with enough heat in it to promote condensation.

Waiting for the right moment, he unfastened the pouch at his waist and checked the contents in the sweltering shade beneath the Land Rover. There was a penlight; twenty spare rounds of 240-grain boattails for the AutoMag; a miniature Malayan parang wrapped in his rolled-up blacksuit; an aluminum mess tin; a pack of solid fuel tablets; and two small tobacco cans sealed with adhesive tape. One of these contained a tiny medical kit, the other Bolan's basic survival package.

Bolan repacked everything carefully—the contents of the tobacco cans insulated with cotton wool—and started to construct his still.

He'd have to dig a hole in the ground two feet across and eighteen inches deep. Because he would eventually need the sun's heat, he could not dig it within the protection of the shadow the Land Rover was now casting.

It was one hell of a job.

The sun was about twenty degrees above the western horizon, but the temperature was still over 100 degrees. To break up the stony terrain, he used a screwdriver from the off-roader's tool kit, and a heavy wrench as a hammer. The earth could then be removed with the flat blade of the parang.

It took him one hour and twelve minutes to complete the chore, and his clothes were totally soaked in sweat after the first ten minutes.

He had placed a handkerchief on top of his head, covered it with a triangulated towel and tied it in place with a strip of cloth torn from the tail of his shirt. But the blood was thundering behind his eyes and he was reeling from the pain of a headache before the hole was half finished.

When he judged it was deep enough, he drained the water from the radiator into an empty two-liter oilcan he found in the rear of the Land Rover, built a small fire from dead brushwood and lit one of the solid fuel tablets beneath it. He placed the oilcan on top of the fire.

The next step was to fashion a length of hose to carry steam from the water when it boiled into the still. With the sharpest of the parang's three cutting edges he sliced up ducts from the utility's cooling system, hydraulics and wash-wipe apparatus, joining them up with adhesive tape from the medical kit.

One end of this complex tube was fitted to the radiator hose, which was suspended just above the surface of the water; the other end dipped into the hole in the ground.

Bolan put the mess tin at the bottom of the hole and then covered it with a four-foot-square sheet of plastic he found beneath one of the seats. He fixed the plastic in place with stones laid around the edge, and then poked down the cen-

ter of the sheet so that it formed an inverted pyramid with
the apex above the mess tin.

With the heat remaining in the air and the relative coolness below the surface of the earth, the steam passing into
the hole through the tube condensed on the underside of the
plastic, ran down the slope to the point of the pyramid and
dripped into the tin.

Bolan emptied the tin twice, but there was no airtight seal
above the boiling water and more steam was lost between the
different parts of the conduit. When the oilcan boiled dry,
he was left with only enough distilled water to fill one of the
condoms from his medical kit—a fraction more than two
pints.

He shrugged. There was no question of choice now; he
had to start walking—or stay with the Land Rover and die.

Folding the sheet of plastic as small as he could, he
stuffed it in the pouch along with the wrapped parang, the
spare ammunition, the penlight and the solid fuel tablets,
lowering the bulging rubber carefully on top. The mess tin
was now hooked to his belt, the tobacco cans in the pockets
of his bush shirt, the towel around his neck.

The sun at last sank behind a misted horizon, leaving a
sky stained crimson in the west. Bolan began to walk.

He ran up against a major difficulty at once.

The trail was hard enough to follow in daylight. By night,
since the distance between the thorn trees was greater than
the width of the track, he soon lost it altogether.

He took out the luminous compass and, guided by the
map, set a course twelve degrees west of true north. This
should leave him, if he made it to the far side of the desert,
fifty miles due south of Ouad Faturah. And after that?
Whether he went that far or branched off earlier depended
on whether his trail was crossed by a caravan track that

could be a prolongation of the route taken by the train carrying the lead canister.

Play it by ear.

Trudging on between the silent thorns, he used the stars as a navigation aid. The Great Bear was not in sight, but as he was only six degrees north of the equator, Orion was almost directly overhead and he was able to see Mintaka in that constellation as a pointer to the Pole Star. Every half hour, he stopped for a five-minute rest, checking the correct deviation with map and compass and the penlight.

By ten o'clock it was penetratingly cold.

During his next halt, he stripped, took the blacksuit from his pouch, put it on and then donned his outer clothing. He hung the parang from his belt, replaced the mess tin at the bottom of the pouch and lowered the water-filled condom gently into it, after he had permitted himself a single sip. He slung the plastic sheet over his shoulders, tied the two top ends beneath his chin and walked on.

Even with this double insulation, he was still chilled to the bone. Hunger gnawed at his belly. He had not eaten for thirty hours. But it was his preoccupation with thirst that was becoming obsessional.

In a detached way, he observed the weakening of his body. From time to time his even stride was broken by a stagger, a stumble. If his thoughts wandered to relieve the monotony of his passage through the interminable thorn trees, there was a tendency to veer off course, to lurch away from his correct line. Twice he tripped on some projection piercing the gravel floor of the desert and fell, grazing his hands and knees.

He knew that the human organism needed salt for survival, that the salt lost in sweat and wasted with physical exertion needed to be replaced. He knew that his excessive fatigue, the occasional twinges of nausea, a muscular cramp that locked his calf, were signs of salt deficiency. He knew that in a normal diet there was a daily intake of half an ounce of salt.

And he remembered the instructor on the survival course in Hereford. "The remedy for this is to take a pinch of salt in a pint of water."

There were salt tablets in his medical kit, but he couldn't waste a whole *pint* of water. Swallowing a tablet whole or taking one with just a sip of the precious water would provoke, Bolan knew, stomach cramps. He gritted his teeth and plodded on.

The first blister appeared at a quarter after four. It was on his left heel. He lowered himself wearily to the ground, removed his combat boot, peeled off the sock and stuck a Band-Aid over the sore place. He permitted himself a second sip of water. No salt. That—the tiniest fragment of a tablet—would have to wait until he allowed himself something approaching a gulp, then he halted at sunrise to rest for the day.

It seemed to him that he took a long time to push himself upright, an undue amount of energy to coax his legs into forward motion.

He stopped when the sky on his right lightened noticeably and the stars began to fade. The spiny silhouettes of the thorn trees surrounded him on every side.

It was not until thirty minutes later, when the sun had already flared into sight above the eastern horizon, that he found suitable shelter.

One of the thorn trees had at some time or other become uprooted. There was a slight hollow where the skeletal strands had pulled free of the gravel, and the dead trunk itself, although it was no more than twelve inches in diameter, would provide the smallest vestige of shade.

Swaying on his feet, Bolan deliberated. Should he use the parang to increase the depth of the hollow?

He rejected the idea. The amount of energy he would have to expend would be counterproductive.

He punched holes on one side of the plastic sheet, threaded them onto the dead roots and stretched the sheet over the hollow, securing the lower side with stones. As a tent it was kind of basic: the sheet was only four feet square and he would have to lie curled up all day if he wished to keep every part of his six-foot-plus frame away from the assault of the sun. It would still be intolerably hot. But it was better than nothing.

He crawled into the hollow, soaked with sweat already.

Preoccupied as he'd been to find shelter, he'd seen no sign of the trail.

He had looked for, and failed to find, evidence of desert vegetation that could be chewed for moisture or boiled up for food—the carob with its edible seed pods; wild gourds; stapelia, the fat-spined plant whose star-shaped "carrion flowers" give off the stench of rotting meat.

There were plenty of thorn trees.

Period.

Bolan had no idea how far he had traveled during the night. He had been walking for nine hours. Dare he estimate eighteen miles? Fifteen? Twelve?

However far it was, he knew it would be less the next night. Less still—if he was able to stand upright and walk— the one after that. Allowing that he had maybe forty miles to cover, and the longest he could hope to survive was three days, the equation matching time against distance against strength and supplies looked increasingly gloomy.

Hell, there was nothing he could do but press on. He took his gulp of water, his pinch of salt, and prepared to sweat out the day.

The day was more hellish than the night.

Cramped beneath his pint-size, inadequate shelter, Bolan suffered the tortures of the damned while the sun, blazing remorselessly down on the dust-dry plain, inched its way across the colorless sky toward the west.

Spiderlike, the iron-hard spiky shadows of the thorn trees moved as slowly in the opposite direction.

Beneath the plastic sheet, the heat was a ferocious living thing, attacking his muscles, sinews and nerves, sapping what little strength he had left, grilling the blood in his veins. His head ached abominably, his belly felt bruised. Each time his swollen tongue stuck to the roof of his mouth, he rationed himself a sip of the water, but this served only to emphasize the sandpaper rawness of his throat and increase the pain clawing his guts.

Four or five times during the inferno of the afternoon he was forced to quit the improvised tent and brave the scorching direct rays of the sun in order to ease the cramps provoked by his hunched position beneath the sheet. Each time the hammer blows of that heat struck him, the ache in his head got worse.

Once an airplane labored across the sky to the east, but apart from that no living thing disturbed the windless silence of the desert. Bolan was reminded of an Australian sheep farmer he met one time in a bar in Singapore. "Traveling the outback," the old man had said, "I get worried when I see no skulls, no bones... because that means I'm lost."

Was the Executioner lost? He was almost past caring when at last the sun sank from sight and he rose giddily to his feet.

Once more he checked over the components of his nightmare trek. Handgun, harness, parang... mess tin in the pouch with knotted condom on top, wadded handkerchief and strip of cloth on one side, medical supplies and basic survival kit in the pockets of the bush shirt . . .

He had stripped off the blacksuit at the start of the day because although an extra layer of clothing trapped cooling air, he knew it would have become sodden with sweat and chilled him when the temperature dropped at night. Now, moving slowly with heavy limbs, he undressed and put it on again, then pulled on his pants and bush shirt.

He applied a fresh Band-Aid to his blistered heel and laced his combat boots.

Then, checking his direction with the compass, he tied the plastic sheet around his shoulders and lurched off into the gathering dark.

Bolan's recollection of that second night was never precise. He retained a confused impression of determination struggling to overcome pain and exhaustion—start . . . stagger . . . stumble . . . stop. Rest. One sip of water. Start again . . . stumble . . . stop . . . take five . . .

World without end.

But for the warrior, no "amen."

When, after countless eternities, the sky finally began to pale in the east, he was plodding on bent almost double, with a pause between each step, the breath rasping in his raw throat.

This day there was no cloud bank to delay the sun's attack. It rose above the desert like a blazing ball of fire, a huge orb of blinding brilliance that splashed scarlet over a sky reflected in the stones flooring the plain, a furnace dissipating the night mist still shrouding the thorn trees.

There were still thorn trees all around.

Bolan cursed the thorn trees. He cursed the whole desert, he cursed his hunger, his thirst, his pain, his total fatigue. He saw with surprise that some of the red staining the stones was blood from his own feet. He cursed the thorn trees again. The spiny, goddamned deadwood—

But wait!

Was he hallucinating, or was there finally, after all, a shape ahead that contrasted with the eternal, endless woody spikes?

He tried to swallow, focusing bloodshot eyes.

It was no mirage.

One hundred . . . ninety . . . eighty agonizing yards ahead, something square-cut, rectangular loomed through the mist.

Bolan forced his unwilling limbs to move faster.

Was it the beginning of an African village? A hut where he could rest up during the hours of daylight? A rock outcrop even?

He strained his eyes, trying to blink away the iron filings strewn beneath the lids.

The veils of mist wreathing the shape withdrew.

Bolan halted in his tracks, aghast. His jaw dropped in astonishment. A croak of disbelief escaped between his cracked lips. Slowly he lowered himself to the ground.

The silhouette rising above the stunted thorns, unmistakable with its soft top and vertical lines, was that of an abandoned Land Rover.

CHAPTER TWENTY

The nearest Central African airport to Zemio was at Bangui, the republic's capital, 350 miles to the west. There was a local field at Isiro, only two hundred miles to the south, but that was still in Zaire and there would be land frontiers to cross. Jason Mettner took a chance, overflew the border and put the Beechcraft down on a strip of savannah a couple miles out of town.

Helmeted police in a jeep arrived before he had time to close the canopy and lock the hatch. What the hell did he think he was doing? Who did he think he was? Didn't he know there were rules?

Mettner played dumb. A man with dollars in his pocket, but dumb. He hadn't realized, he really thought, since there was no field . . .

His papers were okay. And because the *Globe* was one of the few English language newspapers on sale in the republic, his story about an exclusive on the riches of the diamond mines in the interior was believed. He got a ride into town aboard the jeep.

The hotel could have been a mirror image of the one he had stayed at in El Da'ein. He saw the same front porch railed with the same cracked and peeling wood, the same sunbaked yard with the same beat-up pickups parked there. He sat under similar fans stirring air that was equally stale while he emptied his hip flask into the tepid Coke that seemed to have ritual significance in central Africa.

"Funny you should have arrived in a plane," the desk clerk who served the drink said. "Second since the beginning of the month. There's no field here to put down."

"Oh, yeah?" Mettner feigned indifference. "So who was the other pilot? Another scribe from the New World?"

"Search me." The clerk figured he was into the American scene. He chewed gum, slicked back his hair, wore a flowered shirt over striped peg-top pants that could have come from a 1940 Cab Calloway movie. "The man said he was a prospector who lost his way checking out minerals in the Sudan. Dropped out of the sky in a bird, but he never claimed back the chopper when he left. Funny that, don't you think?"

"Very droll," Mettner said. "American guy?"

"You tell me. I never saw his papers. Tall man with blue eyes, stayed across the street at the Excelsior. Maybe they could even tell you his name."

They couldn't. The visitor had filled in papers, but they had since disappeared. "Didn't see much of him," the proprietor said. "Man spent half his time around the cable office."

"No kidding!" Mettner said. "Maybe he wanted to bet on a horse."

The Watusi kid behind the grille at the cable office counter didn't think so. "Man had something on his mind, all right," he confided, "but it wasn't a horse race. Me, I didn't handle all his business. But Kitty there, she had a time, I'm telling you. Tried not to lose his cool, but you could tell. It was important to him to contact these people—phone, cable, telegram, he tried them all. Just *had* to reach somebody."

"And did he?"

The kid shook his head. "Not a damn one. Musta been something screwy with the communications that week.

Sunspots or whatever. Maybe a broken—what you call it?—satellite.''

"And he was mad because you couldn't connect?''

"Was he ever! But I'm telling you—" the kid leaned across the counter toward the grille "—Zemio, it isn't exactly the hub of the world communications-wise.''

"You said 'people.' How many did he try to reach?''

The young man scratched his head. "Two? Three? As I said, Kitty handled most of it. I only came on the scene when we were trying to route the stuff through Zaire. Bukama it was. That time, there was one for Khartoum and a couple for the States.''

Mettner lit a cigarette. He stroked his unshaved jaw. Courtney, Brognola, Langley, perhaps? He could buy that. "Could I speak with Kitty?''

"If you don't mind a six-hour journey in a bus. She went back home to Uganda at the end of last week.''

"Shit!'' Mettner said. "How long ago was this?''

"Middle of last week. Man was here two, three days. I guess he arrived in town maybe nine days ago.'' He grinned. "They say he flew in from the Sudan in a helicopter!''

"So they tell me. But it seems he left without it. Would you have copies on file—" the newspaperman peeled a couple of bills from a roll "—of those cables he tried to send?''

"No. Only those that connect. If we filed the ones that don't make it, we'd have to build a new office.''

Mettner shoved the bills under the grille anyway. "One last question,'' he said. "Or maybe two. Do you recall the name signed on those cable forms, the sender's name? Would it have been Bolan?''

"Could be. I'd like to help you, mister, but to be honest I just don't remember.''

"Okay. Did the guy put through a phone call—did anyone put through a phone call—to Zaire while he was here? To a hotel in Bukama?"

"Not while I was in the office."

Mettner resigned himself to legwork. It was an eighty-five to fifteen chance that the "tall man with blue eyes" *was* Bolan. Even if the kid here couldn't remember it, the girl at Bukama confirmed that at least cables had been signed with that name. But the hotel reservation?

The newspaperman returned to the Excelsior. The blue-eyed guy whose name had been lost had made no phone calls from the hotel.

He checked out the other hotels in town. There were only four that rated. He struck pay dirt at the third.

The owner was a Belgian refugee who had fled from the Congo just before it shook off the colonialist yoke and turned into Zaire. His wife, a faded blonde of fifty, acted as waitress, chambermaid and receptionist. As cashier, too, Mettner suspected. He pushed a little money her way before asking his questions.

"Impossible, tu sais, de trouver du personnel dans cette ville," she told him—no way can you find help in this town.

Mettner backed off from the overfamiliar second person singular. Was every female in this part of Africa suffering from hot pants?

The woman delivered just the same. Everything was written down, logged with two sets of figures against it, one for the tax collector, one for personal use. And, yes, a white foreigner had indeed called through to Bukama some days ago. By chance—quite by chance, you understand; it was not her habit to listen in to calls made by clients, even if, like this one, they were not staying at the hotel; most certainly not—quite by chance she had overheard one end of the conversation. And the man had made a reservation there.

And the name? Bolton...? Bolder...? Boston...? Indeed, yes: Bolan, that was it!

"Tall, dark guy with blue eyes in a rugged face?" Mettner suggested.

The woman stared at him. "But no. Not at all. He was tall, certainly, this one. But thin, with grey hair and brown eyes. He was very chic, very—how do you say?—elegant, distinguished."

"An American?"

She shrugged. "Possibly. I do not think so. More German. Or perhaps Swedish? But he spoke good English. *Très correct*."

"Was he staying in town?"

"I do not think so, *monsieur*. He had some business with a flying machine abandoned out on the savannah. But he arrived and left in a Mercedes. Very expensive. Evidently, from the state of the vehicle, he had traveled a long distance."

Mettner thanked her and left.

Scattering chickens and a starving dog across the dusty roadway as he strode off, the newspaperman was in a pensive mood. He had been expecting Bolan in Zaire and nobody had shown; now he had *two* Bolans in this hick town in the armpit of Africa! Was there any connection between them?

He could find none. Making the round of stores, bars, restaurants and agencies the following day, he ran across a number of people who had seen or done business with the blue-eyed man, very few who had noticed the other, none who had seen them together. The dollar bills he scattered like confetti brought him some interesting intel.

The nameless blue-eyed guy from the Excelsior had bought a used Hasselblad camera from a retired journalist who had once worked for a propaganda sheet owned by the

"Emperor" Bokassa. He had purchased a quantity of small items from a hardware store—items that suggested he was about to start out on a journey overland. He had made a lot of inquiries concerning a printer. Was there a specialized printer in town who was reliable and also discreet?

Mettner's news nose started at once to sniff: Fake certificates? Diplomas? Passes or ID papers? He didn't flush out any printer admitting to that particular kind of work; in fact everyone became unusually "discreet," almost to the point of reticence, whenever the subject was raised. But it was after he had made a zero score at a back street duplicating and secretarial agency that he struck lucky.

It was dusk, and the heat of the day still lay heavy beneath the banana trees and date palms at the end of the street, when he heard a cheerful, "Hey! Watcha know!" as he trod down the steps from the agency stoop to the sun-baked roadway.

He turned and saw the young Watusi he had met at the cable office.

"Don't know if it would interest you," the kid began, "but there's this buddy of mine who ran across your blue-eyed boy last week. And he wasn't trying to send a cable, either."

Mettner reckoned it would interest him to the tune of twenty bucks.

The buddy worked at an auto repair shop behind the town's one gas station. "Got himself a deal there," the Watusi said, stuffing the bills in his pocket. "Hey! You won't forget to put in my name when you write your story, huh?"

Mettner said he'd do his best. The grease monkey at the gas station said yeah, sure, he'd fixed up a deal for the guy with blue eyes, put him in touch with a connection had a good-condition Land Rover for sale. Two more ten-spots bought Mettner the registration number of the vehicle.

"You wouldn't have any papers relating to the deal?" the newspaperman asked. "I mean like receipts or warranties and suchlike?"

"Papers?" The mechanic was at once defensive. "Heck, no. What are you, mister, a cop or something?"

"No way," Mettner said. "I just wanted to check if it was the right guy. Nobody seems to know his name. That's all."

"He had money cabled from Switzerland, I know. It happens that I, uh, I have a girlfriend who works the post office. Could be, in certain conditions, she would be able to check out the name."

Mettner sighed. He knew what the conditions would be. He reached for his billfold.

It was worth the money. The name was Bolan.

But the mechanic's other friend—the guy who'd tanked up the Land Rover and given the driver directions how to make the road to Niangara, in Zaire—just happened to have seen the new owner's ID.

Mike Belasko, photographer.

Mettner groaned. He had beaten his brains out trying to establish *some* firm connection relating the clues he dug up in Zemio with the Executioner.

Now he had three of them: Bolan, Belasko and the mystery man in the Mercedes who reserved rooms in Bolan's name....

But the only hard lead he had was the Land Rover and its destination. He decided to follow up that lead. Reducing still further his depleted store of dollars, he bribed another friend of the gas station attendant to drive him out to the Beechcraft.

Once airborne, he radioed the controller at Isiro, Zaire, for permission to land. The field was less than fifty miles from Niangara.

The gas station attendant heard the plane pass overhead. He went to check with the mechanic, who took time off to go see the girl in the post office. He put through a long-distance call, collect.

"Mister," he said when the connection was made, "you promised to see me if I came up with any additional information on this Bolan character, okay? Well, there's this foreigner who's been asking questions all over town the past two days.... That's right. An American named Mettner. Claims to be a newspaperman...."

CHAPTER TWENTY-ONE

Mack Bolan sat on the graveled floor of the desert and forced himself to stare out between his laced fingers.

Navigating by the stars, checking every half hour with a compass, how could he possibly have made such a gigantic mistake? Given the exhaustion, given the mental fatigue, allowing for the physical damage wreaked by hunger and thirst, how could he unknowingly have the physical damage wreaked by hunger and thirst, how could he unknowingly have walked in a huge circle and returned to his starting point like some fictional castaway in a desert romance?

Even if the working of the compass had been affected—perhaps by a heavy iron lode beneath the floor of the plain—how could he? How could he have continually misread a skyful of stars?

Worse, how was it that he was approaching the vehicle the wrong way—because, the way it was facing, the sun, too, was in the wrong place, rising in the west instead of the east? Or was it in fact setting, and he had lost a whole day? For a moment he felt his reason slipping away. Then the panic was over.

This was not the same Land Rover.

This one had clearly been involved in some desert skirmish—the windshield was starred, bullet holes peppered the tattered canvas top and punctured the hood. The action had occurred some time ago, Bolan guessed, because human scavengers had removed wheels, tires, headlights, anything that could be dismantled or wrenched off the rusted chassis. A thin coating of sand was sifted over the seats.

He rose to his feet, staggered the last few yards and cast himself down in the shade beneath the wreck. He slept.

Bolan awoke with dust clogging his nostrils. A hot wind stirred the dry twigs strewing the sun-scorched surface of the thorn tree desert. His whole body was bathed in sweat.

He looked at his watch. It was well after midday. He struggled out from his refuge below the vehicle. The heat struck him like a hammer blow. Shading his sore eyes with one hand, he looked around.

West, south and east, the atmosphere trembled above the limitless expanse of spiked deadwood, but ahead, clear enough even though they were still blue with distance, a line of low hills undulated against the burnished sky.

As the Executioner heaved a long sigh of relief, the hot wind blew again, a hell breath of desiccated air, dry as dead leaves. Thorny branches rose and fell, clattering their spines.

How far away were those hills? Fifteen miles? Ten? Was there a chance they could be less than that? It was impossible to estimate: details blurred in the superheated air dancing over the plain. But one thing, he saw now with a surge of relief, was crystal clear. Less than fifty yards from the wrecked vehicle, faint but still discernible among the graveled wastes, the desert trail arrowed toward those hills.

At last he was back on the right track.

After nightfall, he would make the far fringe of the interminable plain or die in the attempt.

If he didn't make it during those precious hours of darkness, he thought soberly, he *would* die. Less than half his supply of water remained. Statistically the third twenty-four-hour period without food and with insufficient water was his limit. In these climatic conditions the human organism, even one as tough as Bolan's, could take no more.

He crawled back beneath the Land Rover, stripped off his drenched blacksuit and pushed it out in the sun to dry. He wet his parched lips and tried to masticate a fragment of the tallow candle in his survival kit in the hope that the fat would provide protein for his starved metabolism. But tallow does not keep well in hot climates. The candle had melted into a glutinous mass and the tallow was rancid. He vomited at once, making his raw throat dryer than ever.

He took a second sip of tepid water, was reknotting the condom when the third gust of wind—much stronger this time—rocked the vehicle's body. A loose fragment of metal, displaced from somewhere in the engine compartment, tinkled to the ground.

Bolan realized the light was fading. He looked out from his shelter. The sun was partially obscured by the outer fringe of a dark cloud that had blown up from the west, an iron-gray curtain drawn over half the sky.

As he watched, the incandescent brilliance dimmed, faded to an orange fireball, a silver disk . . . and then vanished behind the advancing cloud.

The wind blew harder. The thorn trees leaned.

Bolan knew the signs. A dust storm was approaching, fast.

He was still half-naked. Hastily he drew on pants and bush shirt, fumbled with the clasp of his belt. The wind was now moaning through the dry branches of the trees.

Above his head, the dust cloud was tumbling, roiling, racing across the sky. And a quarter of a mile away to the west he saw with mounting apprehension an approaching dust devil—a miniature tornado similar to those that occasionally ravage the American Midwest.

Linking the earth with the lowering sky, the dun-colored corkscrew shape spiraled at frightening speed toward the

Land Rover, uprooting trees and whirling stones aside in its crazy course across the desert.

The moan of the wind increased to a howl, a roar. Bolan scrambled out from beneath the vehicle and ducked behind the bodywork on the side away from the blast. A moment later, the storm engulfed him.

The tail of the pint-size tornado whipped across the off-roader with frenzied force. Stones rattled like shrapnel against the rusted steel and lacerated the lower half of the Executioner's legs.

His mouth, ears, eyes, nostrils, every square inch of his frame between skin and clothes, were invaded by the choking dust. It was pitch-dark in the center of the shrieking whirlwind, and for a time he was afraid he would be buffeted into unconsciousness.

When at last it was over, he lay on his face, gagging and retching, some yards away from the battered Land Rover. It was the fierce heat of the sun beating on his back that convinced him the tornado had really passed.

He struggled to his feet and saw the sinister spiral dwindling away toward the east.

It took him a long time to rid himself of the worst of the dust, and he was obliged to use a few drops of the water to clear his eyes. Only then did he get wise to the full extent of the damage wrought by the storm.

The blacksuit had gone, whisked away into the unknown. The AutoMag would be useless until it was entirely stripped down and reoiled. Both tobacco cans with their irreplaceable contents had been blown away. His map, sucked into the air by the violence of the storm, had flapped away like a wounded bird.

He checked over his mental list. He was left with his belt and pouch, containing the penlight, mess tin, condom and a few rounds of ammunition; the gun and the parang at his waist; and the towel. Even the plastic sheet had disappeared.

He risked the heat to make a one-hundred-yard recon in the lee of the vehicle. Many of the thorn trees had been uprooted in the gale; dead branches lay everywhere; dust had piled up in the smallest depressions to form miniature dunes. He found part of the map impaled on a thorn. The plastic sheet was lodged at the top of one of the taller trees, but it was ripped to pieces, not worth the effort of a climb. Of the rest of his missing kit there was no sign.

He trudged wearily back to the Land Rover, trying to ignore the agony in his belly.

Kicking aside a pile of dust that had gathered beneath one of the wheel-less brake drums, he stepped on a hidden stone, turned his ankle and fell heavily.

A sudden gurgle. A rush of warmth over his crotch and thighs, a clamminess of the pants clinging to his legs.

Bolan couldn't even curse.

As he went down, the parang clipped to his belt had twisted, the razor-sharp tip of its blade sliding beneath the unfastened pouch flap to puncture the condom.

Frenziedly he pushed himself upright as warm water gushed from the open pouch. He struggled to wrench the sac upright, to keep at least some of the precious liquid in its waterproof depths. But he could save no more than a few spoonfuls in the mess tin. And even these could not be reserved for the remainder of his nightmare journey: the second condom had been in the basic survival kit carried away by the whirlwind.

Bolan crawled back beneath the chassis and drank the water. If he hadn't, in a shallow open tin in that heat, it would have evaporated in a half hour.

Now he had to make the most difficult decision of all.

In his present state of exhaustion, with no food and no more water, he could only expect to last a certain amount of time. If he waited until nightfall and started the final leg of his odyssey then, there was a chance time might run out on him before he made the hills on the far side of the desert.

If he started now, the sun could destroy him.

Apart from the question of time, there were other considerations.

Now that the plastic was gone, he had nothing but the towel to protect him against the onslaught of the sun. Equally, with no plastic sheet and no more blacksuit, he had nothing to insulate his body from the cold of the desert night.

The compass was gone with the wind. If he traveled in daylight, he could simply follow the trail. If he waited until it was dark, he could use the stars again—unless the weather was bad and clouds blacked out the night sky.

He looked at the western horizon. The sky was stormy.

Final point: without wheels or tires, the Land Rover's chassis was very close to the ground. It was damned uncomfortable under there in this heat.

The hell with it. He would walk now.

It was after four o'clock when he finally left, but the sun, scarcely started on its slide down toward the west, was still hammering the desert with blinding power.

Bolan was a scarecrow figure, his eyes staring, his cracked lips moistened with no saliva. Thick stubble blued his jaw.

He lurched along the trail in the direction of the distant hills, the padded handkerchief on top of his head, the towel draped over that and the two bound in place with the strip of cloth torn from his shirttail. In his weakened state they were not much protection.

In less than a quarter mile he was limping badly. His ankle had swollen and there were blisters on both feet. Only his iron will kept him going; he was past logical thinking now. Because he hadn't a hope in hell of making those hills before dark—of keeping on the right track after dark—of surviving the night to try again the following day...

Yet somewhere at the center of that zero threatening to engulf him a single spark of brightness, the will to survive, refused to be dimmed. Doggedly he would continue to place one painful foot before the other...one foot before the other...one foot...

Whatever the odds.

In the heat that rose in numbing waves from the shaley desert floor he lost all sense of time. Lying on his back among the thorn trees—he must have fallen—crazy!—he gazed sightlessly at the sky and listened to the music of an organ.

At some other time that blinding afternoon, swaying, he stood with his arms wrapped around a tree trunk, staring over a great field of grass rippling in the wind.

He knew that he was hallucinating. "Can't fool me," he mumbled. "I know that's no mirage...mirage is...optical illusion. Actual impression on retina. This is all in...my mind." He laughed weakly. "Even a camera could record...mirage."

Camera?

Where the hell was the Hasselblad?

He knew he should have a camera. He *did* have a camera. Suddenly he was terribly worried about the camera. If he was a photographer he had to have a goddamn camera.

And then he remembered. Of course. The Hasselblad was in the Land Rover. It was stowed in back, behind the front seats. No sweat... He could pick it up when he made the Land Rover. He should reach it soon. All he had to do was keep on walking....

The organ music was louder now. Could it really be the pounding of blood through his own veins? He put a hand into the pouch at his waist. No water. Screwing up his eyes against the glaring light he looked beyond whitecapped waves and watched the blue hills shiver in the sun. Brognola was shouting in the cab and the Land Rover's brakes were squealing.

AT FIRST Bolan was irresistibly reminded of General Halakaz, for the accoutrements glinted and gleamed from the toes of the knee-high leather boots to the lenses of the sunglasses that masked the eyes. But there the resemblance ended.

Although deeply bronzed, his rescuer was white. And a woman.

She was blond, small-waisted, about thirty-five years old, wearing whipcord breeches and a polished military belt with crossed shoulder straps. She wore lipstick, and her hair was gathered on her nape in a black velvet bow.

Bolan didn't believe her.

He moved his head and looked around. He was lying on his back on a camp bed in a forest glade. Tall trees arched overhead to screen out the sky. On the far side of the glade three tents with mosquito nets had been pitched between a Range Rover and a fat-tired Toyota Land Cruiser. Several men, black and white, were busy around a wood fire, and the aroma of roasting meat drifted on the cool evening air.

Bolan cut his gaze to a close-up. The woman was still there.

"Aren't you hot, wearing all that stuff?" was the first thing he said. His voice was weak, not much more than a croak.

She smiled. Even, very white teeth. "It can be uncomfortable in the desert," she said. "But both the vehicles are air-conditioned and the clothes are really designed for forest conditions, as a protection against stings, bites and scratches." Her voice was deep, husky, overlaid with a trace of accent—Swiss?—that he couldn't place.

"How did I get here?" he asked.

"We picked you up at dusk, the day before yesterday. You were lying beside the trail halfway across the desert."

"The day *before* yesterday?"

"You were pretty far gone. We've been pumping you full of glucose and vitamins and concentrated protein." She smiled again. "And knockout drops to allow your body to heal itself without any interference from your mind."

"I don't know how to thank you," Bolan said awkwardly. "But I . . . How far did I have to go? Before the end of the desert?"

She shrugged. "Ten miles. Twelve. Something like that."

"You were heading north? We're north of the desert now? Okay. . . You would have passed two Land Rovers, both abandoned. How far was I from the first one, the one with wheels?"

Blond eyebrows were raised. "About fifteen miles. Why?"

Bolan bit his lip. He had walked through several hells and that was all the distance he had made.

He tried to sit up. There was an intravenous drip in his left arm; an inverted bottle of saline solution suspended from a stand beside the camp bed. She pushed him down again. "You are still very weak," she said. "You must rest."

He stared around the glade once more. The black bearers were setting canvas stools around a trestle table. Between the tents, bales and crates of stores were stacked neatly. Among them, he saw, was a theodolite on a tripod.

"This is an expedition?" he asked. "And you're the boss?"

She nodded.

"You're on safari?"

"Not quite," she said. "We'll feed you some broth and then you must sleep. Tomorrow will be soon enough for the questions."

She strode away toward the fire.

When she returned with the broth in a waxed paper cup, she saw that he was sleeping already.

HER NAME, she told Bolan the next day, was Trudi Finnemann. She was a geomorphologist, surveying and mapping the great triangle of uncharted forest that lay between Ouad Faturah, Wau and the thorn-tree desert on behalf of a German development corporation, which she did not name.

"There are thousands of square miles of jungle in this part of Africa practically unexplored," she said. "What's underneath it is mostly limestone, but the strata are crisscrossed with unconformities and there are igneous, that is to say volcanic, intrusions everywhere. Probably mineral veins, too. It is a most interesting area."

Bolan was feeling much better. Not quite back to his normal coiled-spring alertness, but totally human again. He said, "Surprisingly few rivers, just the same, considering how rich the vegetation is right here. According to the map I had—"

"Ah, that is because they all run underground," Trudi interrupted. "The limestone is riddled with potholes and caves and subterranean channels. Most of them drain finally into the Bahr el Arab, the Bahr el Homr or the Soeh River—and so eventually into the Bahr el Ghazal and the White Nile."

That night, over a surprisingly elaborate meal—they even had ice for the drinks from a portable gas-operated refrigerator—Bolan embroidered the story of his own supposed photographic excursion. He was more than grateful to Trudi Finnemann and her companions, but he knew nothing about them and he certainly wasn't going to tell them the real reason for his presence in this part of the Sudan.

There were five blacks with the expedition and two white men: a bearded, bespectacled surveyor named Hans Voigt, and Jochen Kraul, a pale, balding thirty-year-old. Kraul was a botanist whose task was to relate the forest vegetation and the creatures living off it to the rock formations that might lie beneath.

Voigt was an extrovert, a big man with a big voice he was always ready to use. Kraul contributed little to the conversation. The blacks shared the same table and the same food, but it was clear that they were no more than the hired help.

All of them, Bolan noted, treated the leader of the expedition with a great deal of respect, and he sensed that beneath that affable manner and bandbox appearance there was a determination and force of will equal to his own.

To firm up his story, he cited the fictitious companion he was slated to contact there in the forest, and added, "If you've been traveling across the province, you, uh, you wouldn't by any chance have come across my buddy?"

Trudi Finnemann shook her head. "Nobody but refugees from the burned villages. The jungle's full of them, trying not to starve, wondering all the time what's going to happen to them and their families, whether to risk trying their luck in Uganda or Chad."

"Where exactly was the rendezvous with your partner?" Voigt asked.

"That's the trouble," Bolan said. "Someplace between Ouad Faturah and that so-called forbidden city, Oloron. But we were to fix the precise place of the meet by radio, and mine was taken from me on the other side of the desert by an irregular leader named Mtambole."

"You can raise him on ours," Trudi Finnemann said.

"Yeah. Sure. Thanks." Bolan edged away from the subject. He could go through the pantomime of calling the mythical Courtney only so many times. Apart from which, they might know the real one. "In any case," he said, "I kind of blew it. I lost my camera."

The blonde smiled. "The Hasselblad? I should have told you before. We recovered it from the Land Rover. It seems to be undamaged. You take it when you want it."

"Why, that's great. Once I locate my partner I have to make it fast to wherever he is. I was hoping maybe I could rent a mule, a horse or even a camel at Ouad Faturah."

Voigt laughed. "Forget it," he boomed. "Ouad Faturah is a six-hundred-year-old mud fort with one street of tumbledown hovels leading up to it. If the inhabitants saw a spare beast any time in the past ten years, they would have cooked and eaten it!"

Bolan shrugged. "I might as well try. Are you going anywhere near the place?"

"We're heading northeast," Trudi told him. "We could take you within ten miles, fix you up with a few supplies and point you in the right direction."

"Or maybe Oloron? It wasn't on my map, but they tell me that's an interesting site, like so many of these holy places. Maybe you could explain how I would get there?"

The conversation suddenly died.

Voigt's rumbling laugh preceded an order to one of the porters: certain supplies should be replaced in the Toyota now, since they had an early start in the morning.

Trudi Finnemann's responses to that point had been crisp and precise. Now she appeared suddenly to suffer an attack of vagueness. She wasn't quite sure, she said, where the place was. If indeed it existed at all. As far as she knew they had been nowhere near it.

Jochen Kraul said nothing.

A few minutes later the leader of the expedition rose to her feet and clapped her hands. It was time to bed down for the night.

Bolan was intrigued.

It was perfectly clear that there *was* something mysterious about Oloron. And that the members of the geological party knew about it. Why were they not prepared to discuss it?

Was the scientific story a cover, like his own photographer pose? He didn't think so. He had already seen enough notes and charts and readings to substantiate the story. But even if that was all a carefully worked-out blind, possibly with real scientists taking genuine readings, what could be the hidden purpose of the expedition? Whom could they be working for? He had deliberately trailed a couple of leading questions about radioactive ores, the possibility of deposits in the region.

The response had been genuinely negative. No deposits, no chance of ores in these particular rock formations, no interest.

On the whole the Executioner had decided to accept Trudi Finnemann and her colleagues at their own face value. But there were, nevertheless, a couple of things—apart from the evasions on the subject of the forbidden city—that he found disturbing.

He knew from certain indications—minor techniques of fastening straps, preset tolerances and other personal routines—that the Hasselblad had been stripped down and thoroughly examined before it was returned to him.

Secondly, there was the question of the firearms.

Trudi Finnemann and her two scientists each carried small-caliber automatic handguns. The headman in charge of the porters wore an old-fashioned Colt revolver in a leather holster at his hip. In a dangerous region teeming with half-starved refugees that was normal practice, if only for self-protection.

Equally acceptable were the three hunting rifles—two Mannlichers and a Husqvarna—strapped in custom-built canvas gun cases in back of the Range Rover. There would be enough big game in the forest, as possible food supplies or simply as an ever-present danger, to make the inclusion of such weapons a must.

But what was he to make of his accidental discovery in the forward part of the luxurious vehicle?

He had gone, at Trudi Finnemann's invitation, to get his camera and saw them stowed in the wide elasticized pocket on the driver's door: two 9 mm mini-Uzi machine pistols.

What did such supercompact and deadly weapons have to do with geology?

Bolan was in a thoughtful mood when he crawled under the mosquito netting that night in the one-man tent allotted to him.

Before he went to sleep he dismantled, checked, reassembled and finally reloaded the AutoMag. He slept with the butt of the big gun nestling in his right hand.

CHAPTER TWENTY-TWO

Bolan remained with the geological expedition for most of the next day.

The forest grew denser and steamier; the hills became higher. Progress was slow until, at the foot of the fifth steep-sided valley, instead of climbing the far slope the trail turned and followed the dried-up riverbed along a twisting defile that finally opened out into a shallow depression perhaps ten miles across.

The Range Rover and the Toyota, heavily laden with stores and equipment, increased speed until the top-heavy bodies were bouncing uncomfortably, bottoming on the suspension with each fresh hole in the stony track.

Sitting between Trudi and Voigt in the Range Rover, Bolan saw a trickle of brown water appear in the deep wadi. Birds flapped into the air and a herd of deerlike creatures—there had to have been several hundred—galloped off in a cloud of dust as the vehicles approached. They were the first signs of animal life he had seen since he entered the country.

On the far side of the depression the topography was different, the slopes gentler, the vegetation lusher and greener. To balance this advantage, the trail was frequently hidden by the dense undergrowth. Several times the convoy had to stop while the porters cast around, beating the brushwood down before they could identify the route.

Toward the end of the afternoon, they emerged from a dense tract of forest into a small glade floored with bright violet flowers. The trail vanished among trees on the other side of the open space. But a gorge across the center barred the way.

They pulled up again and Voigt, Bolan and the woman went to the edge of the fissure. Kraul remained behind the wheel of the Land Cruiser.

Some gigantic upheaval eternities ago had split open the earth as though it had been cleft with a mighty ax. Trudi at once started to explain it in geological terms, but the warrior was not listening.

He made a lightning visual recon of the site. On either side, jungle trees closed in and lined the gorge as far as he could see. Two hundred feet below a thread of water glistened in the shadows, and among the smooth rocks he could make out the splintered remains of what had been a plank bridge. The sheer faces of the cleft overhung at the top, leaving a gap no more than ten or twelve feet across where the bridge had been. A high-school athlete or any man in shape could have leaped it after a running start. But for the two vehicles it was an impassable barrier.

"The Arabs!" Trudi exclaimed angrily. "They think they can hinder the black guerillas by destroying the bridge! But there are dozens of places farther down where they can cross."

"That doesn't help us, Fräulein Finnemann," Voigt said. "We can't get the vehicles down there. We shall have to backtrack ten miles to the fork by that water hole, and then take the other trail that leads around the head of this gorge."

Trudi compressed her lips. "And that is at least fifteen miles upriver from here. We'll never make it by nightfall. We'll have to make camp this side of the stream. Really, it is too bad. It will delay us a whole day."

Bolan saw an opening . . . and took it.

"I really am rather anxious to locate my partner," he said. "Since we can't contact him by radio—" they had tried twice, not surprisingly with no success "—I reckon I'd better make it to Ouad Faturah in case he left a message there. The place shouldn't be more than ten or twelve miles ahead, and if I left now..."

"You mean you want to go ahead on foot? To jump the gap and take it from there?" Trudi asked.

"If you wouldn't mind. You said you'd be dropping me off ten miles short of the town anyway."

She nodded. "That is true. You would *gain* a whole day by going ahead. We'll do what we can to help."

They fixed him up with new pants, a bedroll, a water bottle and several other necessities. He slung the camera over his shoulder and walked back to the Toyota to say goodbye to Kraul.

The botanist leaned out the vehicle's window. "I don't know what your motives are," he said in a low voice, "but if you really want to make it to Oloron, it lies no more than a dozen miles due northeast of here."

"I don't know what *your* motives are," Bolan replied, "but I sure appreciate the information. You know the place yourself?"

Kraul glanced quickly at the porters in back of the Land Cruiser and then at Voigt and the woman, who were discussing something by their vehicle. "We have been near there," he murmured. "We have looked down upon the place. But it is necessary to go damn carefully. The town— it was originally only a religious settlement—is tucked away at the bottom of a steep gorge. It is impossible to climb down the cliffs behind it and on either side. The only entrance is along the valley floor that leads directly to the gate, and that is too well guarded to force."

"I'm not aiming to storm the place." Bolan smiled. "Only take pictures."

"Just so. It is well to be forewarned just the same. Oloron is the headquarters of the Anya Nya guerilla forces. There are hundreds of them there, and there seem to be assault courses, training grounds, shooting ranges, lecture theaters—the whole organization and equipment for a military academy—inside the walls."

"Very interesting," Bolan said casually, trying not to reveal the extent to which he *was* interested—and excited—by the intel. "I don't know why you want to tell me—"

"Sometimes it is a fault to be too cagey," Kraul replied enigmatically. And then he clammed up as Voigt and Trudi approached.

The young woman took Bolan's hand in a firm grip as they said their farewells, and seemed reluctant to let it go. "I wish you luck, my friend," she said huskily, "and I ask you to take care. This can be a dangerous region. Remember that if you have need of help, you can always come back to us. We'll be mapping and taking readings for several days about thirty miles north of here." She smiled. "In any case, I have a feeling that we shall meet again."

"Don't get your pictures developed in Africa," Voigt quipped with his rumbling laugh. "They charge far too much and the color processing is hell!"

Trudi ignored him. She stared full into Bolan's eyes for a moment and then, abruptly releasing his hand, turned and strode back to the Range Rover, the switch of blond hair with its black bow bouncing up and down on her shoulders.

Bolan tossed his bedroll to the far side of the gorge. He moved back twenty paces, dashed forward and launched himself over the gap. He was glad to see, as a yardstick of his return to fitness, that he landed on the other side, several yards beyond the edge.

Waving to the members of the expedition, he set off along the grassy trail, staying with it for half a mile in case he was being watched. After that he plunged in among the forest trees in the direction indicated by Kraul. He was playing a hunch, but what the hell—a fighter's hunches had saved his life before now.

Thirty minutes' hard going brought him to another narrow track running roughly northeast. He spread the bedroll beneath a rock shelf that was canted up through the carpet of brushwood and creeper, ate some of the dried food he had been given and prepared to sleep.

He awoke before dawn into a heavy, humid darkness pulsating with the thrum of a million insect wings, rank with the odor of jungle vegetation. There were louder noises, too.

The shifting of birds, perched among the interlaced branches far above the forest floor; a scuttle, from time to time, of small creatures hurrying through the undergrowth; a distant chattering—of monkeys, perhaps, angry at seeing their domain invaded by an alien biped.

Just below the threshold of sleep, the Executioner had subconsciously been aware of these sounds throughout the night. His jungle fighter's sixth sense, recording the impressions and finding them inoffensive, left the alert signals nonoperative.

The noise that woke him was not loud, but it was different. Two noises, actually: a dry twig snapping; a clink of metal on metal, or metal on hardwood.

He was awake in an instant, on full red alert with the alarm bells ringing and all defense systems go. There were no animals in a forest this dense that were heavy enough to snap a twig if they stepped on it. He had yet to hear of a monkey carrying a rifle equipped with a webbing sling and metal D-rings.

The sound, all too familiar to a Vietnam veteran, was definitive. A sniper, less professional than he should be, unslinging his weapon.

Bolan was out of the bedroll and flattened against the rock in seconds, the AutoMag ready in his hand.

Neither of the sounds was repeated.

He had no idea how far away the unseen rifleman might be. As both noises were initiated while he was asleep, it was impossible for him to orient their source, and in any case leaves, branches, creeper and liana were so thickly intertwined that it was a no-go situation, trying to vector in on any specific sound.

He would have to wait for the hunter to make the next move.

The bedroll site was well chosen. From above and on one side it was protected by the rock shelf; the other open side was no more than three feet from a thick screen of mucuna and nettle trees. The trail was ten yards away, on the far side of the rock. To sight directly on the bedroll, a sniper would have to be a considerable height from the ground, lodged in a tree.

Bolan froze in the vibrating dark, every sense on full alert. He had made no more noise leaving the bedroll than a restless sleeper might make changing his position.

While he waited, he ran over a list of questions he couldn't answer. Had the unseen gunman located the place where the Executioner was sleeping and was he simply waiting for first light to make sure of his aim and rake it with a hail of death? Or did he, alternatively, know only that there was *somebody*, someplace, that he could only finger when it was light enough to see? Was the guy a guard? Part of a patrol? A detail sent specifically to waste Bolan? If so, was the planned assault directed at Bolan *as* Bolan, or would it have been unleashed against any stranger wandering into an area that was clearly "sensitive"? Finally was there a chance that the sniper was not hostile at all, that it was a coincidence, that the Executioner had been woken by an innocent hunter stalking some jungle game?

Bolan didn't think so.

Every instinct in his battle-trained mind, every pulse of adrenaline that sent the blood coursing through his veins, told him that he was in danger.

In mortal danger.

The velvet forest blackness thinned imperceptibly. Very slowly, the limestone face of the rock shelf emerged as a paler blur against the dark. High up in the treetops, a tropical bird uttered a harsh call.

The gunfire, when it came, was deafening.

Three shattering bursts from a high-power automatic rifle that echoed thunderously among the forest trees and startled an angry chorus from a family of monkeys somewhere on the far side of the rock.

Bolan heard the stream of slugs thwack into the bedroll, shriek away among the trees in ricochet, splat against the rock. One passed so close to his cheek that the shock wave fanned his ear.

He dived away, careful to avoid the nettle trees with their hairy, poisonous fruit, and hit a combat crouch. The blast—he figured it for an M-16 assault rifle—had come from behind him. And, as he expected, from above.

The sniper was someplace up among that tangle of branches, with a sight line clear to the rock shelf. Bolan edged silently through the undergrowth, alert for a sign of movement up there. Birds were screeching all over; the light grew brighter with every minute.

Three single shots cracked out still from behind him. Bolan swiveled, facing the rock once more. So there were two of them.

He heard a rasp of metal, a tinkle of glass as one of the bullets pulverized the Hasselblad. He figured this second gun was a big-bore sporting rifle. A Mannlicher? A Husqvarna? He tried to put the thought from his mind. He hoped not. In any case, if the enigmatic Fräulein Finnemann and her entourage had wanted to eliminate him for some reason, they could have done so while he was leaping the fissure or even earlier while he was in their care. They could have left him in the desert.

It was now light enough for the riflemen to see that there was no bloodied body between the smashed camera and the shredded remains of the bedroll.

The warrior bellied down beneath a broad-leaved jungle succulent with sickly yellow flowers. He waited.

Crazy situation, he thought. Kind of a civil war, in which he felt no particular allegiance to either side. And yet each side, independently, was after his hide.

Why? Because everyone concerned was desperate to keep secrets; whichever way he turned, it seemed, there were interests prepared to go to any lengths to stop him continuing his mission.

Because the mission was to track down the stolen consignments of uranium 235, it figured that the secrets and the deadly isotope were intimately connected. Any other explanation would be crazier still.

But why were *both* sides on the same kick?

In terms of any warlike use of the fissile material, it made no sense.

Bolan sighed. Interpret them any way you wanted; those were the facts. Before he drew his own conclusions, he wanted more of them.

The warrior heard a noise behind him and to his right. Maybe fifty yards away. A faint slithering sound. A swish of leaves.

He held his breath, peering through the leafy screen, alert for any movement among the complexity of tropical stalks and stems. He reckoned the sniper had shinned down his tree, was now prowling the undergrowth, finger on the trigger, covered by his companion's hunting rifle. Or maybe, like the Executioner himself, he was just waiting.

The bird song had ceased. The monkeys no longer chattered. All at once the forest was deadly quiet.

In the vibrating silence, Bolan heard a tiny ticking noise. He glanced briefly down. Six inches away from his gun hand, a sawtooth beetle was burrowing into a deadwood stump: it was the trickle of sawdust, pattering onto a dry leaf, that he had heard.

The rifleman was an expert tracker: he didn't even make that much noise. Bolan saw the bare feet first, a blur of movement on the far side of a tangle of giant ferns.

He focused his eyes on that sector of the forest.

More movement. A branch swaying. Still no sound. And then, so swiftly that it could have been his imagination, a figure glided across a gap between the ferns and a clump of agave.

The M-16 was no figment of his imagination.

The sniper who carried it at the ready was a Dinka tribesman. Bolan knew that many of these South Sudanese warriors were seven feet high. This one must have been pretty close to the maximum. His lithe ebony body was oiled. Tribal marks were incised on his cheeks and shoulders. The loincloth he wore was a bright yellow.

Bolan had no choice. It was either kill or be killed. He hadn't declared the war. If it hadn't been for his battle-bred sixth sense, his body would have been the one staining the forest floor. And there was still a second killer hidden up among the branches someplace.

He raised his gun arm.

Big Thunder roared.

One, two, three, four times, and then Bolan was rolling frenziedly away as the hunting rifle up ahead returned fire and heavy slugs tore through the leaves where he had been.

Behind the ferns there was a threshing of branches and the sound of a heavy fall. He had stitched the AutoMag's .44 deathstream through an arc covering perhaps six or seven yards, hoping that at least one of the rounds might score on his invisible target.

Reaction positive. But the marksman wasn't dead. Bolan could hear movement along the jungle floor, labored breathing and a metallic click. From his new position he scanned the thickly overgrown terrain.

His vision homed in on the wounded tribesman just in time. Beneath the spiked arms of the agave, he saw white markings on a dark, contorted face. One eye was squinted shut—and the other eye stared coldly behind the notched back sight of an M-16.

Bolan squeezed Big Thunder's trigger once more.

The assault rifle spit flame skyward, and the face vanished in a cloud of blood and bone.

The hunting rifle boomed immediately, but the Executioner had already leaped away. Leaves ripped off by the heavy-caliber slugs fluttered down over him as he dived behind cover.

By now he had a fairly good idea where the second killer was—about twenty-five feet above ground in a group of acajou that formed a solid tower among a collection of taller, thinner jungle trees.

He figured he could identify the rifle, too.

There were not many that coughed out such a thunderous report. From the quality of the sound, his experience told him to put his money on a Weatherby Mark V, a .460 Magnum monster that was almost four feet long and shot 500-grain bullets that flew faster than any slug on earth.

A round from a Weatherby, developing more than eight thousand foot-pounds' energy at the muzzle, would stop an elephant or a charging rhino. But the gun had one disadvantage for a marksman whose prey was armed too: the magazine held only two rounds.

For the warrior, that disadvantage could be an asset.

If his calculations were correct, and if it *was* a Weatherby, he could safely use the few seconds it took the killer to reload to make his own moves.

In the initial attack on the bedroll, the hunting rifle had fired three times. Assume the guy had topped up the box so that it was full again...and then fired three times when Bolan opened fire on the Dinka, and twice again when he finished that sniper off.

There would be a single round left in the rifle. And now that Bolan had shown himself, the guy would be unwilling to take time off to reload until he knew what the score was.

If the Executioner could tempt the man to fire that round, he could use the reload time to get beneath the branches of the acajou—the only place from which he would have a chance of wasting the killer, since the branches themselves would make it hard for him to maneuver the twenty-six-inch barrel of the big gun and take aim.

The way things worked out, it was a piece of cake.

Bolan knew he would have been placed, in his refuge behind the bamboo. Beyond the screen on his left was another fern clump. As there was nothing else heavy enough within reach, he tossed the AutoMag into the center of it.

The ferns swayed wildly as the four-pound handgun crashed down among the fronds.

Right on cue, the big hunting rifle blasted out the remaining round.

Bolan was already on his feet, grateful that the second sniper was less smart than his companion. Snatching up the AutoMag as he passed the ferns, he sprinted for the acajou stand, zigzagging among the undergrowth until he was directly below the broad branches.

From there, looking up toward the rare patches of blue sky among the treetops, he could see the body of the killer bulked against the crisscross of branches. The guy had seen him coming; he had reloaded and fired again. Neither of the bullets came anywhere near the Executioner.

Sighting on the silhouetted shape above, Bolan fired.

The rifle dropped, clattering from branch to branch on its way to the forest floor. Blood spattered the broad leaves of the acajou and dripped to the ground.

Bolan squeezed the trigger again.

A strangled cry pierced the echoes of the report. The bulky shape extended, leaned outward from the tree fork and finally folded forward to plummet down on the carpet of moss and dead leaves below.

This one needed no extra rounds. The warrior's first shot had drilled his right shoulder; the second had smashed open his chest.

Bolan took stock of the armory that had been ranged against him. The second marksman—a Dinka like his partner—had indeed been armed with a Weatherby hunting rifle. There was also a pair of infrared binoculars slung around his neck.

No sweat now to work out how they had located Bolan's hideout by the rock shelf...or, thankfully, to know why they hadn't fired on him before dawn: a man perched in a tree cannot hold binoculars to his eyes and accurately aim an eleven-pound rifle at the same time. If, instead, the sniper had been equipped with an IR nightscope...

Bolan put the thought from his mind. He made his way back to the first man. As he had thought, the gun was an M-16. This man carried regular Apollo binoculars in a leather case. He took the case and the assault rifle. The Weatherby was too cumbersome—and too slow—a weapon to appeal to him.

After he had dragged the bodies out of sight behind the giant fern, he shouldered the rifle, slung the binoculars around his neck, clipped on his pouch and picked up the rucksack containing the supplies he had been given.

The Hasselblad was broken beyond repair. He was examining the bullet-riddled bedroll when the rucksack was torn from his hand and hurled against the rock shelf.

Bolan leaped to the top of the shelf and was lying prone beneath overhanging branches while the whipcrack of the shot was still ringing in his ears.

He hadn't bargained on the possibility that the snipers might have a backup in the neighborhood. The guy must have been posted some distance away, heard the sound of gunfire and come running.

He was much shorter than the Dinkas. And darker. And younger. He was an amateur.

His second shot was fired from the same place as the first, slamming into the rock just below the Executioner and stinging his cheek with stone chips. But it enabled Bolan to get a make on the gunman's exact position.

He was standing on the trail, his head and shoulders clearly visible between the branches of the undergrowth, the rifle still held to his shoulder, questing for a better line at the third attempt.

Bolan pushed himself backward across the top of the shelf. He slid down a grassy slope, wormed his way beneath ten yards of brushwood choked in creeper and came out on the trail.

The young killer was sixty yards away, peering through the dense vegetation at the shelf his target had just vacated.

It was quixotic, it was illogical, it was crazy—after all, the kid had twice tried to murder him—but Bolan couldn't bring himself to gun down the young man in cold blood, as if he was scoring just one more hit on a pop-up target at a fairground booth. He stepped boldly into the center of the trail.

The killer whirled, the whites of his eyes staring in his face. He fired, almost in a reflex action, from the hip. The shot went wide.

Bolan took one-tenth of a second longer, but the M-16 was at his shoulder and his aim was good. Before the backup gunner could trigger a second, three high-velocity 5.56 mm deathbringers had drilled the left side of his chest.

He dropped, lifeless before he hit the ground.

Bolan sighed. One more life wasted for the wrong reasons.

He laid the body with the others, decided to leave the martyred bedroll with the remains of the camera, recovered the rest of his gear and resumed his trek toward the northeast.

He moved warily, five yards away from the trail, in case those who had detailed the snipers had also thought to sow antipersonnel mines or Bouncing Betty gut-busters along the way.

If they had, he didn't see them. Two hours and fifteen minutes later, tough going all the way, he was wedged in a tree fork, focusing the binoculars on the forbidden city of

Oloron from a ridge above and behind the ravine in which the place was built.

Kraul the biologist had been right. It did look like an army camp. Between geometrically arranged buildings—constructed, astonishingly, of red brick in the European style—squads of men marched back and forth, most of them black Africans and all of them in uniform. Bolan could distinguish a parade ground with platoons performing classic drills, a carefully laid-out battle course, and several groups sitting cross-legged on the ground listening to open-air lectures complete with chalkboards and slides. A crackle of rifle fire drifted up from a line of butts just outside the settlement's entrance gates.

If this was indeed the training base for the Anya Nya irregulars, Bolan could see why General Halakaz took pride in his force and why his colonel was so boastful. But was the Parris Island efficiency and the bull that went with it supported in some way by the promise of nuclear clout?

Was it to this hidden bastion of black power that the stolen isotopes were finally directed?

Or was this just one more coincidence? Was the precious radioactive material destined not for the vengeful military beneath the rooftops far below but for some other organization altogether in this most complex of countries? That was for Bolan to find out.

The break came sooner than he expected, but it was not until he turned his back on the forbidden city that he was wise to it.

He had maneuvered himself around in the tree fork and was scanning the miles of wooded hills to the east with his binoculars when he almost exclaimed aloud in astonishment. For a moment he thought... Hell, yes! There it was again! In the magnified circle of terrain revealed by the lenses, he saw a section of modern, metaled highway....

He lowered the binoculars and rubbed his eyes. The road was still there. Now he knew where to look, he could see it with his naked eye: a wide highway running along a treeless crest a couple of miles away that linked up with an undulating concrete swath that could only be an airstrip!

As he watched, a vehicle came in sight. It was traveling fast—a square, blue Renault Espace minibus with a steeply slanted windshield covering the front. He followed its course along the road until it disappeared behind a belt of trees. Then, idly estimating its speed, he mentally traced its path behind the woods and waited for it to emerge on the far side. Promptly, as he had anticipated, the Renault reappeared and continued along the road at the same velocity.

Only now it was red.

For the second time, Bolan rubbed his eyes. What the hell? A blue bus, hitting forty, vanished momentarily behind a stand of trees and came out the far side at the right time, at the same speed, in a different color! What kind of trick was that?

There was no other traffic on the road. The tree line wasn't long enough for a substitution to have been made: there wasn't enough distance behind the trees for a second car to make that speed before it was out in the open again. In any case, why would anyone do that?

Bolan was reminded of the takeover in a track meet relay race, where the second runner gets going before he grabs the baton from the first. Except that there wasn't room for that here!

Hell, he had to check this out. Before he did anything else he would solve the mystery of the Renaults that changed color....

He slid to the ground and made it as fast as he could in the direction of the roadway.

It took him more than three hours to traverse the two intervening valleys. The undergrowth was dense—often he had to hack his way through with the parang—and he had to watch the noise: there was, after all, what seemed to be a fully manned garrison in the neighborhood.

And the natives—yeah, remembering the dawn attack—the natives were definitely hostile!

But despite the proximity of Oloron he saw nobody on the way and finally emerged from a stand of acacia to find himself at the edge of the road.

He reckoned the blacktop had been laid around six months ago. Twenty feet wide, it ran from an airstrip in uncharted, unexplored country to...where? The runway was innocent of buildings. There wasn't even a shack in sight. Beyond it, the forest closed in again, and on the other side the road curved away toward the belt of trees where the metamorphosis of the Renault Espace had taken place.

Bent double behind the bushes at the side of the road, he moved cautiously toward the woods.

Like most conjuring tricks, the explanation was simple once you knew how it was done. In fact there was no trick. There *had* been two different Renaults. The optical illusion was possible because there were also two different roads.

Behind the trees, the road Bolan was following dipped suddenly to run into a tunnel leading underground. Just beyond the tunnel mouth, a little way off to one side, was the exit from a second tunnel...and a strip of blacktop that curved away into the distance.

It was like a city underpass. And it had happened, while he watched, that a vehicle had emerged from the exit tunnel at the same time that another, traveling at the same speed, had plunged into the entrance.

Okay, mystery solved. But what kind of underground complex did these roads and the airstrip serve?

Bolan lowered himself to the ground and wormed his way through the undergrowth until he could train the Apollo binoculars on the tunnel mouth.

It was arched, tall enough to take a ten-ton truck, well engineered in blocks of limestone. The stonework continued out along the sides of the sunken road until it had risen to ground level. Inside the entrance, a row of electric lights in the tunnel roof paralleled the sweep of the roadway as it turned steeply aside and spiraled underground.

The second tunnel, from which the red Renault had emerged, would doubtless mirror the arrangement in reverse.

And the two roads would meet someplace below.

Where?

Why?

And where did the exit road go?

Bolan laid an ear to the ground. A slight breeze sighed through the treetops and creaked the branches, but otherwise this part of the forest was silent. Was it his imagination, or did he hear a faint but persistent thrumming, a constant vibration transmitted through the earth that could have been produced by the operation of heavy machinery?

He crawled farther along, parting wild grasses so that he could see a greater distance inside the curving tunnel.

A little way around the bend, the sandbags and slits of a blockhouse broke the even surface of the wall. He nodded. As he had expected, direct entry was out of the question.

But he was going to get in there somehow.

The sun was nearing its zenith and the heat was becoming too much. The hell with it: he would prospect in the other direction, where the trees offered some protection from the direct rays. He rose warily to his feet and sped across the roadway. If he cut through the woods, inside the wide curve of the blacktop, he could make the airstrip more quickly and more safely.

He began to work his way through the undergrowth.

When he was perhaps halfway there, he pushed through a tangle of thorny bushes . . . and froze.

The ground opened beneath his feet. Half concealed by leaves and branches, the mouth of a concrete-walled shaft yawned before him.

He peered over the lip.

The breeze died away. Over the hum of insects he could hear the thumping of his own heart.

In the shadowed depths of the shaft, reflected sunlight gleamed momentarily on the metal sheathing the slim, tapered nose of a missile.

CHAPTER TWENTY-THREE

During the next half hour, Bolan found three more underground silos of the same pattern, each with a missile in place.

No prizes now for guessing where the stolen uranium 235 ended up. He didn't like to think of the nuclear ramifications that might be going on somewhere below his feet.

No prizes either for guessing why General Halakaz and his sidekick were so confident of victory in their struggle against the rulers in Khartoum.

But who was helping them . . . and why?

Because this was a worldwide operation. This was no crazy plan dreamed up by a few hundred guerrilla irregulars, however efficient their parade-ground drill might be, however much their families learned about the splitting of the atom in school. An organization that could mastermind thefts from heavily guarded reactors in Britain, the Soviet Union and the United States, and activate blocking tactics smart enough to outwit investigators all along the line, had to have almost unlimited funds available . . . and a network of ruthless operators on the payroll way beyond anything the South Sudanese rebel leader could conceive.

The Executioner was thoughtful indeed as he arrived back at the edge of the airstrip. There was a lot more legwork to be done before he decided what action to take, if any.

Maybe he should simply report his findings, refer the matter back to Brognola at Stony Man and let the Fed take it from there.

He was staring into the heat haze shimmering over the concrete strip when he became aware of a persistent, low roaring noise that had for some time been forcing its way into his consciousness. It had nothing to do with the faint mechanical sound he had sensed with his ear to the ground during his recon of the roadway.

He looked up. Above the forest trees away to his left, another kind of haze hung in the air, halfway between a mist and a cloud of thin smoke. He decided to check it out.

The noise increased in volume as he approached. The undergrowth became denser and more luxuriant. The mist resolved itself into a curtain of spume hanging above a waterfall.

Bolan fought his way closer. It was in any case too hot now to venture out into the full glare of the sun by the runway.

That was some waterfall!

The breadth and scale of it amazed him. The river, shallow and fast moving, was much wider than he would have expected. It flowed across a plateau whose existence he had not suspected, divided around a number of islets on the lip of the falls and then twisted away down a steep-sided canyon—perhaps to vanish underground and reappear lower down the valley in which Oloron was built?

The falls were staggering: a semicircle of separate cascades that roared over a fifty-foot ledge between the islands, coalesced in a turbulent pool and then leaped in a single great waterspout over a sheer cliff fully one hundred feet high.

For some minutes Bolan remained fascinated by the grandeur of the scene, his senses battered into quiescence by the volume of sound. Then, as his mind automatically began accepting, rejecting, sifting the evidence offered to his eyes and ears, he noticed a discrepancy.

Surely the flow of water frothing away from the foot of that last waterfall was appreciably...no, markedly less than the amount arriving at the top?

The more he looked, the more obvious it became. Maybe this was one of the places quoted by Trudi Finnemann, where the greater part of the river did vanish underground into a subterranean channel hollowed from the limestone. He scanned the falls, searching for some trace of a sink-hole. It must be someplace in that seething basin that sep-arated the cascades and the final, single fall over the cliff.

Behind several of the initial cascades he could make out dark openings breaching the hollowed rock.

There was something else, too.

Unmistakably he could see patches of concrete among the glistening rock faces. Somewhere behind those deafening cascades, man had been improving on the works of nature!

Concealing the M-16, the binoculars and his rucksack in a clump of bushes, Bolan scrambled down a narrow path zigzagging the steep bank above the pool. In two minutes he was drenched to the skin. But after the fierce heat of the day, the dank, ferny atmosphere of the ravine and the moisture of the spray were as refreshing as a cool drink. Slipping and sliding on the wet moss covering the rocks lower down, he reached the level of the basin.

The surface of the water was in a tumult, shading from acid green near the foaming impact of the cascades to a deep violet in the center of the pool. And once he approached he could see at once that his reasoning was correct. The water spilling over the lip and falling one hundred feet to the gorge below was nothing more than an overflow; by far the greater part swirled back from the bottom of the pool to go racing down a series of conduits slanting into the rock behind the cascades.

As he expected, the falls over the centuries had hollowed out an overhang in the cliff, and it was possible to walk along a shelf between the curtain of falling water and the rock face. Treading with infinite care, he edged along the slimed ledge behind the first cascade, slithered across an open space and ducked behind the second.

Here were two of the conduits—giant ferroconcrete tubes ducting the water into the bowels of the earth at an angle of sixty degrees. Crossing the deep channels that led the twin torrents from basin to conduit were small arched bridges with single guardrails.

Behind the third falls, Bolan found three conduits, similarly linked by concrete bridges. But here the one in the center was larger, a vaulted tunnel with the water thundering down a course laid in its floor. At the far end of the tunnel he could see light, the curved corners of huge turbines, the base of a generator.

He had clearly come across a vast underground power station, the source, he imagined, of the electricity lighting the road tunnel and of the vibrations he had sensed nearby.

Soaked as he was, the warrior found himself shivering in the chill, moist semidarkness behind the falls. He never knew what it was that made him look up at that moment. Certainly no sound could have penetrated the ever-present roar of falling water. But he did look up, up and out over the empty cliff face separating the third and fourth cascades.

They were farther apart than the others, these two, and a guardrail snaked across the wet rock at the side of the pathway linking them.

A black soldier in uniform leaned his hips against the rail. There was a submachine gun in his hands and it was trained, from a distance of about thirty feet, on Bolan.

He whipped Big Thunder from its leather and triggered two 240-grain boattails across the space. The soldier's face split open in an O of astonishment, the gun dropping from his hands and slithering down the rock into the pool. For a moment he teetered against the rail, then slowly slumped over it and fell.

One of the Executioner's skullbusters had fisted through the guy's abdomen; the other severed the carotid artery in his neck, and bright blood jetted far out into the cascade as he dropped.

The body sank at once, for the briefest instant staining the foam crimson. Thirty seconds later it reappeared, bobbing like a cork, in the center of the maelstrom.

Bolan expected it to be sucked toward the conduits, but after a while some undercurrent tugged it toward the side of the pool, where it snagged on a branch, freed itself, spun slowly in an eddy and then started to move, remorselessly and with increasing speed, in the direction of the lip and the hundred-foot drop beyond.

He lost sight of it again then, but the dead man made a final horrifying appearance, rearing grotesquely up from the water on the very brink of the chasm before he plunged from sight.

The warrior heaved a sigh of relief. It would be a long time now before his body was recovered, if it ever was. On the other hand, his absence from his post could be noticed at any time. Maybe it would be wiser to leave after all.

Bolan recovered his gear and resumed his route through the forest to the strip.

He became aware of the change when he was still a couple of hundred yards away. The roar of the falls had drowned the engine noise, but a ship had landed while he was checking out the conduits. As he drew nearer he could hear shouted orders, the whine of machinery.

Peering through a screen of creepers, he saw a twin-engined cargo plane parked near the roadway. A squad of soldiers were unloading the cargo into a convoy of half-tracks drawn up on the concrete.

With his wet clothes steaming in the tropic heat, Bolan lay beneath a bush and watched them through his glasses. Most of the cargo was crated, and judging from the way it was manhandled onto the forklifts, the stuff inside was delicate.

Thirty minutes later the transshipment was completed. The freighter trundled back to the far end of the runway, turned and took off. The convoy had already formed and was heading toward the road and the tunnel before the drone of the plane's two engines died away over the forest.

The trucks passed quite close to the Executioner's hiding place. There were six of them—half-tonners with canvas tops painted in drab camouflage—but so far as he could see, only the first three carried guards: tall men with AKMs, one standing on each side of the cab. On an impulse, Bolan rose to his feet and ran through the long grass to intercept them.

He reached the blacktop just as the last truck slowed to turn off the landing strip. Once it was past him, he ran out onto the pavement. In three quick strides he was level with the tailgate. As the vehicle accelerated, he grabbed the hinged panel, pushed aside the canvas flap and hauled himself up and over into the interior. So far, so good!

Two outsized crates filled most of the space inside, stoutly built containers of half-inch boards reinforced with strips of wood on all sides. There were no contents specifications or delivery instructions stenciled on the wood.

Other than these crates, the truck was empty. And Bolan was thankful that there was no window between the back and the driver's cab. He settled down behind the crates to wait.

He had no idea of what he was going to do when the truck stopped, but he wanted in. He wanted action at close quarters; he was tired, however hectic it had been, of operating on the fringe of the mystery.

Identify, infiltrate, destroy. Okay, he was past the first hurdle created by that guerrilla's creed: identification completed.

The time had come to infiltrate.

And the truck was one way of getting past the guards at the tunnel mouth.

After that?

Well, it was unlikely they would search their own vehicles after such a short trip. He was gambling that he would find an opportunity to slip out unnoticed before the cargo was unloaded.

Soon the floor tilted as the truck began to sink below ground level. The beat of the exhaust and the rattle of the caterpillar half-tracks echoed back from the stone walls dipping toward the tunnel.

They drove straight past the guards. For some time the truck continued to descend in a series of tight curves, then the road flattened out and they drove straight ahead for what seemed about a quarter of a mile. Finally the half-track made a right-hand turn, braked, backed up, stopped again. The driver cut the engine, and the truck rocked as he jumped out, a second time when his mate quit the cab. Two doors slammed.

Bolan's first impression was that of noise, a huge swell of sound that echoed back and forth between the walls of whatever underground fortress they had entered. He could identify the boots of the soldiers as they clambered down from the trucks, a distant hammering, the pervasive hum of machinery, a confusion of voices calling. Inching forward between the crates, he put his eye to the crack between the truck's tailgate and the canvas flap.

The vehicle was drawn up with the other five half-tracks in a bay off an immense cavern in the rock. Both the roof and the farther reaches of the vast chamber were lost in shadows. Nearer, a battery of arc lights blazed on workmen erecting some complicated apparatus from a scaffold.

Beyond a stack of crates similar to those in the truck, an arch in the limestone led to another cavern that was even bigger. In the bright light that shone through, Bolan could see figures in shiny decontamination suits and protective helmets busy around the spirals of great cooling tubes. On one side, a section of a gigantic silver sphere—a cyclotron? a synchrotron?—bulged into view.

The convoy drivers and the escorting guards were grouped around an officer issuing instructions, their backs turned toward the parking bay.

This was Bolan's chance.

Raising the flap as little as possible, he dropped to the ground and slid around to the front of the truck. Here, out of sight of the soldiers, he crouched between the radiator and the rock wall, looking for a place to hide.

A little way to his left, hidden from the men in the cavern by another truck, a six-foot archway had been cut into the wall. It was closed off by a steel door.

The warrior edged along to it, listened, reached out to try the handle. The door was unlocked. He turned the handle, ducked his head and slipped through into a long passage with closed doors on either side.

Electric bulbs glowed in the low roof. At the far end, an opening led to the dark reaches of another cave. The humming noise was much louder now. He had to be approaching part of the generating station he had seen from behind the falls.

The Executioner stole down the corridor and into the cave. It was empty and unlit, but through it was yet another chamber hollowed from the rock. And here, sure enough, reflected light gleamed on the squat shapes of turbines and transformers.

He hesitated. Should he hide in this empty cavern, or would it be better to risk discovery and return to the cave where the action was, hoping to find some place of concealment there?

Perhaps the latter. Because then he might be able to emerge and check the place out systematically when work had stopped for the day.

First, though, he had to hide, at least temporarily, his backpack and the M-16. It wouldn't be smart to try to steal through a heavily guarded fortress with a three-foot automatic rifle slung across his back.

Partway into the cave, he found a niche in the rock wall where he could lean the gun and stow the pack.

He turned and stole back to the lighted passageway.

General Halakaz stood just inside the entrance, a heavy Smith & Wesson Combat Magnum in his hand.

"Not many white rhino down here," he said mildly. "I think you and I had better have a little talk, old chap."

PART THREE

DESTRUCTION

The black sergeant leaning against the barrier pole at the Sudanese frontier was dead.

The body, stiff with rigor mortis, had been fixed there with a loop of rope. The entrance wound was clean, and the little blood staining the khaki bush jacket was lost among the soldier's medal ribbons. The exit wound beneath the left shoulder blade was something else, but Jason Mettner didn't find that out until later.

At first, bringing the Chevrolet Blazer to a stop ten yards from the pole, Mettner didn't make the connection. He was within a few feet of the corpse, his ID and accreditation held out, when realization hit him. With an exclamation, he ducked beneath the pole and hurried to the guard hut.

The stench of recent death met him at the door.

The five men in there among the overturned chairs and shattered table were all naked from the waist down. Each had been castrated. The newspaperman thought they had been killed by gunfire, but he didn't wait to find out. He lit a cigarette and went back outside.

The other huts had all been sacked. Everything in them was destroyed—bedding ripped, furniture hacked, mirrors smashed. Seven more black soldiers lay dead below the back wall of the last hut. White splinters pricked out of the dark wood showed where the execution squad's bullets had slammed into the wall.

Mettner shuddered and returned to the road. Should he pick up one of the rubber stamps from the guardhouse floor and frank his own passport?

Maybe not. If he ran into the murderers, a stamp originating apparently from their enemies could turn out to be a death warrant for him, too.

He shoved the papers back in his pocket, figuring the smartest thing he could do would be to get the hell out. The attack must have been very recent: the fact that the bodies were still locked in rigor mortis testified to that.

· But there was no question of backing off.

He raised the barrier pole gingerly.

The body of the sergeant slid to the ground, bounced once in the dust and turned onto its face. Mettner averted his eyes from the cloud of flies that had been clustered over the raw wound in the man's back, and dragged the body into the guard hut with the others. There was nothing else he could do.

He climbed back into the Blazer, drove past the upraised pole and stepped hard on the accelerator to send the vehicle careering along the rough trail leading to the interior.

Four hours later, halfway across the thorn tree desert, he saw the unmistakable outline of a Land Rover silhouetted against the glare of the sun.

It was parked about ten yards off the trail, apparently undamaged. Mettner slid the Blazer to a halt in a shower of gravel. He walked across to the vehicle, taking a notebook from his pocket. The registration numbers tallied; this was the vehicle Mack Bolan had rented. But there was no sign of the Executioner.

He leaned on the horn button. The two-tone blast died away beneath the thorn trees, but nobody came running; the shimmering desert floor stayed silent and empty beneath the pitiless sun.

The keys were still in the ignition, so he tried to start the engine.

Zero.

Okay, enough juice to sound the horn; electrical systems go...but a dead engine and a blocked starter. In other words, mechanical breakdown.

Where had Striker gone? Had he been picked up? Would he have been crazy enough to walk? Was he lying some-place nearby, a victim of the sun?

Mettner got back behind the wheel of his own vehicle. He turned up the air-conditioning and cruised around the stalled off-roader in widening circles for twenty minutes.

No Bolan.

Frowning, he returned to the trail.

Forty-five minutes later he stopped by the second Land Rover. Clearly there had been a storm recently in this part of the desert. Sand and gravel lay piled against the wheels on the western side, the seats were covered in stones, the soft top hung in tatters from the iron frame. Many of the trees were uprooted.

Once more Mettner clambered out into the heat, but he couldn't find a clue by the abandoned off-roader. For the second time he cruised.

He was maybe two-hundred yards away to the east when a flash of bright light caught his eye. The lid of an open to-bacco can was reflecting the sun's rays. The can was empty.

Mettner shrugged. Maybe, maybe not. He made a more detailed search of the immediate area on foot. He found a tube of antihistamine tablets, unused, among the roots of an upended tree, a limp scrap of plastic sheeting impaled on a thorn, a broken button compass. They might signify Bo-lan, they might not. The compass, certainly, had not been lying long in the desert because the bright metal casing was untarnished.

The newspaperman decided to go on looking, limiting his search to the eastern side of the Land Rover. He got back in the Blazer and slammed it into first.

He was ready to call the whole thing off when he saw the clincher. It was caught in the branches of a thorn tree fifty yards away, a dark amorphous shape he figured at first for a dead bird. He was within ten yards before he tumbled.

Hanging from a thorny spike, he saw a formfitting blacksuit, a one-piece garment suitable for a man around six feet tall.

That did it!

Like Kilroy, Bolan had been here.

But where was he now? It didn't take the brainpower of a genius—a smartass foreign correspondent would do quite well—to work out that the items Mettner found had been carried there by the storm. It was reasonable to suppose that Bolan might have been sheltering by the second Land Rover when the storm broke.

So why wasn't he wearing this blacksuit at the time?

Well, he sure wasn't taking a shower before dressing for dinner, Mettner thought sourly, staring at the barren wilderness surrounding him. Maybe he was too hot; maybe he was resting and got hit by a daytime storm.

Maybe. But that didn't get him any closer to the Executioner's whereabouts right now. And there were no clues around the wreck itself from which he could make any kind of deduction.

The one thing he did see—a punctured condom, shriveled by the sun, half buried in a drift of fine gravel—left him puzzled, but none the wiser.

Sweating in the ferocious heat, he returned to the Blazer, lit a cigarette and continued his journey north along the desert trail.

It was dusk when he reached the water hole, stampeding a herd of gazelles, two prowling hyenas and a great cloud of birds. Where the track divided some way beyond, a pile of stones blocked the left-hand fork. He lifted his foot, shrugged and then swung the wheel to the right. When you were driving blind, one road was as good as another.

Like the geological expedition before him, he stopped for the night at the head of the steep-sided gorge that snaked through the jungle. The spring that issued there from a limestone outcrop had hollowed out a grotto that served as a natural shelter and a refuge from the attentions of monkeys, bats and other nocturnal denizens of the jungle.

Mettner had no idea where he was going. He was following the only clue he had.

The man at the Niangara general store who had tanked up the Land Rover with gas and loaded the supplies had been precise enough with his description—and sufficiently observant—to convince the newspaperman that Bolan and Belasko were one and the same. He knew that the Land Rover was heading north for the Zaire-Sudan frontier because Bolan-Belasko had asked his advice on the best routes to take.

He wouldn't have known that the Executioner had already quit the Sudanese southwest via the Central African Republic, or wondered why he should have detoured south through Zaire before he went back there. Mettner himself could supply the answer to that one: Striker had escaped via helicopter into the CAR; if he reentered the Sudan from that direction, there was more risk that they would be waiting for him someplace along the route.

Whoever "they" were.

What the storekeeper did know was that the driver of the Land Rover had asked a pesky lot of questions about some

armpit shantytown called Oloron, and that he was as mad
as hell because it wasn't shown on his map.

"Maps!" the storekeeper told Mettner. "We keep the best
maps you can get around here. But we're not trying to provide a yard-by-yard survey of the whole equatorial jungle.
That's guerilla country up there in the Sudan. They burn the
towns soon as they build them! How can you expect to find
places on a map where nobody has ever been?"

Mettner didn't know, but he was convinced that was
where the Executioner would be. He had bought the best
map the storekeeper could provide and followed in Bolan's
footsteps.

But it was not until he found the blacksuit that he had any
indication this was something more than a newsman's
hunch.

He took the one-piece combat garment along with him.
The material was dusty but undamaged except for one place
where a thorn had ripped the shoulder.

Mettner left the grotto at dawn, easing the Blazer slowly
along the narrow jungle track. Within a half hour briars and
spines and whippy branches had scratched the paint from
both sides of the vehicle. He had to wait three times that
long before he received further proof that he was on the
right track.

It wasn't the kind of proof he expected. He saw a baboon sitting in the center of the trail, playing with what
looked like a camera.

The Chevy rocked to a halt, and Mettner got out. The
baboon, screaming with rage, swung away into the treetops.

The camera was left lying on the trail. It was broken, the
case deformed, the lens missing, the minor controls
wrenched off. But it was a Hasselblad.

Mike Belasko, photographer.

Mettner made short forays into the dense undergrowth on either side of the trail. Soon he found the rock shelf and a bullet-riddled bedroll beneath it.

He hesitated. Things didn't look too good.

It was then that he heard the whistle, a shouted exchange in a dialect he was unfamiliar with, a stammer of shots from a submachine gun on the trail. Glass tinkled from the direction in which he had left the Blazer. A moment later there was the *whoomp* of a gasoline explosion, a blast of hot air and a view through the close-packed leaves of flames boiling around the forest trees.

Mettner dived beneath the rock shelf and pulled the damaged bedroll over himself.

CHAPTER TWENTY-FIVE

"It would be easier for everybody, old chap, if you would just come across and spill the beans," General Halakaz said to Bolan. They were sitting in a small office off the corridor that led to the reactor. Papers covered the flat-topped desk that separated them. The rock walls were hung with production charts and graphs, and there was a plaster relief map of the Sudan and surrounding countries on one side of the door. The general's Combat Magnum lay heavily among the papers by his right hand.

"There's not much to tell, really," Bolan replied. "I guess I have to plead guilty to being inquisitive. I was trying to locate my partner, Courtney—I explained this to one of your colonels who I ran into earlier—and I came across an airstrip and then a road.... Well, I got real curious when I discovered these in the middle of an unexplored forest."

"I am listening."

"Yeah. Well, the next thing I discovered was a silo. With a missile." Bolan turned down the corners of his mouth in a grimace, and contrived a shrug. "Not that I was spying, but I damn near fell into it. I mean, can you blame a guy for looking around some, after that?"

"But I found you in here, old chap. In here. The place is closely guarded, you know. Very closely guarded."

"That was unintentional. I didn't mean to come in here. How could I? I didn't know the place existed."

"Unintentional?"

"I was bushed. A convoy of trucks passed me and I . . . well, I stole a ride. I swung aboard the back of the last one just as it passed me."

"Just as it passed you. I see. You didn't know where the convoy was headed—you didn't know where you were going—but you stole a ride." Halakaz shook his head, shooting a shrewd glance at the Executioner from beneath his brows. "Mr. Belasko, you had a vehicle of your own when I met you. A Land Rover, as I recall."

"It died on me. In the middle of the desert. I had to decide whether to go on or go back. On foot. I decided to press on. I can show you the blisters if you want." For some reason Bolan was unwilling to involve Trudi Finnemann and her expedition in his cover story. Hell, it was his party; there was no reason to lay anything on them.

"We can do without the blisters, old chap." Halakaz picked up the AutoMag he had taken from Bolan, weighing it in his hand. "My people have strict orders to exclude all strangers from a forest area ten miles across—with this place, of course, as its center. What a coincidence that you should arrive just when we are missing a sentry from the cascades and three of our jungle guards are discovered shot!" He looked down at the AutoMag. "Shot, as I understand, with a large-bore handgun."

"I don't know anything about that," Bolan lied.

"Perhaps. This truck in which you, uh, stole a ride. What did you find inside it?"

"It was a half-track. It was carrying two unmarked crates."

"Yes?"

"When the truck stopped, I waited a minute and then I got out. I could see at once that I was somewhere I had no right to be, so naturally I figured I better leave as quickly as possible. I was trying to find the exit when you found me."

The general turned the AutoMag over and over in his hands, as if he were examining it for hidden flaws. "You have indeed stumbled on something that does not concern you, Mr. Belasko," he said at last. "Although 'stumbled' is hardly the right word, is it? Because I do not for a moment believe your story. Nevertheless, we are ready to strike within the next few days. In a week, we shall be masters of the whole Sudan, probably the whole of Africa."

Bolan said nothing. The man's voice was tinged with pride. It was a good time to clam up, in the hope that he would start spilling secrets.

"Perhaps, therefore, your unwelcome arrival does not matter so much," the general continued. "But I have a feeling.... Highly placed officials of the organization assisting us are due to show up shortly. The decision must be theirs. But I fear they may think you have learned more than is good for you. And even if your life is spared, you will have to stay here as our—shall we say guest?—until after the great day."

"It sounds intriguing," Bolan prompted.

"Intriguing? My dear fellow, if only you knew! Do you realize how much work, how much planning has gone into this?"

"Just building this underground complex must have presented enormous difficulties."

"But of course. There were the natural caverns to start with. We had the advantage of knowing about them. But our friends had to fly in vast quantities of material undetected, instruct the labor force we provided and supervise every stage of the construction. It was a fantastic task. For three years we have been slaving underground here. Three years, old chap. Because the place has to be invisible from the air, you see. The Arabs have reconnaissance planes that fly frequently over Oloron."

"There is certainly no sign of construction work on the surface," Bolan encouraged, "but what about the airstrip?"

"What about the airstrip?" Halakaz echoed. "You'd think it could be seen for miles, wouldn't you?" He was as boastful as a child with a new toy. "Undetectable from the air. Not a sign. From the ground it looks like any runway, but we had the greatest camouflage expert in Europe, an expatriate Russian. Since there are no buildings to cast shadows, you see, skillful variations of tone and texture in the cement mix can blend it perfectly with the surroundings."

"You've been very clever, General."

"Clever? This is only the beginning. We have a cyclotron, and we are building a synchrotron that will have an energy level of ten thousand million electron-volts! That has to wait until we enlarge the caverns still further, because the ring of tubing must be one hundred meters in diameter. But in a year we shall have completed a fast-breeding reactor using tamed plutonium and liquid sodium. Then we shall be able to dispense with the outdated hydroelectric plant, which always risks detection by people exploring the falls.

"After that, of course, we shall be masters, our own masters, at every stage of our weapons program. Right now we have to rely on, er, outside sources for certain isotopes."

Bolan said, "You mention a strike in the near future. If all this is to help you best your enemies in Khartoum, the…organization helping you must be altruistic. What do they get out of it?"

The sixty-four-dollar question. But did he know?

"I said 'organization,'" Halakaz replied. "I use the word loosely. It is, in fact, a consortium of powerful men. And of course, as you imply, it's a two-way deal. In return we pro-

vide free labor, a very discreet site in which certain researches can be carried out unhampered by official
interference and—once we take over the country—the
granting of invaluable mining concessions in what are at the
moment still desert regions.''

Bolan sighed. Mining concessions! ''The missiles I saw,''
he began. ''Your own men are in charge of targeting and
firing?''

''Well, no, old chap. At the moment white technicians
supplied by our friends look after them. We haven't yet acquired the know-how to man the computer room and the
control dugouts. But we are training, we are training. Part
of my force is seconded to a special course in Oloron, at the
foot of the ravine beyond this plateau. There are supple-
mentary courses for the nonmilitary in various outlying villages.''

Bolan nodded, remembering the nuclear formulae in the
gutted classroom, the burned-out huts and the impaled
teacher.

''The accursed Arabs sacked one not too far from here
some days ago,'' Halakaz said, as if reading his thoughts.
''Purely by coincidence, I hope. But they will pay. The time
will soon come—''

A telephone on the desk shrilled him into silence.

''You must forgive me,'' he said when he had listened for
a few moments, made a comment in his native language and
hung up the receiver. ''The members of the consortium I
mentioned have arrived, so I must leave you.''

He holstered his revolver and picked up the AutoMag.
''There are, as you see, no other doors, no means of exit
from this office. The door through which I leave is solid and
will be double-locked. Also there are two armed men on
duty outside.'' He smiled. ''My advice to you, old chap, is
to make yourself comfortable and sit tight until I return.''

Covering the Executioner with his own automatic, Ismael Halakaz backed from the room.

Bolan began to say something and then thought better of it. If this somehow likable patriot had not yet realized that his poor little six-thousand-strong army, his labor force of refugees from the destroyed villages, his offer of mineral concessions, were factors of no importance in some immeasurably vaster project, his awakening would come soon enough.

For Bolan was enough of an expert in modern warfare to know already that Halakaz and his men were being duped.

The missiles whose sleek streamlined shapes he had seen in their silos were no tactical pieces of atomic artillery designed to obliterate Khartoum and its Arab rulers; they were IRBMs, intermediate-range ballistic missiles capable of taking out London, Paris, Rome or Kiev.

CHAPTER TWENTY-SIX

If Bolan had any doubts concerning his reasoning, they were dispelled the moment he laid eyes on "the high-ranking members" of the consortium financing Halakaz and his nuclear arsenal.

Jazzy neckties, striped shirts, white vicuña jackets and two-tone shoes competed with the glitter of rings and the gleam of gold chains. Even the general's habitual spit and polish seemed dowdy in comparison.

They crowded into the office behind Halakaz—a blue-chinned torpedo, another with his arm in a sling, the broken-nose goon who had attacked Bolan in Marseilles and finally the hire-and-fire supremos.

Don Carlo Giovanni and Louis Mancini: the capo of capos and his sidekick; number one and number two of all the East Coast mobs, with controlling interests among the families running Detroit, Chicago, Vegas and the West.

If the bosses of the underworld were turning their backs on prostitution, dope, financial rackets and the protection game in order to go nuclear, Bolan knew that Brognola had been right: there was a situation here that could turn out as dangerous as the Cuban missile crisis, a conspiracy so evil that it could be a potential threat to world peace.

Especially since the mobsters already had their nuclear "persuaders" in place.

Bolan wondered if he could provoke them into revealing the real targets programmed into the sleek and deadly missiles hidden in those silos. And if so, whether they would come across with the purpose of the blackmail operation, the details of what they hoped to gain.

Because nobody could kid him the plot had anything to do with freedom fighters or political clout or military advantage: he knew the Mob too well for that. They didn't help people out; they didn't give a damn for causes. If Giovanni was concerned, there had to be a shakedown someplace in the scenario. And the end product would inevitably be money. Give, brother... or else.

How the Executioner was going to react if he did find out those things, and what means he had available for wrecking the plan... He'd attend to that when the time came.

Right now there were more immediate problems.

Like how to stay alive with Giovanni on the scene.

The capo had stopped dead the moment he laid eyes on the warrior. His flinty expression hardened, and his mouth twisted into a snarl. "It's him, all right," he said through clenched teeth. "I'd know those ice eyes anywhere, Lou. I only saw him behind a shooter before, but this time it's going be different. This time I'm in the driving seat!"

"So you know Mr. Belasko already?" General Halakaz asked.

"Belasko? I don't know any damn Belasko. The name of that man there in the chair is Bolan, and I got good reason—"

"It says Belasko on his papers."

"I don't give a damn what it says on his papers. Haven't you heard of phony ID? Look, I'm telling you I know this man, and the first thing I'm going to do down here is find out who the hell put him up to this, then get the other creeps who are working with him."

"You still want to handle this yourself, Don Carlo?" Mancini queried. "I mean, we got work to do. Maybe we should hand it over—"

"Shut up, Lou. If I need your advice, I'll ask for it. Damn right I'm going to handle it myself, and it'll be a pleasure." Giovanni turned to the blue-chinned gorilla. "Go fetch me some tools to work with, Joe. I'll want a whip made with fine wires, an electric cattle prod, a bench vise, a strong pair of tweezers, a box of matches and a cutthroat razor."

The hood nodded and left the office.

While the door was still open two black officers in uniform entered the room. Bolan recognized Colonel Mtambole and the man who had captured and then tortured him after he had been decoyed by the fake canister in the camel train.

"So you got him back?" this last man said. "That's good. Maybe we can find out a little more about his . . . prospecting now."

"You should have found out everything the first time," Giovanni growled. "When you came to my place in Miami, you promised me results. All I got was a name . . . and the good news that the bastard had split. Big deal."

"Colonel Ogada was unfortunate," Halakaz soothed. "Bolan had an accomplice. He lowered a rope outside the window of his cell. It couldn't have been foreseen, old chap."

"Of course he had an accomplice! Or two or three!" the Mafia boss shouted. "The punk stowed the beeper on that camel for one. That was what you was supposed to squeeze out of this bastard—who, how many and where. But you had to let him fly before you made him sing."

"A business is properly run, nothing is unforeseen," Mancini said. "You couldn't spare a soldier to guard the roof? You didn't think to tie the guy up so he couldn't *make* the damn window?"

Bolan kept his eyes fixed on the floor. He was learning all the time. Like there was already tension between the mafiosi and the Africans. Like it wasn't exactly smart of Giovanni to treat Halakaz and his men like dirt. Not yet, anyway. He wondered what they would say if they knew his "accomplice" was a teenage Arab kid who'd helped out as a favor to his sister!

"What's this prospector thing, then?" Mtambole asked. "Man here is the picture-snatcher, Belasko. The animal photo guy."

"Bullshit!" Ogada retorted. "Bolan. A Russki. He had some kind of laissez-passer from Khartoum. It was signed—"

"I know what I'm saying, man!" Mtambole snatched off his beret and thwacked it against his thigh. "Hell, didn't I spend half a morning trying to talk him out of this crazy trip? He could be the accomplice you're talking about, for all I know. But—"

"For Chrissake!" Giovanni yelled. "Can't you get it into your skulls that Bolan and Belasko are one and the same? Jesus, what do I have to do to knock sense into your heads? It's the *other* guy we want to know about, the one with the damn caravan. And me, I'm going to choke everything there is to know out of this creep right now."

He plunged a hand into the side pocket of the white jacket and drew out a set of brass knuckles. "You guys—" he nodded at Mancini and Broken-nose "—hold him good while I read the first part of the lesson."

The two hoods stepped swiftly in, pinioned Bolan's arms and jerked him to his feet.

Bolan tensed, watching the black hairs on the backs of Giovanni's fingers slide through the openings in the knucks.

"Be proud of your partners, General . . ." the warrior began. And then doubled up choking as one of the two-tone shoes slammed into his crotch.

As his head came forward, the capo hauled off and crashed a murderous roundarm blow to the side of his jaw. Bolan felt the blood warm on his face as his cheek split open. Then a second punch, an uppercut with all Giovanni's weight behind it, exploded beneath his chin and snapped his head back. He sagged, and for a moment the room went dark.

"Okay, take him away," the Mafia boss said. "Maybe we'll stick a meat hook under his shoulder blade later on, and hang him up smeared with honey for the ants. But today I want him laid out nice and tidy, like a fish on a slab. You dig?"

Mancini nodded, and the Executioner was dragged from the room. When he was near the doorway he saw a smirk on the face of the hood whose arm was in a sling, and realized suddenly why the brutish face with its hairline mustache was familiar. This was the guy who had murdered Ahmed Ibrahim in Marseilles, the guy Bolan had winged after the car chase in Alexandria.

The clans were gathering.

Two minutes later Bolan was thrown violently into a chamber cut from the solid rock...and found himself sprawled at the feet of Mahmoud, the camel master.

The man's lips split into a smile, showing yellowed tombstone teeth. "Welcome home," Mahmoud said. "Last time you walked out before the party was over. Maybe now we can persuade you to stay a while longer?"

Bolan said nothing. Mahmoud was the only person there who could tie in the bogus Russian prospector with the "Arab" spy he had caught prowling around the camel train at Wadi Djarzireh. Admittedly he'd assumed the spy was searching for the homer rather than putting it in place, but it didn't take a genius to make the connection once the subject of a missing accomplice was raised.

How come he'd never gotten around to it?

Probably, Bolan reckoned, because nobody had thought to ask him. Also there was the question of language. The camel master spoke French but he had no English and Colonel Ogada had conducted his interrogation in English. Intent about his job as torturer, Mahmoud must have missed out on the drift of the officer's questions; perhaps he thought Ogada was concentrating on the question of Bolan's supposed employers.

One thing was certain: as long as the bosses didn't get wise to the fact that the accomplice was a myth, Bolan would be kept alive.

It wouldn't be the good life, just the same.

"Get this one ready for a session with the *patron*," Mancini said in heavily accented French.

"Pick him up then, and let me put him in the right state of mind," Mahmoud growled.

The two hoods dragged Bolan to his feet and held him while the camel master flattened his hand and rabbit-punched the warrior into unconsciousness.

He regained his senses in total darkness. His head ached like hell, he had been stripped again and he was spread-eagled with his wrists and ankles wired to the four corners of a flat wooden surface, probably a table. A cool draft played over the surface of his body, and the darkness vibrated with the hum of nearby machinery.

Bolan shuddered, listening to the hoarse rasp of his own breathing. He knew that the things Giovanni would do could be much worse than any tortures he had suffered so far, because the hood's aim would be to destroy him psychologically; and he would be enjoying it while he did it, exulting over each new twist of cruelty as the idea came to him. Bolan hoped he would be able to hold out long enough without breaking...long enough, anyway, for unconsciousness to save him again.

Somebody was in the room.

He closed his eyes against the blackness, nerving himself for the unexpected assault, tensing his muscles in anticipation of pain, the searing bolt of agony that would flame through him...where?

Was this Giovanni's first line of attack, the mental anguish of waiting, sightless, dreading the blow, the stab, the jolt of electricity that might come anytime, anywhere?

He could hear breathing above and behind him.

He was unable to repress a start as fingers touched his skin, testing the wire that cut into his left wrist. Prepare for the first blow now? In the belly? The genitals?

Negative.

There was something strange here. The fingers were soft. The wire was loosened; his wrist was free. He smelled a cloying, exotic perfume.

Opening his eyes, Bolan saw the darkness dissolved in the faint illumination cast by a penlight. "You are very pretty like that," a voice murmured in his ear, "but I could admire you better in another place at another time. Come, do you wish to stay here until they return?"

His arms were free. He brought them down to his sides and pushed himself into a sitting position. In the dim light he saw an Arab woman crouched beside the table, her eyes glittering at him over a veil as she untwisted the wires at his feet with a pair of pincers. He recognized her at once.

"Yemanja!" he exclaimed. "What are you doing here? How did you get here?"

"Talk later," she said urgently. "Help me unwind this one. There. I saw them carrying you in here, and I knew what would happen."

Painfully Bolan swung his feet to the floor, his limbs agonizing as the blood coursed back through the veins. He took two steps toward his clothes, where they had been dropped in a corner, and almost fell. There was a thundering behind his eyes, and his head was spinning. Yemanja darted across and snatched up bush shirt, pants and money belt. Big Thunder and the quick-draw rig were presumably in the general's office. "Quick!" she whispered, climbing onto the table. "They will be back any minute now."

In a daze, the warrior watched as she leaned forward and reached up to push at a grating set high in the rock wall. The grille swung away with a metallic scrape. She tossed clothes and belt into the dark opening beyond and hauled herself up after them.

Bolan picked up the penlight and followed, clambering stiffly onto the table and grasping the hands held out to him. He made the climb with difficulty and lay gasping for breath while Yemanja lowered the grating back in place.

They were in a tunnel hollowed out of the rock. It was about three feet high, and there was a moist breeze blowing from somewhere ahead. "Air-conditioning!" the woman murmured. "Very up-to-date, no? Put your things on and follow me."

Bolan squirmed into the pants and shirt after he had buckled on the belt, crawling after her along the damp, rough floor. The tiny light he still held in one hand sent grotesque shadows leaping ahead of them as he moved, and struck gleams of color from the crystals embedded in the rock.

After a while, the passage joined another, wider tunnel, and they were able to raise themselves into a crouch and advance more quickly. Judging by the drafts he felt occasionally against his feet, Bolan guessed there were a number of small subsidiary galleries running into this main one.

From someplace in the distance behind them, he heard the muffled sound of voices raised in argument. His absence must have been discovered.

Soon he saw a dim radiance ahead. Five minutes later they were standing upright at last in a cave illuminated by reflected light from a series of radiating tunnels. "Now we stop for a minute and talk," Yemanja said. "But quietly, for sound carries far in the rock."

"Okay," Bolan whispered. "For starters, you tell me a thing or two. Like what is, or was, this place before they started making an atomic power station out of it? How did you get here, and how do you know all about these underground passages?"

"This is the mountain headquarters of the Anya Nya. The caves and passages have been the secret retreat of my people for many hundreds of years. But now their friends from America have built many new things inside the mountain: factories and bombs and places to make electricity. Airplanes come and bring much for this building, but although my people help with the new things they keep secret some of the old. The Americans know nothing of these ancient passages that bring air to the rooms, for example."

"But how do *you* know, Yemanja?"

"I was born in Oloron," she replied. "My father was Assyrian, but my mother she was an Oloron woman. I lived here as a child, before it stopped being a town and became a soldiers' camp, and we had to come into the mountain sometime to escape the Arabs."

"What are you doing here now?"

"Mahmoud has bring me to entertain troops and workers here, along with some other girls. But I know more than others. See—I will show you all parts of the factory."

She took the Executioner's hand and drew him along one of the passages leading from the cave. The light grew brighter as they advanced; the noises of the base increased in volume. He could hear the humming of generators, voices, a truck engine gunned, a whole complex of tapping and hammering. When they passed a row of grilles set low in the rock he saw it was through these that the light was reflected. Below the metal gratings he glimpsed offices, lecture rooms, stores busy with uniformed clerks.

"The Americans *must* know about these grilles," Bolan said. "They know there's air blowing through their offices. They must know where it comes from."

"Of course they know *about* them. But they do not know they are big enough for people to walk in. Many of our own people, even, do not know this."

"Can all the gratings be moved like the one we escaped through?"

Yemanja shook her head. "Only that one. The others are cemented in place, but we left that one in case any of our own men were tortured in the interrogation room and we wished to help them escape.... Look! Now you can see!"

They had come to a wider opening that was set chest-high in the limestone wall. Fifty feet below it was the floor of the huge cavern Bolan had seen when he first penetrated the base. Once more he gazed at the cyclotron, the half-finished cooling tubes, the swarm of men working on the hundred-foot steel sphere of the atom furnace. He saw banks of dials winking with colored pilot lights and, far above, mobile cranes running on rails set in the roof of the cave. Forklifts whined here and there among the army of workmen; in the background, the sinister, streamlined fish-shape of a missile lay along the frame of a low-loader. Behind that, double doors barred entry to another chamber, each door carrying a red-lettered warning in French, Arabic and English:

DANGER! RADIATION HAZARD BEYOND THIS
POINT!
Entry forbidden to personnel not wearing
protective clothing.

Yemanja tugged at the Executioner's arm. "Come," she
whispered. "There is more to see."

She led the way through a maze of passages continually
branching and dividing, rising and falling in the rock. After a quarter of a mile, Bolan noticed that the limestone
visible through the gloom was glistening with moisture, the
air was much colder and a faint roaring noise vibrated all
around them. A few minutes later they were looking over the
edge of a rock gallery at the giant turbines of the power station.

"Yemanja," Bolan called over the thunder of the conduits, "why do you think these people are offering to help
General Halakaz and the Anya Nya? What is all this great
factory for?"

"They say it is to vanquish the Arab government in
Khartoum," the woman replied, her lips close to the warrior's ear. "But they speak with lying voices, I think."

"You're right. These are evil men. Your people are being
fooled. They're being conned into helping with a much
larger conspiracy. As soon as the work is finished, the
Americans will have no further use for them, and they'll be
killed. The secret work of which I spoke is to try to foil this
plan. Will you help me?"

"Am I not helping you already?" Yemanja said simply.
"You are no longer in the interrogation room. That is why
I show you all this."

"Of course you are. I owe you a lot. And I'm very grateful to you and your young brother."

For the first time Yemanja smiled. "He is a good boy, Ali," she said. "You know what he has done with the money you gave him? He has returned to Wadi Djarzireh and bought himself a place in the bazaar where he will sell small things of electricity—" she held up the penlight "—that he buys from a trader bringing a camel train each month from Zaire up to Omdurman."

"I hope he does well," Bolan said. "There are two more things I have to ask you, Yemanja. I've hidden a gun and a small backpack in a cave near the turbines. I have to get them back. But first, won't Mahmoud and the others guess that we escaped through the hinged grating and follow us? If they locked the door when they went out, there's no other way we could have gone."

She shrugged. "Perhaps. But you were securely tied. They might have left the door unlocked. Even if not, if they did open the grating, they could never find their way through these passages, for Mahmoud is not of our people and the others are nothing."

Yemanja paused, the light glistening on a moist lower lip, silhouetting the curve of one breast. White teeth glimmered through the dark. "There is a third question I would be happier to answer," she said, "but I know you will not ask it."

Warm breath played over Bolan's cheek. "Instead—" she sighed "—I will show you the rooms where the important ones, the chiefs of the organization talk."

Once again she led the Executioner down a narrow tunnel in the rock.

METTNER WOULD PROBABLY have missed the airstrip if he hadn't seen the second helicopter land.

He had noticed the first, a big Sikorsky with civil markings, lower itself behind the jungle trees about a mile away,

assuming it to be a fire prevention ship or maybe a recon
chopper for some survey unit. It was only when the Dassault five-seater droned down from the northeast that he
realized the Sikorsky had never taken off again.

The second bird circled and sank from sight; the whine of
the turbojet faded and died. Mettner scrambled to the top
of a rocky knoll, found a sight line between the tree
branches and raised a pair of binoculars to his eyes.

It had been a bitch of a morning. After the Blazer had
been machine-gunned and set on fire, he had stayed a long
time beneath the rock overhang before he dared continue
along the trail. Strangers, it was clear, were discouraged in
this part of the forest. Logically, just the same, there was
nowhere he could go but on. He was unarmed, and his maps
had been in the gutted Chevrolet. At least he knew he was
heading in the right direction; he was following in Bolan's
footsteps. The Hasselblad proved that. What it didn't tell
him was whether Bolan had been in the bedroll when it was
riddled, whether he was wounded or in shape, dead or alive,
a captive or free.

Apart from the news angle, Mettner was man enough to
check out all the options in an attempt to help a guy he knew
and admired. But where did he start? He was not a warlike
man; he recorded wars and disasters, he commented on
them, but he was no participant. He knew nothing of unarmed combat, and the toughest fights he'd ever had were
trying to stop smoking—he'd lost out on that one—and
convincing himself he should say no to a fourth martini at
the press club.

After two hours in the sweltering, humid jungle heat,
faced with a forest glade with three different trails leading
away from it, he felt about ready to quit for the day. Or
forever.

Then the choppers arrived and relieved him of the decision. Two helicopters landing in the same place had to mean at least a helipad.

And civilization?

The binoculars focused on a ravine, a belt of trees beyond it and then an open space. He saw more trees, the two birds parked on what looked like a strip of concrete painted in different greens, a group of men. A turreted command car with a pennant fluttering at the end of a whippy radio antenna rolled into the shot. The men moved toward it.

Mettner adjusted the focus wheel and saw a tall, thin European with graying hair, a dark guy wearing Arab robes and a distinguished-looking middle-aged man in a white suit. They were followed by the chopper pilot and an army officer, leaving a ring of black soldiers to guard the two helicopters. Mettner didn't recognize any of them, but he could see clearly that there were many rows of medal ribbons decorating the officer's chest.

The command car stopped at the edge of the strip. A black officer wearing a red paratroop beret jumped down and shook hands all around. He ushered the visitors into the vehicle, which moved off and disappeared behind a row of trees.

Mettner slid down to the foot of the knoll and began to make his way through the forest toward the ravine. If the mysterious airstrip had anything to do with Hal Brognola's nuclear thefts, then there sure was one hell of a story here!

With boredom, indecision, even caution behind him, he was eager to follow up the trail again. Especially since he was pretty damn sure it was the same trail that would lead him to the Executioner.

Ninety minutes later, he dragged himself over the far edge of the ravine and advanced warily through the trees.

The helicopters still stood at the end of the runway, though the guards, now that the officers had gone, had split up into several groups and stood smoking and talking beneath the trees.

Mettner found the metaled road and followed it on hands and knees behind the screen of bushes. He went beyond the twin tunnels and discovered that the continuation of the road passed close to the falls and eventually wound down a steep hillside to the valley in which Oloron was built.

He pulled a notebook from his pocket, made rough sketches and scribbled some words. There was a blockhouse halfway down the loops of road that zigzagged into the valley, another outside the gates of the town. He returned to the tunnels and saw that each of these was guarded a little way inside the entrance.

If he was going to penetrate whatever it was that lay below the ground, or find his way inside the fortresslike settlement in the valley, it was evident that a lot of legwork would have to be done first.

And if he wasn't going to waste valuable time, he must find out which way the command car had taken the visitors. Were they underground or in the valley?

Whichever, he was convinced that was where the action would be.

He decided to go back to the airstrip and start over. Maybe if he could get near enough he could overhear the soldiers talking and find a lead there.

While he was working his way back through the forest he happened on one of the silos. Whistling softly, Mettner took out his notebook once more.

Later he pushed aside a tangle of undergrowth and walked several times around the circular opening. Surely there was room for a thin man to slide down between the gleaming skin of the missile and the shaft's concrete wall.

He stole back between the trees and began pulling down strands of liana creeper.

Mettner had read somewhere once that lianas had been known to grow as long as three hundred yards—almost one thousand feet. But here in Equatoria the longest he could make was no more than fifteen feet. He stripped off leaves and started plaiting the lengths together. When he reckoned he had enough, he started to join them in order to form a rope.

Scouting expertise from long-forgotten summer camps came back into his mind. A fisherman's knot was best for vines, the sheet bend secured lengths of unequal thickness. Hell, he'd use them both, just to make sure: it was his own life he would be entrusting to them!

By the time he had a rope long enough to reach the bottom of the silo, his hands were raw from handling the tough, woody fibers.

A round turn and two half-hitches anchored the improvised rope to the nearest tree trunk, and then Mettner paid out the rest into the yawning depths of the silo. He tested the first knot with all his strength. It held. He nodded and lowered himself gingerly into the shaft.

Gritting his teeth as the rope bit into his lacerated palms, he let himself down slowly hand over hand. Relief from the wet heat at the surface was immediate, but as he sank past the slender, pointed nose of the missile, the coolness of the air increased to a point where he was shivering.

He was aware of the monstrous power of the fissile material in the warhead separated from him only by a thin shell of . . . what? Titanium? Manganese steel?

Passing the thickest section of the IRBM, just before it tapered slightly toward the finned tail, his shoulders touched the cold greasy surface of the metal and a rash of sweat broke out all over him. He had to drop the last five feet, landing among the network of cables and tubing that fed into the rocket motor.

Mettner looked up past the swelling, menacing shape that towered above him to the thin rim of daylight circling the nose cone. When was he going to feel that humid jungle warmth on his skin again?

He shrugged. What the hell. The die was cast now.

A steel inspection hatch about three feet wide ran in oiled grooves above a nest of brass pipes. It was not locked in place. Mettner eased it up very slowly and stepped through into the passageway carved from the rock beyond.

CHAPTER TWENTY-SEVEN

"I want this first one, the warning, to be dead on time and dead accurate," Don Giovanni said. "There's a lot of guys who put up a lot of money on this deal, and we can't afford any more screwups."

"Your own technicians wrote the programs and installed the guidance systems," General Halakaz replied, glancing at the row of cathode ray screens that stood on either side of the computer console in back of the operations room.

"My men scheduled the last U-235 run," the Mafia boss returned. "But that didn't stop screwups all along the line—in both the outfits we hired to move it." He walked across to the wide control room window and scowled down at the main cavern, where Broken-nose, Joe and the man with his arm in a sling were organizing a search for the Executioner. "And it didn't stop this Bolan from horning in," he said.

"Maybe it was because you did hire two separate teams," Colonel Mtambole offered. "The confusion, I mean. This need-to-know approach works fine maybe in intelligence, but militarily, man, the right hand's got to know what the left is doing."

"Shit," Mancini said, "we got one crew to handle the transport and another to keep the road clear for them, look after the law and take care of people who ask too many questions. They're *supposed* to work in cahoots. And Bolan penetrates one and ducks the other all the way? He pulls this off although the security team *knew*, ever since Marseilles, that the bastard was on the trail?" He raised his arms and let them fall to his sides. "What kind of operation are you guys running, for God's sake?"

"We took him as soon as we knew someone was following up on the caravan," Ogada said.

"Oh, sure. And then you blew it. You let him go before you had him sing."

Giovanni swung away from the window. "You blew it four times," he accused. "When he was trying to locate the beeper, when he tried to rejoin the caravan, in that goddamn hill village and again right here in this base. You let him travel right up through the country, you lay hands on him here and he's still free!"

"Pretty smart work, leaving that door unlocked," Mancini said sourly.

"He was wired up tightly," Ogada said. "They used a mechanical packer to twist those ends. What I mean is, it proves first of all that he does have an accomplice, and second of all that the accomplice is here. If we catch them both, we won't even need to squeeze Bolan to find out who—"

"We've got to know who hired him," Giovanni snarled. "If you punks figure you can hold him long enough for me to work him over."

"Your own men didn't do much better, did they?" Mtambole retorted. "When we called up your helicopter, I mean. The man wasted both the soldiers crewing her, then used the machine to leave the country!"

"That's another thing the bastard has to pay for." Giovanni ignored the criticism. "The pilot was an egghead, one of the best brains the family had on this nuclear scene."

"Gentlemen," Halakaz interrupted, "could we change the disk? All these problems will sort themselves out once these chaps have been caught. And time is short: the ultimatum goes on the air at midnight. Wouldn't it be better if we—"

"That's right," Giovanni cut in. "A final rundown before we press the button. The second chopper should be setting down any time. While we wait for the others, why don't you guys take a look around, check out your end and see that you got all systems go?"

Halakaz nodded, snapped his silver-knobbed cane under his arm, and led the two colonels out of the room.

Giovanni and his sidekick exchanged glances. "When do we give them the bad news?" Mancini asked.

"Not until we're ready to take them out. We need their help right up to the last minute, Lou. We have to have the workers, and we need these creeps to keep the workers in line."

"You don't think they'll get wise when we start the countdown?"

"Nah. If they were smart enough to get wise, they'd have gotten wise long before now. Listen, the tape with the ultimatum punched into it runs through the transmitter at midnight, okay? One time each for Damascus, Tehran, Riyadh, Bahrein, Abu Dhabi and Rotterdam. The general's bringing those tapes with him in the second chopper, right? Halakaz and his boys won't get a chance to give them the once-over because we're keeping them under wraps until H-hour. And the warning nuke, the small warhead targeted on the Gulf refinery to prove we can do what we say, is scheduled for blast-off ten minutes later."

Mancini nodded. "Time enough for the messages to those countries to be received, but too soon for any interception shit if the defenses are alerted. You don't think there's any chance they might tune in to the transmissions?"

"They saw the script of a message they *believe* will be beamed to Khartoum. For my money, Lou, they'll be on such a high, waiting for that first nuke to take out a military airfield at Omdurman, that they won't be listening to any goddamn radio! Any case, we'll have guys covering the radio room."

"Omdurman!" Mancini laughed. It wasn't a pleasant sound. "I want to see their faces when we tell them. I want to see the expressions on their mugs when they know they're going to die."

"There are a whole lot more damn faces I'd rather see in New York, Zurich, Rotterdam and Paris, when they take in that ultimatum and their experts tell them yeah, we can do it. They said they'd obliterate just this one isolated refinery, like as a demonstration, and they did it!"

"You're a brilliant guy, Don Carlo!"

"Ain't it the truth! The only thing is, I can't figure out why I never thought of it before. Hell, it's the only business worldwide we don't have a piece of already." Giovanni fished a cigar from his breast pocket, bit off the end and leaned toward Mancini's gold lighter.

"But it's got to be right one hundred percent this end, Lou," he said between puffs. "So what do you say we run down the whole routine from the top?"

FLAT ON HIS FACE in the three-foot-high rock tunnel behind the grille in the operations room, Mack Bolan caught his breath as the enormity of the Mafia scheme dawned on him.

He had just heard the blueprint for a conspiracy that was, in effect, an extension of the protection racket on a global scale—only instead of saloon keepers, club owners, truckers or amusement concessionaires, this time the bite was being put on an entire industry worldwide.

The plotters were saying to the oil-producing countries of the Middle East, and to the port where the world's biggest oil auctions were held: give us a percentage, cut us in on your profits or we'll nuke you to hell. And here's the proof we can do it.

A "small" H-bomb explosion in one of the Gulf states. Not more than, say, two thousand dead.

Plus the radiation sickness spreading like a deadly cloud over the densely populated countries neighboring the Gulf.

Plus the continuing threat once the deal had been finalized, for the Mob was insatiable and those IRBMs could be retargeted to put the bite on other victims, to lend clout to other forms of blackmail.

Bolan thought that Giovanni had to be out of his mind, and the other Mafia bosses had to be insane to underwrite him. Did they think they could hold the world to ransom indefinitely? Didn't they realize they could be nuked out of existence themselves once Big Business pinpointed their base? They could start World War III if one of the big power watchdogs was a mite too hasty with a finger on the button.

They could start it at eleven minutes past midnight.

There was a clock on the control room wall. Through the mesh of the grating Bolan could see that it was a quarter to six.

Six hours and fifteen minutes to avert catastrophe.

How could it be done? Because it had to be done.

By individual assassination of the leading conspirators? No way.

Yemanja had left him, promising to return with the backpack and the M-16. Big Thunder was in the general's office. And even if they could get that back, there were three militarily trained black guerrillas, five mafiosi and an unknown number of white technicians put in by the Mob, all of whom would have to be eliminated. And Giovanni had said that "the others" were due to arrive from "the second chopper" at any minute.

The warrior figured he'd wait where he was until they showed. He wasn't even going to consider alternatives until he knew just how long the odds against him were.

Ten minutes later, the door of the operations room opened and Colonel Ogada ushered in four men.

Bolan had seen them all before. He recognized the robed man as the distinguished stranger who had ridden at the head of the caravan—and ordered Mahmoud to call off the search after Bolan had been surprised in Wadi Djarzireh. That must have been because he knew about the lead canister, knew it was a decoy and knew arrangements had been made to locate the "spy" later.

The white suit, Bolan saw with astonishment, was worn by Hamid el-Karim.

He was less surprised to see General Hartley. There had to be a mole who was close to Hal Brognola. It had to be someone who was a party to the Fed's briefing of Bolan, who knew the Executioner was on his way to North Africa and who knew enough of his movements to arrange the attempt on his life and tip-off Broken-nose and his companions when that failed.

It was the last of the four big-shot arrivals who caused the Executioner to shake his head in amazement. At first, when talking to Ogada, who had remained in the doorway, the man had the back of his perfectly cut suit turned toward the grating. Then he swung around to face Giovanni and Mancini, and Bolan got a clear view of the too handsome features.

It was David Courtney.

CHAPTER TWENTY-EIGHT

Once the Executioner had seen the strength of the opposition, more pieces of the puzzle fell into place, enough to persuade him that the picture was almost complete.

It was clear, through listening to the conversation of the conspirators in the control room, that Courtney had been responsible for the "minders," and Hamid el-Karim, in association with the man in the djellaba, for the organization of the camel caravan.

Bolan remembered the last words of Ibrahim, the informer who had been murdered in Alexandria. El-Karim, he had said, could supply any papers Bolan wanted, but the warrior was on no account to reveal that he intended to travel with the caravan. When Bolan had asked why not, Ibrahim had started to say "Because he is the man who..." And then the poisoned dart had ended his life.

Evidently, if he had been allowed to complete the sentence, he would have said, "Because he is the man who organizes the caravan and the secret freight it will be transporting."

The Brit, of course, with his CIA connection and his newspaper contacts, was a perfect choice to act as undercover boss of a team briefed to sniff out anyone too curious and eliminate those rash enough to interfere with the uranium transportation.

But however hard they sniffed, they seemed to have lost the scent. For Bolan, apart from his talent for survival, owed his life to a stack of things that were at the same time related and unrelated.

The attacks on him in Marseilles and Alexandria, and the murder of Ibrahim—unless that, too, had really been intended for Bolan—must have been organized by Hartley.

The corrupt atomic expert would have tipped off Courtney that they had failed, that there was a spy checking on the U-235 still at large. Yet, astonishingly, he had failed to quote the warrior's name.

So that Courtney accepted him as a CIA field agent and made no connection with the supposed spy tracking the isotope.

And then?

Courtney, knowing Bolan *as* Bolan, also knew he was hoping to travel with the caravan under an Arab alias.

El-Karim—who also knew Bolan as Bolan but believed him to be a Russian prospector—did *not* know he was intending to latch on to the camel train, or that he had fake Arab papers as well as the laissez-passer he himself had provided.

The key was that Courtney didn't know Bolan knew el-Karim.

And the Sudanese wasn't going to let on that he had lined his own pocket, accepting a bribe to supply bogus papers to a foreigner.

The way it stacked up, then, was that human error—carelessness, inefficiency, greed—compounded by Bolan's own prudence in refusing to confide in Courtney had allowed him to slip through the net.

Just the same, he thought, he should have gotten wise to the Englishman long ago. He had even been suspicious of the richly appointed apartment, the pricey clothes. But he hadn't realized that Courtney's failure even to go through the motions of alerting Langley to a situation he could himself control was symptomatic of a slackness, a slapdash approach that marked everything he handled.

He should have faked some reply to Bolan's radio messages, from the intel he had, instead of ignoring them completely.

He should have invented an explanation for the nonarrival of the gear Bolan ordered from Brognola.

He should in any case have been smart enough to deduce from the text of the messages that Bolan was getting warm, even if he was too dumb to connect the "CIA field agent" with Hartley's spy.

Above all he should have liaised with Hamid el-Karim, so that Ogada and the others escorting the caravan would have known earlier just who they were dealing with.

The giveaway, however, had been right at the beginning, only the warrior hadn't seen it then. Offering Bolan a rundown on the situation in the South, he had shown far too much knowledge of Oloron—a place that wasn't even on the maps.

El-Karim and the mafiosi obviously shared some kind of distrust of Courtney, because a heated argument had broken out in the control room. "You left trailblazers a mile high all over Africa," Giovanni raged. "Paying that cow who worked for the cable office in Zemio to go home to Uganda, for starters. You think that was smart?"

"I wanted to get that bloody newspaperman off our backs," Courtney said sullenly. "He called me in Khartoum and said he wanted to trace Bolan. I'd sent him down to Zaire on a wild-goose chase, just to get him out of the way. Then I figured he might stay there longer, hoping Bolan might turn up, if there was a reservation in his name. So I called Bukama and made one."

"Yeah. From a public hotel in Zemio," Giovanni growled.

"Look, I was in Zemio anyway. Bolan had been there. I'd tracked the helicopter there. I found out he'd bought a bloody Land Rover, so I slipped a spot of cash to the garage chap to let me know if there was any follow-up."

"Of course there was a goddamn follow-up... after you left signs all over that a ten-year-old kid could have followed."

"I thought I covered my tracks pretty well, actually," Courtney returned.

"So well that this muckrakin' scribbler sticks his nose in every place you went in Zemio and finds out enough to track Bolan right up through Western Equatoria until Halakaz's boys fire his heap and we lose him in the forest."

"At least the garage fellow told us he'd be coming."

"He wouldn't have *been* coming if you'd kept your mouth shut. If you'd just said you didn't know the hell where Bolan was."

The Executioner was making mental notes, taking stock of the situation. There was one thing that still puzzled him.

Why hadn't Courtney, as chief of the Mafia's security, ordered Bolan's elimination once he knew the warrior was determined to join the vital caravan?

There could only be one answer. Believing Bolan to be a high-ranking CIA operative, Courtney wanted at all costs to keep his nose clean with Langley. He had therefore left it to Ogada and the caravan escort to finger the spy and take any action they thought necessary.

The fact that he hadn't tipped them off posed an interesting question.

Was it conceivable that Giovanni, el-Karim and the other conspirators didn't know that Courtney was on Langley's payroll? That they had hired him believing he was no more than a corruptible newspaperman with underworld connections? That the Englishman was, as he himself would put it, playing both ends against the middle?

If that was true, it could be a useful lever in any confrontation Bolan could engineer in the next few hours.

Time was running out. Decisions had to be made, plans had to be worked out. First, however, now that his card was marked, the Executioner decided to take an objective look at the runners, to see what the score was.

Louis Mancini and his boss were dangerous men, ruthless, brutal and callous enough to rise to the top of the Mafia slimebucket. Powerful and persuasive enough to talk most of the other Mob leaders into underwriting their crazy scheme. Men you couldn't talk to because for them the end always justified the means—and the end was money, the means murder.

The man who had been in charge of the caravan—his name, Bolan gathered, was Azziz Habibi—was an unknown quantity.

Halakaz and Mtambole, honorable men by their own standards, were nevertheless so much under the Mafia thumb, so besotted by the conviction that they were being helped to overcome their enemies in Khartoum, that they could not be counted on to listen to reason.

Ogada was something else. As Bolan knew from his treatment at the colonel's hands in the torture chamber back in the hill village, this, too, was a ruthless character and a tough one. He had visited the mafiosi in Florida; he could probably be relied on to stick by the men who had promised him so much.

Courtney and el-Karim were birds of a feather. Each was greedy, rapacious, probably ready to fight viciously in a tight corner if he figured his profits were threatened.

That left Mahmoud and the other heavies, plus the technicians owing allegiance to Giovanni. Bolan had no idea how many of them there were: they had seemed to him liberally seeded through the native work force in the short time he had been able to check out the caverns. In any case, like the torpedoes, they would obey orders; like them they would probably be expert infighters.

Whichever way you looked at it, Bolan thought, this was too heavy a team to be bested by one guy with an M-16 automatic rifle.

Even if the guy was known as the Executioner.

What were the alternatives?

There was only one.

Contact General Halakaz and the Anya Nya. Persuade them somehow that they were being duped and prove to them that they were being taken for the biggest ride of all time. Ask them to run up a different flag, fight with Bolan against the men who had so cruelly used them.

The warrior sighed. Whatever the odds, it was time to start to do what he could.

On hands and knees, he backed down the tunnel to the unused cave where he was to rendezvous with Yemanja.

She was waiting there, but although she held Bolan's backpack she didn't have the M-16.

That was in the hands of a man.

For a moment Bolan wondered if he was dreaming. The guy was tall, saturnine . . . and he was covered from head to toe in a formfitting combat blacksuit.

"Figured you might need this, so I wore it under my own clothes," the apparition drawled.

The Executioner continued to stare. It was a while before he recognized the man in black.

Jason Mettner.

He had been puzzled by Courtney's references to "that bloody newspaperman"; he had asked himself how the mysterious scribe came to be following in his own footsteps. But somehow it had never crossed his mind that it might be the ace reporter from the Chicago *Globe*.

"Mettner! How did you get here?" Bolan held out his hand.

"A man called Brognola asked me to locate you," Mettner responded, shaking the outstretched hand. "Took me some time to find the right frequency, but I finally homed in."

"Welcome home!" Bolan said. "But you might find it a damned sight harder to get away again."

CHAPTER TWENTY-NINE

Bolan's plan, like all long-odds undercover operations, relied for its success on two things: surprise and audacity. With the assets he had—one M-16 rifle, a courageous but untrained newspaperman and a woman who knew the layout of the base—they were the only other weapons available to him.

He had donned the blacksuit and now followed Yemanja through a warren of narrow passages that led to a staircase cut into the rock. Mettner, entrusted with the M-16, had been left with a specific briefing in the maze behind them.

At the foot of the staircase there was an antechamber connecting with the lofty cavern where the atomic furnace and the cyclotron were being built.

Yemanja stopped on the final step, peered into the room then laid a finger to her lips. Bolan soft-footed down behind her and peered over her shoulder. There was a guard posted ten feet away from the staircase, an Ingram cradled in his arms. Bolan recognized Mahmoud, the camel master.

The warrior didn't hesitate. He whispered an instruction in Yemanja's ear, sidled around her, waited until the camel master was looking toward the outer cavern and then launched himself forward.

He landed on Mahmoud's back, one knee crashing with agonizing force against the base of the man's spine, and a forearm snaking around and crushing his windpipe. Bo-

Ian's other hand clamped over the mouth to stifle a cry of alarm.

The camel master's arms flew wide, and the Ingram dropped from his hands. Yemanja swooped forward, as she had been told, and caught the weapon before it clattered to the ground.

There was no question of using it: Mahmoud would know they wouldn't dare when a single shot blast in the big cave would bring scores of workers, running to investigate.

The Executioner was unarmed. He was relying on superior skill and—again—surprise in his bid to subdue the guard. But Mahmoud was tough and he was strong.

Balling both fists, he swung his arms backward to punch Bolan hard on each side of the groin, bending double at the same time to throw the warrior forward over his head with a heave of his powerful shoulders.

Bolan landed on his back on the rock floor with a shock that drove the breath from his body. Before he could recover, Mahmoud was on top of him, callused fingers scrabbling for his throat. Pinned down by the weight of the muscular Nubian, he thrashed and rolled, fighting to claw away the fingers tightening around his neck, trying to place a nerve hold beneath his adversary's ear with his other hand.

Grunting with effort, Mahmoud increased the pressure. He shook off the hold with an angry toss of his head. Bolan felt the breath strangled in his throat; the noise made by the construction crew faded; the light started to dim. He clenched both hands on the murderous wrists, tried frenziedly to pry the fingers loose. He knew that if he couldn't get out from under within the next few seconds he was finished.

Yemanja entered the fray with a vengeance. She swung the loaded Ingram by the muzzle and cracked the lead-weighted sheet steel overhung bolt against her master's head. The blow, fueled by years of resentment, humiliation and disgust, zeroed in just above his ear. It wasn't hard enough to knock him cold, but it shook him, it angered him—and it caused him involuntarily to turn his head.

That was all Bolan needed.

The guy's chin was raised enough for him to jam an elbow beneath it. The head jerked back, and the grip on his throat loosened. Bolan snatched a hand away and jabbed his fingers into the Nubian's eye sockets.

Mahmoud gasped, shaking his head like a wounded bull. His thumbs swiveled upward, gouging for the warrior's own eyes. But Bolan raised his shoulders with a superhuman effort and butted his adversary hard in the face.

Blood spurted from the Nubian's mashed nose. In the second that his eyes were momentarily blinded by tears, Bolan thrust him to one side, lifted the upper half of his body and clubbed the steely edge of one hand repeatedly down on Mahmoud's neck.

He took two punishing blows on the ribs, but a final deadly chop on the carotid artery ended the fight. The Nubian subsided like a deflated balloon.

Bolan dragged himself out from beneath the deadweight. Panting, he managed to grin at Yemanja. "Thanks. That was just in time. Now help me strip him."

Like most of the work force, Mahmoud was wearing blue coveralls with the initials AN worked into the breast pocket. Anya Nya, Bolan reckoned. Nothing like some kind of uniform for promoting loyalty to an idea.

The one-piece garment was long enough—Mahmoud was a big man—but voluminous around the chest and hips. Bolan dragged it on over the blacksuit anyway. He had no choice.

They dragged the body to the top of the stairway. Bolan showed Yemanja how to work the Ingram and left her standing guard. He returned to the antechamber, walked through into the main cavern and strode boldly past the construction gangs on their scaffolding. Broken-nose, Joe and the rest of the search party, Yemanja had told him, were combing the series of smaller caves between the falls and the generators.

Nobody took any notice of the tall man in regulation blue. They would have been warned to watch out for a fugitive wearing a sweat-stained bush shirt. At one point Bolan had to turn hastily aside into a feeder passage: he had seen the torpedo with the wounded arm standing guard at the foot of the ramp leading down from the airstrip.

Later, he found his way back into the cavern behind the half-tracks, and gained the corridor he was looking for walking on the far side of a mobile forklift delivering steel formers to the gang working on the cyclotron.

The corridor was wide and brightly lit. Halfway along there was a heavy wooden door set into an arch, and behind the door Bolan could hear a hum of voices. He crouched and peered through the keyhole.

General Halakaz was sitting behind his desk and staring at the four men grouped beneath the Sudanese relief map on the wall of his office. "You are telling me, old chap," he said to Don Giovanni, "that you want me to withdraw all of my people from the control center and the main cavern one hour before blast-off?"

"That's what I'm telling you," Giovanni agreed.

"And assemble the entire work force in the empty chamber behind the generator cave?"

"You got it."

Halakaz leaned back in his chair and frowned. "May I ask why? Plenty of my people would like—I might say have the right—to be present during the countdown. The gang bosses and overseers in particular, after three years' back-breaking work, have earned a ringside seat. Surely they cannot be excluded from the ceremony we have awaited so long, the moment of truth when the tyrants of Khartoum will at last be called to account for their sins?''

"I want the whole damned lot in that empty cave."

"Don Giovanni figures," Mancini said smoothly, "that it would be kind of unfair to single out individuals when all of them have worked so hard. We're, uh, patching in TV on a closed circuit . . . a giant screen in that empty cave where everybody, but everybody, can share the excitement in the control room as the hour of, uh, triumph approaches, okay?''

Hamid el-Karim nodded.

"Splendid idea," Courtney drawled. "Most democratic.''

"Well, old chap, I don't know about that . . ." Halakaz began.

The door slammed open and Mack Bolan walked into the room.

"Don't believe a damned word of it," he told the general. "It's after eight already. Less than four hours to go. Did you see any TV cameras in that control room? Have you noticed any cables, any sign of a screen, in or out of that cave?''

Halakaz half rose to his feet behind his desk, his mouth open in astonishment. El-Karim stood wide-eyed. David Courtney drew a 9 mm Beretta and leveled it at the Executioner's chest.

"They want all of you together in that cave so it'll be easier to gun you down," Bolan explained. "Unless they plan to seal it off and use chemical exterminators. They're making a fool of you, General. You've been tricked all along the line.''

The four conspirators all yelled at once.

"How the hell did you—"

"Shut your goddamn mouth!"

"What does a Russian mineralogist—"

"Shut up or I'll drill you."

Halakaz held up one hand. "Gentlemen! Gentlemen! Order, *please*. There is no need for panic. Our friend Courtney has Mr. Bolan covered, and he appears to be unarmed. And as for you, old chap," he said, turning toward the Executioner, "I see no point in your making such wild statements."

"They're true," Bolan pressed. "I'm afraid you've been used. Now that the missiles are ready to be fired, you'll be…executed. In that cave. Because I promise you they have no intention of using those rockets to help you take Khartoum or any other city in the Sudan."

"That is ridiculous, old chap," Halakaz said, stemming the chorus of fury exploding from Giovanni and his companions.

"Are you a missile expert, General?"

"No, but—"

"Then how can you explain the fact that these weapons are not short-range tactical missiles suitable for such an operation, but intermediate rockets capable of delivering atomic warheads all over Europe and the Middle East?"

"Bull!" Unexpectedly Halakaz lapsed into the vernacular. "How can you possibly know that? How could a photographer—"

"I have to plead guilty to another deception there, General. I can't tell you who I work for..."

"He's a mercenary! Works for anyone who pays," Giovanni stormed.

"But I *am* an expert on modern warfare. And what I tell you is true."

Bolan's even voice carried conviction, and for the first time Halakaz hesitated. "What's more," Bolan continued, "if they were really going to help you conquer the Arabs in the north, would there really be such a highly placed Khartoum official working for them?"

"A *Khartoum* official?"

"Hamid el-Karim. Do you mean you didn't know? He's the head of—"

"Silence!" el-Karim shouted.

"I don't believe it," Halakaz said blankly. "That cannot be true."

"I can prove it to you. Now."

"I challenge you to do so, old chap."

Very slowly, his eyes on Courtney's gun, Bolan reached into the breast pocket of the coveralls. With two fingers, he pulled out three small photographs and then the miniaturized recorder he had carried with him all the time in the money belt.

"These pictures show him in the official reception office at his home in Khartoum," he said. "You can see the arms, the crest, the wording, the Sudanese flag by the wall map..." He tossed the prints onto the desk.

While Halakaz was staring at them in disbelief, he switched on the tiny recorder. They could hear el-Karim's faint but distinct voice.

"...one or two cutthroat bands of renegade blacks... We Muslims here in the north...continually being misrepresented by the backward Negroes.... The poor fools fancy themselves exploited.... There are, I am afraid, various charges.... Do not worry, Monsieur Bolan. Discretion is assured...."

Bolan thumbed the switch. Over the hubbub of angry

voices he said to Halakaz, "It could be faked, of course. And so could the photos. But since I knew nothing until to-day of el-Karim's involvement with your plan, why would I bother? At least they should show you that my warning must be carefully considered."

"What is this nonsense?" el-Karim's voice rose queru-lously above the confusion. "What is this fool Russian on about? What has a mineral prospector to do with the spy in the caravan? Why should he be here—"

"You greedy bloody fool!" Courtney shouted. "This *is* the spy in the caravan! I hired you to do a specific job—or-ganize that same caravan. You knew I was running the team protecting it. You bloody knew! But you weren't content with the fat sum you were being paid. You had to line your beastly pocket with some dirty deal on the side, and then keep it secret."

"You don't understand! I didn't—"

"I understand that your duplicity could have bitched the whole damned operation, for Christ's sake."

El-Karim had gone a sickly gray color. "I...I don't know what you m-m-mean," he stammered. "I was told there would be a spy traveling with the caravan, that I was to or-der Ogada and Habibi to identify him, but that he was to be allowed to find and follow the decoy canister. All that was done. It was not my fault that—"

"I'm not talking about the caravan," Courtney yelled. "Was it part of your job to receive the spy in your own house and let him bribe you? I *knew* the bastard would be tagging along. I knew he'd be disguised as a pilgrim. If you'd just checked with me as you were supposed to do, I could have told you he was the one to watch. If you'd just mentioned the name Bolan, we'd have guessed he meant to use your papers as well as his Arab ID and the whole ghastly mess could have been avoided."

"But he was a Russian government mineralogist. I saw no connection with the caravan. It was part of my normal cover activity to issue—"

"*You* saw," Courtney grated. "Like all politicians, you saw nothing but the chance to stuff your wallet, and you took it without any heed of the consequences. Bolan will die, but because of your stupidity he has caused us all a fantastic amount of trouble. And for that you're damned well going to pay."

"I swear that I—"

"Shoot him," Giovanni said suddenly. His face had been darkening throughout the exchange, and now the flush of anger suffusing his cheeks had spread to his thick neck.

"A pleasure, my dear fellow," Courtney said. The muzzle of the Beretta shifted from Bolan to the Arab.

The Executioner tensed. But no, Courtney was too far away: he could bring the gun back and fire before Bolan covered half the distance between them.

Hamid el-Karim was on his knees, the fine bones of his swarthy face outlined in a dew of sweat. "No!" he cried. "No, no, I beg of you—"

The Beretta spit fire, its report unexpectedly loud in the rock-walled room. El-Karim jerked back onto his heels, staring with horror at the blood spurting between fingers raised involuntarily to cover his chest. The Englishman fired again, and the impact of the 9 mm slug crashed the man over onto his back. He tried to sit up, groaned then sank to the floor again. Courtney pumped three more shots into the body twitching under the scarlet-stained robes, then trained the automatic back on Bolan.

When finally the convulsive movements had stopped, Giovanni nodded. "I always told you it would be smarter to stay away from the politicos," he said.

Courtney shrugged. "He had the connections."

Halakaz was on his feet behind the desk. His face had blanched at the cold-blooded execution. Now, in a hoarse voice, he said accusingly, "Just a minute. Am I to understand, then, that this man—" he gestured at the body on the floor "—was, in fact, a Khartoum government official after all?"

"Well, natch," Mancini sneered. "Jesus, how do you think caravans mainly composed of Arab mercenaries have been able time and again to pass through the goddamn country unquestioned over the past three years? Who the hell d'you imagine fixed up the escorts that brought them each time as far as the forest?"

"But in view of the plan, old chap, surely it would have been better—"

"The plan!" Giovanni's sidekick laughed. "Shit, are you really dumb enough to believe that persons as smart as Don Giovanni and his associates would really spend all that loot, go to all this trouble just to help a handful of self-seeking guerrillas and chisel a couple of two-bit mining concessions out of them? Be your age...General. And don't call me 'old chap.'"

Giovanni nodded again. "Face it, General," he said. "Now that the base itself is completed, once those missiles blast off, your use is at an end. I mean, like it's curtains for you and yours."

"But the missiles?" Halakaz whispered. "Where...?"

"Read the papers," Giovanni said shortly. "If you still got eyes to see with."

Faced with the ruin of his hopes in a couple of sentences, General Halakaz behaved with restraint. Compressing his lips, he exchanged a glance with the Executioner and subsided quietly into the swivel chair behind his desk.

Courtney kept the Beretta lined up with Bolan's chest. Bolan eyed it speculatively. Assuming he was using at least the 15-round box magazine, and that this had been fully charged, there were still ten shots left in the gun—too many to risk attempting a decoy move, as he had done with the forest sniper, for a second time. He decided to wait.

"As we were saying," the Englishman resumed, "before we were interrupted by this jumped-up native boy—"

"I say, I say! Hardly the way one expects a racially pure English milord to talk!"

Astoundingly, the voice, with its exaggerated mimicry of Courtney's accent, seemed to come out of the air.

Courtney kept his eyes on the warrior, but the other three men swung around. No other person had come into the room. For once Giovanni was at a loss. "What the hell...? Who are... Shit, what did you—"

"I said that's hardly the way for a jolly old Englishman, pillar of the Raj and all that, to talk, by Jove," the voice repeated.

Courtney's eyes glinted. "I'm not an Englishman," he snapped in spite of himself. "My father was Irish."

"Ah, that accounts for it then." This time it was Jason Mettner's normal voice. *"Went to the IRA backstab and bomb-throwing school, no doubt. I thought all that frightfully frightful and deucedly top-hole blarney was laid on a bit thick."*

"The grating!" Mancini shouted suddenly, realizing where the voice was coming from. He snatched a Browning automatic from the pocket of his sharkskin jacket.

At the same time, Courtney, his face black with rage, whipped around and loosed a 3-shot burst at the iron grill-work set in the wall.

Simultaneously they got wise to the danger. As the slugs spanged off the metal and ricocheted with shrill screams around the office, they hurled themselves to the floor.

Bolan was the first to recover. He had been expecting the interruption. Big Thunder was still lying on the general's desk, along with the shoulder rig and waist harness, as they had been when he was taken away to the interrogation cell. Reaching up to seize the belt, he scythed the whole harness across the desk top and swept the AutoMag to the ground in a shower of charts and papers.

He swooped to retrieve the heavy stainless-steel auto-loader—only to find that Courtney was already into a crouch, with the Beretta aimed at his belly.

Still reclining on one elbow, Bolan blasted off a single round. It was a lucky shot. The 240-grain boattail struck halfway along the Beretta's barrel and spun it from the Englishman's hand.

Courtney hollered, snatching his hand back as if it had been plunged in molten lead, shaking his fingers to ease the agony.

Mancini aimed the Browning at Bolan, but the grating had not exhausted its surprises. Before the hood could press the trigger, or Bolan could realign Big Thunder, the muzzle of an M-16 poking between the bars belched flame. At a range of no more than twenty feet the high-velocity 5.56 mm slug drilled Mancini between the shoulder blades, tore away the top of his heart and punched an exit through the sternum that left scarcely a stain on the sharkskin. He went down like a felled tree and didn't move.

Giovanni was unarmed. For a heavy man he could move fast. Before Bolan recovered from the success of his snap shot or took in the fact that Mettner had probably saved his life, the capo, followed closely by Courtney, was through the door and pounding down the corridor toward the caverns.

Halakaz, in the meantime, had placidly regained his seat. He must have been touched by a ricochet because his right hand was clenched over his left bicep and the fingers were red. He made no move to pick up his Combat Magnum, which still lay on the desk.

"General," Bolan said urgently, "are you on our side?"

"I'm afraid I seem to have no side left to be on, old chap," Halakaz said sadly. "From now on, you had better regard us as neutral. And go ahead with whatever it was you came here to do."

"Okay," Bolan said after a moment's pause. It wasn't what he'd hoped for, but it was better than nothing. "Mettner, can you find your way back to the big cave, where the reactor is?"

"Can do, or if I can't there's a lady guide," the newspaperman replied through the grating.

"Right. Go there and we'll join forces. Behind the half-tracks, okay? For weapons we've got the M-16 and my own gun. Courtney's Beretta is buckled and useless. I'll see if el-Karim was armed.... No, he wasn't. But we do have the torpedo's Browning. And—" he paused and looked inquiringly at Halakaz, who stared impassively back at him "—yeah, we got a Combat Magnum six-shot."

He picked up the big revolver from the desk and stuffed it, as well as the Browning, into his waistband. "Anything more lethal," he said, "we'll have to win from the other side. See you there."

"We're on our way."

Bolan left the office, the AutoMag in his right hand. As he opened the door, Halakaz pressed down a switch and started to speak into a desk mike in front of him.

"This is General Halakaz," he heard the words boom from PA speakers all over the underground base. "Here is an urgent message for all Anya Nya personnel. There are two groups of Europeans at large in our fortress—our so-called allies and another. There might be fighting between them. You are not—repeat not—to take any part whatever in this conflict. Stop all work immediately and proceed to Oloron. Retain your arms but take no part in any combat. Do not use them unless anyone tries to requisition them. If they do, you may defend yourselves.... I repeat: stop work immediately and return to Oloron.''

"So far," Bolan murmured to himself as he stole toward the cavern, "so good. All we've got left is the tough part...."

CHAPTER THIRTY

General Hartley was in the control room with Ogada and Azziz Habibi. The American, as well as Habibi and the Mafia physicist killed by Bolan after the helicopter chase, had been responsible for the concept and overall design of the Oloron base—in particular for the installation and programming of the missiles awaiting countdown in their silos. Habibi, a Libyan ex-revolutionary originally financed by Khaddafi, had fallen for the big-money lure after a brilliant hi-tech career had taken him from Leipzig, East Germany, to Silicon Valley via MIT and Oxford University, England.

Watched by the colonel who had safely shepherded the final installment of the precious U-235 isotope halfway across Africa, the two nuclear experts were now checking out every detail of the prelaunch drill before the countdown started at 2300 hours.

"It is essential," Hartley said, strutting up and down in his emphatic birdlike way, "that the radio messages, all of them, are beamed at *exactly* the same time. There must be no chance of any cross-checks until each ultimatum is delivered. So we must verify the coaxial—"

He stopped in midsentence. The voice of Halakaz was crackling from the PA speaker above the computer console.

"What's he playing at? What the hell can that mean?" Habibi said blankly.

"Trouble," Hartley snapped. "I always said the discipline was too damned slack in this outfit." He walked to the control-room window and stared down into the main cavern.

There was a sound of rushing feet along the gallery that led to the operations center. Giovanni and Courtney burst into the room, panting. *"Son of a bitch!"* the mafioso gasped. "Somebody's got to go back down there and shut his mouth."

"What happened?" Hartley demanded. "Who is it? What's this fighting?"

"Bolan," Giovanni snarled. "He got a helper someplace. At least one. The bastard wasted Lou. Now they got irons, too." He joined Hartley at the window. African workmen were already streaming from the sector that contained the partially completed atomic plant, heading for double steel doors set in the far rock face. Among them were several groups of soldiers, their rifles slung.

The sounds of hammering had stopped, the forklifts were silent and the only noise to be heard over the shuffling of feet was the diminuendo whine of the generators as they spun to a standstill.

"Jesus!" Giovanni foamed. He snatched a microphone from the transmitter console and pressed a switch. Now it was his voice that echoed furiously around the underground fortress.

"Get back to work, all of you. Right now. Any technician leaving his post will be shot.... Lanzmann, Delaney, Gianelli, round up these creeps and herd them back. We've got to have them for the prelaunch maneuvers. Plug any that refuse. Get our own boys together and issue the Ingrams. I want this stinking dump working full blast again in fifteen minutes...."

Colonel Ogada had remained silent throughout the drama. Now he walked to the window. "Maybe I could help, Mr. Giovanni?" he offered. "The soldiers have been under my command for—"

"Fuck you," Giovanni raged. "You. and that tinpot doorman with the chestful of medals. Is this the kind of thanks we get for all we did on account of you punks?"

"Maybe the colonel's got something, Don Giovanni," Azziz Habibi put in. "The work force would be more likely to listen to orders if they came from him, don't you think?"

"The important thing is surely to get them back," Ogada said, "so that the Khartoum ultimatum goes out on schedule."

Giovanni's mouth dropped open. "The Khartoum . . . ? Oh, uh, yeah, sure. Of course. The ultimatum. So okay, you get along out there and tell them who's boss here."

"Good. Right idea. A voice they trust," Hartley put in.

"I'll go with him," Courtney said with a meaningful glance at Giovanni. The two men left the control room, the Englishman taking an automatic from Habibi's outstretched hand as he followed Ogada. He dropped the gun into the side pocket of his jacket.

Two-thirds of the labor force had disappeared through the steel doors before Ogada and Courtney joined a dozen armed Europeans at the far end of the gallery.

"*Stop!*" Courtney shouted. "Get back to your work, damn you. Return at once to the machines where you belong."

The file of Africans below looked up impassively and continued to stream through the doors.

"Get back, I say," Courtney screamed, "or we shall start shooting to show who's master here."

The soldiers and workers continued to quietly walk out.

Ogada shook his head. "That is not the way," he said. "Let me."

He advanced to the rail. "Our European friends forget themselves," he called. "But there is, after all, much at stake. The general, unfortunately, has been taken ill. He does not know what he is saying. Now, will you please all return to your jobs and perhaps we can get on with what is really important—the subjugation of Khartoum."

For the first time, the main body of the exodus wavered. Some of the workers halted, milling around the doors. Soldiers stopped and looked up at their officer. A low grumble of questions started at the rear of the crowd and rapidly spread.

"Don't believe him! General Halakaz is in perfect health. We have been used by these white adventurers, and Khartoum is not the target at all!" The voice this time was Mtambole's; it came from another gallery on the far side of the cavern. "So obey your orders, stay neutral, and return at once to Oloron."

There was confusion on the shop floor. The workers continued to eddy left and right; the soldiers looked from one colonel to the other. Then Halakaz himself, uniform as resplendent as ever, appeared beside Colonel Mtambole. He was still clutching his left arm, but his voice was strong and authoritative. "There is nothing the matter with me," he roared. "Pay no attention to these foreign racketeers. They have been using us. The missiles are not intended for Khartoum at all. Now do what you are told. Go home and await further orders."

At once the crowd formed into a single stream, swaying toward the doors.

Courtney was hysterical with rage. "All right, then, you rebellious buggers," he seethed. "You asked for it!"

He gestured to the white technicians surrounding him and a ragged burst of fire crackled from the miscellany of revolvers and automatics wielded by the men on the gallery.

The Africans beneath surged and wavered once more. There were people lying on the ground. But the majority pressed forward to flood through the doors; the soldiers among them wheeled smartly out, unslung their rifles and sank to their knees in the firing position. Their first volley crashed out as Courtney's men were joined by two more technicians carrying half a dozen Ingrams.

Before the deadly little weapons could be distributed, three Europeans were slumped over the iron railing and a fourth was yelling in pain and rage as he nursed a shattered knee.

The others crowded back away from the edge of the gallery. Only Broken-nose, Joe and another torpedo with a sandy crew cut dared to advance and hose a deathstream down into the cavern. But by this time the soldiers had fired again. Several of them were bowled over by the murderous .45-caliber hail, but the remainder coolly sent a third broadside bellowing upward.

They were well drilled, and their aim was good. The guy with the crew cut, who folded forward over the rail and dropped to the floor of the cave, was one of three cored by the Kalashnikov slugs. That did it. The hoods and the technicians withdrew from the gallery.

Courtney was the last to go. He saw Ogada running toward the control room, his face a mask of conflicting emotions. Fear, disappointment, fury that he had backed the wrong horse, bitterness at the knowledge that he, like Halakaz and the others, had been fooled after all? The Englishman didn't know. Perhaps he thought the colonel was out to avenge himself on Giovanni.

Whatever the reason, he raised the pistol he had taken from Habibi and pumped three shots into the soldier's back.

Ogada tripped, fell, somersaulted and then lay still with his limbs in grotesque positions, leaving a huge splash of blood on the rock wall.

The soldiers below waited a few seconds, then hustled the rest of the workers out, dragging the dead and wounded with them. The control room was empty; Halakaz and Mtambole had disappeared from the gallery on the far side of the cavern. In less than a minute the place was deserted.

After the thunderous echoes of weapon fire the cave was eerily silent.

Mack Bolan had slipped out from behind the half-tracks during the firing and dodged into the center of the vast floor. Now he was sheltering behind the crates of machine parts on an abandoned forklift truck, evaluating the courses of action open to him.

His overwhelming reaction was relief that at last there *was* action, however dangerous it might be.

His problem was very different from his enemies'. To Giovanni and his toadies it was no more than a matter of rounding up two interlopers—three if Mahmoud had recovered consciousness and told them about Yemanja—killing them, and then trying to get back on good terms with the workers.

And even if that was impossible, they could almost certainly send the radio messages and blast off at least that first fatal missile.

Bolan, on the other hand, with his limited firepower and restricted numbers, was faced with a question of tactics: he must somehow force the opposition to show itself and eliminate it member by member.

Yemanja had been left in the antechamber with the Ingram they had taken from the camel master. Mettner, no ex-

pert shot, was still behind the half-tracks toting the Combat
Magnum and Mancini's Browning. Bolan himself had retained Big Thunder and the M-16. He figured the woman
was more likely to hit something with a weapon that could
spray knockdown slugs at a rate of more than 1100 per
minute than she was with a single-shot handgun possessing
a heavy recoil. The lightweight Browning and a revolver
carrying only six shots were a natural choice for the newspaperman, who was only expected to give covering fire when
Bolan needed it.

A low murmur of voices from the passage behind the
control room grew louder as Giovanni, Courtney and Habibi appeared on the gallery and climbed down the stairway
leading to the cavern along with Broken-nose, Joe and the
remaining technicians.

"Remember, you guys," Giovanni was saying, "there's
only a couple of these bastards as far as we know. They
won't know the layout of the place, and I don't even know
if they linked up yet."

"Any special order you want us to search?" one of the
technicians asked.

"Yeah," the mafioso replied. "You, Manson and Trottman take the passage leading to the power station. Courtney, you go with Joe and Goldberg and turn over the
administration sector. I'll take Azziz here and Fawzi. We'll
do the reactor cavern. The rest of you can look around
here."

As the men began to fan out through the base, he called
after them, "Don't forget they're armed. So shoot to kill.
But if you *can* take them alive, that's fine. I want they
should die slow if possible. With witnesses."

Bolan shifted silently around to keep the forklift between him and the searchers as they separated. They were all
within easy range, but it would be suicidal to drop one of

them while the others were still in touch. He wondered which of the four groups it would be smartest to attack first.

Giovanni, Habibi and Fawzi—the guy with the broken nose—vanished through the archway leading to the reactor. Three technicians headed for the first passage Bolan had explored, when he found the hydroelectric turbines. Courtney's detail advanced toward the corridor Bolan had recently left.

The Mafia boss's voice, distorted by echoes, boomed out from the reactor cave. "And if any of the blacks show their faces, shoot them, too."

Bolan deliberated. Should he follow the hood and take a chance on silencing him and his two confederates first—cut off the snake's evil head and leave the writhing corpse until later? Or were the odds too long again? Would the others be alerted and come running to corner him in the cavern?

Would it be better to deal with the three men near at hand? Could that be done without shooting? And if he decided that was on, how the hell was he going to contact and brief his own two companions, when the enemy were all around?

He didn't have to decide.

There was a sudden warning shout from Mettner. Bolan swung around to see the torpedo with his arm in a sling. He was twenty yards away, back in position at the foot of the ramp—and the .38 Police Special in his good hand was pointing straight at the Executioner.

Big Thunder flashed up in the warrior's right hand, but before either of them could fire, Mettner leaped from the roof of the nearest half-track and landed on the wounded hood's shoulders. He went sprawling with a cry of pain, the pistol spinning away down the slope. After that it was all movement.

The three technicians in the cavern spun in the direction of the noise, scattering to find what cover they could. There was an abrupt outburst of shooting. Bolan dropped one with a short blast from the M-16, simultaneously forcing another to dive for shelter behind a crate of machinery. The third fired at the same time as the newspaperman with his borrowed Browning.

Both shots went home. The gunman was hurled to the floor with half his face shot away; the slug meant for Mettner slammed into the back of the killer with the wounded arm just as he was rising to close with the newspaperman.

"Make it to the gallery while I cover you," Bolan yelled. "Get the guns from the dead."

He could hear Giovanni's furious voice, and footsteps clattering his way from the reactor cave. He fired two thunderous shots from the AutoMag into the packing case, pinning down the technician behind it, while Mettner sprinted for the stairway. At the same time, one-handed, he sprayed a burst blind toward the reactor. Fawzi and Habibi withdrew hurriedly around the corner of the archway. The mafioso had prudently remained out of sight.

"Any luck?" Bolan called. Mettner's face appeared over the edge of the gallery—for once without a cigarette hanging from the mouth. He shook his head.

"They already thought of that and lifted them," he replied. "Should I— Bolan! Behind you!"

It was way out of range, but he fired the Browning and a deafening sound from the Combat Magnum at the half-tracks as Bolan whirled and flung himself flat behind the forklift.

A fusillade of shots erupted from among the trucks, fanning the air above the Executioner's head and gouging splinters of wood from the crates on the forklift. Courtney and company had returned.

Beneath the low chassis of the loading truck, Bolan stretched the M-16 out at arm's length to get the highest possible elevation of the muzzle and stitched a withering figure eight to crisscross the gaps between the half-tracks. Glass shattered and fell, a ricochet whined, pieces of metal clanged to the rock floor. And one at least of the high-penetration bullets scored. The warrior heard a choked cry, a stumbling clatter of feet and then the sound of a fall. Someone had dropped beneath a half-track.

A moment later a second volley from the parking lot struck sparks from the steel frame of the forklift uncomfortably close to Bolan's face. He couldn't see where the gunmen were hidden, then suddenly a final shot from Mettner's Browning, which had been firing sporadically in his support, flushed out the torpedo Joe. He careened sideways from the cab of one of the trucks, scrabbled futilely at the starred windshield and collapsed to the ground leaving a trail of bloodied fingermarks over the glass and camouflaged metal.

Courtney had had enough. He dashed back to the corridor that led to the administration offices and disappeared from sight.

But Bolan and his companion were now victims of a pincer movement—Fawzi and Habibi firing from the far side of the arch that led to the reactor; Trottman, Manson and a third technician advancing from the hydroelectric plant.

Bolan rose to his feet behind the stacked crates. It was at this moment that the sudden silence was shivered by a woman's scream. Shrill and terrified, it came from someplace behind the control room.

Mettner burst through and into the passage beyond.

Mahmoud, clothed only in his underwear, his swarthy face mottled purple from Bolan's karate attack, was standing over Yemanja. She was lying in a tumble of robes on the ground, with one eye blackened and a trickle of blood oozing from the corner of her mouth.

"You dirty little slut," the big camel master ranted. "I'll teach you to meddle in affairs that don't concern you and help foreign spies to escape, you no-good whore!" He dragged the woman to her feet and slapped her face viciously with the back of his hand.

Mettner landed on his back, much as Bolan had done some time before. But the newspaperman was no match for the muscular Nubian. Mahmoud twisted and dropped to the floor, bringing Mettner down with him. Locked together, pummeling and gouging, they rolled down the passage and back into the control room. Mettner managed to free an arm and caught the camel master with two uppercuts to the jaw, but the blows hardly seemed to shake him.

He rose up onto his knees, arms at full stretch, and closed his great hands inexorably around Mettner's windpipe. The newspaperman thrashed and writhed on the floor, his feet and knees seeking a purchase. But the thumbs pressing into his throat would not relax their iron grip. The thundering behind his eyes was threatening to engulf the universe when there was a whining of hydraulic rams, and Mack Bolan rose slowly into view over the gallery rail, seated on the forklift of the loader truck.

The big stainless-steel autoloader held in his two hands spit fire once, and the pressure on Mettner's throat relaxed. Mahmoud gave a strange coughing groan and plunged downward, a deadweight across his body.

Bolan ducked beneath the rail and helped the sobbing woman to her feet and he rolled the body off Mettner. It was only then that Mettner saw the raw wound, pricked out with bone, smashed through Mahmoud's chest and realized his own bush shirt was soaked with blood.

"We're running short of ammunition," Bolan said quietly. "The M-16 is finished. My backpack and the spare clips for this—" he held up the AutoMag "—are down in the antechamber. You must damn near have exhausted that Browning. How many shots do you have left in the six-shooter?"

"I should have thought that was an academic question," a voice said levelly before Mettner could reply. Courtney stood in the doorway at the far end of the gallery, an Ingram in his hands. "Drop your weapons, both of you. Mettner, take the revolver out of your pocket, very slowly, and throw it beside the Browning. Then I want the two of you back on top of that forklift."

Bolan's M-16, its magazine exhausted, was down below. As he threw the AutoMag at the Englishman's feet he stole a glance over his shoulder.

The *two* of you?

Surprisingly Yemanja must have ducked back into the control room just before Courtney appeared. She was nowhere to be seen.

Courtney was at the edge of the gallery. "Fawzi!" he called. "Habibi! You and the others can come out now. The bloody birds are caged! One of you operate the lift to bring them down to your level while I whistle down the stairs . . . and keep them covered!"

"You really earned a place in the *Guinness Book of Records*," Mettner said as he stepped off the gallery onto the forklift. "Murder, treachery, deceit, inefficiency and the double-crossing of two separate employers at the same time, all in the one worm—that sure takes a lot of beating!"

Courtney flushed. "If you want to live even thirty seconds more, shut your bloody mouth, mate," he said, jerking the Ingram threateningly. He kicked the AutoMag, the

Browning and the Combat Magnum over the edge of the
gallery and called out, "Right you are. Lower away now."

Fawzi was at the controls of the forklift. Perched on top
of the crates, Bolan and the newspaperman sank slowly toward the ring of armed men waiting for them.

Courtney turned on his heel and made it to the staircase.
He was halfway down when Yemanja appeared from the
control room with the Ingram in her hands.

With tears streaming down her face, she clenched the
fingers of both hands around the pistol grip and squeezed
frantically on the trigger.

The explosive rip-roar of the .45-caliber skullbusters
thundered around the rock walls of the cavern and shook the
woman's slender body with the force of their compound recoil. She stood there until the entire 30-round magazine was
empty, then threw the gun down the stairs after Courtney
and sank to the floor of the gallery with her face in her
hands.

Eleven of the ACP rounds struck the man between the
shoulder blades and the hips, shredding flesh, bones and
interior organs, fountaining blood over the walls of the cave.
The impact of the deathstream lifted him from the stairs and
flung his lifeless body through the air to impact against a
concrete buttress. The corpse, cut almost in two by the lethal hail, flopped to the ground as limp as an empty rag doll.

Instinctively the gunmen surrounding the forklift had
raised their eyes to gaze horrified at the carnage. It was the
opportunity Bolan had been waiting for.

He dropped from the top of the crate stack onto Fawzi.

The motor was already running to power the hydraulics.
He slammed the lever into reverse as he grappled with the
hood, and the machine, veering from left to right, began
backing up toward the cavern wall.

Bolan and Fawzi fought frenziedly between the saddle seat and the controls. The Arab's gun was tucked into his waistband, and Bolan was determined it was going to stay there. He had a score to even with the broken-nosed torturer, dating back through his ordeal in the Arab hill village to Marseilles, and he suspected the man also had a hand in the bomb outrage that destroyed the world of Mustapha Tufik. This, the Executioner felt grimly, was a matter he would prefer to settle hand to hand.

Eyeballing among pedals and levers, the two men grappled viciously, each searching for the advantage.

Mettner jumped a fraction of a second later than the Executioner, when the startled killers had already opened fire. He dropped facedown beside the forklift and lay still.

Bolan cursed. He rode two savage chops to the throat, kneed Fawzi in the belly, freed a hand to tweak the wheel and grunted with pain as stiff fingers jabbed his kidney. He lodged a thumb between the man's jaw, probing for the pressure point on the artery, then was forced to back off as Fawzi butted him with paralyzing force in the face.

The rear of the forklift slammed against the rock wall, stalling the motor and spilling the two fighting men to the ground. Bolan was underneath, the hood's fetid breath hot on his face. His hands were pinioned beneath him as Fawzi seized both his ears and began banging his head on the ground.

Half stunned, the Executioner made a superhuman effort and drew up a knee, raising his antagonist's body off him enough to free both arms. He clawed the heels of his hands beneath Fawzi's chin, then straightened his arms violently.

Fawzi uttered a choked gurgle. His eyes opened wide and the pupils rolled up beneath the lids. Blood poured from his mouth and nose as Bolan shoved himself forcefully out from under and stumbled upright.

Bolan looked up at the clock above the control room window. With Hartley, Habibi and the Mafia chief still at large—and the remainder of their forces concentrated now in the big cavern—it was still possible for the blackmailing radio messages to be transmitted and that first catastrophic missile to be fired.

As long as the Executioner was pinned down here on the shop floor.

The one-hour countdown began in fifty-two minutes. The forklift was backed up into a corner. Bolan was protected from the fire of the conspirators by the stacked cases...until the gunmen spread wide enough on either side and a man climbed to the gallery to enfilade him from above.

After that? Big Thunder was on the floor beneath the gallery, and Fawzi's gun was a Colt Python carrying only six shots.

Faced with that situation, what could a cornered man do?

Make use of the little ammunition he had and eliminate the guys capable of launching the missile.

He shrugged. What the hell. Fight to the last man and the last round, the old soldiers used to say. Well, he was the last man all right, and he had six rounds.

He would waste the three bosses and take another trio with him when he went.

It didn't work out that way.

He risked a rapid recon, peering around one side of the crates. Bullets thudded through the wood and splatted against the machine parts inside. Giovanni and Hartley were nowhere to be seen, but Habibi was on the far left of the gunmen encircling the truck.

Crouching behind the wheel, Bolan restarted the engine and engaged the forward lever. He would rush them and hope the surprise might get him through…if the word *rush* could be used for a vehicle whose top speed was four miles per hour.

He spun the wheel and swerved to the right, firing twice at Habibi as the physicist slid into sight from behind the crates.

Both shots missed.

Slugs screamed around him as the unwielding truck lumbered for the shooters. Wood splinters stung Bolan's cheek.

The forklift snaked right, then left again. Bolan was on top of the crates. From that unexpected angle, on the wrong tack, he aimed once more at Habibi. The Python roared, bucking in his hand.

The Libyan staggered, clutching his shoulder.

But it took a fourth shot to flatten him against the cab of a half-track with a scarlet stream pumping through the rent in his robes at belly level. By the time he hit the floor, the forklift was in reverse again, whining back toward the wall beneath the control room.

But it was a no-win situation for the Executioner. Killers were creeping forward on all sides, dodging behind the cooling tubes, sheltered by crates, ducking under steel girders waiting to be placed. In a moment he would be vulnerable from the right as well as the left.

Someone stood up behind a nest of scaffolding and shouted, "Drop the gun. You don't have a chance! Give in and we'll make it quick and easy."

The words ended in a shrill scream, drowned by a thunderous single report that echoed around the cavern. Immediately afterward there was a deafening rattle of automatic fire, a chorus of curses, yells and moans, and a series of ragged volleys from the killers' Ingrams and pistols. Flat on his face beneath the truck, Bolan realized with astonishment that none of it was coming his way.

When at last there was silence in the cave, he cautiously raised his head. There wasn't a torpedo or a technician left alive.

When the heat from the arcs had cleared away the gun smoke he recognized three figures standing on the ramp: Hans Voigt and Jochen Kraul, each toting one of the mini-Uzis he had seen in their Range Rover and Trudi Finnemann, belt, boots and blond head shining, with a Mannlicher Express in her hands.

"The blockhouse was deserted, so we figured we'd come down and see if we could help," she called.

Bolan was hard-pressed to hide a grin. True to tradition, the good ole U.S. Cavalry had arrived in the nick of time . . . only *this* time it was wearing German uniforms!

CHAPTER THIRTY-ONE

"Not actually German," Trudi Finnemann informed Bolan. "I'm afraid I, too, must confess to a certain disregard for the truth. We are not, in fact, a geological team but an investigative unit from the Mossad."

"You're Israelis? What was your particular interest in this?"

"Surrounded by hostile countries, my government is always anxious—vitally concerned—at any hint of a change in the balance of Middle East power. The threat of any nuclear activity in our theater makes us very nervous indeed. So when the whispers of such hints and threats reached us, we were sent at once to check them out."

"There were rumors of a threat to Khartoum," Voigt said. "And suspicions that the menace might reach much further."

Jochen Kraul, as usual, remained silent.

"But how did you know the threat was that serious?" Bolan asked. "That it was nuclear?"

"We knew about the uranium isotope thefts," Trudi told him. "We can run a computer trace as well as anyone. Then we have an arrangement with an offbeat character, a merchant of intel, I guess you could call him, in Marseilles. He told us—"

"Not the Moroccan-Irishman?" Bolan cut in. "Mustapha Tufik?"

She smiled, the network of fine wrinkles around her eyes showing white against the tan. "That's the one. A very useful man."

Bolan nodded. "I get it. And you didn't get wise to my real purpose here when we met in the forest because he never tells one client about another. And that's why he didn't tip me off that *you* were following the same trail."

"I guess so. He alerted us through Le Brocquet, the Marseilles police chief, that someone was curious, but he gave no details."

Bolan sighed. "Too bad these bastards got him in the end."

"Oh, but they didn't," Trudi said. "The place was wrecked and most of the personnel killed, but Tufik and Hassan—the thin man who acts as his bodyguard—both had miraculous escapes. Mark my words, we shall be hearing of Monsieur Tufik again!"

"I'm glad to hear that," Bolan said, and meant it. "But talking of miracle escapes, how's my friend Mettner?"

"He'll be all right," she said. "He was creased above the left ear. A slug plowed a small furrow there and knocked him out, but the skull isn't damaged and he didn't lose too much blood. I'd guess he'll have a bad headache a few days, and that's all."

They were sitting in the Range Rover at the foot of the ramp leading to the underground base. The redoubt had been searched from the top to bottom, but there had been no sign of Giovanni or General Hartley. Later, when they went up to the airstrip, they saw that the smaller helicopter had gone.

Once more the top men had gotten away with murder.

"But they won't get away forever," Bolan said grimly. "I suspect General Hartley will be taking an early retirement.

And Giovanni, I promise you, will find that like Tufik I may reappear more quickly than expected...."

Trudi turned to Kraul. "You're the expert, Jochen. You know what you have to do here?"

Kraul exchanged glances with Bolan and replied, "No problem. I shall need a great deal of wire, detonators that I can probably raise from the stores here and an alarm clock. Plus a lot of manual labor to dismantle those warheads and lower them to the foot of that two-hundred-foot shaft in the limestone that we found near the falls."

"You can use our porters for that," Trudi said, "and if you need more clout on the physical level, I'm sure the general will oblige."

Halakaz had been sitting silently at the rear of the Range Rover with Colonel Mtambole. "My regrets, General," Trudi said formally, "but I hope you appreciate why we have to do this?"

Halakaz retained his dignity in defeat. "I suppose so," he said wearily. "To be honest, we don't have the expertise to use them on our own, anyway."

"Man has to face up to the occasional defeat," Mtambole offered. "Lost a battle but not the war, what?" He snatched off his beret and slashed it across his thigh. "Find some other way, damn it, that's all!"

"We can't offer to help," Bolan said. "But tell me, apart from your own Anya Nya troops and workers, are there any refugees in this part of the forest?"

"None," Halakaz said firmly. "We have rigorously excluded them, as I told you before, from an area ten miles around this base."

"Okay," Bolan said. "Now you've got exactly three hours to clear every man, woman and child of your own people, plus as much equipment as you consider necessary, from that same area. I regret the inevitable destruction of

Oloron, but it can't be avoided. I suggest you take the half-tracks and any other vehicles you can find." He picked up the Combat Magnum that Jason Mettner had been using and handed it to Halakaz.

The soldier was almost in tears. He took the gun, slammed it into its holster, snapped the cane under his arm, saluted and led Mtambole from the Land Rover. They walked smartly away toward the inner recesses of the cavern where the survivors of the Anya Nya awaited them.

Some time later, Kraul looked up from an old-fashioned alarm with a bell on top. It was wired in to a nest of cables, terminals and junction boxes webbing the floor of the control room. Below, at the foot of the ramp, Trudi and Voigt waited in the Land Rover with the engine running. "What time shall I set this for?" Kraul asked.

Bolan glanced at the wall clock. "Give them the full three hours. It'll still be dark then, anyway."

Later still, when the cursing Mettner had been stowed in the remaining chopper and they were waiting to take off for Khartoum, the Executioner drew Kraul aside and asked him, "Tell me—why did you wise me up on the route to Oloron when Trudi and Voigt were being deliberately evasive?"

The Israeli smiled. "That's simple," he said. "I'm the team archivist. I'm familiar with the dossiers. I knew who you really were."

TRUDI FINNEMAN SAT IN the informal conference between Bolan, Mettner, Hal Brognola and Samson, the CIA liaison, thirty-six hours later. "It seems, thank God, to have passed off all right," Samson said, tapping a copy of the Chicago *Globe* that lay on the table between them.

There was a two-column headline halfway down the front page that read: Earthquake In Southern Sudan? Experts Disagree.

Seismographs as far apart as Santa Barbara, Tokyo and Edinburgh registered shock waves the night before last whose epicenter was placed in an unexplored region of the southern Sudan. The shock, registering 7 on the Richter scale, was of short duration and is thought to have been a severe earth tremor. Certain characteristics, nevertheless, exhibited points in common with large man-made explosions, experts said here. The Sudanese government last night accused rebel factions in the southwestern province of Equatoria of responsibility for the explosion. But a communiqué issued by the headquarters of the Anya Nya guerrillas laid the blame squarely on "repressive government elements." Neither side specified exactly what form the disturbance had taken and there have been no reports of casualties in the area.

Jason Mettner II, special correspondent in central Africa, writes: Explosion or earthquake, the shock appears to have demolished a series of waterfalls and altered the course of the Oloron River. This will bring relief to thousands of refugee tribesmen, for the new watercourse irrigates what was formerly a barren thorntree desert, and this should soon be fertile enough to produce crops.

"My God," Mettner exclaimed disgustedly, holding a hand to the bandage that still remained taped in place above his ear, "would you just look at that! I go through seven different kinds of hell and save the world for future generations, and what do I get? Two lousy sentences below the fold, tacked on to the end of a wire service special!" He snorted with assumed anger and set fire to a cigarette.

"Better two sentences on the front page than seven column inches of obit inside," Bolan said soberly.

"I've got to agree, Striker," Brognola said. "You're lucky yourself that human nature is so fallible. If Hamid el-Karim had not been greedy enough to want to line his own pockets—and if Courtney had not been such an egomaniac that he figured he could decoy you to his headquarters and choke our secrets out of you—you could've been written off with that man Ibrahim in Alexandria."

"What about Courtney's own secrets?" Trudi asked. "Do *you* have those?"

"Sure do," Samson said. "That Madison news agency was a front for Mob operations worldwide. Our guys found details of fifty companies they intended to put the bite on— plus listings of all the scientists and technicians suborned to steal the U-235 isotopes in Courtney's office safe. We're contacting the counterintel chiefs in the countries concerned so that the bastards can be weeded out. Your own people will be receiving a digest in the normal way."

"A digest!" Mettner echoed. "Hey, that reminds me of food, reminds me I'm off the foreign circuits and back on the nightclub beat for a while. Fielding figures I need some kind of rest, can you imagine? But I have to be back in Washington at that new Mocamba joint at nine." He grinned. "There's a new Sudanese belly dancer there that they tell me is sensational!"

Bolan and Trudi exchanged glances. "Small world," the Executioner said. "That's where we were heading ourselves...."